Lies
Secrets Can Kill

LINDA LOVELY

Published by Windtree Press
4660 NE Belknap Court, Suite 101-O
Hillsboro, OR 97124
http://windtreepress.com

ISBN 9781943601271

Interior Design by LHI
Cover Art by Karen Phillips, Phillips Covers

ACKNOWLEDGEMENTS

A special thank you to Keokuk, Iowa, history buffs and friends for their generous help with research related to my hometown as it existed in 1938 and the activities associated with that year's fall Street Fair.

Joseph Breitenbucher provided background on law enforcement in the era when his uncle, Harry V. D. Maas (from all accounts a good guy) was Lee County Sheriff.

Mike Krebill provided invaluable introductions to knowledgeable historians Doug Atteburg, Ed Kiedaisch, Mary Murphy, and Bob Wustrow, who shared information and insights. Keokuk Public Library staffers Angela Gates, Tonya Boltz, and Emily Rohlfs were tireless in answering my questions. Dixie Mackie sent a carton of history books. Any historical inaccuracies are mine alone.

Detective Diane Orlando, a violent crimes investigator for the Greenville, SC, City Police Dept., shared knowledge of sex-crime psychology. Steve MacLeod offered suggestions about World War I guns.

As always, I'm indebted to all my critique partners Robin Weaver, Donna Campbell, Danielle Dahl, Charles Duke, Howard Lewis, Ashantay Peters, Maya Reynolds, and Jean Robbins, as well as Beta reader Fara Driver.

I'd also like to thank Karen Phillips, Phillips Covers, for creating the eye-catching cover art for Lies.

Finally, my husband, Tom Hooker, is always there for me to talk through character traits, plot options, and, if necessary, study U.S. Patent drawings to see how a vintage Ferris wheel might have worked.

NOTES

This novel is set in my hometown, Keokuk, Iowa, in 1938. The story is pure fiction and imagines what might have happened in that time and place if the fictional characters had actually lived.

For storytelling purposes, I elbowed real folks out of positions of authority and installed fictitious characters in their stead. This includes the chief of police, mayor, and bank president. These characters bear no relationship to real-life individuals. The same applies to the fictional characters associated with Sol's Liberty Show.

I did try to be as accurate as possible in describing events that occurred during the novel's timeframe, from Hitler's moves and the burning of the Nauvoo Opera House to the 1938 Street Fair acts and unusual fall flooding. I incorporated real landmarks and company names, too. However, I invented several institutions for the sake of plot. To the best of my knowledge, there was no Iowa First Bank or 19 ½ Club in Keokuk, and there isn't a Momiss Cave in Missouri.

I'm sure I'm forgetting other inventions made to avoid sullying the reputation of actual institutions and organizations. I did take the liberty of adopting the surnames of some Keokuk friends for my characters, but again, these aren't the relatives of real people.

Since this is a suspense novel, LIES includes some evil characters. But I hope my love of Keokuk, Iowa, and its people shines through. Keokuk is—and always will be—my hometown, and I love it.

DEDICATION

For my mother—
Marguerite Kennedy Willis
Loving, smart, brave, resourceful

Rita Willis was
Linda's Sister

ONE

Keokuk, Iowa—Monday, September 19, 1938

Ed Nelson knew it was bunk. What an old wives' tale—casting loaves of bread upon the water to find a corpse. But he couldn't afford to argue and rile Chief Dexter more, not with a distraught mother standing vigil on the riverbank.

Mrs. Meister's fourteen-year-old son was last seen at dawn fishing for catfish below Keokuk's lock and dam. The boy's empty johnboat had drifted to shore near the railroad roundhouse a little south of a ragtag collection of fishing shanties.

Ed channeled his frustration into rowing. His long, smooth strokes knifed the boat beyond a swirling eddy. A third of the way across the Mississippi's flood-swollen span, Chief Dexter finally spoke. "Good a spot as any. We're near where that barge captain saw the kid."

The scratchy wool of Ed's long-sleeved police tunic prickled his skin. Despite the unseasonably cool temperature, sweat dribbled down his spine. He extracted a bandana from his pocket and mopped the back of his neck. Though the September sun carried meager heat, it boomeranged off the water's mirrored surface, making his eyes water.

His beefy boss shifted to open the picnic hamper holding the bread. The rowboat wallowed in the murky water. For a moment, he wondered if they'd capsize—a fitting start to what promised to be a colossal shipwreck of a week. When the Street Fair came to town, so did the hustlers and pickpockets. The Depression swelled their ranks.

An hour ago, at Dexter's behest, he'd begged some mercury off Doc Foglesong, who used it in his dental practice to fill teeth. The chief wanted quicksilver to spike bread for his harebrained corpse detection scheme.

Convinced his boss was kidding, he stretched the joke. "'Course once I get us some mercury, we'll need to spit on the ground three times and spin in a circle."

Dexter greeted his chuckle with stony silence.

Ed slogged on. "I read Huck Finn, too. Can you believe some folks really think a loaf of bread basted with mercury will miraculously halt when it floats over a drowned body?"

The chief fixed him with a baleful glare. "I know you're a college boy. Spent a couple a years at Iowa State College of Agriculture. Well, la-di-dah. Maybe that makes you an expert on cow patties, but you don't know shit about police work. I can read, too. 'Bout ten years back, police used this very method to find a drowned lady in a lake up in Connecticut."

Ed forced himself to nod politely and shut his trap. With a third of the town's able-bodied men out of work, he could easily be replaced. *Swallow your pride and kowtow to the foul-tempered ignoramus. Otherwise you'll never learn the truth.*

The chief dumped five tainted loaves overboard. Ed hoped hidden currents would quickly sweep them to shore and end the charade. The muddy water smelled worse than an outhouse. A bloated carp floated by. He wasn't eager to drag *anything* up from the muck coating the river bottom.

"Look." The chief pointed. "That loaf's a-bobbin' in one spot. Row on over."

Ed put his back into it, pulling hard on the oars. Through the blinding glare on the water he spied an object breaking the surface just beyond the bread. Two more pulls on the oars solved the mystery—a loaf snagged on the branch of an uprooted tree.

The Mississippi wasn't quite at flood stage, though warnings were up. Already the roiling river had begun to belch up its spoils as unseen eddies scoured debris from underwater graves.

"Oh, shit!" Chief Dexter pointed. "There *is* a body! Look there, tangled in the branches."

Ed rowed closer and peered into the depths. A body bobbed with creepy energy inches below the surface. Though the corpse floated face down, Ed could tell the victim was a full-grown man, not the missing boy.

"Make yourself useful," Dexter ordered. "Let's see what we caught. Use the grappling hook. Don't worry. The stiff's dead. Won't feel a thing. Snatch his clothes so he don't burst."

Ed gritted his teeth and took aim, swinging the hook back and forth on its rope pendulum. With his first toss, he snagged the man's suit coat and pulled the corpse free of the tree's slimy carcass. The body flipped face up. The pasty visage, framed by an ebony halo of floating hair, turned his stomach.

Dexter's cheek puffed out as he shifted his tobacco chaw. "I'll be. It's Dirk Black. Sure don't look like he dressed for a swim. He's fresh, too. Can't have been floatin' long. Otherwise catfish would've nibbled."

"Who is he?" Ed asked.

"Came to Keokuk four years back, married a local. Turned out the guy already had a wife and kid out east. Never divorced, just got up and get. Clipped money from his boss to bankroll his trip to Iowa."

"Did he go to jail?"

The chief's eyes narrowed. "Nah, it happened afore I took over. The old chief screwed up. Got sweet-talked into dilly-dallying long enough for the new missus—a sneaky wench—to pay off the other wife. Charges were dropped once she repaid the money he'd pocketed and got him a legit divorce."

Dexter grunted as he leaned over and poked at the body. "Bet wife number two got tired of the jerk and drowned him. The mug probably planned another vanishing act." A smile replaced his scowl. "No one'll talk me into doing that bitch any favors this time 'round."

As Ed tied the corpse to the side of the boat, a woman's wails echoed across the water. "Oh, God, Mrs. Meister thinks we're hauling in her son's body."

He cupped his hands to yell. "Mrs. Meister, this isn't your son! It's not Jeremy." As soon as the message echoed its way to the riverbank, the mother collapsed in a friend's arms.

The scene made him wonder. How would Dirk Black's widow take the news? Grief? Panic? Could the chief actually have pegged one right?

"You never said, Chief—who's the local gal this Black character married?"

"Catherine Reedy. Maybe you knew her afore you left town. Family lives over on Second and Timea. Her dad worked at Huiskamp's shoe factory till the Depression. Her mom, Adelaide, passed last year."

Ed's tongue glued itself to the roof of his mouth. Cat Reedy? He'd last laid eyes on her at his high school graduation. Bobbed hair the color of corn silk. Shy smile. Eyes the blue of twilight. Brainy, too. He remembered how her little brother took bets. Call out any pair of six-digit numbers and Cat could multiply them in her head. The girl skipped two grades, graduated a month shy of her sixteenth birthday as class valedictorian.

He did his own calculation. She'd be thirty. How could someone so smart—and pretty—be mixed up with a ne'er-do-well like this Black?

"Well, do you know her?" the chief prodded.

"In high school. Haven't seen Cat since."

"Huh, Cat, is it? Gotta admit she's a looker." Dexter spit out his chaw. "The best gams in Keokuk. Too bad she's worse than a damn Bolshevik." He settled back on the hard boat bench. "Can't wait to hear Mrs. Catherine Reedy Black explain why she didn't notice her husband had gone missing."

TWO

Catherine Black hopped off the bus, tucked her pocketbook under her arm and hurried toward Iowa First Bank. Since Main Street was cordoned off while carnival workers set up the annual street fair, she'd intended to start for work early. That was before two-year-old Jay dumped a bowl of oatmeal on his head, and she discovered one of her dad's vicious minks missing. Evidently it clawed under its backyard cage to freedom.

Dear Lord, please let Dad's next get-rich scheme involve something other than rodents.

"Hi, Cat," Mrs. Gage called. The shopkeeper leaned on her broom, taking a breather from sweeping the vestibule of her family's music store. "You gonna bring that adorable son of yours to town tonight? Imagine he's old enough for some of the kiddy rides."

She grinned at Mrs. Gage. "You bet. Jay's eyes will be bigger than Liberty dollars when he sees all this hubbub."

Great Depression or no, the annual street fair lifted spirits. She pictured Jay's little mouth forming a perfect "O" when he spied the Ferris wheel lit up like perpetual fireworks. Plunging his chubby fingers into fluffy strands of cotton candy would send him straight to heaven.

As she hurried down the block, Cat realized her smile was still in place—and it wasn't forced. She felt genuinely happy. Carefree would be an exaggeration, but hopeful? Yes.

Dirk was gone. For good, thank God. She doubted anyone would ask what became of her husband. The whole town knew his sorry history. The chief of police made sure of that. He'd spread tales about Dirk like honey on a hot biscuit.

Stepping off the curb to cross Main Street, Cat collided with a midget. He backed into her while yelling insults at someone named Geisha inside a tattered show tent. The little man—under four-feet tall—whirled, bringing his bloodshot eyes just below her breasts. His high-pitched laugh resembled a schoolgirl's giggle though it was accompanied by an almost visible cloud of garlic breath. He ran his tongue along dull steel teeth, the most attractive feature in a grimy face, pocked with tufts of coarse hair.

"Hey, lady, why don't I teach you to twirl these?" The Lilliputian positioned two gold tassels nipple high on his chest and vigorously swirled them as he ogled her. "You got the equipment. You could steal the show."

The midget's leer seemed too absurd to offend. Cat's chuckle startled the pint-sized barker, who looked as if he hoped to provoke a shocked reaction.

"Don't think so." She grinned. "Never could get the hang of it."

As she walked away, her smile grew broader. The encounter triggered a memory. At ten years' old, Cat and her best friend Lydia Dexter set out to unravel the mystery of why men packed street fair girly shows. At the time, the adolescent detectives sported breasts smaller than silver dollar pancakes, their nipples the size of unripe gooseberries. They'd waited for a performance to begin, then wriggled through a torn seam on the canvas tent's shadowed side. Spellbound, they watched a woman with bare bosoms the size of honeydews proceed to set one breast rotating clockwise, the other counterclockwise. Her shimmering tassels spun topsy-turvy in opposite directions.

Cat's smile faded. Where was Lydia? Had *her* marriage worked? Was she happy? Her friend deserved a bit of bliss after all those years of living in fear. While she understood Lydia's two-year silence, she sorely missed her childhood friend. Maybe she'd return to Keokuk.

Someday.

But not before her daddy, Chief Dexter, was planted six feet under.

Cat slipped in the bank's small side door, an employees-only entrance.

"Good morning, Mrs. Black."

Kenneth Jacobs, president of the bank, issued the same clipped, impersonal greeting whenever they met by chance. Cat reciprocated, her voice neutral. "Good morning, sir." She never raised her eyes to meet his. Never dared.

Clutching her handbag tight to her chest, she stepped up her pace. A glance toward the mezzanine confirmed her immediate boss hadn't arrived. She sighed in relief. That man made her uncomfortable for a different reason. The tight-lipped prude disapproved of working women—especially mothers—and relished any opportunity to chastise her.

Once she claimed a seat in front of her Comptometer, she relaxed, losing herself in her work. Though the machine's keys were arranged in ten color-coded columns, she never looked at her hands. Her fingers read the keys' concave and convex surfaces like Braille. Adding, subtracting, multiplying or dividing was like playing Grandmother Nell's Wurlitzer. But instead of reading piano sheet music, she scanned bank ledgers and struck numeric chords. In two seconds, she could enter any transaction, her fingers a choreographed blur.

A large deposit—$11,565.45—caught her attention. No surprise about the receiving account—The Hubinger Company. From her work on accounts, Cat knew its manufacture of corn syrup, corn starch, corn sugar, corn oil, and cattlefeed brought in more than three million dollars a year. The local factory filled boxcars with the sticky corn syrup that smothered her son's French toast.

Her gaze skipped to the next entry. Cat had little time to woolgather. Iowa First Bank prided itself on prompt reporting, and a tall stack of customer transactions teetered on her desk. She welcomed the busyness, the distraction.

Figures spoke to her. Numbers were noble—eternally truthful. No matter how many times you added a column, the total never changed. Math was black and white. Not like people. Not like life. If only she could decipher her future like an equation. Yet with so many unknowns how could she ever solve for X? She held fast to one certainty—Dirk would never again wound her heart.

The two-week-old scene flashed through her mind. She'd stumbled down the apartment stairs with baby Jay cradled in her arms as Dirk's screamed obscenities battered her like stones. "Cold bitch! Scheming whore!"

Their landlord, old man O'Reilly, had cracked his door for an earful.

Back now in her childhood home, no one screamed. But the tomblike silence almost felt worse. Asthma had claimed her mom in January of '37, yet Cat still smelled Addie's cinnamon-scented offerings every time she passed the worn pie safe.

Each workday as she stepped off the bus and walked up Timea, her first sighting of home—the drooping porch, the bleak, weathered siding—stole all bounce from her step. A pictogram: broken dreams dwelt here. Next came the self-inflicted tongue lashing. They had food, a roof. Riches compared to the wretched Dust Bowl refugees.

Once she went inside her home, dark thoughts vanished. Little Jay only needed to laugh or coo. Thank heaven for her giggling gift from the gods.

She glanced toward the bank's large wall clock. Grandmother Nell should be putting Jay down for a nap. Cat imagined her curious baby valiantly fighting yawns, coveting every waking second to explore the wonders within his reach as he toddled on wobbling legs like a diapered Charlie Chaplin.

Back to work.

She calculated new balances for a large stack of accounts and rewarded herself with a small break. She flexed her fingers, arched to stretch her stiff back.

Though her desk faced a wall, she sensed the presence behind her before the man cleared his throat.

"Mrs. Black, I need to speak with you."

The voice chilled. Chief Dexter.

Oh, God, what now? I told Dirk's boss I'd pay him back. How did Chief Dexter get involved?

THREE

Cat pushed away from her desk, stood, and turned to face the police chief. How she wished Elmer McPherson was still chief and not this bully.

Dexter's expression seemed different, his usual smirk more sinister. He hadn't come to harass her about her husband's episodic larceny. Something worse. His beady eyes seemed to glitter. Her right hand flew to cover her mouth, ready to smother the moan forming deep in her throat.

"Your husband is dead."

"What?" She grabbed the desk and steadied herself, searching Dexter's face for some hint of what could have happened to a man as strong and healthy as Dirk. "Dead?"

She noticed Dexter wasn't alone. A uniformed policeman loomed behind him. The man stood a head taller than Dexter. Early thirties? Mahogany-red hair, green eyes, a firm jaw. She flashed on a younger-version of the handsome face. *I know him. What's his name?*

Cat realized her brain was desperately seeking mental detours, any excuse to avoid processing the news.

Dirk.

Dead.

For a second, she remembered the night she met Dirk under the Aragon Ballroom's starry canopy. His muscled arms reeling her closer as they danced. His mercurial face. Laughing. Lusty. Then the image shifted to that last sighting of her husband. The cords in his neck etched in high relief as he hurled invectives. Rage dilating his eyes, forming pitiless black holes.

A nerve in her eyelid twitched. Her cold, numbed lips fought to form words, ask a question. "A car accident?" Her voice disintegrated to a whisper.

"No."

She caught the chief staring at her fluttering eyelid. Fear tinged her shock. A hammering pulse roared in her ears. She lowered her gaze to avoid the lawman's eyes.

"What ... what happened?"

"I'll ask the questions." Chief Dexter's gravelly voice carried no trace of sympathy. "When did you last see your husband?"

At that moment, Cat knew—Dirk had been murdered.

Oh, Lord, who did it? Please, please, let it be some desperate hobo. A stranger.

Not him.

* * *

She'd grown more beautiful, Ed decided. Her thick blonde hair shimmered as it brushed the choker of tiny pearls kissing her slender neck. The polka dot dress with its cinched waist celebrated soft curves. The chief's description of her shapely legs hit the target—they were easily the town's sexiest gams.

The girl had been pretty in high school. The woman was stunning, despite the wary eyes and the hands nervously smoothing her narrow skirt. The minute she heard the chief's voice her face froze. She'd had business with his boss before. Unpleasant business.

As Dexter bluntly delivered the ugly news, Ed tried to read her reaction. Shock? Maybe. Her oval face paled beneath its light dusting of powder, and a tiny vein throbbed at her temple. An almost imperceptible moan escaped her lips. Yet word of her husband's death triggered no hysterical wails, no weak-kneed surrender to grief. Could she have killed Black?

"How did he die?" Cat's voice grew stronger. Her eyes met Dexter's.

"We fished him out of the river." The chief paused. Ed sensed his boss studying her. "Looks like someone bashed him on the back of the head and dumped him."

"Maybe he fell—"

"Not unless your husband likes to fish in a suit and tie."

Was Dexter smiling? Good God, he's enjoying this.

No wonder he left two other officers searching for Jeremy Meister's body. He wanted to personally hammer Cat with the news.

"When did you last see your husband?" the chief repeated.

"I'm not sure. I, uh...I don't live with him. I thought he left town."

"Yeah, when?"

Dexter had clamped the bit in his teeth, decreed the woman guilty as sin.

"I moved back home with Dad at the start of September. Our landlord, Pat O'Reilly, watched me pack up and leave. I haven't seen Dirk since. He said he might head to Canada."

"Why'd you desert your husband?"

Cat's chin lifted. Her glare defied the chief. "That's personal."

"I'll decide what's personal. Someone murdered your husband, and it sounds like you had reason to kill him. What? Was he doin' some other dame?"

Cat held the chief's gaze. She didn't answer. The silence stretched for long moments. "Why'd you leave?" the chief demanded.

"He embezzled ... again," she finally said, her voice steady. "I promised his new boss I'd pay back the money—just like I did on his last job. I had one condition. I told Dirk I wanted him gone. I figured he'd already high-tailed it. I didn't want my son to grow up shamed by a father branded as a liar and a thief."

"Maybe Dirk wasn't happy about you giving him the heave-ho. Maybe he came round to patch things up. Maybe you decided to say goodbye permanent-like."

Cat turned her back on Dexter and sat in her chair. "If you'll excuse me, I have arrangements to make." Her slender hand opened a desk drawer and retrieved a handbag.

"Don't think I'm done with you." Menace colored the chief's words. "You know what they do with murderers, don't you? String 'em up at the Fort Madison prison. I hear tell the last one kicked five minutes with his eyes buggin' out and his face turnin' blue."

Cat rummaged in her open purse. Ed was impressed. He wasn't certain he'd be that composed with the likes of Dexter crowding him. The chief reached down and fingered the pearls circling her throat. "Won't need a big noose for you."

Ed watched goose bumps pebble Cat's perfect white skin, but she didn't flinch.

The chief turned and stomped toward the mezzanine stairs that tethered the bank's balcony workspace to the ornate marbled teller area below.

"Come on, Ed," he called loudly over his shoulder. "We got a murderer to nail, and if'n I was a bettin' man, I'd wager on the missus. Maybe the mob will take book."

Ed cast one last look at Cat. Were her shoulders shaking? Had she finally given in to tears? She must know irritating Chief Dexter was damn risky business. Everyone in Lee County knew he was as sneaky and fearsome as a Mississippi River rat.

He stifled a ridiculous urge to comfort Cat, caress her silky hair and murmur everything would be okay. But a stunt like that would cost his job and the chance to keep tabs on Dexter and his cronies. Besides, he sensed Cat would spurn any hint of pity from a virtual stranger.

He recalled a story from his school days. When Cat was about eleven, two boys waylaid her brother, Pete. They were beating the tar out of him when she jumped into the fray. Broke one boy's nose with a balled fist. The other kid grabbed her and she bit his finger clear to the bone. A high school buddy told Ed the story to warn him off the first time he set eyes on Cat. "She's good lookin' but a hellcat," his friend said. "Best forget that one."

He sensed this woman boasted the same feisty core as the child who bloodied the bullies messing with her baby brother. She might look like a kewpie doll, but she was a fighter. Good thing. He had battles of his own.

* * *

Cat refused to look up until she was certain Chief Dexter had gone. She folded her hands in her lap. She would not cry. Her throat tightened, and attempts at deep, calming breaths came closer to gasps. She shuddered as she recalled the chief's malicious taunts. Her fingers touched her necklace where he'd fondled it. Had they ever hung a woman at Fort Madison?

She'd reasoned Jay would be better off growing up fatherless than living in Dirk's shadow. The man lied compulsively and constantly "borrowed" money he had no plans to repay. If prison was Dirk's destiny, she wanted her husband's future cell in a town far, far away from her son.

Now Jay's future looked bleaker. Would he grow up listening to whispers about a mother who hanged for killing his father?

Oh, no! Who will raise Jay if I'm gone?

The thought stole her breath. Grandma Nell was a flinty seventy-one. Rigid and joyless. Though only in his fifties, her dad reeked of bourbon and seemed hell bent on joining her mom under their shared headstone in Oakland Cemetery. He wouldn't last five years. Already his ribs poked through skin as gray as his undershirts.

Cat sorely missed the father she'd idolized as a child—the ice skater who could jump half a dozen whisky barrels on Rand Park's frozen pond, the master brewer of basement beer, the jovial pinochle player, the pillar she could depend on when she needed help. The Depression claimed his job as a foreman at the shoe factory in 1933. He never found work again. His wife's death dealt a final blow. The John Reedy of old vanished. From sun-up to sundown, his gaunt shadow haunted the deteriorating clapboard house like a contrarian vampire.

I won't let anyone take Jay from me.

Cat ran through her options. She could ride the Route 1 bus home, bundle up the baby, leave. Tell no one. Her pragmatism quickly squashed that notion. Dirk had kept the car. Needed it for his work. If she fled by train, Dexter could track her with ease.

Running would cloak her with guilt, bring her one step closer to a hangman's noose.

She would gut it out. Had to. No matter how hard Chief Dexter tried, he couldn't pin her husband's murder on her. Could he?

Who killed Dirk?

Her stomach lurched. She knew one man with an excellent motive. Could that sanctimonious bastard really have murdered Dirk? No matter, she couldn't dish him up as a suspect. If anyone even believed her story, she'd be cast as an accomplice, the Jezebel who goaded a decent man to kill at her behest.

Perhaps Dirk had fleeced some unlucky rube in a scam. Her husband spent plenty of time in Keokuk's gambling halls. Maybe he'd gotten crosswise of management, though most folks knew better. Every week one of the town's wealthiest lawyers hauled bags of money to a gangster's Cicero address. The take from Keokuk whorehouses and gambling dens wasn't chump change.

Give me strength. I have to call Dirk's mother. Plan a funeral.

She reconsidered her stiff-backed reaction to Dexter. A mistake? It probably didn't matter. They had a history as bitter as rhubarb. But she should have asked more questions. She didn't even know where they'd taken Dirk's body.

She refused to run after the chief and beg information. Perhaps she could talk to that policeman who'd stood in the background, straight as a walnut tree. His solemn green eyes looked kind. As if he'd seen his share of woe and empathized. She knew him from years back, but the name wouldn't come.

Ed. That was it. Ed Nelson. She'd graduated with him and his twin sister, Myrtle, the class clown. Myrt could always coax a chuckle from her twin. No laughter today. Having skipped two grades, Cat had been younger than Ed and Myrt. A bookish outcast, Cat had kept to herself, too shy to talk with any of the older teens. Had she ever spoken to either sibling?

Frowning, she tried to remember a snatch of recent conversation. Ed had married Hannah Peele. The Nelsons and

Peeles both lost farms to foreclosure, and Ed moved away. Why was he back in Keokuk?

Cat stood. People were staring. The mezzanine had no walls. Her boss had witnessed the chief's visit, probably heard snatches of the conversation, including his throwaway taunt. She stacked her papers and walked toward her supervisor's desk. He rose as she neared.

"Mr. Thompson, my husband has died. May I leave work early? I need to tell the family."

He nodded. "Of course. How did Mr. Black die—an accident?"

She couldn't answer. Her hand flew up to cover her mouth. "I'm sorry. I'm not feeling well." Fleeing, she caught sight of Maude Burks, eyes wide, mouth agape, eagerly cataloguing all the details of the unexpected drama. How long before Maude's crew of gossipmongers fingered Cat as a murder suspect?

Exiting the bank's dark crypt-like interior, she blinked in the bright sunlight. The cool morning air triggered a shiver, and she pulled her sweater tighter. In seconds, a logjam of bodies and raucous voices trapped her. Her throat tightened. She needed more air. Claustrophobic, she hurried. The smell of rancid hot dogs floating in bubbling lard caused her to gag.

She'd momentarily forgotten. This was day one of the weeklong Keokuk Street Fair. The roustabouts, working since dawn, had already set up the biggest rides, including the Ferris wheel. Weathered canvas tents dotted the streets as far as she could see. Hearing a shout, she looked up at a man stringing cable for one of the high-wire acts. Each act claimed a different intersection. Was this the street corner reserved for Jaydee the Great in his ape suit?

Maybe he can swing down and spirit me away like King Kong did Fay Wray. I wouldn't even scream.

Her heart thudded faster. Feverish chills wracked her body. She broke into a run. As she stumbled past the burlesque tent, the midget she encountered earlier called to her. "Hey, lady, I can learn you how."

She swallowed the hysterical laugh bubbling up in her throat. *Maybe I should take him up on it.* A murder trial would cost her bank job—even if a jury found her innocent. Working women were about as popular as leeches. Leaving church, she ignored the whispered complaints—"Not right for a woman to take a job, not when husbands can't find work."

No matter that Cat needed to put food on the table, to keep a roof over her extended family. Her husband's primary contribution was debt. The rare times he was flush, he brought home flashy, impractical gifts, worth a fraction of their cost when she hocked them.

An image of her mother came to her—lips a thin line, eyes narrowed. Cat earned her mom's glower whenever her "smart mouth" or "bullheaded pride" led to disaster. Like marrying Dirk Black. Like defying Chief Dexter.

Her dad proved more indulgent. "Don't let them break your spirit, Kitty-Cat. But you have to learn—look before you leap."

Well, she'd leapt straight into a heap of trouble and, this time, she wasn't the only person who might suffer.

Use your brain. Think it through.

She straightened her shoulders. She would not let Baby Jay pay for his mother's transgressions. Her high heels clicked on the sidewalk like castanets as she hustled to catch the bus.

I won't run. And I'll be damned if I'll let Chief Dexter railroad me. I'll find a way out.

FOUR

"Where are we headed?" Ed asked.

The chief's beet-red jowls and white-knuckled grip on the steering wheel suggested apoplexy. Dexter hadn't uttered word one since he stomped out of the bank. Now they were barreling north on Blondeau, a side street parallel to Main. The fair had closed off ten blocks of the town's central artery.

Dexter took his eyes off the road long enough to glare at Ed. "I told the boys to drop Black's body at St. Joe's and phone Doc Sprague. If we get anything that looks like it might be murder, Doc cuts 'em open at the hospital to see what's what."

Ed swallowed. Growing up on a farm meant plenty of personal encounters with death. He'd butchered hogs, put down lame mares, wrung the necks of countless hens. Didn't make him any keener to watch the doc dissect a fellow human.

The chief snickered. "You're a little green 'round the gills. If you'd gone to France, like me, you'd have seen enough dying in the Great War to know dead men ain't no different than any other slab a beef. But it don't matter. Doc's probably sewed Black back together by now."

Five minutes later, Dexter's prediction proved accurate. Doc Sprague had reassembled the corpse with helter-skelter black stitches. His nude body looked like a cheap rag doll chewed by a stray dog. Still Ed could tell Black had been fit—muscled arms, flat stomach. A big man. Ed guessed his height at six feet, his weight around two-hundred pounds.

The doctor wiped his hands on a bloody apron as the chief's eyes flicked over the corpse. "Can we prove it's murder?" Dexter asked. "Don't want our killer claiming it was some freak accident. 'Course she'd still have a devil of a time explaining why her hubby went out on the river in Sunday-go-to-meeting duds."

Ed noted Dexter'd raced straight past fact-finding and evidence collection. He'd already put Cat on the witness stand, accused of murder.

Why was he so eager to convict her?

"He was murdered all right." Doc Sprague held up a mangled bullet. "This proves it."

"Well, I'll be damned." Dexter reached for the stumpy piece of lead. "Didn't see no holes in him. Where'd she shoot him?"

Black was positioned face up. Doc Sprague grabbed the corpse's shoulder, lifting the body enough to expose the back of the head. "Bullet entered where the skull's caved in. Looks like your killer bashed him with something heavy—maybe a rock—for good measure. Whatever the murderer used, it had lots of jagged edges.

"That blow came after he was shot and dying—maybe already dead. Can't say exactly when this fella stopped breathing but it was before he went in the river. No water in his lungs."

Dexter fingered the slug. "Why didn't the bullet go clean through his head?"

The doctor shrugged. "How do I know? I'm no expert on guns—ammunition either. Send the bullet to the state lab in Des Moines. If you find bloodstains on your killer's clothes, ship them up, too. They can test dried bloodstains these days. Amazing. Tests will tell whether the blood's type A, B or O."

Dexter smirked. "Think we'll mosey over to the Reedy house. Peek in a few closets and maybe the trash bin."

Ed nodded toward the corpse. "When do you suppose he died?"

Dexter scowled. A reminder the chief preferred his officers to function as mute wallflowers. Doc Sprague didn't notice the chief's squinty-eyed rebuke. The physician ran his fingers through his sparse hair while he considered his answer.

"I'm better on time of birth than time of death. But I'd say he died sometime yesterday. Seen enough bodies pulled out of the

Mississippi. Though it's been cool, he'd be a lot juicier if he'd been bobbing around any longer."

"Yesterday, huh? Hope Mrs. Black went to church." Dexter chuckled. "Course maybe she prayed on the matter in the morning and shot the man Sunday afternoon."

As he looked at the body, Ed tried to imagine slim, five-foot-two Cat muscling the corpse's considerable dead weight into a boat. No way.

"You're thinking an accomplice, right?" This time Ed was savvy enough to direct his question to the chief and suggest his boss knew the answer. "A small woman would have a tough time carting around a body of this size."

The chief took off his glasses and polished them. "Wouldn't put nothin' past Catherine Reedy," he said, using his suspect's maiden name. "You're right, son. She probably had a helper. Maybe a relative. Could be that union-lovin' brother of hers. Or maybe she's doing the hootchie-kootchie with someone new."

Doc Sprague dumped what looked like a kitchen meat cleaver into a nearby sink. "Is the family claiming the body?"

"Mrs. Black didn't exactly swoon and beg for a last look at the dear-departed." Dexter snickered. "But she'll likely pay to bury him—for appearances' sake. Have one of the nuns call the Reedy house and ask which funeral home. No sense Lee County footing the bill for a pine box."

The chief turned abruptly. "Come on. Let's get to the Reedy place before the woman decides to clean house."

Don't we need a search warrant? The question almost popped out of Ed's mouth before he bit his tongue. If he antagonized the blowhard with more questions, his insider tenure would abruptly end. He owed it to his twin sister to stay the course. Only a fellow cop could shovel enough dirt to bury the corrupt chief of police.

He figured tossing the Reedy house would be a total waste anyway. If Cat really did kill Black, she was too smart to hide a gun in her handkerchief drawer or stuff a bloody blouse in the clothes hamper. Any physical clues would be long gone. Buried or burned.

Ed understood that husbands and wives killed one another. Too many men used their fists on women folk, took out their frustrations on loved ones, especially when hard times had everyone spoiling for a fight. Before the chief was widowed, he'd heard rumors Dexter's wife made "falling down" a weekly habit.

She wasn't alone. Abuse escalated when bills piled up and farmers burned their unsold field corn to heat their houses. Maybe this Black attacked Cat and she killed him in self-defense. No, that didn't fly. He was shot in the back of the head, and he hadn't seen a single bruise marring Cat's porcelain skin.

Hell, why are you so sure she didn't kill her husband?

She could have had any one of a dozen trite motives—jealousy, revenge, money. You barely knew her, and that was fifteen years ago. The chief bears a grudge, but maybe he's right.

* * *

Hanging onto the bus strap as the car swayed, Cat's mind skittered from worry to worry like a trapped water bug. She needed to contact the banker without anyone knowing. Impossible to phone. Not with every connection routed through the loose-tongued ladies at the central switchboard.

As she considered a telephone call, her mind leapt to her mother-in-law. How to break the news? Hell's bells, would Mrs. Black come to Keokuk for the funeral? That would be ducky. No matter who killed Dirk, Cat's acid-tongued mother-in-law would lay the blame at her doorstep. "You didn't obey your husband, stand by him. That's why he's dead."

A thought struck her with new dread. Did Greaves Mortuary have a lay-away plan for caskets? And what would her dad say about burying Dirk in the Reedy plot? She couldn't afford to buy another gravesite.

While a dozen alarming questions ricocheted around her brain, one repeated over and over: Who killed Dirk—and why?

The minute she hopped off the bus, Cat shucked her high heels, stuck them in her purse, and ran. The sidewalk's rough concrete chewed at her prized, oft-darned Rayon stockings. She didn't care. Her breath came in gasps. She needed to reach home, close the door on the outside world. Maybe then she could order her thoughts.

She dashed up the porch steps. The screen door banged as she burst into the hallway. The noise exacted a startled squeak from Grandmother Nell, slumped on the prickly horsehair davenport with her head lolling on her ample bosom, napping.

Cat scanned the room. Baby Jay teetered beside one of the tall front windows. In a fit of giggles, the toddler tugged on the heavy drapes to maintain his precarious balance. Cat ran over and scooped up her baby boy. "No, no, Jay. Don't touch."

The child wailed, and Cat feared her head might explode. Don't scare your son. You're frightened enough for the whole family.

She rocked Jay in her arms. The contact soothed her as much as it did her boy. "It's okay, sweetie. I'm not mad. I just want to keep you safe. Yank on those drapes and that big, heavy rod—" she pointed —"could fall on your head. Ka-boom. Now that would be a big ouch-ee."

Straightening, Cat's grandmother assumed her usual ramrod-stiff bearing. "Sorry, dear, I must have dozed off. What are you doing home at this hour?"

The old lady's brow wrinkled with worry. "Heaven help us—the bank didn't fail, did it?"

"No," Cat snapped, then chastised herself. Her anger dissipated as quickly as it had flared. Cat knew Grandmother Nell obsessed about losing their home. She raved about widowed friends who suffered the ultimate indignity, living in crumbling boarding houses where they were forced to stand cross-legged waiting to piddle in grimy, shared commodes.

"I'm sorry, Grandmother. I know you're worried, but Iowa First is in no danger of going belly-up."

Her grandmother had grown up wealthy, though the family fortune had vanished before Cat started school. Cat guessed that's why the woman obsessed about losing the family's remaining pittance. While the current Reedy residence was a giant step down from the mansion Grandmother Nell once presided over, the family's abode was a palace compared to alternatives like the county farm—the last stop for crazy people, orphans, and penniless old folks.

Unfortunately, the Reedy "palace" was mortgaged to the hilt. Her out-of-work dad had pledged it as collateral when he borrowed to repair the leaking roof. Her brother, with a family of his own to support, contributed what he could, when he could. Still every penny from Cat's job was spoken for. Barely enough to pay loan installments and feed the Reedy survivors who called 218 Timea Street home.

"I didn't mean to bark at you," Cat spoke softly, rocking the baby. "It's just that I have terrible news. Dirk ... Dirk is dead—"

"That's good news," a male voice chimed in. "Hell, we should celebrate."

Cat hadn't seen her father enter. He leaned against the doorjamb, his fingers curled around a lit pipe. It pained her to look at his bony body. He'd used leather scavenged from the shoe factory where he once worked to fashion the belt holding up his baggy pants. With every passing week, it seemed he bored another hole to cinch the belt tighter.

"Dad, please don't let anyone hear you talk that way. Someone murdered Dirk, and I'm pretty sure Chief Dexter hopes to hang me for it."

"That horse's patoot!" Her father waved his pipe and a tiny red ember escaped. Cat watched it wink out just before it reached the threadbare carpet.

"Dexter's been gunning for you ever since you helped Lydia elope," he continued. "Smartest damn thing his daughter ever did, escaping that brute of a father."

Grandmother Nell, now fully awake, locked eyes with her son. "John, don't you go hunting up more trouble for us by mouthing off to Chief Dexter. He may be an idiot—and a ruffian—but he's got powerful friends. He could toss Catherine in jail for no good reason." The old woman sighed. "Things would be different if my father were still alive..."

Cat watched the light go out of her dad's eyes. She put her squirming baby down and crossed the room to hug her father. "I'll be okay, Dad. Don't worry about Dexter. He's a bully, but I don't think he has enough brains to frame me for murder—not unless I confess. And since I didn't kill Dirk, I can't imagine how he could force me to plead guilty."

She turned to her grandmother. "Can the two of you watch Jay a little longer? I need to call Dirk's mother and make funeral arrangements. I'll phone Beth, too, and ask her over. She worked the weekend, so she's off today. We'd planned to take the little ones to the fair tonight."

Cat's spirits lifted at the thought of talking things over with her good-natured sister-in-law. She'd bonded with Beth as soon as the younger woman started dating her brother. Having skipped over petty childhood rivalries, the two women were closer than most sisters. The like-minded ladies shared laughs, worries and confidences. Even shameful secrets proved easier to bear if you could whisper them to a trusted friend.

I'll ask Beth to relay a message for me. I can't talk to him. She can. Did he kill Dirk?

* * *

Ed stood a step below Chief Dexter on the porch as his boss twisted the bell ringer on the Reedy front door. A mix of voices—male and female—drifted through the open windows.

A pleasingly plump brunette answered the door. Her mouth thinned into a grim line when she saw Chief Dexter. "Yes, can I help you?"

"You can step aside, Beth. Me and my officer here need to search the house."

The woman Dexter called Beth stood her ground, blocking the entry. "Chief Dexter, what in heaven's name are you talking about? Search for what?"

Dexter pushed through the open door, shouldering Beth aside. "We're looking for the gun that killed Dirk Black and any other evidence of the crime."

A skinny old man entered the hall, creating a fragile roadblock to the chief's offensive. Ed figured the man for Cat's father even though his blue—almost purple—irises appeared to be the only shared trait. "Stop right there, Chief," the man barked. "Who says you have the right?"

"I say it, John," Dexter answered, his voice lazy. "Law says I can search without a warrant if'n I think someone's planning to destroy evidence. Your daughter high-tailed it out of the bank soon as she heard we found Dirk. Figure she's tryin' to cover up her crime."

"Oh, for God's sake," John swore. "Don't be an ass. You know full well Catherine didn't kill anyone. You just want to punish her for helping Lydia elope."

Ed watched Dexter's complexion darken to barn red. His meaty hands balled into fists.

Lydia? The daughter the chief claimed was dead to him. So that's his beef with Cat.

Fearing Dexter might slam a fist into the frail man's midsection, Ed pretended to stumble, wedging himself between the men. Before anyone could do or say anything more, Cat rushed in. She still wore her work dress, but her slender feet were bare. Absent high heels, she looked even more petite, more vulnerable.

The baby boy balanced on her hip took in the fracas with huge eyes, the same twilight shade as his mom's and granddad's. He'd inherited his mother's silky blonde hair, too.

The toddler focused curious eyes on the policeman and giggled. For a second, Ed couldn't breathe. *My son would be his age.*

Cat's voice snapped the spell cast by the baby. "It's okay, Dad. For all I care, Chief Dexter can search till the cows come home. I have nothing to hide. The sooner we clear up his ridiculous suspicions, the sooner we can get on with our lives."

"Fine," said the chief. "John, do you keep a gun in the house?"

Glaring at the chief, the man answered. "Brought a Webley back from the war. A Brit gave it to me as a souvenir. Since we have a little one in the house, I hid it in the basement."

"Ed, go with John, and collect that gun. Meanwhile I'll check Mrs. Black's bedroom." He turned toward Cat. "Where do you sleep? I want to see your closet."

Cat gently transferred the baby to Beth. "Follow me."

"You stay with him, Cat," John Reedy warned. "Don't leave Dexter alone or he'll plant something sure as shoot."

Ed trailed Cat's father, who paused at the top of the basement's darkened stairway.

"I'm sorry, sir. I know this is difficult. I'm sure it's a misunderstanding." Ed wanted to say more, tell John Reedy he agreed the chief was a total ass. The need to keep quiet tore at his gut.

John gave him a hard look. "Son, I've been out of work for years, but I'd kill myself before I'd kowtow to that bastard."

Though the man muttered, Ed understood him perfectly. Unable to reply, he felt blood rush to his ears. They burned with shame. Until today, he'd only seen the chief badger fellow cops and bums, not young women or beaten-down old men. Though he'd promised himself to tough out his charade, he felt complicit. For the umpteenth time, he gritted his teeth.

How long before I give in and bloody Dexter's nose?

Halfway down the basement steps, the senior Reedy yanked on a string that dangled from a bare bulb. The damp air smelled sweet and smoky. When they reached the cellar floor, John turned left, passing an almost empty coal bin. Unlabeled dusty brown bottles lined shelves on both sides of the passageway. Sunlight leaked into an opening at the end of the basement, highlighting a short set of stairs that undoubtedly led to a backyard entry.

John stood on tiptoe to retrieve a fishing tackle box from a high shelf. "The gun's in here." He set the box on a nearby stool and undid the clasp.

"What the hell?" The old man gaped at the empty box, then fixed Ed with frightened eyes. "I-I don't understand," he stammered. "I must have moved it and forgot." His fingers trembled. "I forget sometimes if I've had a drink or two."

* * *

Cat stepped aside as Dexter bulled into her bedroom and scanned the room. It didn't have a closet. He walked directly to the battered armoire her dad had salvaged from an abandoned farmhouse. The chief yanked clothes from their hangers and flung them to the floor. Once he freed the last dress from a swinging hanger, he walked over it. A boot print soiled the white double collar on the jacket of her favorite dotted Swiss dress. She'd paid $1.98 for it at Sullivan and Auwerda. A splurge—more than a full day's pay.

She clamped her mouth shut, struggled to control her temper and her breathing.

Dexter opened her dresser drawers and pawed her underwear. He wadded her silk panties into balls and discarded them with studied nonchalance.

She wanted to scream at him. But that was what he wanted. She bit her lip. *I will not react. I will not give him the satisfaction.*

She forced herself to look away from his malicious degradation. That's when she noticed Ed Nelson in the doorway, glaring at his boss. The young policeman's eyes were narrow slits.

His nostrils flared. A redheaded bull ready to charge. Yet he made no move.

His eyes cut to Cat, and his expression softened. He held her gaze for a second and shook his head ever so slightly. A warning? What was he trying to tell her?

"Chief," Ed said, his tone clipped, "looks like you've finished. You may want to speak with Mr. Reedy. He hasn't seen his gun in months. Forgot where he put it."

Dexter's eyes gleamed. "Now there's a likely story." He wheeled on Cat. "Don't you want to help your daddy find his gun? Why don't you remind him where you hid it after you shot your husband?"

She fought an overpowering urge to slap Dexter. Wipe the sneer off his pug face. Her fingers twitched with the need as adrenaline jacked her pulse to hummingbird level. Pounding blood whooshed in her ears. Her eyes caught movement. Ed shook his head again. Though he stood behind Dexter, she could clearly see the taller man's face and troubled green eyes. With the exaggerated pantomime of a silent movie star, his lips repeated an emphatic command—"Don't." Then Ed tapped his chest and mouthed, "I'll help."

Cat dug her nails into her palms. The compulsion to smack the chief ebbed.

Don't. Dexter's egging you on to do something stupid. Then you're his. Locked away in his jail.

She glanced at Ed once more. His eyes looked cold now, green ice. Did she need a friend so badly she'd imagined the exchange?

Ed moved aside to let Dexter pass. As Cat walked past, he bent to whisper in her ear. "I'll help. Come to the street fair tonight. Corner of Seventh and Main. Eight o'clock."

FIVE

Ed's jaw unclenched once the chief and John Reedy ended their shouting match. As he passed Cat's dad in the hall, a stale stench of booze radiated off the old man's loose skin. Had to be half in the bag—probably stayed that way. Still he'd rallied to stand up to Dexter and attempt to shelter his daughter.

Not that Cat Reedy couldn't stand up for herself.

Cat would surely have embossed a scarlet handprint on his boss's face if he hadn't distracted her. The corners of Ed's mouth lifted at the thought though he couldn't afford an outright smile.

Intent on getting in the last lick, Dexter paused with his hand on the car door handle and glared at Cat. "I'll be back to arrest you, Catherine Reedy." He bellowed loud enough for the entire block to hear. "I know you murdered your husband. Every time you see me, I'll be hammering another nail in your coffin."

Ed snuck a glance over his shoulder before ducking into the car. Cat crossed her arms as if to ward off a winter chill. Would his promise of help be anything more than cold comfort? If Dexter got any inkling he was butting in, things would go even worse for her. And he'd fail his sister.

What have I done?

He'd let emotions color his thinking. The vision of Cat cuddling her son prickled the hairs on the back of his neck. It felt as if his wife and baby were communicating from beyond the grave. He simply knew—Cat wasn't the killer. Didn't mean he could fix things.

Would she even show tonight? He suggested meeting at the Street Fair because everyone flocked to the carnival. Rich and poor. Young and old. Farmers and townsfolk. A chance encounter with a copper on patrol wouldn't look suspicious.

Then it hit him. Not suspicious? A woman widowed less than a day trundles off to the carnival for laughs. Keokuk's pious busybodies wouldn't need a trial to convict Cat.

What was I thinking?

* * *

Cat watched the police car drive away. "Grandmother, would you mind the children? I heard the basement door close. I'm sure Dad's searching for his gun. Beth and I should help."

The stairs creaked as the women descended. Though the dangling bare bulbs offered meager illumination, Cat spotted her father huddled on rough planks near the coal bin. His bony arms hugged his knees. She walked to him, touched his quivering shoulder.

"It's my fault." He wouldn't raise his head to look at her. "I swear the gun was here. I can't...can't remember."

"Dad, go upstairs. We all forget things. Beth and I have plenty of practice hunting for things we've misplaced. Maybe we'll get lucky. Let us take a look."

She clasped one of her father's elbows and Beth took the other to help him stand. His skeletal frame crackled as he unfolded, bone scrapping bone. He shuffled forward, never lifting his head, never meeting her eyes.

She felt the tears welling. She swallowed, waited a second until she could control her voice, stop the building sob. "You take the shelves on the right side, Beth. I'll take the left."

Cat searched the lowest shelf first, her fingers probing every crevice, even ones far too small to house a gun. On tiptoe, she foraged on the upper shelf where her dad's empty fishing tackle box sat open. A sharp stab of pain. She jumped back, stared at her bleeding finger, a fishhook still imbedded. "Hell and damnation. What next?"

In an instant, Beth stood at her side. "Let me get the blasted thing out. Believe me, Nurse Reedy's seen a few fishhooks stuck in worse places. Let's go upstairs. I'll clean it with peroxide. We're done here anyway. The only place we haven't searched is the coal bin."

Cat sighed. "You're right. Maybe Dad hid the gun under his bed."

After Beth doctored her finger, the women resumed their frantic treasure hunt. Cat sank to her knees to peer beneath her dad's bed. "Heavens to Betsy, these dust bunnies are big enough to qualify as hares. Poor Mom would be mortified at how low Reedy cleanliness standards have sunk."

Beth chuckled. "Glad to know I'm not the only one who'll never win a Good Housekeeping Seal of Approval."

"At least poor housekeeping isn't a hanging offense." Cat's chuckle sounded hollow to her own ears.

After scouring the upstairs rooms, the women tackled the first floor. Their frenzied search yielded four stashed bottles of hooch.

The phone rang and Cat's heart tap-danced. What if it was some reporter for the *Daily Gate City*? The phone trilled again. *Don't be a coward. You can't stop answering the phone.* She squared her shoulders, lifted the receiver. "Reedy house."

"Hello, this is Sister Pearl. Catherine? I'm sorry to hear of your loss, and I hate to bother you at this time, but, um, Chief Dexter asked us to phone. Have you selected a funeral parlor to receive Mr. Black?"

"Greaves," Cat answered after a slight pause. Greaves Mortuary always handled Reedy burials. "But I haven't made arrangements. I hope they're not..." She stumbled, not knowing the appropriate term. *Booked?* She regrouped. "I hope they can accommodate us. Thank you for calling."

Though she didn't intend to be rude, she hung up to avoid an exchange of mandatory yet meaningless condolences. Sister Pearl probably found the conversation equally uncomfortable. Before Cat's dad was excommunicated, the nun and Grandmother Nell were close friends. After John Reedy divorced his first wife and wed Cat's Methodist mother, Sister Pearl never stepped foot on their sidewalk. In Keokuk, religious ties and labor union sympathies—or their absence—could launch or end friendships.

Beth walked over and hugged Cat. "Why don't I go to the funeral parlor and handle arrangements? You should rest a bit."

"No. There's too much to do. I'll call Greaves Mortuary and tell them Dirk's coming. Selecting a casket can wait for a bit."

Her conversation with the undertaker proved mercifully brief. She scheduled the service for Wednesday and thanked him profusely for offering to send *The Daily Gate City* a pithy "survived by" obituary. As it was, Cat was certain the local newspaper would devote too many column inches to the gruesome details. Would they go so far as to hint she was a suspect?

She hung up and slumped against the wall next to the party-line phone—a rare luxury her brother, a phone company employee, helped them cling to despite the hard times. She looked at Beth, seated at the kitchen table. "Now comes the tough one. Dirk's mother." She shuddered. "I can't postpone it any longer."

Beth frowned. "I'd call, but hearing the news from a stranger would make it worse. Maybe I should pour us a stiff one from that bottle we found in the potato bin."

Cat sighed. "Hold that thought." She tapped the telephone cradle to signal an operator. As she waited for long distance to connect to the Illinois number, she twisted the cloth-covered cord, weaving it between her fingers.

"Hello." A man's voice.

"Yes, I'm calling for Mrs. Black."

"She's sleeping," the brusque voice answered. "This is her son. What d'you want?"

"Ralph? It's Cat. Catherine Black, your sister-in-law." What a relief. Breaking the news to Dirk's brother instead of his mother. Her words tumbled out in a torrent.

"There's no question he was murdered?" Ralph asked. "Any suspects?"

Cat hesitated. "Nothing concrete." She wasn't about to name herself as a prime candidate.

"I'll tell Mother," Ralph said. "She's too stove up to travel to Keokuk."

Thank, God, Cat thought. Then a wave of shame washed over her. How could she feel glee about an old lady too sickly to see a son buried? As a mother, she understood—no matter what Dirk had done, he'd always be Mrs. Black's little boy.

As she prepared to say goodbye, Ralph spoke. "You say the service is Wednesday, right? I'll leave for Keokuk tomorrow. Should be there by nightfall."

The announcement surprised her, though she couldn't fathom why. Of course Dirk's brother would want to pay his last respects.

"You can stay at the apartment." The offer came as a reflex—one she instantly regretted. What if Ralph found the damned letter? Would he accuse her of murder, too? *Sweet Jesus.*

"No, I'll get a room somewhere." Ralph's voice sounded gruff. "It, uh, wouldn't be proper for me to stay with you."

The comment eased her worries a mite. Ralph didn't know she'd left Dirk. "The apartment's empty. It's on the second floor. The address is 401 ½ North Fourth Street. Jay and I are staying at my dad's house. Besides most of the boarding houses are full—it's Street Fair week."

Cat's hands shook as she hung up. Her throat felt even tighter than when fall ragweed choked her. She accepted a mug of hot tea from Beth and drank greedily. Burned the roof of her mouth. *Dear God, can't I do anything right?*

"Thanks, Beth. I know it's cool outside, but would you mind sitting on the porch? We need to talk. In private."

The women sat side-by-side on the cushioned glider, nestled under a crocheted throw. Beth rested her feet against the porch railing and pushed, starting a gentle rock-a-bye sway. In the shade, it felt as if winter had arrived. A gust of wind carried the tinny sounds of a calliope, a reminder that come dusk half the town would scurry to the Street Fair.

Beth took Cat's hands in her own. "I figured I'd be bored on my day off. Play paddy cake with Amy. Shuck corn. Clean house.

Can tomatoes. You and the police chief certainly know how to add excitement."

She squeezed Cat's hands. "Someday this will sound like a tall tale, a bunch of hooey. I just hope Chief Dexter takes sick real soon. Nurse Reedy here will shove a thermometer so far up his caboose it'll pop out one of his hairy ears."

Cat gave her good-natured sister-in-law a wan smile. She couldn't manage a laugh. "Thanks for coming. The more witnesses the better if Dexter's around."

When Beth released her hands, Cat hugged herself. "It's a wonder the chief didn't drag me off to jail. I'm sure he's picking out his best Sunday suit to wear at my hanging."

"He can't arrest you." Beth sounded indignant, certain. "He doesn't have a shred of evidence. So your dad misplaced his gun, so what? Doesn't mean a thing."

Cat slumped against the glider's soft, tufted back. "Things would have gone even worse if the chief hadn't brought Ed Nelson along. I remember seeing him at school with his sister, Myrtle. I thought he was a dreamboat back then, but I never said boo to him."

She tucked a leg beneath her and turned sideways to face her sister-in-law. "I thought Ed left town after the bank foreclosed on the Nelson farm."

Cat hoped a conversational nudge would prompt Beth to deliver the man's unvarnished biography. As a nurse, her sister-in-law interacted with every element of the town strata and knew—even better than Undertaker Greaves—where the bodies were buried. She didn't dare ask the questions that weighed heaviest. Why did Ed say he'd help? Could she trust him?

Beth chewed on her lip, apparently marshalling her memories. "Ed and his wife, Hannah, moved to Peoria. Then Hannah died in childbirth about the time Jay was born."

"Did the baby live?" Cat asked.

"No, the boy came too early, only weighed a few pounds. I don't think he lasted a day. Heard folks talk about the double funeral, the tiny casket. Ed buried Hannah and his son in the family plot on his wife's farm. Got special permission from your bank since the cemetery's on Iowa First property now."

Poor soul. Losing two loved ones at once.

"Ed joined the Civilian Conservation Corps afterward." Beth paused, setting her mug of tea on a rickety side table. "Worked on some park project out West. Came back when Myrtle's husband, Al, went missing. Now there's a mystery. Al was a good man. Not the type to skedaddle. Folks figure he must be dead."

The biographical sketch made Ed sound a decent sort. That didn't mean Cat could trust him. Once upon a time, she'd trusted Dirk. She glanced at her sister-in-law. Beth's lips had vanished, mashed together in a temporary dam. A giveaway. Her face always contorted as she calculated how to voice some unpleasantness.

She raised her chin, looked Cat in the eye. "You must have some idea who murdered Dirk. Why not give the chief some suspects, get him off your tail? Dirk gambled, cozied up to prostitutes. You know it. I know it. Can't you push Dexter in another direction?"

Cat shook her head. "The chief knows full well how Dirk spent his time. That gambling hall between Second and Third Streets is practically Dexter's second home. He'd never look at his cronies and risk losing his payoffs."

But maybe Ed would.

She hung her head and paused. "I'm scared, Beth. There's something I didn't tell Dexter. Dirk was blackmailing Ken—"

"Oh, my Lord in heaven." Beth's eyes grew wide. "You think Kenneth Jacobs killed Dirk. No wonder you're scared. Did Dirk find out about the, uh, incident?"

Cat nodded. "Dirk was in a rage when I left him. I just stuffed things in a suitcase and ran. I forgot I'd taped Jacobs' last letter to the back of the drawer in that gate-leg table Dad made for me.

Dirk wasn't searching—just destroying things I loved. The letter fell out when he smashed the table."

She closed her eyes and shuddered. "My dear husband paid me a visit at the bank. Said he wanted to thank me for dealing him a straight flush. He claimed Jacobs agreed to buy him off."

"Jesus, Mary and Joseph. That letter—did it spell out *everything*?"

Cat's head drooped, and her breath caught. "Yes." She raised her gaze to meet Beth's. "I need to talk to Jacobs. Will you get word to him? Arrange a meeting? I have to know."

Beth frowned. "You sure about this? Maybe it's better if you don't know. What if Jacobs tells you he killed Dirk, won't that make you some sort of …I don't know…conspirator?" Her eyes widened. "Oh my God. If Jacobs killed Dirk, maybe he'll kill you. Are you willing to trust that man with your life? You know he's capable of violence."

Cat didn't answer instantly. "Mr. Jacobs still grieves for his dead son. I've seen how he looks at Jay. I don't think he wants to leave my boy without a mother and a father. I'm sure he's the 'anonymous' donor who leaves cash in unmarked envelopes when I'm desperate. So, no, I don't think he'd harm me."

Cat squeezed Beth's arm. "I need to know if Dirk handed over that damned letter. If not, I have to find it, destroy it. I'll search the apartment when I pick up burial clothes. I hope to God Chief Dexter hasn't beaten me to it."

Beth patted Cat's hand. "So how do I reach your bank president? I don't exactly hobnob with the titans of local industry."

"No, but one of your bedridden patients, Mrs. Anderson, does. Think real hard and I bet you'll recall a conversation with Mrs. Anderson—some private matter she asked you to share with the bank president and him alone. You can say your patient wasn't strong enough to attend to the business herself."

Beth nodded. "That'll work. She's one of the few folks in Keokuk who still has money."

"I have one more favor to ask. I need to go to the Street Fair tonight. I don't want to explain, okay? Not now. I need to meet someone, and it has to look accidental. Will you go with me?"

Beth bit her lip. "You're certain you want to go out on the town the day they fished Dirk's body out of the river? That won't exactly win town sympathy."

"You're right, but this can't wait. Please. Come with me."

When Beth nodded agreement, the breath Cat held escaped in a relieved whoosh. Why was she keeping Ed's offer of help secret from Beth? Her sister-in-law was the only soul she'd trusted to tell about Kenneth Jacobs. Superstition? Or did she fear she was losing her mind—that she'd imagined Ed's words. She'd find out tonight.

SIX

The police car bounced across the cobblestones running parallel to the train tracks. The humid breeze reeked of scorched corn. Rendering corn kernels into syrups and starches produced fumes so potent they seemed to have actual weight—and taste. Ed tugged at his shirt collar.

Caught up in his hindsight game, Ed didn't ask where they were headed. Once they bumped past the Hubinger plant, he guessed the destination—a cluster of fishing shanties by the river. The place poorer folk, like the Reedys, kept decrepit johnboats.

Dexter stopped the car and both men climbed out. A sharp cry prompted Ed to look skyward. A bald eagle, one of dozens that fished the Mississippi, circled above. The chief spotted a human fisherman hauling a rowboat ashore and trudged his way. "Hey, you. Does John Reedy keep a boat 'round here?"

The man gave the police chief a hard look. The set of his jaw said he didn't want to answer. He sat on an overturned boat and slapped a string of catfish on the grass. He pulled a jagged knife from a scabbard to gut his catch. "Down the bank, to the right. Name's Addie. It's painted on her side." The man slid a knife into the belly of the fattest fish. Yellow guts spewed to the ground. End of conversation.

Ed trailed Dexter toward a helter-skelter assortment of weather-beaten boats. Addie was the third boat in. He figured the faded name had once been cherry red. Now the ghostly letters were barely visible on the turtled boat.

"Help me flip her," Dexter barked.

Ed walked to the stern and pried his fingers under the lip. Rough, jagged splinters dug at his fingertips. The flat-bottomed johnboat teetered on its side before it flopped upright with a thud.

Dexter began to chuckle before the boat quit rocking. "Well, looky, here." He pointed at a reddish-brown stain coating the tip of an oar. "Looks like blood to me."

"Could be fish blood," Ed ventured.

The comment earned a shut-the-hell-up glare. "Nope, that's Dirk Black's blood or I'm a monkey's uncle. Now all I need is to put Cat here on Sunday with Dirk. If'n she got her hubby to row them out into the river, the little witch wouldn't have needed no accomplice. She could'a shot him before she used that oar to bang him upside the head and topple him in the water."

Ed bit his tongue. The doc had said Dirk was hit with something jagged not the smooth oar. Even if the blood belonged to Dirk, the circumstantial evidence didn't point a finger at Cat. Hell, Dirk could have gone out in the boat with some low-life buddy who killed him over a high-stakes poker pot.

"Go find that fisherman," Dexter ordered. "I wanna know every idjit who keeps a boat here's about. Make a list, and we'll pay 'em visits."

The chief's tone vibrated with dark intent. He would browbeat, hell, beat some bloke until the poor sod swore he saw Cat and Dirk launching the Addie together on Sunday.

Damn. Dexter's railroading scheme had a full head of steam.

SEVEN

Beth Reedy squared her shoulders, trying to project confidence she didn't feel, as she entered the bank. Quarter till five, almost closing time. She hoped the man at the helm kept banker's hours and hadn't slipped out early. She'd dressed carefully—her best Sunday frock, a demure felt hat, white gloves never worn before. She bypassed the teller cages and marched to the burnished mahogany railing that fenced off the bank's vault and executive offices. She stood before the hinged gate, unsure of her next move.

Inside the barrier, a middle-aged functionary with a glistening black moustache looked up from the sheaf of papers on his desk. "May I help you, ma'am?"

"Yes." She smiled. "I'd like to speak with Mr. Jacobs on behalf of Mrs. Anderson. I'm Mrs. Peter Reedy, Mrs. Anderson's nurse."

The man wrinkled his nose, and Beth regretted introducing herself as Pete's wife. She was proud of her husband, but everyone knew about his best friend's role at Corn Products Workers Union No. 19931. Last July, the labor union had called a strike that virtually shut down Hubingers for two months.

Many of the men who bankrolled Keokuk's factories had little use for what they called union rabble—or their sympathizers. Feelings were still raw over the two-month strike. This starched shirt obviously identified with the fat cats paying his salary.

"Surely there's no need to bother Mr. Jacobs." The man pasted on a crocodile smile. "Why don't you tell me what Mrs. Anderson needs? I'm certain I can handle any request."

Beth shook her head. "No. Mrs. Anderson was quite clear. She asked me to speak to Mr. Jacobs, personally. In private."

The man's eyes narrowed. Beth mentally ran through her options if the squinty-eyed sentinel dismissed her. Should she raise her voice? Make a fuss to flush Mr. Jacobs out of his swank hidey-hole?

"Mrs. Anderson is one of Iowa First's best customers," a voice cut in. "I can certainly make time to see her representative."

Focused intently on the fusty gatekeeper, Beth hadn't seen Kenneth Jacobs, the man himself, saunter out of his office. He idly fingered the brim of the hat in his hand. On his way out the door? The bank president looked like he always did—elegant, aloof. His pinstriped, double-breasted jacket hung perfectly, his silk tie picked up a thread of blue in the weave of his suit coat. Calculating gray eyes maintained a steady gaze over a practiced smile.

A cold fish if I ever saw one. Hard to believe he'd stoop to violence. But he'd proven he could. Was that frenzy really the one-time lapse he claimed?

Jacobs strode forward, unlatched the gate, and swung it aside for Beth to enter. "Please come back to my office, Mrs.—I'm sorry, I didn't catch your name."

"Beth Reedy," she answered. "I'm Mrs. Anderson's nurse."

The man's confident stride stuttered slightly. She felt a perverse pleasure at ruffling his feathers. A visit from any Reedy relation had to tighten his sphincter. Understandable after Dirk's blackmail.

"Won't you have a seat?" He motioned to an office sofa bracketed by side tables and Queen Anne chairs.

Jacobs closed the door. Instead of moving behind his desk, he claimed the side chair nearest her. "What can I do for you? I hope Mrs. Anderson hasn't had a setback."

"No. She's getting stronger every day." Beth hesitated then rushed ahead. "I *am* Mrs. Anderson's nurse, but she didn't send me. Catherine Black, my sister-in-law, asked me to hand you this note and wait for a reply."

She thrust the envelope forward. Jacobs' mouth fell slightly open, a stress crack in his granite exterior. His eyes darted to the closed door and back again. He bowed his head and stared at the envelope. Didn't speak. Beth shivered. Was he contemplating how to get rid of another dead body?

"Look, Mr. Jacobs. I'm just a messenger. I didn't read Cat's note, and I won't peek at your reply. I'm doing a favor for someone as dear to me as my own flesh and blood. Someone who felt it would be awkward to call on you personally."

"I understand." Jacobs took the note and walked to a window. He kept his back to Beth while he opened the envelope and read.

Beth watched the mirrored pendulum of a grandfather clock tucked in one corner of the office mark time, and then glanced at a *Daily Gate City* neatly folded on the side table beside the sofa. Today the fighting in Europe took a backseat to Street Fair news. The paper predicted a crowd would brave the cold to see Jaydee the Great in his ape costume as he performed his amazing high trapeze novelty act on rigging one-hundred-feet high. B.B. Hickenlooper was one of four GOP politicians planning to speak. Opening time for the livestock show was one o'clock. Beth could vouch that part of the fair was on schedule. The cattle and horses might be vying for prizes but their manure smelled all the same.

Seconds passed, then minutes before Jacobs turned and walked to his desk.

"Give me a moment." His gold pen flashed as he scratched out several sentences. He slid the note into a new envelope and sealed it tight. "I hope my trust in you isn't misplaced." His steel gray eyes bored into hers.

Beth didn't flinch. "And I hope to heaven Cat isn't wrong to trust you."

Jacobs opened his office door for Beth. The functionary's desk sat empty. The bank had closed. The good little worker bees had flown home. With the center lights switched off, the temperature in the bank seemed to plummet. Beth shivered.

"I'll walk you out," Jacobs said.

Their footsteps echoed on the marble floor. Her heart skipped a beat. She hadn't considered she might wind up alone with this man—with someone capable of murder? She picked up her pace.

"Do give Mrs. Anderson my regards," he said as she hurried out the front door.

The heavy door banged shut and a lock clicked.

Had a door opened or closed for Cat?

EIGHT

Bad memories swamped Cat as she climbed the rickety stairs to the apartment she'd shared with Dirk. Her gut twisted in fear. Could she find the damnable letter?

"Where's my rent!" Old man O'Reilly's angry shout startled her. *Crud.* Standing with skeleton key in hand, almost inside, she peered down through gaps in the outside stairway. The splintered steps blocked most of her landlord's head as it poked out of his ground-floor window. Still, she could see strands of greasy gray hair. That and his caustic tone identified the man.

"Rent's due first of the month. Ain't seen you or that husband of yours 'round. Took a look in your apartment to see what was what. Heaven all mighty, broke dishes all over tarnation. You folks feudin's none of my business, but you'll make good on any damages, by God."

Cat almost told O'Reilly to take the matter up with Dirk. He couldn't know her husband was dead. The rumor mill wasn't *that* speedy. Let the mean old coot try to wring money from a corpse. She swallowed a tart retort. Couldn't afford for her landlord to change the locks. Not yet.

"I'll pay for the month. Don't worry, my husband won't be coming back. Neither will I. There'll be no more fights. But Dirk's brother arrives tomorrow. He'll stay here a day or two. Please don't bother him."

O'Reilly wriggled further out his window. His pinched face popped into view. He smacked his gums like a hooked fish flopping on a dock. Definitely winding up for one of his sanctimonious rants about her sinful, bound-for-hell generation. Her anger boiled. Damned if she'd stand here and listen to his spleen.

"As long as I'm paying rent, Mr. O'Reilly, this apartment is mine. Don't enter again without an invitation."

Shaking with fury, she slammed the door. Her back sagged against it. Where in hell would she get the rent money? When she repaid Dirk's boss for her husband's last sticky-fingered visit to his employer's kitty, Dirk had promised to pay the rent until he left. Another lie. What a shock.

And I just made matters worse. Sassing O'Reilly. Sweet Jesus, what if he calls Chief Dexter to evict me or throws our belongings on the front lawn? Hell fire.

The lowered oilcloth shades shut out the dazzling sunlight, turning the cramped three rooms into a gloomy cavern. Her eyes slowly adjusted to the twilight. As her gaze slid over the jumbled mess, she sighed. Not so bad.

Even in his rage, Dirk had restrained himself. He'd only targeted the few pieces Cat had brought in to spruce up the furnished apartment. Items with sentimental rather than dollar value. The rocker with Grandmother Nell's needlepoint cushion had been reduced to a pile of matchsticks, but the landlord's barebones furnishings—a knock-off Tiffany lamp, a scarred end table, a threadbare sofa—remained untouched.

A sour odor of decay prompted her to head to what she jokingly called a one-butt kitchen. Her shoes crunched on a shard of glass. Pieces of the heavy crock she used to steep iced tea added jagged blue accents to the strewn rubble. Dirk had swept clean a narrow corridor of linoleum to create a passage to the sink and icebox. She minded her step.

When she reached the chipped cast-iron sink, Cat gagged. Though a dozen furry bodies clung to a flypaper strip, fat survivors buzzed insolently as they feasted on the rotting sauerkraut and pork glued to a pile of dirty dishes.

Breathing through her mouth, she flung open windows to let in fresh air while she tackled the crusted dishes. As she furiously scrubbed, her agitated brain posed new questions. When did Dirk leave the apartment? Had he planned to come back? Chief Dexter said he found him floating in his Sunday best. Why? Was he meeting someone he wanted to impress?

She corralled the cracked pottery and glass shards in a dustbin, and stashed her splintered heirlooms in a corner. An hour of hard, fevered labor restored the apartment to order. For once, Cat was glad the rooms were tiny. While the apartment wasn't spic and span, the floors were broom clean and the kitchen no longer stank.

She'd searched for the letter as she cleaned. Nothing. The pockets in Dirk's clothes and his trumpet case remained the only unexplored options. She opened the instrument case first. The trumpet gleamed. *Dirk planned to come back. He'd never leave his horn.* Her fingers explored the purple velvet lining. No holes or torn seams.

As she sat on the floor and stared at the trumpet, her eyes brimmed with tears. How the man could play. Clear, sweet notes as distinct and delicate as lilies of the valley. He could improvise, too. He'd stunned her the first time he joined a jazz group—eyes closed and body swaying as he intuited a syncopated harmony.

Her fingers danced over the polished metal. Golden, untarnished. Like those first two months of courtship. She allowed herself a good memory, though it now seemed more like a Hollywood movie starring Cary Grant and Katherine Hepburn than something she'd lived.

She'd taken the train to Chicago with two younger cousins—a rare indulgence in the Depression. But Cat's dad, guilty that her earnings kept the family afloat, insisted she spend a little money on fun. "What's the point of living, if you can't kick up your heels once in a blue moon?" he asked. So away she went—and turned her world upside down.

Five minutes after she entered the ornate Aragon ballroom Dirk asked her to dance. On Cat's return to the table, her cousins oohed and aahed. "You two dance like Ginger Rogers and Fred Astaire," one of her relatives gushed.

Dirk's dark eyes and rugged Bogart looks turned her grown cousins giggly. More astonishing, the men who courted these ladies liked him as well. A master storyteller, Dirk orchestrated laugh after laugh as the couples sat knee-to-knee at the crowded table.

Little did Cat know Dirk could improvise new versions of himself as easily as he ad-libbed tunes at jam sessions. A chameleon, he changed colors constantly to suit his surroundings, his audience. Had she ever known the real Dirk?

Maybe Ralph would want the trumpet. She seemed to recall Dirk's brother had played in a band, too. She'd only met Ralph the one time. He'd been on a business trip and made a forty-mile detour to lunch with the newlyweds. While they sat on stools at the Grand Annex Tavern eating chili and pork tenderloin sandwiches, Ralph asked Dirk how his leg felt.

Cat immediately pictured the jagged scar on her husband's calf. "You mean his war wound?" she asked.

Ralph howled with laughter. "Dirk? In the Great War? What a hoot. He was seventeen, no thought of enlisting. No, Dirk fell on a broken beer bottle at a picnic. Drunk as a skunk."

The smile on her face froze. She'd already caught Dirk in a dozen lies—needless, pointless fabrications. Tall tales about why he was late for dinners. Fibs about how much he'd spent on a new Fedora or tie. But this revelation shocked her.

She never told anyone except Beth about the humiliation. "For cripe's sake, you heard the war story Dirk spun," she reminded her sister-in-law. "He made it sound as if he single-handedly saved a dozen doughboys while blood gushed from his leg. Can I believe anything he says?"

She learned the answer. The hard way. Why did he lie? Had his mother started it all by changing the family name from Schwartz to Black, instructing her boys to prevaricate about their absent father? Did it begin with shame, snowball into habit?

Cat sighed and snapped the trumpet case closed.

She stood and walked to the wardrobe where Dirk's clothes hung and meticulously checked every pocket. After a fruitless search, she selected clothes for his burial, bundled them into a satchel, and closed and locked the front door. She hoped her brother Pete could cart the broken furniture away before Ralph arrived.

She glanced at her watch. Five o'clock. Had Beth reached Jacobs? What was his answer? Now that her hands were no longer busy, fatigue and frustration tugged at her body. A dull pain commenced a steady throb behind her eyes.

And she still had to go to the funeral home.

The bus rattled down Concert Street. One more stop. The satchel with Dirk's blue suit sat at Cat's feet. The suit he'd be buried in. His brown three-piece—his best—wasn't in the closet. He must have been wearing it when he was killed. Why? The chief implied Dirk was murdered yesterday, on a Sunday. The man never crossed the threshold of a church. Not even when baby Jay was baptized before the United Methodist congregation.

She leaned down and reached inside the satchel. Her fingers fidgeted with the suit's cheap gabardine fabric. Did she want to see her dead husband's face? She swallowed. No, but she'd look at him. She'd look at anything and everything that might hint at how he died and who killed him.

A somber Mr. Greaves greeted her when she rang the bell on the side door, the trade entry. "Mrs. Black. Please come in." He took the satchel from her arms.

"Are his clothes inside?" he asked.

She nodded and he ushered her into his office.

"I can't afford much," she blurted out before she even sat down.

Mr. Greaves patted her arm. "No one can these days, dear. I'm sure Mr. Black wouldn't want you to spend money on anything more than a pine box. He knows you have to care for his son."

Cat appreciated the kindness, though she felt confident Dirk would have wanted to go out of this world in the same fashion he barreled through it. Flashy. Well, he'd just have to haunt her for denying him a mahogany and satin bier.

She met the funeral director's eyes. His face revealed only sympathy. Either he was a master actor or the police chief had yet to broadcast his opinion that Catherine Reedy Black had murdered her own husband. She signed papers, a formal IOU.

Cat swallowed hard. "I'd like to see him."

Greaves shook his head. "Oh, dear, it would be best if you wait until we've, um, prepared him."

"No. I need to see Dirk now. Please. This isn't real yet."

Greaves stood. "If you're sure. Follow me."

The man shuffled down a winding corridor to a back room. A ripe smell tickled the back of her throat. She swallowed bile. Dirk lay on a table, a sheet drawn over his body. Bare feet poked from beneath the white drape. At the other end of the sheet, tiny bits of debris threaded through thick black hair. The funeral director lifted the sheet to reveal his whole face. Thankfully, closed eyelids hid his angry onyx eyes. His skin's gray tint aged him another decade. Dirk looked almost as old as her father.

She felt nothing. Not grief, not relief, not happiness. No, that wasn't right. She felt something. Fear made her mouth dry as a cotton ball. Someone killed him. And the odds were astronomical the killer wouldn't confess. He'd be all too happy for her to hang in his stead.

Cat sucked in a deep breath and nodded at Mr. Greaves. "Thank you."

She turned and noticed a sodden heap of clothes in the corner. Dirk's brown suit. "May I take his clothes?"

This time an emotion flicked across the funeral director's face. Revulsion. "Oh, Mrs. Black. You don't want them. They, uh, smell. I don't think they can be salvaged. There are no valuables. No watch or wallet. Perhaps the police kept them for safekeeping?"

"I understand. I'd still like to take the clothes. Do you have a sturdy sack?"

* * *

Cat snuck in the back door of her home and headed straight to the basement. The grocery bags, three layers thick, had grown soggy from toting the garments. The sacks fell to pieces as she extracted the suit and then the shoes. Mr. Greaves hadn't included undergarments, and she certainly hadn't objected. She didn't imagine she'd find any clues in his boxers.

Dirk was a secretive man. He had every reason to be. She knew his penchant for hiding damning pieces of evidence, like sales slips and doxie phone numbers. Maybe she'd find some note the Mississippi River hadn't dissolved into paste.

The suit yielded nothing. She reached inside the shoes, and fingered a bulge under the innersole. She pulled the inset free and retrieved a thin brass key. Her find gleamed under the bare bulb's glow. It looked new. What did it open?

An image formed in her mind. Dirk's strongbox, a heavy wooden box, the corners reinforced with iron. A padlock hung from the iron hasp. It opened with a brass key. She closed her eyes. Pictured their old apartment and the spot on the bedroom floor where the strongbox usually sat. Until this moment she hadn't realized it was missing. Had Dirk hidden it?

NINE

The woman slowed her car when she reached the midpoint of the bridge connecting Keokuk, Iowa, to Hamilton, Illinois. Below her, the muddy Mississippi roiled, a fitting repository for a piece of garbage like Dirk Black.

The sinking sun burnished the horizon with streaks of gold. An omen for the future? God provided for those who smote the devils in their midst.

In Illinois, she followed the winding river road toward Nauvoo. She'd have to find a new rendezvous soon if the Mississippi continued its rise. Soon it would swamp the ribbon of curved road beside the river.

Too bad. Nauvoo was a good choice. Ever since God-fearing Christians ran off the Mormons, the town looked closer to dead than sleepy. A movie playbill at the Opera House was practically the only reason for outsiders to bother with Nauvoo. Not likely anyone from Keokuk would spot her haunting a Nauvoo cemetery. Still she took precautions.

Just short of the forsaken town, she veered onto a dirt road and drove behind a dilapidated barn. Once she made certain her car was invisible to passing motorists, she cut through a copse of black walnut trees to the moldering cemetery.

She wore widow weeds—a long black dress three sizes too big with a pillow belted in place to add pounds. She stooped to camouflage her generous height. A nearly impenetrable veil secured to an antique hat completed her ensemble.

She'd watched *Snow White and the Seven Dwarfs* with her daughter. While the fair princess and her devoted "little men" captivated her sweet little girl, she'd sympathized with the queen. The animated character's transformation from beauty to old crone inspired her, too. Disguises had their uses. For weeks, she'd practiced throwing her voice, forcing deeper, guttural sounds from the back of her throat.

The Disney film premiered at Keokuk's Grand Theater in February, more than six months ago. That's when she started planning Dirk Black's demise along with a way to feed Catherine Reedy Black her own version of a poisoned apple, one that promised infinitely more pain than Snow White's deep sleep. She had no intention of sharing the queen's ill-fated end. That's why she willingly paid for competent criminal assistance. Jimmy Cloyd, the mob's local head knocker, met her needs—burly, no scruples, connected, affordable.

She spotted Jimmy the minute she entered the cemetery. The thickset man slouched against a cracked mausoleum. As soon as he saw her, Jimmy sucked a final puff on a glowing cigarette butt and ground it out on a canted headstone.

She wrinkled her nose. He reeked of tobacco and cheap whiskey. She handed him his pay. "Here's five hundred. You did a good job with Black's body and our little drowning victim."

"Yeah, I heard they found the floater today," Jimmy replied. "Worked just like you wanted." He gave a little chuckle. "I paid that brat Jeremy to maroon hisself on an island and give the heave-ho to his johnboat. Once someone spotted it floatin' like a ghost ship, we got word to his ma the kid mighta drowned. She ran to the cops begging 'em to search the river."

She frowned. "You're sure the child won't confess his sins, maybe tell his mother?"

"Nah, even if he gets a hidin', he won't squeal. He's got more money than he ever seen, and he knows he'd get worse than a hidin' from me, if'n he told."

Jimmy turned his head and spit a stream of colored saliva on a nearby leaf. She shuddered. Did the man smoke *and* chew at the same time?

"I schooled him what to say—that he stopped on the island when nature called and his boat floated off, accidental like."

She studied her employee. While she found his hygiene objectionable, she liked his lack of curiosity. He never asked questions. "Tomorrow you call the police chief and tell him where his prime suspect hid her gun. Phone from some hotel in Burlington. Play the good citizen who doesn't want to give his name and get tangled in some sordid muddle."

"Can do." Jimmy shook another cigarette from an almost empty pack of Camels.

The woman backed up a step. Sweat soaked the coarse fabric between her shoulder blades. Her veil seemed to stymie air flow. She felt queasy enough without acrid smoke blowing in her face.

"Have someone follow Mrs. Black. Make sure he's discreet. Let's see where our poor little widow goes—who she meets. No doubt the tart was in on it with her husband. The little con artist may try to bamboozle some other male into playing Sir Galahad. Fortunately Chief Dexter shares my antipathy for Mrs. Black. She won't con him. I don't want anyone else poking a nose in where it doesn't belong."

"Sam can keep an eye on her. I doubt she strays far from home, what with the funeral."

"I want a report tomorrow. Leave it in the usual place. Check there every day for messages. I'll leave instructions when we need to meet again."

The fickle breeze switched direction, and Jimmy's smoke wafted her way. She coughed and cleared her throat, hoping her employee might take a hint. "You recruited some carnies at the Street Fair, right?"

Jimmy nodded. "Yeah, I lined up some toughs. They'll do whatever. Don't care what I need 'em for so long as I grease their palms with enough greenbacks."

"You're certain they'll disappear before anyone thinks to question them?"

"Don't you fret none. Them gypsies know how to vanish when coppers come around. Leave the details to me."

* * *

Jimmy watched the woman mince her way out of the graveyard. No doubt she'd rise to her full height and streak like a banshee once she reached the woods. He chuckled. Did the hoity-toity dame really think her disguise fooled him? She could stoop as much as she wanted but the lady couldn't hide the fact she'd tower over most every dame in Keokuk. Then there was the time she forgot to doff her ring. Diamond bigger than a lump of coal. He knew exactly who she was—an edge he might need someday.

He was smart enough to be careful. Never met a soul—man or woman—better at cookin' up ways to skewer somebody she hated. Popping a bloke with a gun or shoving a shiv in his gut weren't enough. The dame liked her enemies to see trouble coming like a freight train and know no fresh-faced hero would untie 'em in time. The *Perils of Pauline* except the train sawed ol' Pauline in half.

He just wished she'd quit insisting on meeting in the boonies. What a pain. Much more convenient to sit on her fancy porch, high on the Mississippi bluff, and sip a nice lemonade while they did their business. Nevertheless, Jimmy would never let Mrs. Moneybags tumble to the fact he knew where she lived.

Pretending to be stupid paid too good.

TEN

Cat crept upstairs to bathe. She poured bath salts in the claw-footed tub. A luxury she normally hoarded. She wanted to scrub away the smell of death clinging to her skin before she greeted her son.

Back downstairs, she scooped up Jay. "How's my big boy?" He giggled as she lifted him above her head and twirled him in a greeting game. "You hungry? Ready for supper?"

Grandmother Nell paused in her knitting. "John cooked. Said we'd eat soon as you were ready."

"It smells delicious." Cat balanced her son on her hip and walked into the kitchen. "What's for supper, Dad?"

Her father kept his eyes fastened on the concoction stewing in a cast-iron pot. "Navy beans and cornbread for the adults. Don't know about Jay. Your grandmother said she'd kill me if I let him eat beans again."

Since the cheap meal demanded minimal culinary fussing, her dad fixed it often. He slow-cooked the beans with ham hocks and chopped onions until the mixture resembled porridge. Served with a side of cornbread, it provided a filling supper.

Cat smiled. "We'll limit Jay to a bite or two. I'll cut up some leftover chicken and carrots. He'll love it. Is it just the three of us or are Pete, Beth, and Amy joining us?"

"Beth's bringing Amy over after supper. Pete's working late." Her dad swung round. A vein twitched at his temple.

"Are we just pretending everything's normal? That your no-account husband isn't over at Greaves Mortuary being fitted for a casket...that Chief Dexter isn't licking his chops because I lost track of my gun?"

Cat looked at her son and consciously softened her tone. She teased Jay's hair to distract him from the adult conversation. "Yes, Dad, we're going to pretend everything's normal for a spell. I just left the funeral parlor where a man I once loved was laid out rigid and gray as a slab of granite. I need to eat supper, play with Jay." She tweaked the little boy's nose. "Maybe even listen to the radio. Reality will clobber me soon enough."

Her dad's eyes looked haunted. She touched his arm. "Dad, please, I don't blame you. We'll find the gun. Let's relax a few minutes. Right, Jay?"

She put her son in his high chair, tied on his bib, put down a dish of applesauce, and handed him a spoon. "Remember, my little man, we use our spoon to eat applesauce, don't we?"

"Yes, Mommy." His wobbling spoon carried a dollop of homemade applesauce toward his mouth. He swallowed the prize and grinned. "Where's Dadda? I wanna show him I can use a spoon."

Cat felt the burn of unshed tears. "He'd be proud of you."

Time enough later to explain he'd never see Dadda again. Dirk never lowered himself to diaper, feed, or bathe the boy, but when the mood struck, he played with Jay, tickling and teasing him into fits of giggles. She understood her son loved his big playmate. Dirk could be very charming when he wanted to be. Once upon a time, he made her laugh, too.

* * *

At six-thirty, Beth and four-year-old Amy breezed in.

"Aunt Cat, are we really going to the Street Fair?" The little girl did a fair imitation of the jitterbug. As she wiggled, her polka dot dress flounced up and down, showing off a snow-white petticoat.

Grandmother Nell jerked upright. Thinned lips revealed her opinion. The very idea of a widow traipsing off to the fair was social blasphemy. "Catherine Reedy Black, you cannot go to the Street Fair. What will people think? You're supposed to be in mourning."

Cat sighed. "Any minute, Chief Dexter may cart me off in handcuffs. Tongues will wag regardless. Might as well enjoy my freedom while it lasts. Half the town already knows I left Dirk and moved home two weeks ago. That made me a social outcast, a pariah. Not exactly a new role. What do I have to lose? I'll bet Maude Burks has already spread word I'm a cold-blooded killer."

She wanted to say more. Wanted to tell her grandmother how much she regretted letting concern for appearances and worry about gossip lock her in a marital prison for four years. What was the point? Grandmother Nell would never understand. And young ears soaked up emotional content if not meaning.

Please grandmother, drop it. The elderly matriarch shook her head and twisted the ball of yarn in her lap like she was wringing a chicken's neck.

Cat turned her attention to her niece Amy. "Honey, we'll leave for the fair in a few minutes. First your mommy and I need to talk. Why don't you play with Jay?"

Beth followed Cat into the kitchen where they sat at a small scarred table. Cat's dad had disappeared as soon as supper was over. The conversation would be private.

"Did you see Jacobs?" Cat kept her voice low

"Yes, he gave me this." Beth handed her the envelope.

Cat tore it open. The paper shook in her hands. She sucked in a deep breath and read, then she answered the question written on Beth's face. "He says he met Dirk on Saturday and gave him five hundred dollars once Dirk promised to leave town but wouldn't give him the letter. Claims he never saw him again."

"Do you believe that?"

"Maybe. Oh, God, I don't know." She crammed the note back in the envelope, stood, and walked to the sink. She pulled a kitchen match from a metal box above the stove, struck it, and held the flame under the envelope. She dropped the burning note in the cast-iron sink. In seconds, fire reduced it to char.

"I don't know," Cat repeated as she washed the ashes down the drain. "I want to believe him. Wish I knew what happened to that five hundred dollars. There wasn't a wallet or a money clip with his things at the funeral home."

Beth harrumphed. "Bet Dirk had it on him. Chief Dexter isn't above picking the pockets of any corpse he finds."

"Possible. Or maybe someone killed Dirk for the money. He could have bragged about it, flashed it in a poker game. The going wage is twenty-three cents an hour. Five hundred dollars is a fortune. People kill for a lot less."

Beth's face lit up. "If Dirk had five hundred dollars on him, robbery's a likely motive. Maybe if Dexter knew about the missing money, he'd let you be?"

Cat sighed. "And where would I say Dirk scrounged up five hundred dollars? No, Beth, I can't mention the money. The blackmail gives Mr. Jacobs—and me—even more reason to kill my low-life husband."

"Damn." Beth's smile crumpled. "Did Mr. Respectable Banker offer help, or was he too busy proclaiming himself to be pure as Ivory Soap?"

"He offered to bend the mayor's ear about Chief Dexter trying to railroad a bank employee. Jacobs lives in a dream world if he thinks anyone will lift a finger. Most everyone in this town's afraid to cross Chief Dexter and his gangster cronies."

Cat took Beth's hand. "Let's head to the Street Fair. Do you suppose there's a booth where you can toss rings and win a knight in shining armor?"

Beth's look held a question. Cat lowered her eyes.

"Please don't ask about my meeting. And, no, I quit believing in fairytales a long time ago."

The women returned to the living room where Amy and Jay played with wooden blocks and Grandmother Nell's knitting needles clicked like loose dentures. Cat's father had vanished. He'd probably slunk to the basement. Sometimes Cat wondered if he went there to lie on the damp earthen floor and prepare himself for the grave. The way he drank it wouldn't be long.

***

Ed sat on the couch, bookended by his squirming twin nieces.

"Read it one more time, please," Sarah begged.

"Yes, Uncle Ed," Susie added. "Show us how the big wolf huffs and puffs."

He grinned and closed the frayed picture book. "Sorry, kidlings, no more tonight. It's time for me to go to work."

Ed ruffled the carrot-colored curls of the five-year-olds then headed to the kitchen. Myrtle stood at the sink, her rigid back to her brother.

"My husband's dead." She whirled to face Ed, her hands kneading a threadbare dishtowel. "You can't bring him back. Stop this. I can't lose you. Quit the police. Please."

Ed placed his hands on his sister's shoulders and turned her around. "That man is evil. Remember Cat Reedy? We dragged her husband's body out of the river today, and the chief's determined to see her hang for it. My gut tells me the woman is innocent."

Myrtle shrugged off his hands and picked up a dish towel. "Sorry to hear that. If Cat's smart—and she is—she'll run. Take a powder before he locks her up."

His sister's head snapped up. "Oh, no. Tell me you haven't got it in your head to protect the little lady? You're skating on thin ice already. Don't butt in."

Ed didn't answer. He kissed his sister's cheek. "Time to go. I'll be late."

* * *

Ed paused on the fringes of the crowd surrounding a tattered canvas tent while a barker catalogued the freakish wonders they'd see inside. For a mere nickel, he promised a three-armed man and a two-headed calf, a squash that looked like Abe Lincoln's death mask, and a lady so fat she traveled in her own box car.

The carnie leaned down to pat the head of a chubby boy whose mouth had opened wide enough to swallow horseflies. "You'se probably too young, Sonny. We's got a half-man, half-wolf creature inside. We chained the beast up just to keep him from eating little boykins like you!"

The carnie lunged and the wide-eyed youngster squealed and stumbled backward in fright. The audience guffawed at the shenanigans. The barker knew his banter. He was a master at winning over a crowd. He watched him lure a dozen more folks into his canvas lair.

Ed couldn't imagine giving the man any of his hard-earned nickels. Yet he understood how badly folks needed something, anything to take their minds off their troubles. Trying to make a living was hard enough, but the newspaper headlines scared him more. Today's *Daily Gate City* said that Hitler fellow'd seized more land, and the Brits and French sounded mighty worried. A World War hovered on the horizon. If America entered it, he'd volunteer. But only if the government paid enough to provide for Myrt and his nieces. Patriotism was one thing, but his kin had to eat.

He watched more folks enter the freak show. His neighbors. Ordinary people whose behinds polished church pews every Sunday morning. Did it make them feel better, knowing that even if they were dirt poor, they had two arms, two legs, and one head?

He checked his pocket watch. Just after seven. An hour to go before he met Cat. Would she show? A part of him hoped not. He hadn't figured out any way to help her. Not yet.

He scanned the crowd. Chill temperatures hadn't kept folks home. Old men hobbling on canes. Young mothers holding tight to chubby toddler hands. Women gossiping about people they hadn't laid eyes on since last year's street fair.

Like the other coppers on patrol, he had two main duties—keeping an eye out for pickpockets and breaking up fistfights. Laughter punctuated conversations, and smiles transformed normally dour faces. Yet this many bodies rubbing against each other could kindle trouble in a flash.

His roaming gaze snagged on a trio of men. Why was Jimmy Cloyd huddled with two carnies? Jimmy defined bad news. The thug broke bones and worse for anyone who paid. Worse, he seemed to enjoy his occupation. Was he recruiting muscle for a job? If so, it would happen soon. The fair would roll out of Keokuk in less than a week.

He studied the two men jawing with Jimmy. The big, burly one had enough tattoos to join the freaks inside the tent. The shorter fellow's aggressive stance made him look even more menacing. Meaner. A Bowie knife in the bandy man's belt confirmed Ed's first impression. *Bad news.*

ELEVEN

Cat watched Beth and Amy settle into the Ferris wheel gondola. Her young niece snuggled in the crook of her mother's arm as the roustabout snapped the safety bar shut and advanced the wheel to load the next passenger car. In an instant, her niece's grinning face disappeared. Cat stared at the swaying soles of Amy's patent leather slippers. They looked tiny. Doll shoes. Her gaze traveled to the lighted top of the wheel. Taller than any Main Street building. Were these swaying baskets safe? Her heartbeat quickened.

Cat's arms ached. Despite her son's gallant fight, sleep defeated him an hour back. Since then, she'd carried Jay. His warm, even breath tickled her neck while his sturdy body pumped out waves of heat like a coal stove. Her chest felt on fire while goose bumps sashayed down her back. The town clock struck eight. *How long should I wait?*

The roustabout started the Ferris wheel even though one of the gondolas was empty, and at least ten would-be riders were queued with nickels at the ready.

"Hey, how's come you didn't let us on?" a teenage boy objected.

Cat couldn't see the carnie operator's face, but his look was enough to prompt the impatient kid to shut up.

Calloused fingers brushed her arm. Cat whirled and found herself inches from the shiny brass buttons on Ed's uniform. She glanced up. Sad eyes looked back. No smile.

"I'm going to walk into that alley." He nodded toward a darkened cut. "Wait a minute and follow me. It's best if people don't see us talking."

Follow him into an alley? Her breath hitched. Was this a trick? The mysterious cop disappeared before she could object. Cat glanced back at the Ferris wheel. The ride would last at least five minutes.

She'd give Ed that much time. No more. She forced herself to saunter toward the inky slit between buildings.

At the mouth of the alley, he pulled her into a niche formed by stacked cartons. A scream caught in her throat. But the hand gripping her arm fell away as soon as the alley's twilight swallowed her and her baby.

"We have to hurry," Ed began. "I don't know how much I can help, but I'll try. At least I can warn you what Chief Dexter's up to. After we left your house, we drove down to the river to search for your dad's johnboat. Looks like one oar might have bloodstains on it. Now Dexter's looking for witnesses. Someone who'll say you rowed out on the Mississippi with your husband Sunday."

"But I didn't," Cat interrupted.

"Doesn't matter. He'll browbeat someone into saying so. Maybe you should leave town."

"I can't. He'd find me. I don't have money to run far, and I'd look even more guilty when they caught up with me."

She paused, wondering how her question would sound. *Oh, hell. I need to know.* "Did you find a wallet or any money on Dirk's body?"

Ed shook his head. She wished she could see his eyes in the darkness. See if suspicion narrowed them. "No wallet."

How much should she trust him? If Ed didn't know already, he'd find she had motive soon enough. Obvious reasons to wish her husband dead. She'd share those. Maybe it would keep the real reason, the most important reason, secret.

"I'd come to hate Dirk," she whispered. "He was a liar and a thief. He frequented whores and gambling houses. I can't pretend to grieve. But I didn't kill him. I'd never do that to Jay. Brand him as the son of a murderer."

Ed shifted and watery light from an upstairs window feathered his face. He made no comment on her confession.

"I'll keep tabs on Dexter, try to find out more," he said. "You know the old Peele house on River Road? It's empty. Meet me at seven tomorrow evening."

Cat nodded in agreement, even though the Peele place was miles from her house. Too far to walk at night. "I'll be there."

If I only had a car. Car? Where was Dirk's Ford?

By the time the question fully formed in her brain, Ed had bolted. She'd ask tomorrow. Could she borrow her brother's car?

Cat strolled back onto Main Street just as the Ferris wheel shimmied to a stop. She waved at Beth and Amy, who wiggled with delight as their car hovered two slots above the burly man operating the ride.

As soon as the safety bar on Beth and Amy's gondola released, her niece ran to her and hugged her legs. "Aunt Cat, you have to ride it! The Ferris wheel carried us high enough to see forever."

Cat smiled and stroked Amy's hair. "Glad you had fun."

She turned to Beth. "Guess it's time to head home. My arms will fall off if I hold Jay much longer."

Beth reached out to take Jay. "Let me carry my darlin' little nephew a while."

They made the short walk to the bus in silence. Cat wondered what tomorrow would bring. Should she go to work as if it were a normal day? Perhaps. People had seen her at the fair. Mr. Thompson would get a report. She could hear his scorn if she failed to show. "The woman went gallivanting off to a fair, but couldn't be bothered to come to work." The modicum of compassion he'd shown today would evaporate overnight.

Thompson itched for an excuse to fire her. His out-of-work son-in-law apparently had half a clue about operating a Comptometer. She'd be long gone by now if Kenneth Jacobs hadn't intervened. Of course, as always, the banker made certain his gesture seemed impersonal, the decision strictly business.

* * *

Ed walked briskly until a full block separated him from Cat. He'd barely been able to keep his hands to himself. She'd looked so vulnerable. At the very least, he'd wanted to spell her by carrying the boy. Exhaustion dulled her bright eyes. At least he hoped it was exhaustion and not guilt. She'd shown no signs of grief. She admitted she hated Dirk Black.

He knew what Myrt would say. He had no call to ask for more trouble. Was he compromising his position on the police force to help a murderer?

TWELVE

Tuesday, September 20, 1938

Ed figured he'd seen Chief Dexter smile a total of three times and never so early in the day. He worked to keep his own expression blank as he considered his boss's Cheshire grin. That smirk meant some unfortunate would suffer and soon.

Dexter looked downright giddy when he hung up his desk phone. "We got her. Damned, if we don't."

"Who?" Ed's stomach dropped. Might as well nudge Dexter into gloat mode.

"That bitch Catherine Reedy Black. Just got an anonymous call. Fellow wouldn't give his name, just said he was a Good Samaritan. He happened to see Mrs. Smartypants bury something in her backyard under an empty cage. Says it looked like a gun."

Dexter popped up from his swivel chair raring to go. "Fetch you a shovel from storage and meet me at the car."

Ed didn't bother to ask how anyone but a neighbor or Peeping Tom could see any activity in the Reedy backyard. Could Cat really have buried her dad's Webley?

"When did this fellow claim she buried it?"

Dexter's forehead wrinkled. "Who cares when? If'n she hid the gun, she's guilty. Let's go get her."

While Ed retrieved the shovel, he tried to think of any reason Cat would hide her father's gun. Any reason that didn't involve her putting a bullet in Dirk Black's brain. Could she be shielding her dad? Old Man Reedy looked puny, but he'd shown fire when it came to protecting his daughter. Then again the call could be a hoax. Maybe they wouldn't unearth a gun. Yeah, right, and that Hitler fella would disband the German army any day now. The call meant there was a gun. It just didn't answer the question of who put it there.

Dexter chortled as they barreled toward Timea Street in the police car. Once the house came into sight, he yanked the wheel. The tires bumped over the curb and the vehicle slewed cattywampus—half in the street, half on the Reedys' patchy front lawn.

The chief jumped out on the grass. "Grab the spade. Hurry it up."

Ed had never seen his boss so frenzied. Dexter practically crackled with energy and sizzling hatred.

The chief bulled his way around the side of the house and unlatched the back gate. He didn't bother to knock, to see if any Reedy kin might be home.

High-pitched screeches greeted them. Dexter stopped short in front of a row of cages. "Damn hairy rats. Listen to 'em squeal."

Ed shuddered. With little room to maneuver inside their wire enclosures, the agitated minks slammed their bodies against the screen mesh, bared their teeth, and hissed. The ruckus grated.

An end cage stood empty.

Dexter motioned toward it. "Move that contraption and start digging. If these rats don't stop caterwaulin', I'm gonna plug one of 'em." He fingered the gun at his belt as if the minks would understand his threat and pipe down.

On its first thrust, Ed's shovel hit metal.

"Hallelujah." Dexter chortled as he knelt. His meaty hands flung soft dirt like a dog pawing for a bone. "We got the bitch." Seconds later he raised the gun.

The back door to the house jerked open, and John Reedy teetered in the doorway. "What the hell you doing, Dexter? Get off my property."

The gaunt man brandished a butcher knife. Fearing Dexter would plug Reedy instead of one of his varmints, Ed jumped up and put himself between the combatants.

"Mr. Reedy, sir, we received a call from someone saying your daughter buried a gun." He raised both hands in a pantomime of surrender.

"We have a right to be here. To take the gun and see if it's the one that killed Dirk Black."

The old gent's red-rimmed eyes widened. His mouth hung open. Then his eyes narrowed to slits and his jaw clenched.

"My daughter buried it to protect me." Reedy dropped the knife and held his hands out in a cuff-me-now gesture. "Arrest me. I killed Dirk Black. Never liked the S.O.B. Damned lyin' kraut. Didn't want my Cat to suffer any more heartache."

Ed's gaze ping-ponged between the adversaries. Reedy seemed resigned, but his mouth and eyes showed no tension. He looked almost peaceful. Dexter's eyes blazed. He hadn't come to arrest John Reedy. The police chief wanted Cat.

"That's so much bullshit," Dexter said. "You're covering for your bratty kid. That slut is the murderer."

Reedy straightened, the trace of a smile tugged at the corners of his mouth. "No. You're wrong. I did it. I confess. I murdered Dirk Black. Put a gun to his head and pulled the trigger."

The old man had Dexter. For the moment, anyway. The evidence, such as it was, could implicate Reedy as easily as Cat. If this gun had killed Black, it was Reedy's gun, not Cat's. Even the johnboat supposedly used to row the corpse to a watery grave belonged to the old drunkard.

"Handcuff him." Dexter spat out the order in disgust, never taking his eyes off Reedy. "Wait till the drunk starts pissin' his pants, tremblin' with the shakes. Let him stew in a cell. Soon enough he'll say anything for a swallow of hooch."

Ed gently shepherded the alcoholic to the police car. Reedy spared a quick glance back toward the house. A yellowed lace curtain twitched. Cat's grandmother watched. Good. Ed didn't want her to think her son had simply vanished.

He climbed in the backseat with the old man for the short ride to the stationhouse. As he helped him out of the car, Reedy stumbled.

When Ed bent to help him, the old gent whispered, "Please, son, tell Cat I confessed. Make her understand it's what I want. She's got a baby to raise. My life's over."

* * *

Sitting at her desk, Cat felt like one of her daddy's backyard minks. Caged. Frantic. On display with no place to hide. Ready to bite someone—even the hand that fed her.

Head down, she heard her co-workers' whispers, sensed their stares. They'd passed around the *Daily Gate City* with its front-page headline: LOCAL MAN MURDERED, DUMPED IN RIVER.

The story hadn't received top billing. That was reserved for world news "Peace Plan May Fail," plus a story on the nighttime fire that burned the Nauvoo Opera House to the ground. Cat guessed she ought to be happy the world was going to hell in a hand basket. Europe's wholesale murders kept the account of Dirk Black's death to a barebones three paragraphs.

"Local resident, Dirk Black, was found floating in the Mississippi, dead from a gunshot wound to the back of his head. The authorities believe he was killed sometime Sunday. Doctor Samuel Sprague estimated the body had been in the river less than twenty-four hours."

The second paragraph listed Dirk's occupation as salesman and Cat and Jay as next of kin. No conjecture about suspects. Yet Chief Dexter's end quote, the third paragraph, chilled her. "I plan to arrest the murderous coward by week's end. When the culprit dances from the end of a rope, I'll do my own jig on the ground."

Given how much the police chief despised her, Cat doubted his comments had been circumspect. Did the newspaper edit Dexter's remarks to make it appear the murderer who'd hang could be male or female?

She jerked, startled when a bony finger tapped her shoulder. Kenneth Jacobs, all six-feet of pious banker, towered over her. "Mrs. Black, would you please come to my office. I need a word."

He strode off without a backward glance. She sat for a moment, gathering herself. She couldn't recall Jacobs ever visiting the mezzanine before. If he deigned to address staff, it was after a flunkey gathered the peons in the marbled rotunda.

Cat's stomach flip-flopped. Would he fire her? She could well imagine the uptick in catty gossip. After his daughter Lydia ran off, Dexter, who wasn't yet chief, made sure the whole town knew Cat's husband Dirk was an embezzler who only avoided jail because his employer agreed to restitution. Cat had been lucky to keep her job through that shit storm. Guilt by association. Any bank that had so far escaped collapse guarded its reputation with a vengeance. Her employer need not prove impropriety to toss her out on the curb like yesterday's trash.

She straightened her shoulders. Damned if she'd entertain looky-loos by slinking back to her desk to fetch her purse after she got the boot. Cat clutched her handbag, her fingers tightening around the straps in a white-knuckled fist.

Her high heels clicked as she descended the stairs and crossed the polished floor. She threw back her shoulders, lifted her chin. Jacobs' office door stood open. She walked inside. The banker waited beside his desk, arms folded across his chest, face closed. A bad news portrait.

"Close the door, please."

The heavy mahogany door clicked shut. Their conversation wouldn't escape.

Cat's belly churned. She felt she might jump out of her skin. She had to know. "Are you firing me?"

Jacobs blew out a breath. "I wish I had a choice. Yes, I'm president, but you know my father-in-law founded Iowa First. My wife read the morning paper." His eyes pleaded. "Martha insists it would tarnish her dad's memory if we kept someone on the payroll who was involved with a sordid murder."

Cat thought she was prepared until the words slammed her. How would her family survive? Her pittance of a salary was all that let them cling to their home, eat without begging for food. Who would hire her now?

She sank onto the sofa. Jacobs walked over, held out a fat white envelope. "You know I'd never let your family starve. There's five hundred dollars here. It's from me, not the bank. Take it."

Cat kept her hands in her lap. She wanted to throw the money in his face. Scream at him. Was it the five hundred he claimed he gave Dirk?

His voice softened. "Please, Cat, take the money. If not for you..."

She reached for the envelope. "I'll pay you back...when this ends." This was the first time he'd handed money directly to her. Before, the cash mysteriously appeared in a plain manila envelope whenever she needed it most. Of course, she'd known the source. But somehow taking money from his hand made her feel like a whore.

Jacobs' fingers tightened over hers. "It's yours. I'd do more if I could. Someday—"

Cat wrenched her hand free. "Of course, someday." She stood.

"Your note? Was it a lie?" She stuffed the envelope in her purse so she wouldn't have to look at him. "Did you kill Dirk?"

Jacobs captured her face in his bony hands, forcing her to meet his eyes. "I swear on my son's grave. All I did was give Dirk five hundred dollars. He promised to leave but refused to give me the letter. Called it insurance. Tell me you found it."

She noted the tremble in his voice. She shuddered, remembering the last time she'd seen Jacobs shed his banker personae and free his inner demons.

"No, I have no idea where it is. Guess you'd better hope Chief Dexter isn't the one who finds Dirk's *insurance*. If he does, your missus may demand a lot more than some peon's job."

Jacobs' Adams apple bobbed. "I think about you all the time. If it weren't for my little girl—"

"And don't forget your son." Cat turned, opened the door, and walked out of the bank.

THIRTEEN

Bright sunlight forced Cat to squint at the large outdoor clock, barely visible over the Street Fair's city of tents. The clock had yet to strike ten. God, what more could the day hold?

A gaudy poster touted the daring, high-wire feats of the Blondin-Kellum Troupe. Could their three-bicycle balancing act be any more dangerous than her own? She couldn't bear to think about her firing. The news would crush her dad and Grandmother Nell. The bills stuffed in her pocketbook wouldn't support her family forever—especially if her future included a hangman's noose.

She turned off Main Street toward a bus stop. A horn blared. Startled, she stumbled. A beat-up, black Model T jumped the curb on the side street.

Her brother Pete rolled down his window. "Get in. What are you doing here? I was headed to the bank to fetch you."

She slid into the passenger seat. Pete's frantic gestures made her heart stutter. She'd thought losing a job in the tenacious Depression was the worst she'd have to live through this day. Her brother's uncharacteristic gruff demeanor suggested worse tragedies. "What's happened? Is someone sick?"

Dead is what she feared, yet she flinched at voicing the horrid thought. Her dad? Grandmother Nell?

Pete shook his head. "No. Nell called me at work. Chief Dexter arrested Dad for your husband's murder."

"What?" Cat moaned. She hadn't seen this curve ball coming. Dexter wanted her, not her father. Was he persecuting her dad to coax her to confess?

"There must be some mistake."

Pete put the car in gear. "That's what I intend to find out. I'll demand to see Dad. They have to let us, don't they?"

She swallowed. "They don't have to do anything. Chief Dexter makes his own rules. But he might get pleasure out of watching a teary reunion."

As the Model T sputtered forward, Pete glanced her way. "Sis, you never said—why aren't you at work? You sick?"

She took a deep breath. "I was fired. According to Mr. Jacobs, employing a woman implicated in an unseemly murder case would sully Iowa First's reputation."

Pete's fist beat the steering wheel. "Pious bastard. Dammit." His eyes narrowed as he glared at the road. "You, Nell, and the baby will move in with us. Dad, too, once we clear up this ridiculous arrest. The phone company won't fire me."

"No. You take care of Beth and Amy. I have money enough to tide us over." Cat didn't dare admit where the money came from. It would raise too many questions.

"Don't kid a kidder," Pete replied. "You're barely scraping by."

Cat sighed. "The bank gave me six months' wages to leave quietly. I'll find another job before the money runs out."

"Really?" He glanced her way. "That's a first for those cheapskates. Iowa First certainly hasn't shown any compassion with its foreclosures."

She shrugged. "You can't tell anyone. That's part of the deal. No one can know the bank gave me money."

Pete's forehead wrinkled as he looked back at the road. Did he buy her story?

The combination firehouse and police station came into view. Cat knew the jail cells sat in the building's damp cellar. Lydia—Dexter's daughter—had often tagged along when her mother delivered prisoners' meals. Relatives of locked-up folks sometimes crouched outside to talk to the prisoners through ground-level casement windows.

When Cat asked Lydia if she got scared walking past those caged men, her friend laughed. "No. Mom says they're mostly hoboes or drunks. Just need a bed and a hot meal. They send the really bad men to prison in Fort Madison."

She prayed Dexter hadn't managed to ship her dad to Ft. Madison without a trial.

Pete parked and turned off the engine. Silence. For a moment, neither sibling moved. Cat reached over to touch her brother's arm. "We have to do this."

No one greeted them when they entered the stationhouse. "Bet we could engineer a jail break," Pete whispered.

"Anybody here?" Cat called. No answer. A minute passed before footsteps sounded on the stairs that led down to the jail cells.

"Hold your horses," a man grumbled. "I'm coming."

A door creaked and a balding head emerged, followed by a hunched, rail-thin body. The man's grayish pallor made Cat wonder if he might be a TB survivor.

"What'cha want?" The man scratched a hind-end itch Cat would rather not have known existed.

Pete stepped forward. "You're holding our father, John Reedy. May we see him?"

"Guess so." The officer shrugged. "Just head down them stairs. The old coot's our only customer. I'd take you, but I'm here alone. Everyone else is off somewheres."

"When will Chief Dexter come back?" Cat asked.

The man extracted a tobacco pouch, took out a plug, and shoved it in his cheek before he answered. "Search me. Said something 'bout roustin' bums down by the river."

Relief. She wouldn't come face to face with Dexter any time soon. Then her gut churned as she realized why Dexter was at the river. He was hunting up a convenient witness, someone to help him dig a grave big enough to accommodate both her and her dad.

Pete's footsteps echoed in the narrow stairwell leading to the basement. "Five minutes," the officer called after them. "This ain't tea time at the Ritz."

They found their father in the first cell, curled in a fetal position on a filthy mattress. Cat's stomach somersaulted. She gripped one of the cold steel bars to steady herself.

Pete spoke up. "Dad? Are you all right?"

The old man didn't open his eyes.

"Dad, please talk to us." Pete raised his voice a notch. "Cat's here, too. We only have five minutes. Tell us what happened."

Their father's eyes fluttered. He uncoiled his skeletal frame to sit on the edge of the bunk. Looking at his son and daughter, he blinked rapidly as if to make sure they weren't a mirage.

"I confessed." His raspy voice barely rose above a whisper. "I killed Dirk Black."

Cat's hand flew to her mouth. "You did not. Why on earth would you say you did?"

She swung around to make sure the jailor hadn't tiptoed down the stairs. They were alone. "Did that bastard Dexter beat a confession out of you?" Her hands tightened on the cell's bars.

"Tell us what happened," Pete broke in. His voice sounded much calmer than it had a minute ago. "Somehow we'll stop Dexter."

Their father shuffled over, stretched a bony finger through the bars, and ran it down Cat's cheek. "Kitty-cat, let me do this, and, Pete, don't you go interfering."

The old man swallowed. "Remember how one of my minks disappeared Sunday night? Well, Dexter and that young deputy came to the house this morning. They dug under the empty cage. Next thing I know Dexter held up my gun like he'd found the Holy Grail. Said the pistol gave him all he needed to hang you, Cat. That's when I confessed."

A sly smile lit her dad's face. "Took the wind right out of that ugly bastard's sails."

Cat gasped. "Dad, do you think I killed Dirk? That I need you to protect me?"

Her father shrugged, refused to look her in the eye. "Doesn't matter. He deserved killing."

"Dad, he'll hang you," Pete objected.

"I can't let you do this," Cat jumped in. "You don't need to protect me. I didn't do it."

"Listen to me." Their father's voice gained strength. "I been living on borrowed time. Hell, I may die before they scare up a judge to try me. Cat, you have a son to raise. It's been years since I provided for my family. I finally found a way to be a man again. Doesn't matter if you're innocent, Cat. Not so long as Chief Dexter wants you guilty. Now go home. Both of you."

"Dad, no. There has to be another way," Cat pleaded.

Her father turned away. "I love both of you." Though whispered, his words were clear. "If you love me, you'll leave. Now."

The old man shambled back to his cot. His body coiled to face the wall. Pete pried Cat's hands from the steel bars and pulled her into a fierce hug. Sobs shook her body.

"Dad's right, Cat." Pete patted her back. "Let him do what needs doing."

A door creaked. "Time's up." The policeman's scratchy voice floated down from above.

Cat gulped air to regain control. Dexter would love to hear tell she'd fallen to pieces. She steeled herself to deny him that pleasure.

***

The scarecrows Ed slapped together for Myrt's garden looked a damn sight healthier than the first hobo Dexter corralled. The bum's eyes peered from sunken orbits. The white skin stretched over his skull gave way to occasional patches of flaky red scalp. Ed had no idea how old the man might be. Thirty? Fifty? One hundred?

Chief Dexter kicked the bum's leg. The blow released a stench of sweat and urine from the rags wrapping the mummy-like body. "D'you hear me, old man? Sit up and listen real good. Were you down here by the river Sunday?"

The man scrunched into a sitting position and scooted his butt against the shed, putting a few extra inches between himself and Dexter's shiny black boots. His forehead wrinkled in concentration. "Cap'n, sir, is today Sunday?"

Dexter grabbed the man's raggedy shirt. "No, you imbecile. It's Tuesday. You were here Sunday, too, right?"

The hobo's frightened eyes searched Dexter's face looking for an answer that wouldn't get him hurt. "Yessir, cap'n, if you say so."

"Good." Dexter grinned. "Now we're talking. We're having us a fine conversation."

The police chief waved toward the Reedy boat. "See that rowboat, the one with Addie painted on her side. I bet you saw that boat, didn't you?"

Dexter extracted a silver dollar from his pocket and twirled it in front of the man's nose. "A dollar will buy a man a lot these days. Plenty of good corn liquor."

The man licked his lips, his gaze glued to the shiny coin. "Yessir. Reckon I saw that boat there."

Dexter chuckled. "And you saw three people row out on the river, right?"

The man nodded. He was starving, not stupid.

"There was one man in the front of the boat in a suit, right?" he asked.

The hobo's head bobbed up and down. "Yup, that's exactly what I seen."

Dexter dropped the coin in the man's lap. It disappeared into the folds of his rags.

The police chief produced another coin. "And who sat in the back of that rowboat? I'll bet it was an old gent and a woman with blonde hair, chopped off about here." Dexter positioned a hand below his ears to show the length of Cat's hair. "Am I right?"

The man's chin dipped up and down, a regular agreement metronome. "Yessir, right as rain. Three of 'em. Two gents and a lady."

Dexter dropped the second coin in the man's lap. "Can you write?"

The hobo frowned. "I can put me name on paper."

"Good enough. I got me a college boy to write down your testimony. You sign it when he's done."

He turned to Ed. "Get some paper while I fetch me someone to witness this here deposition."

All saliva vanished from Ed's mouth. Dexter planned to hang Cat and her dad. He'd claim father and daughter did it together, that John Reedy confessed to being a solo killer just to save Cat's neck. Ed felt certain the old man's confession was bogus. He was even more sure the father and daughter hadn't schemed together to murder Dirk Black.

He'd heard about Dexter's talent at trolling for "witnesses." With a hot meal and a taste of whisky, he could bribe just about any starving bum to say what he wanted, especially transients with no ties to town folk. Now he'd watched the bastard at work with his own eyes.

What the hell could he do? If he refused to write the words Dexter put in the hobo's mouth, the chief would sack him and get another stooge to manufacture testimony. Yet he couldn't live with himself if he helped the bully frame Cat and her dad.

Play along…for now. If he couldn't nail Dexter before a murder trial, he'd testify for the defense.

He swallowed the bile that burned his throat and soured his tongue. The more he knew about Dexter's dealings, the better equipped he'd be to help Cat when the time came.

Too bad he wanted to throw up.

FOURTEEN

A thin veneer of mud coated the black boots Dexter had worn to the river. Didn't stop him from tilting back in his swivel chair and plopping his feet on his massive oak desk. He hummed as he sorted through the papers resting on his paunch.

Ed fidgeted in the doorway, waiting for his marching orders. Since he'd been summoned, he knew the chief had thought up some new distasteful chore. He swallowed hard. "You planning to arrest Catherine Black?"

"Nope. Not today." Dexter smiled and a gold incisor twinkled. "Don't want it to look like I'm rushin' things, given her daddy just confessed. That woman ain't going nowhere. Not with her baby and old granny actin' like leg irons. Mrs. Black likes to play the martyr."

"What do you mean?" Ed asked.

Dexter chortled as he swung his feet off the desk and straightened in his chair. "My daughter…" The chief's nostrils flared and all amusement fled his voice. "My daughter and the Reedy whore became bosom buddies when they was little kids. Stayed that way. Afore Lydia quit bein' my daughter, she got all teary-eyed repeatin' how Cat broke her engagement so her brother, Pete, wouldn't have to quit school."

Ed stepped into the room. For once, the chief was jawing about something he wanted to hear. "Sorry, I don't follow. What did breaking an engagement have to do with her brother?"

"Her fiancé landed a job somewheres out in the Dakotas. Asked her to marry him right quick and come away. She said no. Boo hoo hoo. She was the only one working in the Reedy house, so if'n she left, Pete woulda had to quit high school, get a job."

"What happened to this fiancé?" Ed asked.

"Who cares? Joker's been gone eight years anyways. Never heard a him after."

Ed had things he wanted to say. He bit his tongue. The chief looked like he'd forgotten why he'd hollered for him to come. "Chief, what did you want?"

"Go visit Pat O'Reilly, the Blacks' landlord and bring me back a motive for the murder. The Reedy bitch claimed old man O'Reilly saw her the day she walked out on her husband. I figure they had one helluva row. Search that apartment, too. Look for anything that might give the little lady another nudge toward guilty."

Ed didn't trust himself to speak. Didn't move either. He wanted no part of Dexter's railroading. Should he quit?

"Well, git!" Dexter spat. "You need to visit O'Reilly afore he's totally in his cups. You can go home after, get a bite. But I need you to patrol the Street Fair again tonight. You'll relieve Smith at eight o'clock. College boys don't get no special treatment from me."

***

Nell's swollen eyes and splotchy red complexion told Cat her grandmother had been crying—something the corseted lady of the stiff upper lip seldom permitted herself. Seeing her son carted off to jail must have breached her formidable wall of self-restraint.

Cat rushed to hug her, but Nell backed away, arms crossed over her ample chest.

"I'm fine." Nell inhaled what might have bloomed as a sob. "What happened at the jail? Where's Pete?"

"He had to get back to work." Cat looked around for her son. "Is Jay down for a nap?"

"Yes."

"Good. I'll make tea. Have a seat in the dining room, and I'll tell you everything."

Cat's fidgeting fingers drew patterns on the chipped china cup as she told her grandmother she'd been fired, quickly adding that five hundred dollars in hush money would keep their heads above water for the time being.

She glanced at Nell. The revelation evoked no response.

Cat put her hands in her lap and forced herself to look her grandmother in the eye. She watched for some reaction as she described her dad's determination to sacrifice himself to save her. Nell's face gave nothing away.

After she finished, her grandmother nodded. "I'm proud of John. It's been a long time since I could say that. Your mother's death killed him…his spirit anyway. I know you always thought your mother was too strict. Someday you'll realize Addie had to be that way. I love my son, but he's always been a dreamer. Addie was his anchor. Kept him from going adrift. My son's finally found purpose. A way to save his family. Don't fight him."

Cat couldn't read the emotions that briefly flickered across the woman's face. How could she be so stoic? The skin on Cat's neck prickled. What if someday she was told her son, Jay, would hang as a murderer? Her heart said she'd fight tooth and nail to save him. Damn the consequences.

Nell shook her head. "You're wrong," she said as if she could read her granddaughter's thoughts. "I love John with all my heart. But there are worse things than dying."

Cat stood, her throat so tight she couldn't swallow. "I need to go back to the apartment. I found a key in Dirk's clothes. I think it opens his strongbox. I didn't see it when I cleaned up. Doubt it's there, but I'm going to look for it. Maybe Dirk hid money in it. We can use it."

"I'll watch Jay. Don't worry." Nell paused. "Where's Dirk's car? Maybe he put the strongbox in the trunk. Or perhaps you can sell the car for cash."

Where did the car go?

Cat wondered why she hadn't raised the question herself. Was it parked down by the johnboats? Did Dirk drive to the river to meet someone, or was he shanghaied from another spot?

FIFTEEN

Ralph Black took a seat on one of the swivel stools at the counter of the Grand Annex Tavern. The hole-in-the-wall décor didn't impress, but his stomach growled as he remembered the chow. He'd come here with Dirk and Cat shortly after they wed, about four years back.

"Tenderloin sandwich and a Schlitz," he called to the short-order cook behind the counter.

The cook wiped his hands on his grease-streaked apron and did a double take. "Fellow, you 'bout gave me a heart attack. Thought I seen a ghost. You sure look like Dirk Black. You kin or something?"

"Yeah, Dirk was my older brother. Came for the funeral. Drove straight through and I'm hungry."

"Sorry for your troubles," the cook mumbled, turning his back and avoiding Ralph's eyes. He sensed the man hadn't cared for Dirk.

Ralph wasn't surprised to be tagged as one of Dirk's relatives. Though he and his brother were far from twins, they sported the same coal black hair, square jaw, and Roman nose. People commented on their eyes, too. His mother said their eyes peered out of their pale faces like lumps of coal in a snow bank.

He wondered if Dirk's hair had started to silver like their dad's did when he hit forty. Would the casket be open? Cat said his brother was found in the river. They often closed casket lids on floaters. Didn't matter. Ralph hadn't come to kiss Dirk goodbye. He was sorry he was dead, but no point weeping. He'd driven over to see if his brother left him anything.

That depended on the status of Dirk's latest scam. If he'd gotten lucky, he would have hid his take from the missus. Ralph knew his brother and his favorite hidey-holes for stashing treasure.

He chuckled to himself when he recalled Cat's shock at discovering her husband might bend the truth a mite. Actually, Dirk seldom found a conversation that couldn't be enhanced with a lie—usually a whopper. Dirk a soldier hero? What a laugh, but Cat had bought it for a spell.

Spotting a newspaper lying on the lunch counter, Ralph pulled it toward him. He quickly read the brief account of his brother's death. He'd pissed someone off good this time. As he munched on his sandwich, Ralph assessed the possibilities. He had high hopes Dirk had double-crossed someone and hid the loot. Time for a little treasure hunt. Lucky for him Cat had vacated the apartment. He could search at his leisure.

He drained his beer and plunked the correct change on the counter. The cook wouldn't expect a tip—not if he knew his brother.

He drove to the address Cat gave him. What a dump. As instructed, he knocked on the downstairs' door to ask the landlord for a key.

"I'm comin'. Stop the damn hammering. You people are giving me a headache."

A scrawny old coot swung the door open then jumped backward as if he'd been singed. "Hell, I thought you was your brother, raised up from the dead. Hold your horses. I'll get the key."

The landlord's hand snaked toward a hall table and snagged a brass skeleton key. "You just missed your sister-in-law. She paid the rent, but that don't mean you can do whatever you want. Keep it quiet and hand over the key when you git."

The man's gaze slid up and down Ralph as if he feared a beating. Then a sly grin slid over his face. "I'd be careful if'n I were you. From what I hear Mrs. Black may have done your brother in. Wouldn't turn my back on that firebrand."

The landlord slammed the door.

Interesting. Cat a suspect? That possibility hadn't crossed his mind. He figured the killer was someone Dirk bamboozled. Ralph had no illusions about his brother's character.

He climbed the stairs and unlocked the apartment. A first glance disappointed. Brother Dirk didn't appear to have been on one of his more prosperous rolls. He spotted a note propped on the kitchen table and walked toward it.

He grinned as he read. Yes, indeed, he would like his brother's trumpet. He walked into the small bedroom. The instrument case rested on the bed. He sat, put the case on his lap, and unsnapped it. The metal gleamed. More importantly, a wooden mute nestled in one of the case's velvet-lined cavities.

Holding the mute's bulging bottom firmly in one hand, he twisted its neck. When it separated, he stuck his fingers inside and extracted a folded paper. He chuckled. Dirk still relied on his favorite hiding place. So what made this piece of paper so valuable?

Ralph finished reading and laughed. Looked like he'd need to hang around a couple of days after all. He definitely planned to call on Mr. Kenneth Jacobs.

SIXTEEN

Ed's eyes burned as he walked toward the back of the gambling den. Smoke hung in low layers like a December cloud bank. At mid-afternoon the place seemed almost drowsy. Lethargic card players sat at just two of the room's ten tables.

Though Ed wore his police uniform, the players didn't flinch as he entered. No surprise. While Keokuk, Iowa, might be in the hinterlands, the Chicago mob's tentacles embraced it. Ed's boss was well paid to make sure the law turned a blind eye to gambling and prostitution.

Ed spotted Jimmy Cloyd and walked over to his table. "Can we talk a minute?"

Jimmy, who'd just mucked a hand, ground out a Camel cigarette and tipped back his chair. "Whadya want?"

"How about we talk in private?" Ed suggested.

Jimmy seemed to debate the request a moment before he nodded and followed Ed. They stopped in a corner of the room where not even a dribble of sunlight lessened the gloom.

The mob henchman looked the cop up and down. "Never seen you in here before. You looking for some action?"

Ed shook his head. "No, just information. I hear Dirk Black came in here regular. Did he owe any of your customers money?"

Jimmy's open-lipped smile released a wave of pungent onion breath. "I'm happy to report Dirk checked out with a clean slate. True, he owed money to my friends regular as clockwork, but he always paid up before the stroke of midnight. Had a knack for finding swag when he needed it. So how come you're asking? A little birdie told me the missus did him in."

Ed shrugged. He knew anything he said would wend its way back to his chief. "Just getting our ducks in a row. Looks better if we say we explored all possibilities. So you don't know anyone who had a recent beef with Dirk?"

Jimmy's grin widened. Why was the hoodlum so amused?

"Dirk was a ladies' man," Jimmy offered. "If I was doin' the investigatin', I'd stick with that. My guess is the missus found out he blew a wad on some new whore and decided she'd had enough. You know how Keokuk town folk look down their noses at women who divorce. Much more respectable to be a widow lady."

"Was Dirk seeing one woman in particular?" Ed pressed.

"Don't know. You could ask at the 19 ½ Club. 'Course I doubt they'd answer."

"You say Dirk always managed to come through with money when he needed it. How? No gambler's that lucky."

"He knew how to work a con. Pretty damn good at it. He traveled plenty. Just never knew when to fold up his tent. And he didn't always play straight with his partners."

Ed saw a lifeline for Cat. "So he could have gotten sideways of some fellow con artist or even the mob, right?"

Jimmy's eyes narrowed. "Don't go sticking your nose where it don't belong. Your sister's a nice kid. Already lost herself a husband. Would be a real shame to lose another bread winner. No need for you to look beyond Dirk's little woman."

The henchman cocked his head and grinned. "You're not sweet on the new widow, are you? Is she givin' you a taste? If so, you better saddle up and do some rodeo riding real fast. From what I hear, that filly has a date at the glue factory."

Ed flushed and his fists curled. Jimmy's drink-reddened nose loomed as an inviting target. Yet he knew better than to pick a fight with one of the chief's cronies—not to mention mob muscle.

He shrugged as if Cat didn't matter. "Just asking for the sake of appearance. Nothing personal. Appreciate your time."

Ed turned his back and hustled out of the gambling hall. He didn't want to spend one more second in the presence of the foul-mouthed thug.

Outside the building, intense sunlight bleached all color from the street scene and the glare off plate-glass windows blinded him. Still he welcomed the chance to escape the smoke filled-room. He sucked in a deep breath and instantly regretted it. A cool breeze from the river carried the smell of manure from the livestock show—a Street Fair staple. It mingled with the usual corn-rendering fumes. Sometimes the air felt thick enough to chew.

He hurried down the street toward the 19 ½ Club, named for the address of its upstairs entertainment. Two categories of prostitutes stayed there—locals and gals from St. Louis and Chicago brothels who'd come for "the cure." One of Keokuk's doctors had gained regional fame for treating venereal disease.

Cutting across Public Library property, Ed spotted a riot of red and pink ladies' underthings dancing on a clothesline at the back of the Club. He smiled remembering the first day his sister spotted a similar display. She'd giggled, calling it a billboard, and whispered the risqué undergarments might give the prudish librarian some new ideas.

At night, red lights glowed from the 19 ½ Club windows. In the daytime, the clothesline's frilly bras and garter belts waved like gay pennants.

He raised his arm to rap on the door. It opened before his knuckles struck wood. Ed decided the clowns at the Street Fair could give the woman who answered a lesson in makeup. Red lipstick jutted well above her actual lips. Her rouge resembled giant polka dots. Still, he recognized her. Emily. Couldn't remember her last name. She'd trailed him by two grades. Quit school when she got knocked up. No husband. Parents dead.

"Ed?" She recognized him, too. "Haven't seen you here before. We have a special arrangement with police." Her hands slithered down her tight dress, caressing her own curves, urging him to ogle the merchandise.

His breath hitched. He hadn't made love to a woman since his wife died. His pants suddenly felt tight. He felt the color creep up his neck and heat his cheeks.

He swallowed. "Hello, Emily," he choked out. "Just need to ask a few questions. Police business."

"Sure you don't want to mix business and pleasure?"

Enjoying his obvious discomfort, she winked and crooked a finger to beckon him inside. "Have a seat. I won't bite ya. Whatcha want to know?"

He perched on the edge of a settee in a pocket parlor. "Did Dirk Black ever come here?"

Emily leaned against a doorjamb and pulled a cigarette from her pocket. He jumped up to light it. Her fingers grazed his hand as he held the match. She sucked in a deep drag, making her titties jut out further before she answered. "You're talking about Cat Reedy's husband, right? The guy who got hisself murdered."

"Yeah, that's him. Did you know him?"

"Never met him but I seen him round. He waltzed in maybe once, twice a month. Never wanted the same lady twice. Heard tell he liked each new one to rave about his equipment, how it made other men look like they belonged in the minors. Didn't ask for nothin' perverted though. Just wanted billing as top stud. Why you askin'?"

Emily's eyes narrowed. "You're not trying to pin his murder on one of us gals, is you?"

"No, no," he assured her. "Just hoped I could talk to the ladies he knew. Maybe find out if there'd been any pillow talk about his troubles. Maybe he had gambling debts. Or maybe he picked a fight with some tough."

Emily's laugh turned harsh. "Honey, men don't come here to chitchat. If I recall, Dirk went upstairs with Millie last time he dropped by, and she ain't here no more. Her mom down in Missouri is doin' poorly. She went home to be with her till she passes."

A knock on the front door ended the conversation.

"Can't help you," Emily said. "Come back if you want to do something besides talk. I gotta get to work." She peeked out the window. "Stay in here outta sight till I take this gent upstairs."

Ed admitted defeat. He couldn't waste more time. Chief Dexter was probably pacing the floor by now, wondering why he hadn't returned with the dirt from O'Reilly. The chief would delight in using the busybody's gossip to tighten Cat's noose. All he could do was keep his report brief. "They fought. She left."

Tonight, he'd see Cat. Only three hours until their meet. He'd let her know her father's confession didn't mean salvation. Would that be enough to convince her to leave town?

He longed to explain his actions, why he'd taken a job under Dexter. He couldn't. Only two people knew his real reason—Bart and his sister. Bart warned any leak might be his death warrant.

SEVENTEEN

Ed rapped hard on Pat O'Reilly's door. Peeling paint flaked to the ground with each knock. A radio blared inside. The old man lived alone. Definitely home. He pounded harder. "Mr. O'Reilly, it's Ed Nelson…from the police. I need to speak with you."

The door swung open. A mingled odor of cooked cabbage and cigarettes assaulted Ed. "What d'ya want?" the landlord grumbled.

"I need to ask a few questions about your tenants, the Blacks. Mrs. Black said you saw her pack up and leave a couple weeks ago—early September—after a fight with her husband."

The landlord grinned, flashing a panoply of rotting teeth and tobacco-stained gums. "Think she killed him? I read about it in the paper. Sounds like Dirk riled someone good and proper. Murdered and dumped in the river. Guess it could have been his missus. She's one cold fish. Never let on he was dead when I collared her yesterday for the month's rent."

Ed frowned. "Mrs. Black came here yesterday."

"Sure did. 'Round three o'clock. Heard her sneaking up the stairs. Braced her about rent. She promised to pay. Admitted Dirk weren't comin' back and neither was she, but her husband's brother would be stayin' a piece. Think she said he'd arrive today."

Ed hoped the brother, another wildcard, wouldn't show before he finished. He needed to search the place to appease the chief. "How long was Mrs. Black here yesterday?"

O'Reilly lifted his eyes as if the answer might be written on the ceiling. "Maybe an hour. Heard her rootin' around, bangin' drawers. She got real snooty. Told me I'd better not go in her apartment when she wasn't about. I said the hell with that. Went in soon as she left. Gotta say it was a helluva lot cleaner. Her old man left it a real mess, a damn pigsty."

Had Cat come to clean up before her brother-in-law arrived? Unbidden, another thought popped into Ed's head. Maybe she wanted to get rid of incriminating evidence.

"What do you remember about the day she walked out?"

"Well, son, I opened my window soon as I heard 'em yelling. Saw the missus barrel down the stairs with that baby in her arms. Dirk yelled after her. Called her an ungrateful whore. I figure she musta stepped out on him."

Ed edged back to escape the man's fetid breath. "Did they fight often? Did it get physical?"

"You mean did he punch her? Can't say he knocked her around, but they had words. Plenty of 'em. Mostly late at night. Ol' Dirk liked his booze, his gambling, and his ladies." O'Reilly chuckled. "From what I heard, the missus bailed him out more than once when he got in hot water for shorting a boss or losin' a poker hand."

Ed swallowed. Whether he wanted to recognize them or not, Cat's motives kept piling up. "The day she left, were they fighting about money?" he pressed. "Could it be Dirk owed somebody a lot of dough?"

He held his breath, hoping the old coot would tell him Dirk had played fast and loose with the wrong folks. The mob had little sympathy for deadbeat gamblers.

"'Nah. Didn't hear what started that fight. Coulda been money. Do you think she popped him?"

Ed didn't answer. Tried to keep his distaste for the man off his face. "I'd like to look in the apartment. Can you give me the key?"

"Sure thing, officer. Want me to come along?" He sounded gleeful.

"No, I only plan a quick look. Just give me the key."

* * *

Cat hopped off the bus a couple of blocks away and cut through a neighbor's yard to the rear of the two-story apartment house. As she rounded the sideyard, she heard Ed interrogating her landlord.

She shook with anger. She'd convinced herself Ed was a decent fellow who truly wanted to help. But here he was, all by his lonesome, sniffing for dirt to help his boss nail her for murder. How she longed to wring O'Reilly's scrawny neck and kick Ed where the sun didn't shine.

What now? Should she follow Ed upstairs and confront him or wait for him to leave?

A thorn from a scraggly rose bush snagged the well-worn cotton housedress she'd changed into before heading to her old apartment. Soft-soled canvas shoes muffled her footfalls as she edged forward. Good thing she'd forgone heels.

Stay put—at least for a few minutes. She leaned against the clapboard siding and splinters pierced her back, making her feel like a live pin cushion. How long would Ed stay? How thoroughly would he search?

Cat got her answer less than ten minutes' later when he pounded down the rickety stairs.

O'Reilly instantly answered Ed's knock. "What d'ya find? Did she have a gun hid up there?"

The policeman ignored her landlord's questions.

"Should I let her back in, or that brother-in-law, if'n they come?" O'Reilly wheedled.

"Yes. As long as she pays the rent, it's her apartment," Ed answered.

As soon as the police car left the curb and rolled out of sight, Cat marched to the front of the house and hammered on O'Reilly's door. When he answered, she pushed a wad of rent money hard into the man's chest. Cat had scrounged the offering from the dollars Jacobs gave her to ease his conscience.

O'Reilly staggered backwards.

"Keep your nose out of my business or I swear I'll break it with my fist."

His eyes narrowed as the bills she shoved at him fluttered to the floor. She spun and headed for the stairs.

"Bitch. You always acted high n' mighty, like your shit didn't smell. Don't guess your next landlord will have to put up with your lip. Jail's your next stop."

The epithets hurled at her back didn't slow her pace. She took the creaky stairs two at a time. Hands shaking with fury, Cat had to try twice to unlock the apartment. Once inside, she slammed the door. A deep breath helped bring her anger under control. She knew she had to keep her head. No one else to count on.

A quick visual scan indicated little had changed since her last visit, except Pete had carted away the broken furniture. When had her brother found time?

If Ed had searched, he'd been neat as well as hasty. No open drawers. Nothing out of place. Unfortunately her walk-through didn't turn up the missing strongbox either. She'd watched Ed leave. The box was sizable, he hadn't carted it away. She stood on a kitchen chair to search above the metal cabinets and probe the back of the wardrobe's top shelf. Her fingers fastened around a stack of papers.

Cat climbed down to scan the paper-clipped documents.

"Oh, no."

The top sheet held a list of people who shared Hamilton as a surname. Delores Hamilton's name, atop the list, had a fat checkmark beside it. Delores, a prominent widow, had lost her husband in an auto accident that also took her little girl's right leg.

As Cat shuffled through five-year-old newspaper clippings about Oscar Hartzell and the "Drakers," her sense of dread deepened. Hartzell swindled thousands of gullible Iowa farmers with an inheritance scheme before his arrest in 1933. The con man convinced folks that Sir Francis Drake died without an heir and his fortune—multiplied by more than a century of interest—sat in a London bank just waiting for unknowing heirs to stake their claims.

Hartzell asked for contributions to pay the legal fees needed to claim the money, promising investors they'd make their money back one-hundred times over.

Cat's hands shook. What was Dirk up to? Had he promised Delores and the other Hamiltons on the list some bogus inheritance? She stuffed the papers in a sack to study at home.

She was almost out the door when she decided to leave a note for her brother-in-law. Maybe if she left a note, she wouldn't have to speak to Ralph before the funeral.

Ralph—
Dirk's funeral service is scheduled for 3 p.m. Wednesday at Greaves Mortuary on Concert Street. Our family will arrive at 2 p.m. to receive folks paying their respects. You are welcome to join us. Please call if you need anything before then.
Catherine Black
P.S. I know Dirk would want you to have his trumpet. If you'd like any of his clothes, please take them.

Cat propped the note against a salt shaker so he'd see it when he walked in the door. She hoped O'Reilly wouldn't give Ralph an earful before the funeral. All she needed was someone else out to extract a pound of her flesh. Chief Dexter was enemy enough. And then there was Ed, the chameleon. What were his true colors?

Should she meet him tonight as he asked? Time to fret about that later. She had another mission first. Find Dirk's car and pray the strongbox was inside.

EIGHTEEN

Cat claimed a seat near the back of the bus. Only one other passenger. She hoped any newcomers would sit up front and leave her be. As the bus jerked ahead, a burly man ran alongside, beating his fists on the closed door. Sweat coursed down his beet-red face. The bus braked, and the panting man heaved himself aboard

"Didn't you see me?" he growled at the driver, then doubled over to catch his breath.

The beefy passenger lurched down the aisle as the bus shot forward. His beady eyes drilled into Cat. The man sat three rows up. Air whooshed out of the seat cushion as his heavy frame settled. She let out a breath she didn't realize she'd been holding.

Her unease hitched back up when he swiveled. Was he glaring at her? Did she look as disheveled and frantic as she felt? She gazed out the window, but kept him in her peripheral vision.

The bus slowed to a stop and several people hopped on. Where was everyone going mid- day? The Street Fair, of course. Even minus the gaudy nighttime lights, the fair pulled at town folk like a receding tide. She recalled someone mentioning a matinee by the Anderson's Dogs and Ponies show. Monkeys were part of the animal act, too.

She exited at the last stop near the Hubinger complex. The other passengers had all hopped off earlier—everyone but the angry rider. The tiny hairs on the back of her neck signaled danger. They stood at attention as if static electricity held them hostage. Was the burly stranger following her?

Cat walked away, her pace brisk not quite a run. When no footsteps thudded behind her, she slowed slightly and risked a backward glance. The man leaned against a lamppost near the plant entrance and lit a cigarette.

She sighed. Chief Dexter had infected her with paranoia. That man was probably meeting someone at Hubingers, wasn't the slightest bit interested in her. Just mad at the world.

Cat spotted her dad's johnboat in the jumble of overturned boats that served as a poor man's yacht club. The sight of her mom's faded name brought tears to her eyes. She traced the letters—Addie. "How I wish you were here," she whispered.

Water lapped a few feet away from the boat. She recalled the bus driver telling a passenger that the river was expected to reach flood stage within days. First time there'd been a fall flood like this in sixty years. Another calamity for the handful of bottomland farmers who'd sidestepped foreclosure. Should she wrestle her dad's boat up the bank? No, she was too tired. Let the damn thing sink. Too bad the waters hadn't crested and claimed it before the chief's visit, before he took a bloody oar.

Standing in the Mississippi's flat floodplain, she could see at least a quarter mile in every direction. Nothing. Dirk's car wasn't here.

"Cat, is it true?"

The deep voice startled her. She turned and saw Mr. Weaver, one of her dad's fishing cronies. They'd worked together at the shoe factory before the layoffs began.

Mr. Weaver's expression reflected no malice, only concern. "Is it true your dad's in jail?"

"Afraid so," Cat answered.

"There's no way John killed anyone. Dexter's just up to his dirty tricks. I hear he's been down here twice. Last time he collared some hobo, bribed him to say he saw you and John row out on the river with your husband last Sunday."

Cat's stomach sank. "Can you help me find the hobo he talked to? Maybe I can bribe him to recant, to tell the truth."

"Too late. Heard tell he hopped a freight train soon as Dexter drove off."

Cat's forehead wrinkled. "That's good, right? The man can't testify if he's not here."

Mr. Weaver shook his head. "Sorry, Cat, it don't matter. That young deputy wrote down the lie. Dexter forced Billy Daniel to witness when the bum printed his name. Dexter must figure that's all he needs. He knew the bum would be in the wind."

Bile rose in Cat's throat. "Were you around on Sunday, Mr. Weaver? Did you see anyone with Dirk?"

"Sorry, no. I was here Sunday, but didn't see Dirk. Wish I had. Dexter wouldn't scare me. I did see one thing that sorta left me scratchin' my head. Your husband drives a red Packard, don't he? I saw a woman drive off in what looked like his car."

A woman? Cat's heartbeat quickened. Could a woman be the killer? Maybe Dirk's murder had nothing to do with blackmail or gambling. It wouldn't surprise her to learn he'd sweet-talked a bimbo who caught him in a lie. A woman who wasn't as forgiving as she'd been.

"Did you recognize her? What did she look like—blonde, brunette, pretty, young?"

Mr. Weaver held up a hand to halt the machine-gun barrage. "The lady looked more like his mother than some young filly. Walked all hunched over and she was bundled up like chunks of ice already floated on the river." His arms stretched wide. "Real broad through the beam. Didn't see her face."

The description stopped Cat cold. What on earth? The woman certainly wasn't Dirk's ailing mother, and no way would he chase after some old, portly dame—even a rich one. Not his style. Dirk had no relatives near Keokuk.

"You're sure about the woman? Did you see where she went?"

The man shook his head. "I was cleaning fish. Just happened to glance over and see her actin' like some Indian scout, eyes shaded, starin' off every which way afore she climbed in the Packard. The next time I looked up Dirk's car was gone."

Cat forced a smile. "Thanks for asking after Dad. Plenty of folks won't come near us now that Dexter has us in his sights."

Mr. Weaver pressed her hands between his calloused paws and gave an encouraging squeeze. "I admit it. Dexter can throw the fear of God in me. I know what he can do to me and mine. But you don't abandon friends 'cause you're scared. I wouldn't be here jawing with you if an Army pal had left me in a hayfield in France when I took one in the leg. The missus and I will see you tomorrow at the funeral parlor."

Tears sprang to Cat's eyes. Keokuk had its share of bullies and gamblers, drunks and cowards. These riffraff were far outnumbered by kind, generous neighbors. Her spirits lifted knowing her dad and her family still had friends, people they could count on.

She flashed back to Mr. Weaver's story about the hobo's testimony. Was Ed the young officer who transcribed the bum's damning words?

Dexter seemed capable of manufacturing evidence with the speed of a runaway train, and it looked as if Ed Nelson helped stoke the boiler. Was yesterday's offer of help a seedy ruse to gain her confidence and make it easier to frame her?

Her heart argued no. Her brain said don't be a chump.

Again.

All energy oozed from her body as she backtracked through town to her home. She wanted nothing more than to sneak into her bedroom and pull the covers over her head like a little girl afraid of the boogeyman.

She opened the flap of the tin mailbox mounted beside the front door and pulled out two envelopes and a postcard. The fierce likeness of Chief Keokuk, the town's Indian namesake, decorated the front of the postcard. How odd? Who sent a postcard from their hometown? She flipped it over. No stamp. The message was printed in big block letters.

HAND OVER THE MONEY TONIGHT OR YOU'LL BE NEXT. RIDE THE FERRIS WHEEL. SET THE BAG OF CASH DOWN JUST BEFORE YOU BOARD. I'LL BE WATCHING.

Cat's shell-shocked system short-circuited. She collapsed on the front stoop. Laughter doubled her over, then hiccups began. Tears rolled down her cheeks. Were her neighbors—or perhaps the note's author—watching her come unglued? For a moment, it all seemed hysterically funny. She longed to shout at the idiots threatening her. "Clues, please, what money? Where?"

Cat reasoned Dirk had stolen or bamboozled "the money" from someone. Was it the someone who murdered him?

She felt confident the threat had nothing to do with any hush money Jacobs paid to silence Dirk or the "gift" the banker had given her to salve his conscience for firing her. Jacobs wouldn't have told a soul about either transaction. He had too much to lose if he opened his mouth.

Of course, Dirk could have bragged about collecting the blackmail.

Perhaps the note was sheer bluff. She'd been stupid shoving a wad of rent money at O'Reilly. Maybe the nasty old bugger decided Dirk scored before he died, and she'd found his stash. Could her landlord believe she was ditzy enough to hand over money because he threatened her with a postcard?

Cat stood up. She took a swipe or two at her backside to brush away the dirt clinging to her skirt. What had Mr. Weaver said about fear? You couldn't let it paralyze you. Well, she was at war. Not in some European trench. Right here in her hometown. She would not let some vague threat make her quake like jelly. She'd meet Ed tonight, see if she could squeeze information out of him. Might work even if he wasn't in her camp. Then she'd head to the Street Fair and ride the damn Ferris wheel.

A sudden inspiration prompted a chuckle. Yes, indeed, she'd leave a bag, and she knew exactly what treasure she'd put inside.

NINETEEN

Ralph whistled as he drove down Keokuk's Grand Avenue searching for Jacobs' home. He'd dropped by Iowa First on the pretense of wanting to meet the bank president before depositing substantial funds. A punctilious flunky told him Jacobs was "under the weather" and might not be in for a day or two.

Ralph figured the hotshot was sick all right—worried sick his dirty little secret would pop up in public. Though Dirk was no longer around to squeeze him, the jerk had to wonder who might find the letter, his tearful mea culpa.

He shook his head. His sister-in-law was such a sap. Cat could have been bleeding the bloke dry. A nice steady annuity. And Jacobs? A total idiot to lay it out in writing to ease his conscience. Ralph smiled. Bet the guy's having second thoughts about the value of his moral cleansing.

He drove past Jacobs' abode, parked a block away, and sauntered toward the two-story mansion. With its grandiose white pillars and stone lions, it looked schizophrenic—an Old South plantation crossed with an English castle. Was the guy trying to convince himself he lived somewhere besides Podunk, Iowa?

Ralph scanned the neighboring houses. Money, money, and more money. He grinned. Yep, his mark could lay his hands on boatloads of cash. Had Jacobs killed Dirk to stop the blackmail? If so, he'd been stupid to shoot him before he held the letter in his hot little hands. With the jury out on the killer's identity, Ralph decided caution was the order of the day.

He rang the doorbell. After an extended footstep shuffle—someone clumping down a flight of stairs—a sturdy black woman in a maid's getup peeked through the glass sidelight. The door cracked open a smidgeon to acknowledge his presence.

"Jacobs residence," her soft voice said. "May I help you?"

Ralph studied the stout maid, who wouldn't look him in the eye. Nothing gray about the woman. Everything—her face, eyes, dress, apron, cap—were either darkest ebony or snowy white. How did a person work and stay so starched? Was answering the door her only duty?

Ralph puffed out his chest, lifted his chin. "I'm here to see, Mr. Jacobs. A business matter."

The maid's eyes flitted up to meet his then quickly fell to his shoes. "Mr. Jacobs is indisposed. If you'll leave your card—"

Expecting a run around, he'd come prepared. Ralph handed her a calling card with a private message printed on the back: *We need to discuss something of great value I inherited from my brother, Dirk Black.*

"Give this to Mr. Jacobs. The matter is urgent. He'll want to see me."

Ralph wondered if the meek maid had enough moxie or book learning to read his message. Didn't matter, who would she tell?

The woman bobbed her head in response, took the card, and shut the door in his face. Several minutes ticked by. As he cooled his heels on the porch like some Fuller Brush salesman, his anger built. He wore the suit and bowtie he brought for his brother's funeral. Yet some stupid maid thought he didn't look respectable enough to be invited inside to wait.

The slight took him back to the days when his last name was Schwarz. His father, Harold Schwarz, had emigrated from Germany, his mother from Austria. They settled in a small Illinois town. When the Great War first threatened in Europe, his dad boasted the Fatherland would crush the European scum. "Be proud you're Germans," he told his teenage sons. Before long, kids began to taunt Dirk and Ralph, calling them filthy Huns. En route to school, the brothers passed storefronts plastered with posters of bloody, bayonet-wielding Germans. Someone painted a yellow stripe on their front door—reprisal for the Schwarz's refusal to buy Liberty Bonds. A week later, their father spouted off in a bar. He died in the alley behind it, a knife stuck in his gut.

Their mother whisked the boys to a new town. "Your last name is Black," she said. "Means the same thing as Schwarz, just more American. You're Polish, not German. You understand, right?"

Ralph recalled the other changes. Their mom tossed all sheet music by German composers, smashed their dad's ornate beer steins, and ordered her sons to lie about their dead father. "Tell people he died fighting for Poland against those bloodthirsty Germans."

The lies brought rewards—sympathy, work, acceptance. Lies paid dividends. A life lesson.

The Jacobs' front door flung open, startling Ralph back to the present. The gangly man didn't look like a financial titan. His wispy hair clumped in patches like yellow squash run amok in a garden. Red squiggles shot through the whites of his eyes. It looked like his blue irises were trapped inside a bloody barbed-wire fence.

An easy mark. No question. No question at all.

"You're Dirk Black's brother." The man stated it as fact, not question. Ralph figured the family resemblance wiped away any niggling doubt.

"Here in the flesh." He smiled and offered his hand. Jacobs didn't take it.

Ralph shrugged. "We have business to discuss. Best done in private."

The man grimaced but stepped aside so he could enter. "We'll talk in the library."

Jacobs led him down a marble hallway to a sun-drenched room. Latticed windows offered expansive views of the Mississippi River that sparkled far below the high bluff. The banker closed the library door and motioned to two club chairs. Ralph doffed his fedora and sat.

"I came for Dirk's funeral and discovered the letter you wrote my sister-in-law among his possessions." Ralph ran his fingers along the fedora's rim. "Imagine you'd like it back."

Jacobs' eyes narrowed and his lips pinched tighter. He didn't speak. Ralph watched him wring the hands he tried to keep still in his lap. "I paid your brother to return that letter. It belongs to me."

"I figure maybe you 'paid' Dirk with a bullet. I'm gonna be more careful. We ain't gonna meet anywhere except in places where it wouldn't look sporting for a hoity-toity banker to shoot a grieving mourner in the back."

"I did not kill your low-life brother." Jacobs' voice shook. "I handed him five-hundred dollars, and he promised both he and that letter would disappear for good."

"You'll pardon me if I don't believe you." Ralph grinned. "You gotta admit it's a stretch to assume Dirk pissed off another bloke while he had the screws to you. No, my bet's on you as his killer. Maybe I should visit the cops—or the newspaper—give 'em the letter and see what they think."

"No!" Jacobs spat out his response like a wad of sour chewing tobacco.

He stared at the floor. "What do you want?"

"You claim you gave Dirk five-hundred. With him dead for his trouble, I reckon the price should double. You can pay me afore the funeral, noon tomorrow, then I'll leave town."

"I can't lay hands on a thousand dollars," Jacobs protested. "Not without questions being asked. For God's sake, it's the Depression. I've had setbacks. I gave Dirk all I could afford."

"What a pity." Ralph stood, slipped his hat back on his head. "Guess I should be going. Do you happen to know the newspaper's address?"

"No. Wait. Let me think. I'll see what I can do."

Jacobs opened the library door, and the men walked together to the front of the house.

"Glad we had a meeting of the minds," Ralph said. "How's about we meet at the Grand Annex Tavern, tomorrow noon. Great pork tenderloin sandwiches. I might even treat."

Ralph didn't bother to glance over his shoulder. He had the mark.

Never let them know you have a single doubt. Gives 'em ideas.

Prospects were looking up.

TWENTY

Back in his brother's apartment, Ralph whistled as he pulled five almost new shirts from an armoire and tossed them on the bed. Since he was almost as big as Dirk, he hoped the shirts would fit. Dirk didn't chintz playing the Dapper Dan.

He smiled as he smoothed the front of the starched cotton shirt and looked in the mirror. Almost perfect fit. This trip was proving quite profitable. If his big brother were around, he felt sure Dirk would applaud. He'd want Ralph to squeeze the balls of the bastard who'd knocked up his wife.

And Goody-Two-Shoes Cat. He shook his head. For two years, the woman let Dirk believe Jay was his own flesh and blood. Ralph had wondered about the picture Dirk sent. A son with blue eyes? First he'd heard tell of such a thing in the Schwarz/Black family tree.

He walked into the kitchen, hoping to find a snack in one of the cupboards. The wall telephone surprised him. He hadn't noticed it before. Then he remembered Cat's brother worked for the telephone company. Musta got his sis a really good deal. Maybe he'd ring up Mrs. Black. He smiled. Should he rattle his sister-in-law? If Jacobs told the truth, it was possible that Cat killed Dirk. Could be she'd pocketed the banker's blackmail. Maybe he could shake some money out of that tree, too.

He picked up the receiver and clicked the telephone's cradle until an operator came on the line. "Would you please connect me with the John Reedy residence?"

He listened to a series of clicks. "Hello." Definitely Cat's voice.

"Hello, Cat. This is Ralph. How are you holding up?"

"I'm doing all right. How is your mother? I'm so sorry illness prevented her from coming to the service for her son."

"Mother is weak, but she has an iron will. Of course, she repeats over and over again what a tragedy it is for a mother to outlive a child."

Ralph paused when he thought he heard a click. "Is this a party line?"

"Yes, it is," Cat answered.

"Well, perhaps it's best if we wait to discuss our family business face to face. Mother will want a full report on her *only* grandson. She finds great consolation in the fact that a *blood relative* will carry on the Black name."

Ralph listened as Cat sucked in a breath. He figured he'd delivered his message without cluing in any eavesdropper on the party line. He stifled a chuckle as the uncomfortable silence stretched on.

Cat finally spoke. "Ralph, do you know anything about Dirk corresponding with a Mrs. Hamilton—a Delores Hamilton?"

"No, can't say I do." *But thanks for another lead.* "Unfortunately, I last spoke with Dirk in July. He called right after the Fourth to check on Mother. Did you find a letter to this Mrs. Hamilton? Perhaps she's a customer. Wasn't Dirk peddling housewares?"

"Yes, that's probably it. A customer."

Ralph sensed her answer came too quickly. What was she hiding?

"I happened to see her name on a list," she added. "Nothing important. Will you be joining us for the visitation before the funeral service?"

"Wouldn't miss it. I'm looking forward to seeing my little blue-eyed nephew. Such a novelty for the Black clan. Will Jay be there?"

"No, uhm, no. A neighbor will mind him. He's much too young for a funeral service."

"Guess I should drop by your house to see the little bugger. It'll give us more of a chance to talk."

Another long stretch of silence. Cat had clammed up.

"Goodbye, Cat. I look forward to seeing you tomorrow afternoon."

Ralph hung up and sauntered into the small living room. Delores Hamilton? Who was she, and why did Cat care? Maybe Banker Jacobs wasn't the only chicken ripe for plucking.

A sagging shelf held only a handful of books, but one title caught Ralph's eye—a biography of Alexander Hamilton. He plucked the tome off the shelf and sat down to flip through it. A library stamp marked the front cover. Hadn't stopped Dirk from writing in the margins. Ralph laughed out loud when he puzzled it out. Genius. Picking Alexander Hamilton for an inheritance scam. The Town of Hamilton sat square across the Mississippi River from Keokuk. Plenty of Hamilton descendants in the vicinity. How many would just love to learn they were long-lost relatives of the nation's first Secretary of the Treasury?

Now all he had to do was find Delores Hamilton. Unsure of the details of his brother's con, he'd play it carefully. Vagueness never seemed to bother marks—especially women. What patsies.

TWENTY-ONE

The woman drove her own car. Being chauffeured about town reinforced the notion women were helpless. Her father had forbidden her to drive. When she first sat behind a wheel, her husband harrumphed and labeled it unseemly.

Her days of playing meek victim were over--forever. She'd teach her daughter to be strong. Her little girl would grow up knowing she didn't need any man.

She parked and walked into the alleyway behind the Scott & O'Reilly drugstore. Glancing around to ensure no one watched, she wiggled a loose brick, retrieved a hidden note, and shoved the brick back in place. The bell above Scott & O'Reilly's front door tinkled when she entered.

The proprietor hustled to greet her. He held out a chair at a table beside the window. "The usual cherry Coke?"

She nodded and tugged off her white gloves, frowning at the ocher smudges left by the brick dust. She waited until Joe brought her soda fountain drink, then pulled the note from her handbag.

John Reedy cunfessed. Hes in jale fir Dirks murder. A new coppers pokin around askin who had raison to kill Dirk.

Jimmy's atrocious spelling didn't stop the woman from realizing her plan had lurched off the tracks. Who was this meddlesome policeman? Was he the reason the Reedy whore hadn't been arrested?

She sipped her fountain drink, tasteless cold fizz. She shoved the half-empty glass away and extracted a fountain pen from her purse. As she uncapped it, a blob of ink fell on Jimmy's note. It reminded her of the blood spatter on the boat's oar. The oar wasn't a weapon. Just used to help tuck the corpse into his floating bier.

She sucked in a deep breath. She'd been too intent on making her revenge a game, wanting to savor the deaths one at a time. *Keep the main objective in sight.* Dirk was dead. Now it was Cat's turn. The sooner the better. No need for a trial.

She turned over Jimmy's note and penned precise instructions.

TWENTY-TWO

Though the temperature had nosedived to forty degrees last night, tonight's forecast was for warmer weather. Could it really be September? The month usually wore down hot and dry. Cat felt as if she'd been in a coma. Slept right through to November.

She considered wearing the bright red, fitted trousers Dirk bought for her two years back "to show off her cute little behind." The pants were one of many presents purchased with "borrowed" funds she had to repay.

She shook her head, closed the dresser drawer. Grandmother Nell would have a tizzy. No widow could wear scarlet pants while in mourning. For the life of her, Cat failed to see why respect and discomfort seemed inextricably bound. But there was no sense in upsetting Nell more. The woman had enough heartache with her son in jail. And Cat couldn't afford for her grandmother to back out of minding Jay while she snuck off on her secret mission.

Cat dressed quickly, tucking a long-sleeved blouse into a loose skirt and slipping a cardigan around her shoulders. She hoped the chain guard on her Schwinn bike would keep the skirt from catching. Last thing she needed was to take a tumble on River Road. Or maybe that was the answer—a broken neck.

No. Think about Jay.

She'd decided against borrowing Pete's car for her rendezvous. She wasn't keen on answering her brother's questions about where she was going or why. Truth be told she wasn't sure about the why. While she longed to believe Ed might help, his actions argued the opposite. Strike one—he'd braced her landlord. Strike two—he'd scribbled down some hobo's false testimony. Should she wait for strike three? Wasn't it obvious he played for the other team?

Cat walked downstairs. She picked up Jay for a goodbye hug then settled him on the floor in the middle of his toys. Her grandmother's knitting needles sang in angry rebuke. Cat squeezed one of Nell's hands, stilling it and forcing her grandmother to look at her.

"I appreciate you minding Jay. I hope to be home by nine. I'm sorry to be so secretive, but it's better this way. If Chief Dexter asks where I am, you can say you have no idea. I loathe the man, but he seems to have a sixth sense about lies. Probably because he's such a skilled practitioner. He'll know you're telling the truth."

She hurried outside, swung onto the seat of her Schwinn, and started pedaling. By the time she reached Rand Park, sweat trickled down her back. The exercise felt good. Each push of a pedal relieved a small measure of stress. A few cars swung wide to pass. No problem. Her concern rested with the one car that dawdled well behind her, poking along in her wake. She swiveled again to check over her shoulder. The car maintained a respectable distance, never getting closer, never falling back. Had Chief Dexter assigned someone to follow her?

She swerved around a curve, hopped off her bike, and pulled it behind a thick cluster of bushes. Breathing heavily, she crouched to watch the road.

The beat-up black Model T moved forward at a snail's pace. She risked raising her head above her green blind to study the driver. Jesus. The man from the bus. The one who trailed her from her apartment to the river. No coincidence. He was keeping tabs on her.

She didn't know the man. Who did he work for? Chief Dexter seemed convinced he had her dead to rights. Would he bother with a tail? Maybe this man had authored the threatening postcard. Maybe he'd killed Dirk.

Goose bumps pebbled her arms. Shivering, she pulled her cardigan tighter around her shoulders. Should she still rendezvous with Ed? Only a mile and a half to go. How long before her follower realized she'd slipped his leash? With her luck, he'd double back and spot her just as she met Ed.

I've come this far. No turning back.

She muscled her Schwinn back on the road at the crest of the Rand Park bluff, and sucked in a breath of chill evening air. Hurry. The section of River Road before her looked as steep as a ski run pictured in some fancy magazine. Kids shrieked as they careened downhill to reach the bottomland below. She began to coast and immediately stood on her brakes. The bike shimmied as she barreled downhill. Her skirts billowed. Her hair lifted from her face.

Letting up slightly on the brakes, she abandoned herself to the reckless sensation of speed and wind. Nearing the bottom, she spotted a patch of gravel. She swerved, attempted to slow. Not enough. Trying to stay upright, she skidded sideways across the road. She glimpsed an oncoming car. A horn blared as she bumped off the pavement, and the grassy verge rushed up to meet her.

***

Ed turned onto River Road and spotted a bicyclist rocketing downhill. Wind whipped her golden hair and ballooned her skirt. Cat? She was going too damn fast. He'd traveled only halfway down the slope when the bicycle spun out, flinging its rider across the road. A surprised driver in an oncoming car laid on his horn as he blew by with inches to spare. The motorist waved a fist but didn't stop.

Ed's heart raced. The woman lay on her side, unmoving. He parked his car on the verge, jumped out, and ran across the road. His breath caught when he saw Cat's face. Her eyes were closed. Except for her contorted position, she looked as though she were sleeping. Was she breathing?

He knelt beside her. "Cat, can you hear me?" He placed two fingers against her throat. Her pulse seemed steady. Thank God. He lifted her head, cradled her body.

"Talk to me."

No answer.

His throat tightened and he rocked her in his arms. "Please, Cat, can you hear me?"

Her eyelids fluttered. Her eyes seemed to have trouble focusing. "Ed?"

"You scared me to death. I'd just started down River Road when I saw you skid. That car almost ran over you. Are you all right?"

She blinked and lifted a hand to her forehead, gingerly probing a spot near her hairline. "I may have a little bump." She shifted position. "Ouch. And I think I twisted my ankle." She stared at her left foot.

He frowned. "Let's see."

Cat's tumble had bunched her skirt high on her thighs, revealing the full length of her shapely legs. Ed swallowed. Stop it. Not the time to fantasize about those luscious legs twined around his waist.

He slipped off her canvas shoe and rolled down a thin anklet, baring her dainty foot. His hands circled her injured ankle. He gently squeezed. She flinched but didn't utter a sound. His left hand traveled up to her muscled calf, while his right rotated her foot. He watched her face. She bit her lip as he tested the injury.

"I can't feel any broken bones. But your fall knocked you out. That's not good. In the CCC, I got to be friends with our doc. The kind of work we did, people had plenty of accidents. He warned us about concussions."

As Ed replaced her sock and shoe, Cat pushed to a half-sitting position, bracing herself on her elbows.

"Want to help me up?"

"Of course. Sure you're ready?"

He moved behind her and slid his hands into position. He felt her ribs as he lifted. Cat stood. As soon as he let go, she swayed. He snaked his arm around her slim waist and pulled her to him. Her body molded to his, sparking inappropriate thoughts. She felt so good in his arms. When she lifted her head to look at him, the impulse to kiss those inviting lips proved almost irresistible.

The spell broke when she looked away.

"I felt dizzy for a moment. Just stunned I guess. Now I'm fine. Really."

He loosened his hold and a space opened between them. Cat attempted a smile. It never fully formed.

"Oh, God." Her lower lip trembled. "We need to get away. Fast. You can't be seen with me. He'll be back."

"Who'll be back?" Was she hallucinating? "Take a deep breath. Relax. Tell me what you're talking about?"

Cat rolled her eyes. "I hurt my ankle not my brain. I'm not imagining things. A man followed me this afternoon. The same thug tailed me tonight. I pulled off the road and hid in the bushes until he drove past. He'll be back once he realizes he missed me."

Ed scanned the road, listening intently for the sound of a distant motor. Nothing. "Okay. I'll drag your bike out of sight. We'll come back for it later. Can you walk to my car without help? If so, go now. Get inside and lay down on the front seat. There's a hidden pull off, a piece down the road. We'll be out of sight there. Safe."

He kept one eye on Cat as he hid her bike. She walked with a slight limp. He hoped a twisted ankle proved the worst of her injuries.

When he climbed in the car, Cat started to sit up. He placed a protective hand on her shoulder. "Stay down. You can sit up in a minute or two."

In less than a quarter mile, he swung onto a dirt road that appeared to go nowhere. In seconds, a clump of bushes and bramble hid them from passersby. He turned off the engine, and Cat struggled up. One lonely tear meandered down her right cheek. A tough lady. Before he could censor himself, his thumb flicked the tear away. He trailed a finger along her soft skin. Who the hell was following her?

Ed cupped her chin and lifted her face, forcing her eyes to meet his.

"Tell me about this man, the fellow who followed you. Do you know him?"

"No." Her forehead wrinkled. "He's big. Maybe six-foot, heavy set. He's dark complexioned, swarthy." She stopped to shiver. "He has black hair and beady eyes. He chain smokes."

Ed sighed. At least a dozen local ne'er-do-wells fit that description. "What did he drive?"

"A beat-up Model T."

That narrowed the field slightly. "Did he speak to you? When did you first notice him?"

"He never said a word." Cat paused and studied his face. He couldn't interpret her questioning look. Mistrust? "I spotted him when I left my old apartment and headed to the river where Dad keeps his johnboat."

Her look challenged him. "It was about two o'clock, maybe fifteen minutes after you finished interrogating O'Reilly and searching my apartment."

Damn. She'd seen him. Ed doubted O'Reilly had clued her in. How much had she heard of his chat with her landlord?

TWENTY-THREE

The sputtering sound of an approaching auto gave Ed a momentary reprieve. He motioned Cat to stay put and keep quiet, then scooted out of the car to peer through the bushes. He could walk faster than the battered Model T crawled up the road. Every few seconds, the driver's head swiveled from one side to the other, scouring the landscape.

No question. The man was hunting Cat. As the car came even, the driver seemed to look directly at him. Ed's heart thumped. Had he been spotted? The car inched forward, and the driver focused on the opposite side of the road.

The reprieve didn't lessen his dread. He recognized the driver—Sam Fox. The thug was all brawn, no brain. However, his boss, Jimmy Cloyd, was clever, amoral, and vicious. How was Jimmy involved? He had ties to the mob, but that didn't necessarily mean he was shadowing Cat for gangsters. Jimmy freelanced for anyone with coin. Ed suspected Chief Dexter might even be a client. Was Jimmy planting evidence for Dexter?

Ed's frown deepened as he recalled seeing Jimmy at the Street Fair cozied up with a couple of tough-looking carnies. If he was recruiting, the job might involve Cat.

He returned to the car and answered Cat's question before she could ask. "You're right, that man was definitely looking for you. His name is Sam Fox. Do you know him?"

Cat shuddered. "No. But it's obvious you do."

"He works for Jimmy Cloyd. You've heard of him, right?"

Cat closed her eyes and swallowed. "Of course. He's a go-to guy for the mob. The whole town knows who he is. Why would Jimmy have one of his goons tail me?" Her eyes challenged him. "And why should you care? You're working for Chief Dexter."

He held up his hands. "Whoa. We need to get some things straight. Yes, I questioned O'Reilly. Dexter sent me, ordered me to search your apartment and ask your landlord about your relationship with your husband. If you listened, you know I asked about other folks who might have wished Dirk harm. I can't stop Dexter's pretense of an investigation, but I can attempt some real police work, stop the chief from railroading you. Whatever your history with my boss, he clearly views your conviction as a holy crusade."

Fresh tears rolled down Cat's cheeks. "I know you scribbled down what that hobo said about Dad and me rowing Dirk to his death. How much more 'investigating' do you need to do? Are you going to buddy up with Dexter for my arrest?"

Double damn. How the hell had Cat learned he helped document that pack of lies?

"Listen, it's not what it seems. God forbid you ever come to trial. If you do, I'll testify. I'll swear on a stack of Bibles that Dexter's alleged witness only talked because the chief bullied and bribed him."

Cat sat up straighter. "Would that even matter? Dexter has the gun hidden in our backyard. Dad didn't shoot Dirk. Someone swiped his Webley, used it, and buried it behind our house. What's going on?"

She swallowed, then stared at the hands clasped in her lap. "Who hates me enough to frame me?"

He reached over and covered her hands with his. "Look at me."

She raised her eyes.

"I'll be honest. The hobo's testimony isn't worth much. But a lawyer *can* convince a jury you had motive. Then there's the weapon. We both know that gun killed your husband. Who'd bother to hide it, otherwise? Discovering it in your backyard looks bad. Finding blood in your dad's rowboat looks worse."

She gulped in air and turned to stare out the window. A vein in her neck pulsed in panicked rhythm. He reached across the seat and captured her face in his hands.

"We need to be straight with one another. Trust each other. That's the only way I can help. Your father's confession doesn't absolve you. No one believes him, least of all Dexter. As far as the chief's concerned, the confession only raised one tiny doubt—whether you killed Dirk alone or your dad helped you do it."

Cat shook free of his hands, scooted as far away from him as she could within the small car's confines. "Why should I trust you? Why do you want to help me?"

He kept his voice soft, his tone measured. "I believe you're innocent. The evidence is too damn neat, too pat. The buried gun, the anonymous call. You're too smart to kill someone and hide a gun in your own backyard. That I know."

Ed shook his head. "You have absolutely no reason to trust me. Just my word. I hate Chief Dexter. He hired me because he's illiterate. He needed a copper to handle his paperwork. He loves to see me at his beck and call. Making the college boy jump when he snaps his fingers gives him his jollies."

He couldn't read Cat's expression. Did she believe him? *Stop talking, you idiot. Don't say anything else.* He couldn't admit his real reason for putting up with Dexter. That knowledge would do Cat no good. If she talked to anyone, the consequences wouldn't be pretty. He'd pay. So would his sister and nieces.

Keep your mouth shut.

***

Cat tried to read the emotions flickering across Ed's face. She sensed he wasn't being totally honest. Living with Dirk had done one positive thing, given her the gift of knowing when people lied or Gatling-gunned half-truths to hide even bigger secrets. She'd bet anything Ed hid some secret, something big. Still she couldn't see a down side to confiding a bit of information. She knew how to play the cat-and-mouse game. She'd share her own half-truths.

"Even if I trusted you, how can you help me?" she asked.

Ed interrupted before she could say more. "If we find out why Dirk was murdered, the motive will lead us to the killer. You asked who hated you enough to frame you. The killer may not know you, may have nothing against you. A wife—especially an estranged one—is always a prime suspect. Laying the murder at your doorstep may simply be a ploy to keep Dexter from digging deeper. The killer might know Dexter well enough to realize he'd welcome a reason to hang you."

Ed paused. "I want the truth, and I'm willing to dig to find it."

Cat slumped. "Dig how? Where would you even start? With Jimmy Cloyd? Dirk never mentioned him, except as a fellow poker player. I suppose they might have hatched something together—some new con. Dirk didn't confide in me."

She studied her fingernails, chewed to the quick. She couldn't tell him about Kenneth Jacobs and the blackmail. It would just give him reason to doubt his tentative verdict that she was "innocent." But she should tell Ed about the threat in her mailbox and her plans for the evening.

"What is it?" Ed asked. "You're holding something back."

Cat almost smiled. Ed had his own talent for detecting dishonesty. She had secrets big and small. She would fork over a medium-sized secret. The big one about Banker Jacobs, never.

She sighed theatrically to heighten the drama. She'd encourage Ed to clamp onto her revelation. Maybe then he'd stop peppering her with questions.

"When I came home this afternoon, I found a postcard in my mailbox. It hadn't been mailed. Someone walked right up on our front porch and slipped it in the box."

Her shudder wasn't part of any act. The idea of some miscreant being so close to her son stabbed icicles into her heart.

She sucked in a deep breath. "Nothing subtle about the message. It ordered me to 'bring the money' to the Street Fair tonight. Whoever wrote it wasn't talking about Jay's piggybank. I was instructed to ride the Ferris wheel and drop a bag of money just before I climbed aboard. It claimed someone would be watching. If I failed, it said I'd be the next corpse."

Ed's fist beat the steering wheel. Splotches of red sprouted high on his cheeks. His eyes darkened as he glared at her. Fury contorted his handsome face. "Why didn't you tell me before now? Good God, someone's threatened to kill you."

She stiffened. His misplaced anger caused her to second-guess her decision. She'd never dreamed Ed might be the type to use his fists on a woman who disappointed. Could she be wrong? Well, she'd married Dirk, hadn't she? Once a fool…

She returned Ed's glare. "Exactly how and when was I supposed to tell you? Sashay into the police station with my news and give the chief a chuckle? For all I know, Dexter sent the note. Maybe he figures Dirk scored on a scam, and I killed him for the money. Maybe whoever sent the postcard is bluffing just to see if I'll play. Even if Dexter isn't involved, the threat would give him a belly laugh. He'd claim I'd penned the note myself."

Ed closed his eyes, shook his head. "Sorry, Cat. I'm not mad at you. Just angry someone's threatening you. Surely you're not planning to go."

"Of course, I am." She bit off her answer. "If I don't show up, maybe I *will* be next. If I do nothing, I lose—even if it's a bluff. I'll ride the damn Ferris wheel and leave a bag, it just won't have money in it. Maybe I can find out something. I'll keep a sharp eye out, look to see who takes that bag. I might even follow them."

Ed's lips thinned, and his eyes narrowed. "No. No. No. It's too dangerous. The note may be designed to lure you into a kill zone. Last night I spotted Jimmy Cloyd talking with a couple of shady-looking carnies. One operated the Ferris wheel."

He suddenly stopped talking. His mouth hung open. "Oh my God." He raked a hand through his hair. His eyes pleaded understanding as he looked at Cat.

"Maybe it's my fault. I braced Jimmy today at a gambling joint. Pumped him for information on Dirk. Asked if your husband could have double-crossed a partner on a score. Maybe Jimmy decided I had it right. Figured someone killed Dirk over a pile of cash, and there was a chance his widow had the dough."

He paused. "That might tempt him to send a note and give him a reason to have you followed..."

"Hoping I'd go collect the cash wherever I'd hidden it," Cat finished. "That makes sense."

Reading what looked like anguish in Ed's eyes, her doubts about his motives eased. He'd been trying to prove someone else killed Dirk. He hadn't intended to cause her more grief. She reached across the seat and let her fingers brush his cheek.

"It's not your fault. Your theory gives me even more reason to ride that damn Ferris wheel. I'll leave the bag. Just like they said."

Ed's brow furrowed. "I don't understand. What are you planning to put in the bag?"

Cat laughed, releasing a small bit of the tension coiled in her stomach. "Black gold. A bag full of black gold."

"What in Sam Hill are you talking about?"

Cat grinned. "That's what Dad calls the poop he collects from the mink cages in our backyard. He uses the manure for our vegetable garden."

The corners of Ed's mouth lifted. The hint of a smile. He took her hand, raised it to his lips, impulsively kissed her palm. Electricity shot through her. Even after the quick kiss ended, her palm tingled. When he released her hand, she wanted to stop him. *Kiss me again.*

His smile broadened. "You're brave, Cat. I'll give you that. Guess those childhood stories about you fighting off your little brother's tormentors were true. But this. This is foolish."

He pleaded with his eyes. "If I can't stop you, talk some sense into you, I'll be there. I'm scheduled to work the Street Fair, starting at eight o'clock. It's almost seven now. We'll pick up your bike, drop it by your house, then I'll drive you downtown."

She interrupted. "No. Someone might see us."

He shook his head. "I'll park on a side street. You can walk the rest of the way. I'll follow."

She opened her mouth to object. He cut her off. "I won't let you out of my sight. You deliver that bag, and I'll shadow whoever retrieves it. Just promise me you'll stay put, right by the Ferris wheel, until I come back to collect you. I'll see you safely home."

TWENTY-FOUR

"Are we almost there?" Cat asked.

Scrunched down in the front seat of Ed's car to hide from prying snoops, she felt like a teenager sneaking off to make whoopee. The notion almost made her giggle. Her imagination meandered in that direction for a reason.

She could smell Ed's aftershave. Sharp, clean, piney. From her unusual vantage point, she could see the well-defined muscles in his arm as he downshifted. Clearly he'd done plenty of manual work during his CCC stint. Earlier, when his hand circled her ankle to test for broken bones, his callused fingers left their fiery imprint on her skin. His big hands felt strong, and all too good.

"Half a block and I'll park."

Ed's voice snapped Cat from her daydream. Pull it together. You're not on a date. He just wants to keep you out of prison.

The car swerved and shimmied to a stop. "You can sit up now. Not a soul in sight."

Cat rose, happy to uncurl her body from its convoluted twist. It was nearly seven-thirty. While the sun had set, the sky retained a mellow glow, burnishing Ed's rugged face in golden light.

Scanning the alleyway parking spot, she recognized the vacant factory. Three blocks from Main. Most people would ride the bus to the fair. Those who actually owned cars wouldn't park this far from the action. Good choice. No one would spot her with Ed.

He hustled around the car, opened her door, and took her hand to help her out. "Sure you want to go through with this?"

"Absolutely. Nothing to worry about, right? You'll be lurking nearby."

Ed nodded. "You bet. I'll stick to you like silk on an ear of corn."

Cat laughed. His corny analogy took her mind in a bizarre direction—first to corn tassels, then to the midget's tassel-twirling, girlie-show invite. Maybe she should run off and join the carnival.

Ed took the burlap bag packed with black gold from the back seat and handed it to her. He'd helped her wrap manure scraped from the minks' cages in several layers of newspaper. She hoped the padding would keep goo from leaking through the burlap. A whiff of feces escaped its gift wrapping.

She was about to leave, when Ed bent down and kissed her. A light, feathery kiss on the cheek. Had he sensed her daydream? He smiled. "For good luck."

"Thanks." Did he notice her voice held a breathless wobble? His kiss rooted her to the spot like a lovesick puppy. Okay, more like a puppy that had been kicked and finally found someone who might take her home. *Move.*

She took two steps before her left ankle revolted. It hurt like the dickens each time she put weight on it. She gimped ahead. At the end of the alley, she glanced back. Ed trailed her by fifty feet. She wanted to wait for him to catch up and wrap her in his arms. If only he would tell her to wake up from this nightmare.

She could almost hear her mother scolding her dad when he entertained her with fanciful stories. "Don't fill the girl's head with Irish nonsense. There are no fairies, no leprechauns. I have no illusions about any pot of gold. I'd be happy if you brought home a pot of beans."

Back then, Cat had bristled at her mother's harsh put-downs, the way they snuffed out her dad's laughter. Now she understood, but didn't completely forgive. "Okay, mother," she whispered. "I have no illusions. None at all."

She'd limped two blocks when she heard scuffling sounds and a sharp yelp of pain.

"Hey, blackie. What ya think ya doin'?" a boy's voice challenged.

"We don't want no nappy-haired snots ruinin' our Street Fair," another voice chimed in.

"I ain't done nothin'. Leave me be."

The plea ended with a whoosh—like air escaping a blacksmith's bellows. A little kid in trouble. Incensed, she shambled as fast as she could toward the voices.

Three scraggly teens surrounded a small, dark-skinned boy in a corner of the alley running behind the Main Street shops. Their victim lay curled on the ground. One of the hooligans raised a boot to deliver a kick. Cat screamed bloody murder and hobbled in their direction, each step sending a shooting pain up her leg.

"You leave that boy alone. Do you hear? Stop it now!"

The pimply-faced boys, maybe thirteen or fourteen, abandoned their fun to stare at her. All stood taller than her five-foot-two height. They outweighed her, too. The biggest one wore a blue ball cap. He grinned at her. "Whatcha gonna do, lady? You a darkie lover? You wanna join him?"

Staring into the frightened eyes of the child huddled on the ground, her anger surged.

"You don't want to try me," she growled between gritted teeth. "I'm closer to your size."

Cat knew Ed was only a couple of minutes behind her. Surely she could hold her own with the little devils until he arrived. She threw back her shoulders and marched straight toward them.

Blue Cap laughed. "Come on, boys. This is gonna be fun. You know who she is? My ma pointed her out at the Street Fair last night. She's the witch who kilt her husband."

The words stopped Cat cold. My God, these hooligans knew her. Did everyone in town believe she'd murdered her husband?

She took a deep breath. "Well, now. If I 'kilt' my own husband, what makes you think I won't murder you?" She punctuated her question with the most evil cackle she could muster. She held up her purse, made a show of unsnapping the clasp. "Maybe I got me a gun in here? Want to see?"

The smallest of the toughs broke first. "I'm leavin'." He barreled down the alley away from Cat.

The second bully swayed on his feet like a bowling pin that couldn't decide which way to topple. A minute later, he turned tail as well. That left Blue Cap alone. He spit on the ground, turned, and sauntered away. After he'd gone a piece, he called over his shoulder, "I'll come to your hangin', witch."

Cat rushed to the boy huddled on the ground. When she knelt and saw his face, she recognized him. Ruth's son, Howie. He had to be eight, though he seemed small for his age.

"Howie, are you all right?" she asked.

The boy nodded. Tears left shiny tracks on his mahogany face, but she saw no blood. "Where's your mother?"

"Waitin' for me at the Street Fair, ma'am. I just run some clothes she mended up to Miz Helen."

"We'll go to the Street Fair together then." She smiled to encourage the boy. "I'll bet there aren't any toughs willing to take on the both of us."

Howie scrambled to his feet, and she took his hand. Ed stood at the alley opening, hand on his night stick. He smiled. "Is there a problem here, ma'am?"

She smiled back. "No, Officer. Not at all. Howard and I are going to the Street Fair."

Ed nodded, turned, and walked away. A man with responsibilities. She believed his promise: he'd stick to her like corn silk.

She looked down at the boy. Eyes opened wide, he chewed on his lip. Was he still frightened?

"Do you really have you a gun?" he asked.

"No," she laughed. "Though there are times I wish I did."

She scanned the crowd on Main Street for Ruth Taylor. She didn't know Howard's mom well, but they always nodded and exchanged greetings. Ruth was the Jacobs' maid. Sometimes Ruth brought the little Jacobs girl, Dorothy, to the bank to visit her dad while she ran errands. Cat and Ruth shared common bonds stronger than their black-and-white differences. Both had to work to feed their families. Cat knew—like one does in any small town—that Ruth's husband had Dirk's affinity for gambling and spent most of his time in one of the gaming halls.

Cat spotted Ruth and yoo-hooed a greeting.

Howie's mother turned. When she saw her son holding Cat's hand, she looked puzzled. Howie pulled free and ran to his mama.

"What happened?" Ruth asked.

Before Cat could answer, Howie blurted out the story. "Some boys were a beatin' on me. They ran when the white lady threatened them with a gun."

Oh, great. That'll help my reputation. With the mention of a gun, the sidewalk crowds thinned around them. People gave gun-toting crazy ladies a wide berth.

"Ruth, I'm not packing heat." Cat laughed, stealing slang from a gangster movie she'd seen. "I just took advantage of childish imagination to send the bullies running for the hills. I hope Howie isn't hurt."

The boy clung to his mother. Ruth hugged him to her side. "Thank you, Miz Black. You're a brave woman, and a kind one. I won't forget."

* * *

Ed watched Cat deliver the Taylor boy to his mother. The more he saw of Cat the more his admiration grew. He'd been poised to run into the alley to defend her when she sent the young ruffians running using her wit.

Smart and brave. And, oh God, was she beautiful.

He'd been unable to resist a kiss. One kiss on her silky cheek. Even now his lips burned for more. Maybe when this madness was over. *If we're both still alive.*

TWENTY-FIVE

Cat slid the purse handles up her forearm to free the fingers clutching her sweat-coated nickel—her Ferris wheel admission. Two couples stood on line ahead of her. Behind her, a little girl laughed as she held hands with her mom and dad. Bracketed by lovers and families, she felt loneliness edge in and join her fright. God, how she wished Ed could climb into the car with her.

She scanned the street. The tall policeman's head easily cleared the milling revelers. Less than thirty feet away. Gaudy lights strung along the Ferris wheel's metal bones lent coppery highlights to Ed's dark red hair. The sight of him calmed her.

I'm not alone. I can do this.

Only one couple to board then it was her turn. She studied the man collecting nickels and operating the ride. Was he one of the carnies jawing with Jimmy Cloyd last night? Had they talked about her? About the money bag she was to set down before she climbed in the Ferris wheel gondola?

The attendant looked rough. She doubted even her father's gun would scare him. He'd lift her by her scrawny neck, wring it as easily as a doomed hen's. Though still three feet away, she could smell the stale sweat wafting from his tattered, unwashed undershirt. His hair might be blond. Grease made the color indeterminate. Bulging forearms decorated with cartoonish tattoos poked out from his ribbed undershirt. One scary brute.

He turned and she saw him full face. Her thoughts froze. Scar tissue puckered the right side of his face from temple to chin. A milky white eye swam in the sea of red. Jesus. What happened to him? A fire?

His good eye seemed to bore a hole clean through her. His malevolent glare turned her insides to mush. Her heart galloped, and her brave thoughts fled like a flock of crows after a shotgun blast. *Heaven help me.*

The attendant focused once more on the passengers ahead of her, snapping the safety bar closed on their gondola. The couple giggled. The young man draped an arm around his date's shoulders as she snuggled against his chest. Their carefree smiles should have lifted Cat's mood, eased her anxieties. They didn't.

She hated being confined in any small space, and heights gave her the heebie-jeebies. In younger days, she whistled her way past her minor phobias to ride the Ferris wheel with friends or her dad. Then she shared a gondola with Dirk. When they crested the top of the Ferris wheel, he rocked the car and tipped them forward. He'd laughed at her panic. Dirk claimed he intended no harm with his horsing around, but he knew heights scared her. She sensed her panic pleased him. He liked it when she begged him to stop the car's raucous bucking.

The Ferris wheel operator yanked back on a waist-high lever and the just-seated couple swung up and away. A new empty bucket arrived in the loading zone. The carnie swiveled toward Cat.

"Money," he mumbled with onion-laced breath. She handed over her nickel. Cat avoided looking at his gruesome face. Her eyes locked on the empty gondola awaiting her. She steeled herself to move, climb into the compact torture chamber. As she stepped forward, a beefy arm shot out and barred her way.

"Not that one, lady."

He pulled the big lever back, and the Ferris wheel's metal skeleton creaked in protest as it hoisted three empty cars through the loading zone. He pushed the lever forward and the wheel stuttered to a stop. "Here's your ride, lady. Leave the bag and get in."

Why had he bypassed three empty cars to lock her in this one? She remembered how he'd left one gondola vacant last night. Was this the same car, a special one for her? Should she refuse?

Cat set down her "money" bag. One of the brute's meaty paws snatched it away.

"Get in, lady. Folks are waitin'."

It took all of her willpower to take a seat in the swaying contraption. *Dear God, let my fear be just my wild imagination.*

The iron safety bar locked into place. Its solid thunk mildly reassuring. She tucked her purse behind her legs so it couldn't fall out. She wanted her hands free for a tight hold on the bar.

The operator reached up, one of his ham-like hands closed around something metal. A wrench? His other hand held the end of a coil of sturdy rope. Her cart rocked side to side as he fiddled with something at the top of the car, then the bottom. What in blazes was he doing? Was anyone watching him?

He gave her gondola a rough push. She yelped in surprise as the wheel jerked upward, heaving her fifteen feet off the ground. Cat's blood pumped faster than the Mississippi River breaching a levee. It felt as though Dirk's ghost settled beside her, gleeful at the prospect of frightening her silly.

She screwed her eyes closed. Ed watched, right? He must have seen that creature at the Ferris wheel snag the burlap bag. He'd see who took delivery. All she had to do was sit tight through a few revolutions of the big wheel. *Don't be a baby.*

The darkness imposed by squeezed-shut eyelids intensified her nausea. Not the answer. Her eyes snapped open. She recalled her dad's advice. "Just look at the horizon. Don't look down."

She resisted the temptation to search for Ed in the crowd below. Staring into the distance above the fair's tents and twinkling lights, she noticed a dark strip at the edge of the sky. Though her gondola had climbed only a quarter of the way to the top, she could make out the ebony ribbon of the Mississippi River, the water blacker than night itself.

Without warning, the image of Dirk's bloated body invaded her mind, triggering a new wave of nausea.

Sweet Jesus, let this be a short ride.

She sucked in a breath and glanced up for reassurance that the rusty bucket carrying her skyward remained securely attached. She sighed in relief as her gaze traveled up the thick steel rod that supported the right-hand side of her gondola. It appeared firmly locked to the axel connected to the Ferris wheel frame.

She looked left. What? The axel looked like it was bending. Below the gondola a twisting flash of yellow caught her eye. If the wheel were a clock, her car had arrived at three. *Not that high, just lean forward and look down. You can do it.*

A second later, she wished she hadn't looked. One end of a rope was tied to the bottom of her gondola. The other end wound around a steel girder below. The Ferris wheel's climb had stretched the rope tighter than a banjo string. Surely it would snap before the strut or axel, right?

Metal screeched. Cat tightened what was already a death grip on the safety bar. Crack! The left side of Cat's car lurched, dropped precipitously, and tipped backwards. Cat's feet flew above her head, her body slammed against the left armrest. The car dangled like an upside down teacup from its single remaining support. She glanced over her shoulder and watched the snapped rope tumble to earth. It did its dirty job before it broke.

Cat's stomach somersaulted as her gondola imitated an out-of-kilter pendulum. Sweat popped out on her forehead and bile inched up her throat. My god, the wheel wasn't stopping. She was headed to the top.

The handbag Cat's father had crafted from shoe factory scraps plummeted. She never saw it land. Her scream blended seamlessly with the other passengers' cries of delight.

As the Ferris wheel crested its three-story circuit, it shimmied to a stop. No, stop wasn't the right word. The metal skeleton moaned and shuddered in protest to the whiplash of its halt.

Groaning metal warned the worst was yet to come. The right-side axel that tied the car's support to the frame no longer looked so sturdy. How many minutes—or seconds—before the car's right side broke free?

The shoe on Cat's injured foot slipped off and flew past her as the cart twisted on its metal thread. Gravity's heavy pressure was nibbling at her piece by piece. A current of air off the river ruffled her gingham skirt, snapping it in her face, blinding her. She felt like a human sheet flapping upside down on a clothesline.

Screams rose from the crowd below. A bitter wind snatched her own raw cry from her throat. *Think.*

As a kid, she'd been fearless, spending hours climbing the black walnut tree in her backyard, swinging from branches to drop to the ground when her mom called Pete and her to supper. *Pretend you're in that tree.*

Maybe there was a way out. She repositioned her hands on the iron safety bar. Could she lever herself up, get her feet back below her? Fighting her terror, she made her move. Hand over hand, Cat mustered all her strength to pull herself up the safety bar like she was climbing a rope. Though the canted seat seemed slicker than a greased playground slide, her fevered squirming worked. She was almost upright, her legs below her head once more.

She felt the toes of her shoeless bare foot touch the left armrest. *Yes.* She wriggled more until both feet touched and she crouched upright in the swaying gondola. The left arm rest had become her undulating floor. *Please, God, let this work.*

She took a deep breath and gathered her courage to take one hand off the iron safety bar. It had to be done if she wanted to make a grab for the Ferris wheel frame. Then she could step off—okay leap—to the nearest metal girder.

A cacophony of screams reminded her that the fair-goers watched. Better show than the Cavots she thought bitterly. She hoped a few members of her audience prayed.

Ed, where are you?

Her hopes dimmed. Ed had followed the bogus money bag. He wouldn't know she was about to die—about to be murdered.

An ominous screech from above told Cat her dangling weight was aiding gravity, making the gondola's final freefall better than an even bet.

She wanted to scream at the unfairness. She'd never see her darling son again.

The hell with this. I won't die without a fight.

Cat had no illusions about pretending to be a high-wire daredevil, competing with the Cavots or Jaydee the Great. *Don't think. Go.* She sacrificed one hand's stranglehold on the safety bar and stretched until her fingers found purchase on the Ferris wheel frame. She gripped the steel support. Using her feet to push off, she leapt into empty space.

Her body slammed into steel, knocking the breath out of her. But both her hands now gripped the wheel's frame. She hung by her arms alone, her feet scrabbling for a toe hold. Her arms felt like they might pull clean out of her shoulder sockets. Her right foot touched a strut on the wheel's skeleton. *Thank god.* Her right hand tightened around a grease-coated beam as her left foot, the injured one, squeezed into a small crevice. She slipped sideways. Was her heart still in her body? Its galloping beat pummeled her rib cage. *Don't look down.*

"Cat! Hang on."

The voice startled her. It sounded close by. An arm circled her waist, pushing her tight against the steel. Ed? She couldn't look. She smelled his cologne. Caught a glimpse of mahogany hair. One of his arms circled her waist, the other looped through a support.

"Thank heaven," she breathed. The hunk of metal she'd latched onto felt as slick as winter's black ice.

"If I brace you, can you get a better grip?"

"Yes." Knowing he wouldn't let her fall, her fingers scuttled over the framework, searching for a metal span that wasn't slippery with grease and grime. Good. Solid contact.

"We'll climb down together," Ed said. "I don't trust that bucket you were in to stay put. We'll work our way down the frame, put as much distance as we can between us and that damn pile of rusty bolts. Ready? Together. Slowly."

"What if that maniac starts the wheel?"

"He's long gone. Once he stopped the wheel with you at the top, he ran like the devil. One of his buddies had already split with the bag."

Ed's firm grip seemed even less important than his encouragement, his confidence their feet *would* reach earth. Once they climbed within a few feet of the ground, Ed whispered, "I'm going to jump. I'll yell once I'm in position. Then you can drop. Don't worry. I'll catch you."

She sent up a silent prayer of thanks.

"It's okay," he yelled. "Let go."

Cat fell into his arms. She only vaguely heard the cheers and applause. Men slapped Ed's back as he helped her limp away.

The Ferris wheel restarted with a groan and she spun around and looked at it like it was a mechanical monster that hadn't given up on killing her.

"My God, is that bastard back?" she screamed.

"No. I asked Smith, a fellow cop, to find someone who could operate the Ferris wheel. We have to get the other riders safely to the ground."

TWENTY-SIX

The woman squeezed her daughter's hand in a death grip as all the people in the surrounding crowd screamed and pointed.

"Mama, look. Look up there!" The child gestured feverishly at the top of the Ferris wheel, using the mounded cotton candy in her free hand as a pointer. "Some lady fell out of her seat way up high. Oh, Mama, I think she's going to fall."

The little girl began to bawl and dropped her pink fluff of sugar in the gutter.

The woman stared at the gyrating bitch at the top of the wheel. She wanted to yell, to tell Catherine Black to let go. Yet she had to admit the drama thrilled her. The Jezebel had to be terrified. She smiled, imagining the horror that would fill the tramp's last minutes.

She stopped breathing, gleefully anticipating the fall, the body splattering on the ground. Greaves Mortuary could cram what was left in the coffin with her good-for-nothing husband. Save a little money. The Reedy clan would need it soon enough, not long until it would be time to bury the last of the line. She wouldn't rest until then.

"Mama, did you hear me?" The girl tugged harder on her mother's hand.

"Don't look, honey." She pressed the child's face into the folds of her pleated skirt. "It'll all be over in a moment. Then the woman will be with Jesus."

The Reedy woman would go straight to hell. No doubt about it. Still there was no need to upset her daughter. Give her nightmares.

She stroked the girl's shiny curls. *I'm doing this for you.*

The woman startled when she picked up on a new round of excited chants. "Go, son, save her!"

What?

Her head snapped up. A man in a police uniform was shinnying up the Ferris wheel scaffolding. What did he think he was doing? Was it that nosy cop Jimmy warned her about?

In dismay, she watched the bitch she hated—hated almost as much as her sanctimonious father. She bit her lips to keep from cursing as the witch maneuvered herself from the tipped car to the wheel's outer steel structure. All the while, the policeman climbed steadily higher.

"Fall!" she screamed. Her anguished cry caused the man in front of her to snap around and stare. "Don't fall!" she called out. The dolt would probably think that's what she yelled the first time. That he'd heard her wrong.

The excited onlookers cheered as the cop and Catherine Reedy weaseled their way to safety like a couple of mangy monkeys. All around her, people slapped each other's backs. Snatches of excited conversation washed over her. "Thank God, thank God."… "Better show than the Cavots."… "Who was the woman?"… "You'll never get me on a Ferris wheel again."

Her daughter clapped her hands. Her cheeks rosy, radiant with joy. "Oh, Mama, that lady's safe. She doesn't have to go to Jesus."

She patted her daughter's head. "I suppose it wasn't her time."

Catherine Reedy must be a witch. I can't believe her luck. Doesn't matter. I swear she'll be dead before the week ends.

This time, she promised herself, the end would come in private, away from witnesses. There'd be no escape. This time mother and child would die together.

TWENTY-SEVEN

A roustabout handed Ed a checkered horse blanket. "For the lady."

Ed nodded and wound the smelly wrap around Cat's shoulders. He had no illusions it would stop her shivering. Cat wasn't just cold. She was in shock.

The roustabout tugged his sleeve. "Ya ain't gonna shut us down, are ya, mister? Mick musta been three sheets to the wind. He's the mug twas runnin' the wheel. He musta see'd there was sumpthin' wrong. Took outta here faster than a hound after a skunk's squirted him."

Ed didn't answer. He ground his teeth to bottle up his anger. If he found 'Mick,' he'd throttle him with his bare hands. He directed equal anger at himself. He shouldn't have let Cat climb aboard that Ferris wheel alone. What was he thinking?

He longed to put an arm around Cat and tuck her petite body into his side, almost as if they were dancing. Instead he stood behind her, hands on her shoulders as he shepherded her toward the black lady he saw her talking to earlier. He knew dozens of eyes followed their every step. He kept space between their bodies and acted as if the woman meant nothing to him. More than a few gossips would try to make something indecent out of any physical contact that resembled an embrace.

While he didn't care if tongues wagged, he didn't want gossip to exacerbate problems for Cat or prompt Chief Dexter to freeze him out of the investigation. Dexter couldn't learn how he felt about Cat.

He located the black lady and her little boy and guided his charge in their direction. As soon as they drew close, the woman put her arm around Cat and tugged the horse blanket tighter around her shoulders. Ed bent and whispered in the lady's ear. "Can you walk her to that alley where those toughs attacked your son? Ask your boy. I'll meet you there in five minutes."

The woman nodded and maneuvered Cat toward the side street, the little boy took his rescuer's hand. Though Cat looked like a dazed sleepwalker, she smiled at the boy. It killed Ed to take his eyes off the trio, to pretend his involvement was over.

He strong-armed the gent who'd asked if he planned to shut down the Ferris wheel. "Let's look at that gondola. I want to see how it broke."

One look confirmed Ed's suspicions. The left axel had bent and sprung free after the operator removed the nut holding it to the wheel's frame. Mick had probably loosened the nut before Cat ever climbed in the gondola. Then he only needed a few turns of a wrench to take it off. As the car climbed, the rope tethering it to the ground exerted enough force to ensure the unsecured axel pulled free. Once the dangling car reached the top of the wheel, the operator stopped the ride and ran. He must have figured Cat had no chance of holding on long enough for some slapdash rescue to succeed. Not exactly precision engineering, but the ploy worked.

"Close the ride for the night," Ed said. "We'll let the city fathers decide if you can make repairs and put it back in operation."

He leaned in tight to ask pointed questions about Mick. How long had he been with Sol's Liberty Show? Who were his friends? Had he done jail time? He didn't like the pipsqueak's "don't-know-nuttin'" shrugs. If it weren't for the need to reach Cat, he'd coerce some meaningful answers from the cagey showman. But time mattered. He wasn't keen on the idea of two women and a boy waiting for him in a dark alley.

He speed-walked to the shadowed meeting place. Cat and the black woman sat together on an overturned crate, while the boy tossed rocks toward a crumbling building's foundation. The black woman nodded toward her son. "We saw a rat. Howie's trying to keep it away. If you want, I'll see Miss Cat home."

Ed shook his head. "No, ma'am. I thank you kindly for helping. I'll see she gets home safely. The woman called to her son. "Howie, come along now. Time to go."

Once they were alone, Ed clasped Cat by her shoulders and forced her to look him in the eye. "Should I take you to a doctor? Tell me what you want to do."

She fingered the scratchy blanket draped around her shoulders. "No, but I can't go home just yet. I can't quit shaking, and I don't want Grandmother Nell—or Jay—to see me like this. Nell might have a stroke, and I'd frighten Jay."

Ed squeezed her shoulder "All right. We'll go for a drive."

He helped her stand and cinched her to his side. Fortunately, the car was only parked a block away. Once he bundled his charge into the front seat, he headed the car south away from downtown, toward the Iowa-Missouri border, and the countryside. Without conscious thought, he swung onto the dirt road leading to his family farm—or rather what had been the family farm for four generations of Nelsons before Iowa First Bank, Cat's employer, foreclosed.

Neither Ed nor Cat spoke. Just short of the old farmhouse built by his great grandfather, he let the car glide to a stop and switched off the engine.

"Where are we?" Cat asked. "Is it all right to get out? I feel like I'm suffocating. I need fresh air."

"Sure, we can stretch our legs," Ed answered. "I grew up here, on this farm. After the foreclosure, Iowa First hired sharecroppers to work the land, but no one lives here. The old farmhouse is falling down, it's a disgrace. I'm almost glad Dad's not around to see it."

He reached for his door handle. "Hold on. I'll help you out."

He scooted around the back of the car and opened her door. Still cocooned in the horse blanket, she stumbled into his arms as she attempted to stand. "Sorry. I'm a little wobbly."

Ed held her. "You're entitled. What you did tonight was amazing. Not sure I know another woman—or man, for that matter—who'd have thought so quickly or acted so bravely."

He guided her toward a patch of grass under one of the big elms lining the farmhouse drive. "Want to sit a spell?"

She nodded. "Please, could you hold me a moment? I can't seem to get warm."

They sat. Ed leaned against the trunk of the tree with Cat cradled in his arms. He rubbed her arms vigorously. "Better? Warming up?"

"Yes. That helps." She sighed.

He tilted his head and scanned the night sky. His dad had taught him a fair number of constellations. Away from Keokuk's lights, the sky looked like a pincushion, dotted with countless stars in every inch of its ebony fabric. As his eyes adjusted to darkness, a waning moon cast just enough light to study Cat's lovely face.

For a while, neither of them spoke. Katydids sang in the bushes. The cold snap hadn't killed them. Lightning bugs frolicked around the tree. A breeze ruffled the dry cornstalks still standing in the field. A barn owl joined the chorus with its forlorn hoots.

Minutes passed. Maybe hours. Ed wasn't sure, didn't care. He kissed the top of her head. Cat's hair was as soft and silky as he'd imagined, spun gold. He told himself he meant the gesture as comfort. Deep down, he knew he lied.

"I can't believe I almost let you die tonight," he whispered. "I was so stupid. I should have asked why they wanted you on that ride." He swallowed.

Cat tilted her head and searched his face. "You saved me, Ed. None of this was your fault. I'd be dead now if you hadn't climbed up to help me."

Her warm breath caressed his skin. Inches away, her soft lips invited.

He kissed her. Gently. His lips barely grazing hers. He wanted her, but he refused to take advantage. Told himself he'd back away at the slightest hint he'd overstepped, that she didn't feel the same pull, the same need to connect.

Their lips no longer touched, but her sweet taste lingered. One of her hands snaked out of the blanket. She threaded her fingers through his hair. This time she took the initiative and let her lips brush his. The fleeting kiss flamed his desire. He would stop if she asked. But, dear God, how he prayed she wouldn't.

His breathing quickened. The blanket around her shoulders fell away, baring her swanlike neck. He feathered her neck with kisses. Her chorus of soft moans excited him more.

He kissed her lips once again. Her mouth opened, inviting his tongue to explore. The kiss deepened. Urgent. Probing. As their arms entwined in a tight embrace, Ed felt the soft swell of her breasts against his chest. He wanted more, much more.

He pulled back, opening a space between them. "Shall I spread the blanket?" Desire turned his voice hoarse. He realized his withdrawal was a gamble, giving her time to reconsider, an opportunity to say "no."

He respected this woman. If they came together tonight, it would be a joint decision, a shared longing to feel alive.

"Yes, please." Cat stood. Her breathing sounded as ragged as his.

Did she feel the same drive to feel loved?

He quickly smoothed the blanket over the ground. Cat reached over and caressed his cheek. Her fingers trailed down his chest as she gracefully lowered herself to the makeshift bed. God, she looked beautiful. He took a seat alongside her, leaning on his elbow so he could memorize her face. Her long eyelashes fluttered as his free hand stroked her neck, inched its way to her clavicle, and finally tiptoed inside the lacy edge of her blouse.

"It's been a year since I've made love," Cat stammered.

"Shhh. It's been almost as long for me." He smiled. "I'd say it's like riding a bicycle, you never forget. But I don't want you remembering how your bike ride ended on River Road."

Cat laughed. "Somehow I doubt I'll fall off this bicycle."

"Not if I can help it." He paused. "Should I withdraw, you know…" It was his turn to stutter.

"No, it's a safe time of the month."

After he undid the tiny pearl buttons on her blouse, Cat sat up to wriggle her arms and shoulders free. When Ed undid the snap at her waist, she reached out and grabbed his hand. Ed's heart tripped. *Oh, God, she's changed her mind.*

Cat smiled. "Maybe you should undo your own buttons. This is a tandem bike, right? Aren't we riding together?"

He laughed as his heartbeat settled into a less chaotic but speedy rhythm. In moments, they were both nude. He marveled at her creamy skin, the delicate pink of her aureole. His tongue lazily circled one nipple and then abandoned it for its twin.

Cat writhed as he twined her hands in his hair. While he suckled one breast, he gently pinched the other nipple between his thumb and forefinger, setting up a rhythm of the lovemaking to come.

Ed trailed kisses down her smooth torso, stopping to stab his tongue into her belly button. She gasped with pleasure. The time for conversation had ended—except for the eternal language of love.

Their symphony of sighs and murmurs blended perfectly with all the other night songs.

* * *

Cat's breathing gradually slowed as she lay in Ed's arms. God, she felt alive. If this was a mistake, so be it. It had been too long since she'd thrilled to a lover's kiss, a lover's touch. Ed was a considerate, gentle lover. She sensed he would never treat a woman the way Dirk had treated her. Her husband never wondered if she enjoyed their couplings.

Within a year of their marriage, she'd come to feel like an ashtray on the rare occasions Dirk asserted a claim on her body instead of using one of his whores. Invariably, he was drunk and intercourse consisted of him grinding into her until he emptied himself. Cat was left with ashes.

How different this night. Every inch of her skin sizzled as if she'd been touched by a live wire. So what if this proved a one-time thing? Hell, people wanted her dead. They very well might succeed. Carpe diem.

As a night zephyr ruffled the leaves overhead, goose bumps rose on her sweat-slicked skin. She shivered, and Ed folded the blanket around them.

"I have to go home soon." Cat sighed. "Time to return to reality."

He captured her face in his hands and kissed her lips. "Don't imagine this isn't reality. Since my wife died, I've spent a few nights with other women. For the women and for me, it was release, nothing more. Tonight is different. I promise. This is real."

She pressed her fingers against his lips. "Yes, but tomorrow, you'll still be a policeman, and I'll still be the murder suspect your boss plans to hang. You can't even afford to be seen with me in public for fear of losing your job."

Ed pulled back. She sensed her words wounded him. Words he couldn't deny.

"It's all right," she said. "I have no regrets. I'm not asking you to promise anything, do anything. You have your sister and nieces to think about. I have my son, my dad, Grandmother Nell." She sat up and reached for her clothes.

"We need to leave."

"Not just yet." His hand settled on her forearm. "Not until we talk. It's true. Unless Dexter fires me for saving you, I'll be a cop tomorrow. That's why you need to talk to me. Trust me. Tell me everything you know about Dirk's extracurricular activities. I need help. Clues to find out who really killed him. Not to mention who wants you dead."

Cat paused as she shimmied into her slip. God knew she needed help. How far could she trust him? How much should she tell?

Though she realized her silence suggested a lack of trust, she didn't speak.

Ed tried a different tack. "Listen, all the signs point to Jimmy Cloyd's involvement. His lackey Sam tailed you and I caught Jimmy jawing with the carnie who arranged your special Ferris wheel ride. Can't be coincidence. But how does Jimmy fit in? Maybe some mobster asked him to make an example of Dirk, and Cloyd decided you knew too much. Or maybe Dirk worked a scam with Jimmy and cheated him."

Cat shook her head. "Dirk didn't like Jimmy, and my husband didn't share his scams with anyone. Not a chance in hell he partnered with that man." She paused, trying to decide which puzzle pieces to provide, which to safely hold back.

"My husband was blackmailing someone. I don't know who. Last time I saw Dirk, he told me he planned to leave town as soon as his mark paid him five-hundred dollars."

"Five-hundred dollars?" Ed's eyebrows rose. "Who has that kind of money these days?"

She made no attempt to answer, didn't want to go there. "You were with Chief Dexter when you fished Dirk's body out of the river. Is there any chance Dexter pocketed the money? I sure didn't find five-hundred dollars in our apartment."

Ed's forehead wrinkled. "No. Dexter isn't above stealing from a dead man. But Black had no wallet, no money belt, and no cash in his pockets when we fished him out. Of course, any money on him might have floated away."

Cat bit her lip as she ran through possibilities. "If the blackmail victim killed Dirk, he would have taken back any money he found on my husband. Then again, Dirk could have hidden the hush money before the killer found an opportunity to get him alone."

Ed frowned. "You're sure you don't know who he was blackmailing?"

"No. But I might have a lead. Have you found my husband's car? It wasn't parked anywhere near where Dad keeps his rowboat. In fact, one of Dad's fishing pals said a woman drove off in what looked to be Dirk's red Packer sometime Sunday."

Ed looked up from buttoning his shirt. "Why didn't you tell me this before? It could be important. What did the woman look like?"

She repeated Weaver's description of an older, heavy-set woman who walked hunched over and dressed as if it were the middle of a January freeze.

Ed's puzzled expression told Cat the eyewitness report made as little sense to him as it did to her.

"Do you think he was blackmailing an old lady?" he asked.

She shook her head. "I doubt it. Dirk said his mark was a man. But when I looked through the apartment, I found a newspaper clipping about that fellow who swindled folks with his Sir Walter Raleigh inheritance scheme. Dirk had a list of people; all had Hamilton as a surname. My guess is he was working an inheritance con."

She shut her eyes. *Should I give Ed more?* "I knew the name at the top of the list—Delores Hamilton."

His head snapped up. "Delores Hamilton. Surely you don't think she'd consort with Jimmy Cloyd or pay hoodlums to bump people off?"

"No." She sighed. "But I fear Dirk either planned to sweet talk the widow out of part of her fortune or he'd already succeeded."

"Maybe I can find a diplomatic way to speak with Mrs. Hamilton. See if she volunteers anything about being bamboozled." He stooped to lace his shoes. "Dexter never mentioned Dirk's car was missing. Can't believe I didn't question how Dirk got to the river. I just assumed he rode with the killer. Strange that your dad's friend thinks a woman drove his car away. Don't know what's less likely—an old lady being the murderer or the woman being some killer's accomplice."

Cat grabbed Ed's arm and squeezed. "Please don't mention the missing car to Dexter. I need to find it before he does."

"Why? It's your property, the chief can't steal it."

How could she answer? She couldn't mention the missing blackmail note. "Dirk kept valuables in a strongbox. I can't find it, either. I'm hoping it's in the boot of his car. Chief Dexter might not try to get away with stealing a car, but he wouldn't think twice about prying open a dead man's strongbox and taking whatever's inside."

Ed's eyes narrowed. "Do you know what's inside?"

"Honest to God, I don't. But I have the key, and I damn well think I have the right to look before Dexter does."

"All right. I'll quietly put out word I'm looking for an abandoned Packer, a red one. I won't mention it to Dexter. With any luck, we'll find it first."

TWENTY-EIGHT

Cat practically jumped out of the car before Ed pulled to the curb in front of her home.

"No need to see me in." She nodded at the porch where a shadowed figure rocked in the swing. "Looks like someone's waiting up for me."

"Like it or not, I'm walking you to the door." His tone brooked no argument. "It's too dark to tell for sure who's there."

She laughed. "Whoever it is weighs about eighty pounds less that Jimmy, Sam, or Mick, and I'm betting none of them wears a skirt. Has to be my sister-in-law, Beth Reedy, itching to give me a tongue-lashing."

"Nonetheless, I'll walk you to the porch."

Each time the swing rocked forward the rusted metal chains creaked in protest. When Cat and Ed reached the stairs, silence descended.

Beth jumped up and marched to the railing, hands on hips. "Where the hell have you been? We've been crazy with worry, wondering what happened to you."

"Beth, I'm sorry. I'll explain." Cat's hand sought Ed's for a reassuring squeeze.

"I believe you know my sister-in-law, Ed. As you can see, I'm in no danger now—unless she takes a swing at me. Thanks for escorting me home."

Ed was slow to relinquish her hand. "My pleasure, Mrs. Black."

He nodded toward her riled relative. "Nice to see you, Mrs. Reedy. I'll be going."

Beth held her peace until the policeman moved out of earshot, then she resumed her diatribe in a stage whisper. "If you were my daughter, I'd hide you." She grabbed Cat's arm and dragged her toward the swing. "What in the name of all that's holy are you thinking?"

Understanding that concern drove her sister-in-law's wrath, Cat didn't attempt to defend herself. Instead her eyes brimmed with tears. Family. If she could count on nothing else, she could count on her family. They loved her.

"Let's sit." She patted Beth's hand. "There was an accident at the Street Fair..."

"An accident?" Beth broke in, her voice rising. "That's what you're calling it? The switchboard went crazy two seconds after you set foot on the ground. Everyone wanted to be the first to tell Pete how they'd watched his sister shinny down a three-story Ferris wheel like some trapeze artist."

"Shhh." Cat placed two fingers against her sister-in-law's lips. "No need to wake the neighborhood. Is Grandmother Nell asleep?"

Beth yanked Cat's fingers away. "Don't shush me. Pete wanted to come over and wait for you. I told him to stay home with Amy, said I'd have a better shot at talking sense into you. I'm sure Pete's still awake, sleepless until he hears you're safe."

Cat risked patting Beth's arm again, hoping to calm her. "I'll tell you everything. First, tell me if Nell and Jay are okay, if they're sleeping."

"They're sound asleep. I checked a few minutes ago. Jay hasn't a clue his mother almost died tonight. Exhaustion claimed Nell the minute her head hit the pillow. Of course, she made me promise to wake her if there were any new catastrophes."

"You should go home. Tell Pete I'm fine—thanks to Ed Nelson," Cat added. "Did the telephone gossips mention he helped me climb down?"

"Yes." Beth paused. "But I'm not ready to pin a medal on his chest for having his way with you as a reward."

"Stop it, Beth. You don't know what you're talking about."

"Oh, don't I? I saw how he looked at you. The way he couldn't seem to let go of your hand. Our hero messed up when he dressed in such a hurry. Didn't quite line up the right buttons with matching button holes. I'm not blind. Besides the drive from downtown certainly doesn't take two hours."

Cat sighed. "Leave it, Beth. It's none of your business. Ed's a good man, a decent man. I needed time to pull myself together. I asked him to take me for a drive in the country. He did. Leave it, will you?"

Beth rolled her eyes. "Fine. We have plenty of other bases to cover. Do you think Jacobs arranged your 'accident'?"

"I honestly don't believe he's involved. Jacobs wouldn't frame me for Dirk's murder. He already paid hush money to bury our history. It would be stupid to back me into a corner. That would hand me a reason to finger him as someone else with a mighty strong motive to kill Dirk. Jacobs is many things, but stupid isn't one of them."

Beth shook her head. "That's quite logical if Jacobs actually paid Dirk. We only have the good banker's word for that. Nobody's seen the money. And why not frame you, if he planned to kill you before you could shoot your mouth off? Quite the tidy solution—the blackmailer and his murdering wife both dead."

Headlights swept across Timea Street as a car turned onto their block. Cat had no desire to speculate on who might be driving past her home this late at night. "Let's go inside."

Seated at the kitchen's weathered table, Cat listened in as Beth phoned Pete. "Your sister's safe. The verdict's out on whether she's playing with a full deck. Don't wait up."

As soon as Beth hung up, she played nurse, fixing Cat a hot toddy—light on water, heavy on bourbon from the flask they'd found stashed in the potato bin.

The entire evening's theatrical, slight-of-hand feel made Cat wonder if she'd imagined the drama. While she knew she could confide in her sister-in-law, she was reluctant to add to Beth's worries. As a compromise, she told Beth everything—except how she felt about Ed and her fantasy about a future together.

Beth took it all in, her spare comments nonjudgmental.

When Cat finished, Beth stood. "There's nothing more you can do tonight. Go to sleep. Can't have you falling off your perch tomorrow when people come to pay their respects."

Cat snapped to attention. "I can't believe I put Dirk's funeral out of my mind. Why didn't I tell Mr. Greaves I wanted a private service? I'm not sure I can do this—stand and shake hands with people who show up out of curiosity. People dying to know if I murdered my husband, and wondering if I'll get away with it."

"You'll do fine. You've weathered worse. Going to work and seeing Jacobs day after day, week after week, acting as if he hadn't—"

"Please, I can't talk about that, think about that now. You promised me you'd never breathe a word to a soul. I need you to keep that promise, now more than ever."

Beth closed her eyes and sat down again. "I wish I'd never made that promise. I think your silence may get you killed." She paused. "I know you're a lot smarter than me, but your reasoning escapes me. For the life of me, I can't fathom why you said 'I do' to Dirk a second time. Why did you repeat your vows after you learned what kind of man he was? After you found out your first wedding didn't count because Dirk was already married. A bigamist. Did you still love him?"

"No." Cat gripped the hot toddy mug tighter, willing its warmth to reach her heart. "Dirk and I had lived with Mom and Dad for three months after we said 'I do' in front of Reverend Pfaff. By the time I learned he'd abandoned a wife, skipped out on her and his little girl, I thought I was pregnant.

"From that moment on, I hated Dirk, but I couldn't shame my parents or abide the thought of being an unwed mother. I didn't want my baby branded a bastard. So I helped Dirk get a divorce and married him before a Missouri justice of the peace. I wasn't sure I could live with Dirk, but I knew I couldn't live with myself if I hurt all the people I loved."

Beth bit her lip. "I had no idea. Did you lose the baby?"

"No. I just skipped my period for two months. I wasn't pregnant. Guess nerves turned my system upside down. Even before I learned Dirk was a bigamist and a first-class liar, I sensed I'd made a huge mistake.

"The Dirk who courted me vanished as soon as we married. He could still be charming, the life of the party. It's just that he no longer needed to waste his talents on me. That conquest was over, done with."

Beth poured a jigger of bourbon into her own cup. "Now I need a drink." She cocked an eyebrow. "I wouldn't ask anyone else this—but did you, uh, continue to live as man and wife."

"We had intercourse if that's what you're asking. But I never got pregnant. I'd always wanted children, and I was crushed. Since Dirk had fathered a daughter with the first Mrs. Black, I thought I was barren. Then, one time when Dirk's brother Ralph phoned, I learned Dirk and his first wife had adopted a child because she couldn't get pregnant."

Beth looked down at her hands and twirled her wedding band. "So why didn't Dirk suspect earlier that Jay wasn't his son?"

"Ego, I guess." Cat shrugged. "Dirk never believed he was to blame with wife number one. His problems were always someone else's fault. He just figured he'd had bad luck, wed two infertile women."

Beth's eyebrow arched up. "Well, we know that's not true. Jacobs only needed one—"

Cat reached over and gripped Beth's arm. "I love Jay—more than anything—and I don't ever want my son to know. Please keep your promise. Tell no one. Not even Pete. Especially not Pete or someone else in this family might be charged with murder."

Cat pushed her chair away from the table. "Go home, Beth. Go home to Pete and Amy and say a prayer of thanks for what you have. I'm going to take your advice. Try to get some sleep."

TWENTY-NINE

Wednesday, September 21, 1938

Ed rinsed the dregs from his coffee cup. His nieces were at school, his sister hanging wash on the backyard clothesline. He hoped to leave before Myrt came back inside.

His twin had heard about his Ferris wheel adventure hours before he came home, and she was furious. Myrt tried to pry details from him, ferret out how involved he'd become in Cat's troubles. She could always sense his feelings. Prevarication was pointless. A twin thing?

He knew the idea of losing him terrified Myrt. Ever since he'd taken the job with Chief Dexter, she worried he'd disappear just like her husband had. No warning. No note. No body.

He saw no reason to voice how he felt about Cat, or tell Myrt how much he'd risk to save Catherine Reedy and her son. He glanced at his pocket watch before he slipped on his coat. Nine o'clock. Almost an hour until he reported to the police station. Plenty of time to call on Delores Hamilton.

Almost everyone in town knew who she was. Mrs. Hamilton lived in a substantial, two-story red brick poised high on the bluff above Keokuk's dam and locks. Before her husband died in a terrible car crash, he'd owned several downtown stores as well as hundreds of acres of rich Mississippi bottomland worked by sharecroppers.

Ed enjoyed a nodding acquaintance with Mrs. Hamilton and her six-year-old daughter, Caroline, whose broad smile made it easy to keep your eyes fastened on her face instead of her peg leg.

Mrs. Hamilton promptly answered Ed's knock on her front door. "Officer Nelson, isn't it?" Her forehead wrinkled and her eyes widened. Her hand flew to her mouth. "Oh, mercy, nothing has happened to Caroline, has it?"

"Oh no, ma'am. Sorry if I alarmed you. I've merely come to see if you can shed some light on a bit of a puzzle. Would you mind if I come in?"

Mrs. Hamilton nodded and held the door open. "Of course, come in."

She turned abruptly. As Ed followed her to a formal sitting room, his gaze locked on her mousy brown hair. He could almost count the comb marks that swept it back into a tight, no-nonsense bun. She reminded him of the schoolmarm at the one-room schoolhouse he attended his first three years of school.

The widow motioned him to sit. "What's this about a puzzle, Officer Nelson?"

She claimed a seat halfway across the room, forcing him to raise his voice a notch to answer. "As you may know, Dirk Black recently died."

"He was killed," she interrupted. Her eyes narrowed. "I read the papers. What does that revolting man have to do with me?"

She didn't blink. If anything, her scrutiny devolved into a glare. She would not make this interview easy. He wriggled in his seat. The chair's horsehair covering punctured his britches like prickly cactus.

"When we searched Mr. Black's possessions, we found a list. Your name was written at the top, and it had a checkmark beside it. All twenty people on the list shared the same last name—Hamilton."

A minute ticked by. The woman's lips pressed into a thin, stern line. Ed got the picture. She might answer direct questions, but she'd volunteer nothing. "I'm sorry, ma'am, but I need to ask: do you know why Dirk Black listed your name?"

Her nostrils flared. "I'm not certain that's any of your business, especially since I saw you consorting with that floozy, Mrs. Black last night."

Consorting? Ed felt his face flush. "Mrs. Black was in danger of falling when a Ferris wheel gondola came unhinged. I helped her to safety. I'd hardly call that consorting."

He watched his interview subject lift her pointed chin. "And just what was a new widow doing on a carnival ride? Answer me that, will you?"

Mrs. Hamilton had turned the tables to grill him. Would he ever be able to get this visit back on track? He feared she'd telephone Chief Dexter the minute he walked down her sidewalk. *Great idea, coming here.*

He straightened in his seat, returned her unblinking stare. "We're investigating a murder, ma'am. If we can form a picture of Mr. Black's activities prior to his death, we may be able to determine why he was killed."

The widow stood. "Are you suggesting I had a motive to kill Dirk Black? I want you to leave this house. Now. Did you know my husband was kin to Artois Hamilton? The town of Hamilton, Illinois, is named for Artois. Remember those Mormons who claimed to be saints, the ones shot to death in Nauvoo? Well, Artois put their bodies in pine boxes. Too bad he's not around to provide more boxes for today's scoundrels."

Ed stood. Didn't bother to say goodbye. Didn't trust himself to speak. In his car, he rested his head against the steering wheel. *What genius.* He'd just given Dexter another reason to fire him—or worse. But he'd discovered one thing. Delores Hamilton spelled it out quite clearly without ever putting it in so many words. She not only hated Dirk Black, she loathed his widow.

Enough to murder Cat? He wouldn't bet either way.

THIRTY

Jay squirmed. Twenty-five pounds of determination. Attempting to escape his mother's wrestling hold, his pudgy fingers poked at her restraining arm. Awakened from his nap, he wanted freedom. Cat tightened her arm around her son, trying to keep him on her lap and under control.

Reverend Pfaff tickled her fussbudget son's chin. "Don't you wish we all had that kind of energy? I believe Jay's given me my cue to leave. First, though, let us pray together."

He clasped one of Cat's hands and closed his eyes. "Please Lord, grant Catherine Reedy the strength to see her family through its travails. We ask your help and guidance in the name of our savior, Jesus Christ. Amen."

The pastor's gentle concern touched Cat. He never hinted she might be better served asking the Lord to save her black, murdering soul. His soft shoe around the subject of her father's incarceration proved tact personified. To the consternation of some of his congregants, Reverend Pfaff wasn't a fire and brimstone minister. His God was a loving one, a forgiving one.

Oh, how Cat hoped the good reverend had it right.

Reverend Pfaff stood, and Cat set Jay on the floor so she could walk the minister to the front door. She smoothed her gray skirt as she rose. Grandmother Nell had reluctantly approved the muted funeral attire given that Cat didn't own a black dress. There was neither time nor money to shop. Nell insisted, however, that Cat borrow one of her veiled black hats and don gloves for the funeral.

As the pastor pushed open the front door, he almost knocked over Sister Pearl.

"Sorry, Sister." The minister extended a hand to help the birdlike woman over the threshold. "I know the family will be glad to have you visit. No such thing as too many prayers."

Cat wasn't so sure about the family's welcome. Once upon a time Grandmother Nell counted Sister Pearl among her closest friends. The nun quit socializing with Nell after Cat's dad divorced and remarried. Apparently the nun felt John Reedy's sins tainted his mother—even though Nell faithfully attended mass every Sunday. Maybe Sister Pearl couldn't bear knowing her friend's grandchildren were unprotected by Catholic baptism, their souls presumably doomed.

Cat forced a smile. "Thank you for dropping by, Sister. Did you come to see Grandmother Nell?" *Or to gloat about God's punishments for us sinners.*

"Yes, dear, and to see you. I'm very sorry for your loss." The nun's gaze wandered to Jay as he toddled toward Cat.

"It's so sad when a child loses a parent." Tears glistened in Sister Pearl's eyes. "My own father died when I was three. Your baby won't even have a scrap of memory."

The nun clasped her hand. "It's good he has such a strong mother, a mother who loves him so much. I've watched you play with him in the yard, carry him on your errands. He's a lucky boy."

Seeing Jay's chubby hand reach to tug on the nun's long skirt, Cat scooped up her son. She chided herself for her uncharitable thoughts about Sister Pearl. The woman clearly meant her visit as solace not rebuke. Cat's throat tightened and unshed tears blurred her vision.

"Thank you, Sister. I'm glad you came. Grandmother's in the kitchen. Have a seat and I'll tell her she has a caller."

"No need." Nell's voice told Cat her grandmother had walked in while they talked.

Cat watched the two old friends join together in a fierce hug. "I'm sorry it's been so long," Sister Pearl whispered. "Please forgive me."

The nun's words tipped Cat's emotions over the edge. Throughout the morning neighbors and friends from Cat's childhood had stopped in to pay their respects. Many came bearing casseroles, food they couldn't afford to give away. These folks weren't glad-handers, publicly pretending sympathy in order to glimpse a suspected husband-killer. No, these private condolences were heartfelt, shared grief for the family's troubles.

She stumbled toward the kitchen, holding tight to her son. "Are you hungry, Jay? Should we get ourselves a little something to eat?" The attempt at a light-hearted tone failed. Her voice skipped like a phonograph needle over a scratched recording.

Thankfully, Jay didn't seem to notice. She set him in a high chair made by her dad. After slipping the chair's tray into place to safely pen her wriggling son, she spooned homemade apple sauce into a chipped bowl.

A knock at the back door startled her, and Cat looked up to see Ruth Taylor's face framed in the Dutch door's glass panes.

As soon as she opened the door, Ruth handed her a warm, fragrant parcel wrapped in a checkered tea towel. "I made bread this morning. Thought you might have family to feed today."

Cat took the bread and gave Ruth a hug. The maid's gesture touched her, but she felt ashamed that Ruth felt she had to slip in a back door. "You should have come around front. You know you're always welcome in this house."

Ruth's eyes raked the kitchen. "Are we alone?"

"Grandmother and Sister Pearl are in the living room. They can't hear us. What's wrong?" Cat's heart raced. *What now?*

"Your brother-in-law, Ralph Black, called on Mr. Jacobs yesterday," she whispered. "At the time I didn't find it strange. Mr. Jacobs was feeling poorly and didn't go into the bank. Your brother-in-law insisted on seeing him. He gave me a card with a message wrote on the back."

Ruth's words tumbled out between pants. It sounded as if she'd been running. She paused long enough to catch her breath. The sudden silence seemed endless to Cat, who dreaded hearing the rest of the story. Deep down, she knew. Ralph's comment about Jay's blue eyes had warned her. He'd found the letter.

"Sit down. Take your time."

Ruth shook her head. "No. I have to get back before Mrs. Jacobs knows I'm gone." She gulped more air, stood a little taller. "Your brother-in-law's note said he'd inherited something valuable from your husband and needed to speak to Mr. Jacobs about it."

Cat swallowed and nodded at Ruth to continue. "Did Mr. Jacobs talk to Ralph?"

"Yes, they went in the library, closed the door. A little while later, Ralph left, smiling like the cat that et the canary. Mr. Jacobs looked even more poorly. I've no notion what theys talked about, but wanted you to know. I's worried your brother-in-law took sumpthin that should rightly be yours or your boy's."

"I don't know how to thank you. My husband left no will so I don't know what inheritance he could mean. I'll speak to Ralph this afternoon."

Ruth's eyes widened. "Oh, please, don't mention me."

"No, no. I'd never do that. Thank you so much." Cat hugged the black woman.

Released from the embrace, Ruth took a step back to look Cat in the eye. "No need to thank me. Howie told me how you stood up for him last night, saved him from a terrible thrashin'. Those mean boys mighta killed my boy. No, it's you I'm thankin'."

Having said her piece, Ruth shot out the door. Cat stood motionless for a moment, watching the maid's retreat. Her son's singsong voice called her back. "Mommy. More applesauce."

She scooped applesauce into a spoon. Her hand shook and blobs of the mashed fruit fell on the table. Jay giggled. What the hell was Ralph up to?

She dropped the spoon back into the bowl. "Be quiet for a moment, honey." She tousled Jay's hair. "Mommy has to make a phone call."

She asked the operator to ring the number for her old apartment.

"Hello." Ralph's voice sounded chipper, cheerful. Cat wanted to strangle him.

"What do you think you're pulling? Are you insane? Your brother tried his hand at blackmail and wound up dead. Do you want to follow in his footsteps?"

Ralph laughed. "You threatening me? Or passing along some pillow talk from your boy's daddy? I'm not scared. After the funeral, we'll have a nice chat. See you this afternoon, Sis."

Cat heard a click. The bastard had hung up on her. She gripped the phone like a snake she wanted to strangle. Then she heard another click. Dear God, had she lost her mind. She'd said too much, way too much on their party line. Who'd listened in?

THIRTY-ONE

Ed dawdled at the entrance to the police station. His enthusiasm was only slightly less than a condemned man watching an executioner test a noose. He pictured Chief Dexter pacing, apoplectic about his Street Fair escapades. If Mrs. Hamilton had reported his visit to the chief, the punishment wouldn't end with a tongue-lashing. He'd be sacked.

"Morning, Ed." David Hooker glanced up from his paperwork and smiled. "Hey, the Cubs are playin' the Phillies today. Wanna bet? You think Dizzy Dean can bring home another pennant?"

Ed's shoulder muscles, strung tight as piano wire, relaxed a fraction at the fellow cop's cheerful banter. "Morning, David. Afraid I can't afford to bet on anything these days. Chief in yet?"

"Nope. Don't 'spect him till afternoon. Been real quiet. Only thing I done was take John Reedy his breakfast."

"How's the old gent doing?"

"Got the shakes bad. He's a boozer, and dryin' out's a bitch. Gotta give credit where it's due. No complaining. No beggin'. Just scrunches up like a nightcrawler wrigglin' away from a fish hook."

Ed flashed back on John Reedy's look of triumph when he confessed to Dirk's murder. The man had grit, same as his daughter. His stomach roiled with shame at being a party to Reedy's arrest.

"Now that you're here, I'm gonna take a whiz." David stood.

He'd made it three feet past his desk when the telephone rang. "Get that, will ya?"

Ed picked up. "Police." He pulled the receiver away from his ear. The woman was shouting. Hysterical. His frown deepened.

"Shirley, please, slow down. I can't understand you."

David stopped in his tracks, an eyebrow hitched in question as he eavesdropped on one side of the conversation.

Ed stepped the caller through her story three times, trying to sift out the facts. "Okay, let's see if I have the gist of it. Your little boy wandered into the woods and claimed he found a man all covered in blood. You figured it was a tall tale. But you took a look and found a dead stranger with a bashed-in head."

He listened to her reply. "Okay, Shirley, we'll be right there."

"Sounds like we got us another dead body," Dave said. "A murder?"

"Looks that way. That was Shirley Scheevers, one of my sister's friends. The way she tells it the bloke was probably beaten to death and dumped. Scavengers haven't picked over the body, so it's recent."

David swallowed repeatedly, his prominent Adam's apple energetically moving up and down like a toilet plunger. "You go. I better stay—what with a prisoner in the jail."

The officer's blanched face communicated his druthers. Viewing a bloody corpse was right at the bottom of his to-do list.

Ed let him off the hook. "Right. I'll go. You call the chief. He'll want to come."

David frowned and tugged on his moustache. "Chief told me not to call. He's at the 19 ½ Club. Said not to disturb him even if Jesus Christ hisself walked in to press charges 'gainst the buggers what nailed him to the cross."

Ed shrugged. "You know Dexter better than I do. You decide. But phone Harry and Mark. Have them meet me at the Scheevers' place out Middle Road."

"Sure." David nodded. "Uh, good luck."

As he drove away, Ed wondered who the victim might be. His first choice would be the carnie who operated the Ferris wheel. No, wait, Chief Dexter had earned top billing as an autopsy table candidate. Too bad neither man was likely to be the stiff.

Ed's mother claimed some good resided in every human—man, woman, or child. He'd yet to find a kernel in Dexter. The man viewed women as punching bags and hated colored folks, union members, and Jews. He was mean as a snake to anyone he could lord it over.

As Ed turned down the gravel road to the Scheevers' farmstead, he spotted Shirley on a front porch swing. A shotgun rested in her lap, her little boy curled by her side.

He leaned out the car and yoo-hooed. "Shirley, it's me, Ed. How about putting that shotgun away?"

"All right." Her voice sounded an octave too high. "Got me the willies thinking whoever did this might still be round these parts." She leaned the shotgun against the porch rail and ordered her son inside. "I'll walk you part way. But I ain't looking at that mess again. I'll have nightmares a week of Sundays as it is."

He waited for Shirley to join him. "Ever see this fellow—the dead man—around before?"

She shuddered. "Hard to say. Only half his face was turned up, and it was stove in something awful. But nothing about him looked familiar."

After they walked about a hundred feet, she pointed toward a copse of trees. "You go straight ahead. He's in them woods. It's Henderson land. Well, guess I should say Iowa First property. The bank foreclosed three years back."

"Thanks, Shirley. Go on home. More officers are coming. Just point 'em this way, will you?"

She nodded and bustled off.

The body sprawled not far from the tree line, fairly close to the dirt road that led to the Henderson place. The killer probably figured an abandoned farm would be a convenient dump site. If Shirley's little boy hadn't chased after a puppy, months, maybe years, could have gone by before the body was discovered in the wooded tangle. By then, the flesh would have been devoured by coyotes and vultures or rotted away, leaving bleached, unidentified bones.

Ed studied the corpse. The neck, corkscrewed at an improbable angle, exposed the right side of the man's face—what was left of it. A fringe of thick black hair surrounded a sticky mass of red pulp. Someone had been very angry. If the other side of his face matched this mess, identifying the victim would be tough—unless his pockets held some identification.

He knelt to search the man's clothes. He wore a Sunday-go-to-meeting suit and shiny shoes, almost looked like he'd been church bound. Ed plunged a hand in one pocket, then another. No wallet, no keys. He tried the suit's vest pocket and pulled out a lone calling card.

Ralph Black.

Jesus Christ, was the dead man Cat's brother-in-law?

He'd only been in Keokuk a day. "Must've gotten crosswise of Dirk's killer," Ed mumbled.

"Talking to yerself again?" Harry asked.

Ed hadn't heard the officer arrive.

"Yeah, that happens when you live with three women," he agreed. It was a standing joke between Ed and Harry—the inability to get a word in edgewise in their respective households.

"So who is he?" Harry asked.

Ed handed over the calling card. "Figure he contacted whoever murdered his brother. I understand Dirk was a con man. My guess is Ralph stumbled on his brother's latest scam and wanted a piece of the action. Either he failed to realize the mark was a cold-blooded killer, or he thought he was smarter than Dirk and wouldn't make the same mistakes."

Harry's head swiveled to and fro, looking to see if anyone stood within earshot. "Ed, I like you. But you better not share your theories out loud—not unless you say Cat Reedy killed both brothers."

Ed rolled his eyes and gestured at the corpse. "You think a five-foot-two woman could have beaten this big man to death?"

Harry shrugged. "I ain't paid to think. Dexter will say she got some man, maybe her brother, to do her dirty work."

Ed shut up. Harry was right. Good God, would Dexter try to frame Cat's brother, Pete, too? Or maybe the chief would settle on

Ed as Cat's male accomplice. That was a real possibility if Dexter got wind he was playing footsie with his prime murder suspect. *Damn.*

Ed waved his arm toward a trail of broken branches and matted weeds. "Looks as if the killer dragged the body in from the Henderson side. I'll scout around the trail. If we're lucky, the killer dropped something."

After ten minutes of poking about, Ed gave up. No footprints. No snagged pieces of cloth. No fallen scraps of paper. Just several sets of tire tracks crisscrossing the dirt road. A recent thunderstorm had turned the road to mud in low places.

"Harry, stay with the body, will you? I'm going to ask to use Shirley's phone to call David Hooker. He can direct the folks picking up the body to use the Henderson driveway so they won't have as far to lug the body."

Harry shrugged. "Fine. I'll wait here."

"After I phone, I'll drive around to the Henderson side. Looks like the tire tracks continue past where the killer dumped the body. Doubt I find anything, but I'd like to see where they lead."

He didn't mention there were three different tire treads. Was there another exit? Was this a mob rendezvous spot?

He traveled down the dirt road until it dead-ended behind the farmhouse. The tire tracks stopped outside a dilapidated barn. Ed peered through a space between two slats. Inside a black model-T cozied up beside Dirk Black's shiny red Packer.

I'll be damned.

THIRTY-TWO

Cat sat between her grandmother and brother on the straight-backed chairs Mr. Greaves had arranged for family in his smallest reception parlor. Every so often, Pete reached over to pat her hand or give it an encouraging squeeze. Cat felt blessed she didn't have to face this ordeal alone. She wished Beth were here, too, but someone had to mind the children. A funeral home was no place for babies, for the innocent.

She glanced again at an unoccupied chair in the "family" semi-circle. Where could Ralph be? The funeral service would begin in ten minutes, and he still hadn't arrived. Should she delay the service?

"I'll be right back," she whispered to Pete. "I'll ask to use Mr. Greaves' phone and call the apartment. Maybe Ralph misunderstood the time or has car trouble. He drove a long way to be here. It doesn't seem right to go ahead without him."

She wasn't about to tell Pete she feared something more than car trouble had detained Ralph. Detained him permanently.

Mr. Greaves ushered Cat into his office and closed the door to give her privacy. She asked the switchboard operator to ring her apartment. When no one answered, she reluctantly suggested the operator try her landlord.

O'Reilly picked up after two rings. "What?" His telephone manner matched his irascible face-to-face demeanor. She barely got out a question about her brother-in-law before O'Reilly spat out a reply. "He ain't here. Left afore noon right after you called him a blackmailer, and he ain't been back."

O'Reilly hung up. Lord Jesus, O'Reilly had been the second hang-up on the party line. He'd listened in on her conversation with Ralph.

She opened the office door. Mr. Greaves stood a discreet distance away at what appeared to be parade rest. "Is everything all right? Should we begin now? It's ten after two."

Cat nodded and clasped her hands together to keep them from shaking. "Yes, thank you."

No point waiting longer. If Ralph weren't here by now, he wouldn't be coming. A cold hard knot formed in the pit of her stomach. Was Ralph dead? Had Kenneth Jacobs killed both brothers?

Logic pointed toward that chilling conclusion. Once Dirk blackmailed Jacobs, her husband turned up dead. And thanks to Ruth, she knew Ralph had visited the Jacobs' household yesterday. Only one reason for her brother-in-law to call on the bank president. Ralph didn't know anyone in Keokuk but her. Somehow he'd found Jacobs' letter among Dirk's things and decided he'd squeeze the banker, too. Would it never end?

As she walked toward her family, icy fingers seized her arm just above her elbow. "Your husband will burn in hell. And you'll join him soon enough. I promise you'll never enjoy a cent of that money."

The woman's harsh whisper arrived on a column of breath so hot Cat felt it might singe the tiny hairs on the back of her neck. She wrenched free of the painful grip and turned to face her accuser.

Delores Hamilton's hand dropped from her arm. "You don't fool me. You were in on it."

The woman's chest heaved as if she'd sprinted up a flight of stairs. Her cold glare raked Cat from head to toe. "Don't you think my little girl has suffered enough? I need that money. It's her future."

Shocked speechless, Cat watched as the tall woman's long strides carried her into the vestibule and out of sight. Mrs. Hamilton's loose black dress fluttered as she moved. It reminded Cat of a crow in flight. What in heaven's name had Dirk done?

THIRTY-THREE

As Pete coaxed the car up one of the cemetery's steep gravel roads to the family plot, Cat stared at the jumbled gravestones and crypts dotting the lush green hills. She'd always found peace in her prior visits to this place where birdsongs floated from the trees and the spread wings of carved angels sheltered those resting below the green earth.

In May, she'd borrowed Pete's car to drive her grandmother here. Nell liked to decorate the family graves when the pink and purple peonies in their backyard burst into bloom. Cat preferred to place fragrant lilies of the valley next to Adelaide Reedy's final resting place. How her mother loved the annual appearance of the dainty white bells.

Family members were buried in two separate sections of the cemetery. Sometimes Nell shook her head at the wasted plots in the Catholic sector. She would occupy the grave beside her husband, but the three remaining spots reserved for Reedys would only be home to worms. Shortly after John Reedy married Cat's Methodist mother, he purchased six "Protestant" gravesites. This was where Cat's mother, Adelaide, rested and where shovels of rich, black Iowa dirt would soon smother Dirk's coffin.

As the car climbed toward the crest of a hill, Cat's gaze snagged on the imposing Jacobs' crypt, built to house generations of descendants, its stone frieze and decorative bronze doors screamed that those entombed within ranked among Keokuk's elite. How ironic. Dirk would be buried in a spot that looked down on the modern day Jacobs' pyramid.

Pete helped Nell from the car, then offered a hand to Cat. She was glad only a handful of people had accompanied her family and the pallbearers to the burial site. The gravediggers stood silent, shovels at the ready to fill the grave once the family departed.

Cat fiddled with her veil, thankful the closely-hatched netting shadowed her face and hid her dry eyes. She could not cry for Dirk, a man whose reckless greed now threatened her entire family.

The pallbearers lowered the coffin. As custom dictated, she tossed a handful of dirt on the pine box. That's when she said her only silent prayer.

Father in Heaven, please don't let Jay come early to one of these graves.

Afraid Nell might trip on the bumpy terrain, Pete held his grandmother's elbow as they returned to the car. Cat walked a step behind, alone. When an unexpected hand gripped Cat's arm, she whirled, ready to confront some new demon unleashed by Dirk's machinations.

Seeing Ed's face didn't slow her heartbeat. His hooded look and the grim set of his jaw indicated he planned to add to her misery.

"Don't say anything," he whispered. "Walk out your back door in an hour. I'll pull around to the alley. I'll tell you everything then. Ralph Black is dead, beaten to death. I found Dirk's strongbox. I have it. Dexter knows nothing about it."

THIRTY-FOUR

The woman sipped her tea while she restlessly scanned the newspaper. Her mother, God rest her soul, had been a proper English lady, who derived great pleasure from tracing their distinguished and allegedly royal lineage. Not her. Past glories and heraldic emblems didn't enamor her. All she cared about was in front of her. A future with money, independence. She'd win it for her daughter, and maybe for herself.

The golden days of the British Empire were over. A week ago, Hitler had annexed Czechoslovakia, and what did England do? The Prime Minister met with that pipsqueak mustached Nazi. Winston Churchill condemned the takeover. Big deal. More hot air. More wasted breath.

Had the English forgotten how they got an empire? You need to crush your enemies. Grind their bones to dust. The only way to ensure they'd never rise up to harm you again.

She polished her eyeglasses and consulted her watch. About now gravediggers should be patting down the dirt covering Dirk Black's casket. Would his widow shed a single tear? Crocodile maybe.

It pained her to think some folks would cry at Catherine Reedy's funeral—an upcoming event. That bitch fooled men and women alike, pretending to be a saintly little church mouse and doting mom.

I know better. She was just as bad as her black-hearted spouse. Maybe worse. No doubt about it. Everybody oohed and aahed about how smart she was. Yet they never asked why such a brainy bitch married a con man and stayed married to the scoundrel. The answer was plain as the nose on your face. Dirk Black was her fall guy. She dreamed up the schemes. He handled the face-to-face part, the dangerous part. Well, honey, you're on your own now.

At least she hoped so. Hoped that young cop wouldn't interfere with her plans again.

Time to leave for Nauvoo. She wanted to get to the graveyard early.

* * *

Waiting in her scratchy wool get-up tried her patience. Did it really matter if Jimmy Cloyd knew who she was? He was in so deep now he could never—what was the popular term?—rat her out. Maybe it was time to end the charade.

Jimmy's car bumped off the road onto the grassed bank, and he hurried her way. *Good man, don't keep your employer waiting.*

He took a final puff on a disgusting cigarette butt before he tossed it in the weeds. "Sorry about the Ferris wheel." Jimmy kept his focus on the ground. Her heavy veil seemed to spook him. "Didn't expect that cop to go King Kong on me. Climbed up like he was rescuin' Fay Wray from the top of the Empire State Building."

"Stop. Enough excuses. I bear some responsibility for suggesting a public demise. I think it best to go private this time. My family owns property in Missouri, near Hannibal. Do you know how to get to the Mark Twain Cave or Mt. Olivet Cemetery?"

Jimmy's forehead wrinkled. "Yeah. My granddaddy got hisself killed in the Civil War. He's buried in Mt. Olivet."

"Good. I'll give you directions to our property starting from the Mt. Olivet Cemetery. It's easy to find."

"What is it with you and cemeteries?"

She leaned toward Jimmy, and his mouth snapped shut. His Adam's apple bobbled. Not as tough as he looked.

"The cemetery's a waypoint, not a final resting place," she said. "You're going to order the Reedy woman to meet you at Momiss Cave. You've heard of it, right? We'll conduct our final business underground."

He paused. "Whoa, lady, I ain't planning no hole-in-the-ground excursions till they plant me six-feet under. Already paid for my spot in a legit cemetery."

"Don't be a ninny. My family owns an abandoned farm that backs up to the Momiss land. My father tried to find another entrance to that cave system on our land. It has more passageways and hidey holes than Mark Twain's, and no one's conducting tours yet. We can walk over from our farm. That way Mrs. Black won't see a car. She'll think she arrived first. Very private."

Jimmy folded his arms across his chest and scuffed one foot in the loose dirt above a recent grave. It grated that he didn't even try to disguise his lack of enthusiasm.

"I thought you were smart, Jimmy." Her tone sharpened. "You should love the idea. Much less risk. Surely those carnies you hired aren't afraid of the dark."

His eyes narrowed as he looked up at her. "And just how do we get the new widow to meet us inside a cave? We'd need to hogtie and carry her. Talk about public. Too many chances we'd be seen."

"Oh, she'll come willingly." The woman felt her lips curl in a smile. Fortunately, her heavy veil hid it. "Nell Reedy, a seventy-year-old, watches Mrs. Black's two-year-old boy whenever the mother leaves the house. Mrs. Black's father's locked up in jail. Nobody else at home. We just need to distract old granny long enough to snatch the kid and leave a note. Who is Mrs. Black going to call for help? Chief Dexter?"

"You want me to kidnap a baby?" Jimmy's voice rose in pitch and he held both palms up as he backed away.

"What? Your high moral principles won't let you?" The woman abandoned her hunched-over persona and straightened to her true height. "Do I need to remind you I can prove you killed both Black brothers?"

Sweat beaded Jimmy's forehead and upper lip. He swiped a handkerchief across his head.

"Okay, lady. It's time to stop play actin'. I know who you are, too. And don't think I haven't arranged insurance. Don't you go schemin' to bury me along with everyone else you want dead."

He grabbed her arm. His grip tightened. "Try something like that, and I'll bury you, too—you and your daughter."

The woman stared hard at Jimmy. The cheeky bastard was smarter than she thought and dumber, too. She lifted her veil, let him see her smile.

No one threatened her daughter.

THIRTY-FIVE

Ed eased his foot off the gas as he turned into the alley, allowing his Model T to coast to a standstill behind the Reedy house. He had no notion how many folks lingered inside. Based on the sparse graveside turnout, he assumed only immediate family remained. Yet it paid to be careful. If anyone told Dexter he was consorting with Cat, the chief would do more than box his ears.

He'd barely finished that thought when the screen door edged open and Cat slipped outside. She held the door handle and gently nudged the door shut. No telltale bang. But the smell of a human prompted a series of high-pitched shrieks. Her father's caged minks thwarted any attempt at a quiet exit.

Would someone look to see what caused the hubbub? Ed scanned the back windows. A curtain twitched. Someone watched. Ed wished he could make out a face.

Cat's gray skirt swirled around her shapely calves as she sprinted toward the car. The ugly hat she'd worn at the cemetery was gone. Sunlight turned her hair to liquid gold. God, she was beautiful.

He longed to unbutton her white blouse, pull it free of the belt that anchored it at her slender waist. His fingers flexed involuntarily with the desire to touch her, bury himself in her sweet warmth. He swallowed. *Get it together*. Remember your priority—keeping her alive and out of jail.

He reached over and opened the door for her. As soon as she climbed in, she ducked her head and scrunched low in the car seat. "I know. I know. We can't be seen together."

"You won't have to hunker down for long," he said. "We're lucky the Street Fair's here. Anyone who isn't at work is strolling the thoroughfare. Soon as we pass K Street, we should be safe."

He headed the car toward his family farm. After last night's lovemaking, his image of the property would always be bound up with Cat—the glow of the moon on her soft skin, the hoot of an owl blending with her moans.

He gunned the car until cornfields replaced street signs. "We're in the country. No one will see us now."

As she sat up and stretched, he licked his lips. Sensitized by their lovemaking, he read sensuality into her every move, no matter how mundane.

Cat glanced his way. "Are you sure Ralph's dead?" Worry etched her face. "What happened?"

"Somebody bashed in his head and dragged him into the woods that run alongside the old Henderson farm. His body might have gone undiscovered for months if Shirley Scheevers' little boy hadn't run pell-mell after his frisky Collie pup."

"You're sure it's Ralph?"

"Yes. Unfortunately I saw the body. I also found his business card in one of his pockets."

Cat touched his sleeve. "The strongbox?" She swallowed. "Was it beside Ralph's body?"

He shook his head. "No. I found Dirk's car in the Henderson barn. Ralph's car was stowed there, too, right beside it. The strongbox sat unopened on a bale of hay nearby. Good thing you have a key. The box is iron, and the lock looks substantial."

Cat fumbled in her purse and pulled out the shiny key. "I found it in one of the shoes Dirk wore when ..." She looked down. Her fingers rubbed the metal, and she swallowed.

"This key must have made walking plenty uncomfortable. I bet Dirk hid it on the spur of the moment. He must not have trusted whoever he was meeting."

Ed drove past his family's falling-down farmhouse and stopped next to a dilapidated barn. "Believe it or not, the old barn's in better shape than the house. The sharecroppers shouldn't have any reason to come round these buildings, but we might as well play it safe. Let's go inside to open the strongbox."

He hurried to Cat's side of the car. The urge to pull her into his arms proved irresistible. The damn strongbox could wait.

He captured her in a fierce embrace and buried his face in her hair, breathing in its sweet-tart apple scent. When she tilted her head to look at him, he kissed her. Eyes wide open, unwilling to miss a single detail. As her eyelids fluttered, he marveled at the thick fringe of dark blonde lashes outlining her turquoise eyes.

Cat's lips parted, inviting, welcoming. His brain provided instant recall of her delicious heat. His body pinned hers against the hood of the Model T. He ached for her.

She placed her palms against his chest and gently pushed back, opening a small space between them. Her breath came in pants almost as frenzied as his.

She traced his lips with her index finger. "We can't do this now, though God help me, I want to." She squeezed her eyes shut and gave her head a little shake. "Beth lied for me. Told the rest of the family I went upstairs, needed to lie down for a spell. I can't be long. Someone will come looking for me."

Ed took a step back, his hands slowly traveled down her slender arms, caressing. With sheer willpower, he ignored his body's fevered demands, the blood surging through his veins.

"I understand." He cleared his throat. Speech came hard. "Go inside. I'll bring the strongbox."

He hefted the heavy box he'd hidden beneath a blanket on the backseat floor and muscled it into the barn. Inside, tiny bits of chaff floated in the air, reminders of decade upon decade when horses and cows filled the empty, forlorn stalls. Light streamed through the hole-pocked roof, allowing the winnow to dance in the sunbeams like artificial lightning bugs.

Cat claimed a seat on a rickety pine bench. A buckled leg canted it at an awkward angle.

"Why in blazes did the killer hide the cars but leave Ralph's body in the open?" Her fingers massaged the back of her slender neck. "It makes no sense."

He set the strongbox on the floor beside her bench.

"The body wasn't exactly in plain sight," he answered. "You know who owns the Henderson place? Iowa First. It's one of the few foreclosed farms the bank hasn't bothered to sharecrop. Soil was too spent. I doubt even hogs could digest those last sorry ears of corn the Hendersons harvested."

He shuddered. "Just remembering our last crop. We burned the corn in our fireplace to stay warm. Whole damn house smelled like popcorn. Can't stand that smell to this day. Something I once loved turned to ashes."

He looked into her sad eyes. She had enough bad memories without him heaping his on the pile. He forced a smile. "That's the past. I plan to leave it there."

Cat waved a hand at the strongbox. "I'm still confused. The killer could have broken this open or hauled the whole thing away, and left Ralph to rot inside the barn. Less risk."

Ed frowned. Valid points.

"Maybe our bad guy hired thugs—like Mick, the guy who ran the Ferris wheel—to do his dirty work. Could be he promised to give his helpers the brothers' cars as part of the pay-off. If so, they might have decided to stash them at the Henderson place until people quit looking for them."

He kicked at a pile of moldering hay. "Seems most men willing to hire out as murderers are arrogant and think they'll never get caught, or too desperate or stupid to think beyond the cash. If these mugs fall in the second category, they probably didn't want Ralph's corpse stinking up the cars they planned to drive away."

Cat's fingers rambled along the cold iron of the strongbox lid. "Hard to believe they wouldn't find some way to see what's inside. I would have. My curiosity would have been killing me."

"It's killing me now," Ed said. "Let's open it."

"No argument." Cat slid the key in the lock. It turned easily. Ed helped her lift the lid.

"Oh, my God."

Bundle after bundle of twenty dollar bills sat stacked in neat rows. Her fingers rifled through one of the packets. She turned to Ed, mouth open, eyes wide. "Where did Dirk get so much money? There must be several thousand dollars in here. What was he doing?"

Tears slithered down her cheeks. She slumped and cradled her head in her hands. "Dirk stole this money. It's dirty. But who did he steal it from?"

Ed lifted several bundles of cash to reach a layer of papers lining the bottom of the war chest. He quickly skimmed the top two letters.

"You were right. Dirk was running an inheritance con. Targeted anyone he could find with Hamilton as a last name."

Cat's head snapped up. "Delores Hamilton cornered me at the funeral home. She didn't come to pay her respects. I don't remember her exact words—I was too rattled. But I caught the gist: Dirk was in hell, and I'd soon follow. She promised I'd never enjoy a cent of the money. I wanted to tell her I had no money, so she was right—I'd never see a penny. Dirk didn't clue me in on his schemes."

She dropped the bills as if they'd singed her fingers. "What should I do? Do you think it's all Delores's money? If I give her money back, she'll be more convinced than ever that I helped steal it. She'll never believe I found it by pure chance."

Ed wrapped her in his arms and rocked her like a frightened child. Each time a tremble wracked her body, it reverberated inside his chest.

"Don't fall to pieces. It's not like you. I just skimmed two of the letters. We need to study them—together. You're the smart one. Use your brain. Let's make sure we understand what Dirk was selling. I seriously doubt all that money came from one mark."

Cat sucked in a ragged breath, picked up another letter, and began to read. "Who would fall for this?"

Her breath caught in her throat. "That son of a bitch! Why did Dirk bring me into it? No wonder Delores Hamilton thinks I'm a she-devil."

Ed tightened his grip on her shoulders as he leaned over to read.

> *My wife, the former Catherine Reedy, did the painstaking research that's enabled us to trace Alexander Hamilton's descendants and discover you are among the rightful heirs to his unclaimed fortune.*

The bastard had used Cat's super-high IQ reputation to bolster his claims. With unbelievable chutzpah, her dear husband had fingered her as an accomplice.

Cat looked up, tears streamed down her face. "Do you really believe Mrs. Hamilton's behind the murders? That she paid someone to kill Dirk and me?"

"It's possible. After you told me her name was on the list you found, I paid a visit. She threw me out of her house. The woman was more than indignant. She was outraged."

Ed bit his lip. Something didn't gibe. Then it came to him. "But how does Ralph fit in?" he blurted out. "What reason could Delores have to kill him? Would she even know he existed?"

Cat raked her fingers through her hair. "I gave Ralph her name. Dammit. I was simply trying to find out if Dirk had told him anything about Mrs. Hamilton."

Ed sighed. "Then it's possible."

Cat stared back at the piles of bills. "I'm so confused. My head feels as if it's going to explode. Plainly, the same monsters killed Dirk and Ralph. But maybe the killers weren't hired hands. Could it be someone else on Dirk's list? Perhaps Ralph was just in the wrong place at the wrong time. Maybe Ralph walked in on a scam victim who was searching our apartment for the cash Dirk swindled."

She let the letter she'd just read fall back on top of the cash. "I've stayed too long. We have to go."

Ed stood, pulled her to her feet, and hugged her body to his. "We'll sort this out. I'll hide the strongbox until we can sift through everything. Maybe we'll see a pattern, something that might help us figure who had reason to kill both brothers."

He saw no point in reminding Cat the killer wanted her dead. The Ferris wheel operator hadn't decided on a whim to put a strange woman in a broken gondola, start the wheel spinning, and run like a bat out of hell. Ed had yet to meet a thug with sufficient brains to frame Cat for her husband's murder. No. If it wasn't Mrs. Hamilton behind the murder spree, someone else with an equally good reason to hate Cat was pulling the strings. Someone determined to kill her.

THIRTY-SIX

Cat's foot had barely hit the top porch step, when her sister-in-law yanked open the screen door. Beth's scowl advertised the tongue-lashing to come.

"Pete wanted to look in on you. I had to tell my husband another lie. I said you woke up and wanted some alone time to clear your head. I threw in that sunshine made you crave a bit of fresh air. Your brother practically bit my head off for letting you wander off by your lonesome."

Cat rested her palm against Beth's cheek. "Sorry. I seem hell bent on making my honest sister-in-law into a bald-faced liar. Where's Pete? I'll smooth things over."

"He's gone," Beth said. "Got a call from Bruce. His family still hasn't recovered from last year's strike. He's so desperate for cash he's growing tomatoes on some of his granddaddy's bottomland. This weird fall flood is fixin' to wipe out his whole crop. He's trying to harvest what he can before nightfall. Pete's helping. The Mississippi's already up eleven feet. One more foot to flood stage. Feels like everyone I love's being washed away in a sea of trouble."

Beth's eyes swam with unshed tears. Cat pulled her sister-in-law into a hug. Beth sobbed and her fists beat a chaotic rhythm on Cat's back. "Dammit, dammit. I'm scared for Dad Reedy, and I'm terrified for you. Please don't do anything stupid. Don't make me worry any more than I already do."

"I'm a selfish idiot. I wasn't thinking. Please forgive me."

Beth shrugged out of the embrace and swiped at her tears with her apron. "Nothing to forgive. I'm not myself. Didn't want to break the news with everything else happening. I'm pregnant. That's my excuse for being a basket case. I'm either laughing or crying."

Cat grinned and kissed her sister-in-law's cheek. "Beth. How wonderful. Does Pete know?"

"Yep, told him this morning. Warned him to be danged careful wading around in the muck picking tomatoes. Don't want some stupid snake to take a bite and leave me two Reedy hellions to bring up on my own."

Beth took a deep breath. "Enough of my blatherskiting. Jay and Nell are napping and Amy's playing with dolls in the front room. There's no one to interrupt us. Come on, Sis, it's your turn to talk."

Cat scooted a chair out from the kitchen table and sank onto it. She patted the seat of the chair beside her. "Sit. I'll tell you everything I know. Not that it makes any sense."

It took ten minutes to fill Beth in on Ralph's death and Ed's discoveries in the Henderson barn. She saved details about Dirk's inheritance scheme and Delores Hamilton's wrath for her closer. Beth gasped when she heard the wealthy matron's whispered threat.

"God in Heaven, don't make me keep this secret. Let me tell Pete. He can help figure out a plan. You need to use that strongbox money to get as far from Keokuk as you can. I know it goes against your grain. But you can pay it back later. Do it for Jay, if not for yourself. He needs his mother alive. Go to California, hell, even Alaska. Pete and I will cover your tracks."

Cat closed her eyes. All that cash was tempting. She and Jay could travel far, stay hidden a very, very long time. But how could she live with herself knowing she'd financed their escape with money swindled from old widows, young mothers, and out-of-work fathers—people made so desperate by the Depression they latched onto any fairytale promising a pot of gold?

Dirty money wasn't the only impediment. How could she abandon a father in jail, a grandmother who needed her?

She slowly shook her head. "Beth, I can't, and I don't need to. I know who the killer is, and I know how to make him stop."

Cat straightened in her chair and took her sister-in-law's hand. "I really wanted Mrs. Hamilton to be the villain. That made it less personal—the woman's hatred is second-hand. I even tried once more to believe Dirk's gambling triggered the deaths…that he'd bragged about a score…started a murderous chain reaction."

Beth squeezed her hand. "Stop rambling. Are you saying you know who killed Dirk and Ralph? Out with it. Who murdered them?"

Cat let go of Beth's hand. She rested her elbows on the table, her head dropped into her hands. Saying the name out loud made it real. Her throat tightened, balking at her verdict.

"Who?" Beth pressed.

"Kenneth Jacobs." The answer came as a whisper.

"You really think he killed Dirk and tried to frame you for your husband's murder? I despise the man, but I can't imagine him paying some thug to jury-rig the Ferris wheel so you'd break your neck. And why would he kill Ralph?"

Cat lifted her chin, met her sister-in-law's eyes. "It's the only answer that makes sense. Ruth Taylor told me Ralph visited the Jacobs' house yesterday. I phoned Ralph, demanded to know if he was blackmailing Jacobs. He all but admitted he was. No one but Kenneth Jacobs had a good reason to kill Dirk *and* Ralph—and to want me dead."

A tension headache bloomed. Cat's fingers massaged her temples. "In his last letter, Jacobs said he admired me, that he'd come to love me. When his daughter's older and less vulnerable, he said he'd recognize Jay as his son. The man convinced me he had feelings for both of us. He acted as if he already carried a heavy load of guilt. I couldn't imagine him harming us and adding to that burden. But I've proven quite easy to fool."

"Oh, honey. I'm sorry. If Jacobs is behind this, you have even more reason to skip town. He's connected. He can shell out dollars to thugs from now till Doomsday. Eventually one of his henchmen will succeed. Nell can move in with us. Pete and I can take care of Dad Reedy. You and Jay need to vamoose."

Cat shook her head. "No. I'm going to confront Jacobs. Tell him I've prepared and signed a dozen accounts of his rape. If anyone in my family dies unexpectedly, those letters will be mailed automatically to all his Grand Avenue neighbors. I'll make sure he understands that one of those letters will be hand-delivered to his wife."

She lifted her chin. "If blackmail triggered this insanity, I think I'm more than justified to use blackmail to end it."

Beth leaned back in her chair and pursed her lips. Cat read the woman's body language. Too much danger. Too many risks. Her practical sister-in-law thought the plan half-baked. She'd hold up one finger at a time as she enumerated each flaw.

Good. Beth's skepticism would help her plug holes in the plan. She wouldn't dare tell another soul. Including Ed. Especially Ed.

"Mommy." Amy's soft voice startled both women. The little girl stood in the doorframe between the kitchen and living room. "I'm hungry. Can I have a cookie, please?"

"Come here, sweetie." Beth wrapped her arms around Amy and lifted her onto her lap. "Of course you can have a cookie. Why don't you bring one for your Aunt Cat and me, too? We could all use a little sugar."

Cat seized on the interruption. A perfect opportunity for an intermission. Give Beth time to prepare her arguments. As Amy scooted off her mother's lap, Cat tousled her niece's curls. "I'll have my cookie later, honey. You two enjoy, while I check on Jay."

Cat turned toward her sister-in-law. "Go home. Don't you have hospital duty later this afternoon? In your condition, you need plenty of rest. We'll talk. I promise. If you still want us to come for dinner, I'll bring the food. Our neighbors contributed enough to feed an army."

"But—"

Cat didn't' let Beth finish.

"I promise to tell Pete everything. Secrets have only brought this family grief. It's time to tell the truth, no matter how painful. Tonight."

She kissed the top of Beth's head and climbed the stairs. She paused outside her dad's room. Her mother had taken her last tortured breath inside. Asthma. The treatments seemed like witch doctor remedies, not modern medicine. Inhaling smoke from bella donna leaves, injections of epinephrine that nudged her strict mother over a depression cliff.

Cat held her mom's hand to the bitter end. Her dad refused to enter the room, couldn't watch his wife gasping, dying. Part of his guilt? Why he seemed hell bent on his own early grave?

How would Mom feel about my lies? Pretending Jay was Dirk's son.

In childhood, Cat learned falsehoods were unforgivable offenses. Her mom punished any lie by cutting a green switch from a backyard plum tree and whipping her youngins' bare legs until red welts bloomed. Once she cried when her mom ordered her to get a switch to punish Pete. Cat's tears earned her the first whipping. A hard woman. Cat had never so much as swatted her boy's rump.

She opened the door to her own bedroom as quietly as possible. Her breath caught when she saw Jay asleep in his crib. She didn't want to wake him, but she needed to touch her baby. Leaning over the crib railing, she trailed a finger over his chubby cheek. Though Jay didn't wake, one of his tiny hands flexed in a fist for a second before it relaxed. What did he dream?

THIRTY-SEVEN

Cat slipped off her shoes and stretched out on the bed's coverlet. The roller blinds had been lowered to darken the room for Jay's nap, but enough light leaked in through the crackled oilcloth to paint the space a murky twilight. Pete had fired the coal furnace to take the edge off the fall chill. The rising heat draped a hot, invisible blanket over her body. She knew she should sleep. Let her mind escape, perhaps find comfort in a soothing dream, an antidote to her waking nightmare.

She closed her eyes. Was Kenneth Jacobs really the killer?

She'd been wrong about him before, never imagined the staunch church deacon and conservative bank president capable of rape. Her mind rewound to a night of terror that ultimately brought her Jay.

Whenever she saw Jacobs, her mind began to replay the scene. She never let the mental movie advance. She simply pictured Jay's face and the terror faded away. Today, though, she let the silent movie flicker forward, hoping to understand the madness.

Dirk had driven to Des Moines on a two-day sales trip. When the bank closed at five o'clock, she gave herself a rare treat and stopped at The Rialto Cafe for a roast beef sandwich. While counting out change to pay for supper, Cat realized she'd forgotten to correct a discrepancy she'd spotted in the Hubinger account—a teller had accidentally recorded a deposit as a withdrawal. Though she hadn't made the posting error, Mr. Thompson would lambaste her for failing to find and fix it.

She sighed. Nothing to be done tonight. Cat handed a dime to the Grand Theater's friendly ticket agent, snuggled into a good seat—the theater was almost empty—and wriggled off her high heels. Nothing like stocking feet and that cute little dent in Cary Grant's chin to improve a girl's mood.

Cat whistled as she walked from the movie theater toward her bus stop. Passing the bank, she noticed lights. Someone working late. Maybe she could correct the books tonight. Cat rapped on the employees' side door. It swung open, banged against the wall, and bounced back.

Kenneth Jacobs towered over her. The punctilious banker reeked of alcohol and sour breath. Sweat stained his half-unbuttoned shirt. He wore no tie, no jacket. And, my God, no shoes. The notion of the bank president parading around barefoot when no one could see brought a giggle to her throat. The wild look on Jacobs' face forced her unborn laugh into a strangled gurgle.

He grabbed her arm, yanked her inside, slammed the door shut. "D'you know what today is?"

She had to concentrate to understand his slurred demand. "No. Well, I mean yes, sir," she fumbled. "It's Thursday, uh, November 4."

"November 4. The date carved on my son's tombstone. He died one year ago today."

Jacobs' hot, heavy breath crowded the space between them.

"I'm so sorry, sir." She'd never imagined this man with his hoarfrost demeanor felt any human emotion, much less the crushing pain painted on his face. The thought of anyone losing a child broke her heart. She reached out and touched his sleeve.

His body swayed. Fearing he might fall, she placed both hands on his chest to steady him. He snatched her right hand, dragged her into his office. The sweater she'd draped around her shoulders fell on the rug.

"Have you seen a picture of my boy?" He didn't acknowledge her. He just stared at a framed portrait. "He was so smart, so handsome. I killed him."

"What?" Panic seized Cat. She tried to back away. Jacobs still didn't look at her, but his iron grip offered no give.

"Took him fishing. You didn't want me to, but I did." He sobbed. "I tried to save him. Jesus, God, I did. I held out an oar. I jumped in but I can't swim. I barely made it back to the boat. Oh, God. The muddy water swallowed him."

Her arm throbbed. What was happening? Was he hallucinating? Who did Mr. Jacobs think she was?

He spun on her, his face a mask of rage. "Stop punishing me."

Cat couldn't believe this was the same man she'd wanted to comfort. Her pulse raced. She had to escape.

He pushed her down on his office sofa. A bony knee pressed between her legs. A hand followed. He straddled her. "I need my son. You give me back my boy. I won't let him die."

Jacobs ripped her blouse open.

"No, no. Please. For God's sake, let me up." She shoved at his frantic hands. He gripped the lace on her slip's bodice and yanked. The thin spaghetti straps broke, and the nylon fell away, baring her breasts.

"Please stop!" She pleaded again.

Jacobs screwed his eyes shut, refused to look at her. God knew who he pictured in his sick brain. Did he even know who she was? She dug her fingernails into his neck, saw the dark blood well.

Jacobs' eyes flew open. A backhanded slap. The force made her teeth rattle. Jacobs the banker was gone. Reason had fled. He grunted like an animal. Fear squeezed her throat shut. She couldn't breathe. Would this madman kill her?

"Damn you!" He grabbed her shoulders and shook her. "Hell isn't fire. It's ice. You are ice."

He slapped her again. The room turned gray then faded to black.

Pain pried her eyes open. A searing pain between her legs competed with her throbbing jaw. Goose bumps prickled her flesh. Cat raised her head. Dizziness turned to nausea. She fought the urge to vomit or to sink back to unconsciousness. One look had been enough.

Rape. The word formed in her head. He'd raped her. She felt the thin skin covering her temples throb with the drumbeat of her pulse.

Mind-numbing fear kept her screams silent. *Think*. Where was he? Could she sneak away? How could she get out of the bank alive?

She scanned the room. Where had Jacobs gone? She couldn't see him. Couldn't hear him. Had he run? Was she alone? She levered herself up on an elbow. Her torn slip fell away from her bruised, tender breasts.

Cat sat up and knotted the silk straps of her slip together to cover herself. She pulled her tattered blouse closed. With shaking hands, she retrieved her panties wadded on the floor a few feet away. She slid the panties up her legs. When her fingers grazed the sticky wetness on her thighs, her dizziness rebounded. She grabbed her torn stockings and scrubbed at the wetness, making her skin even more raw. She tossed the balled stockings on the floor.

A moan issued from a corner of the room behind the bank president's polished walnut desk. She stood and took a couple of wobbly steps toward the door. She spotted Jacobs, curled in a ball, rocking to and fro. She wanted nothing more than escape. As she approached the door, she stooped to pick her sweater off the floor and wrapped it around her shoulders. She held her breath as she crept from the office, trying not to whimper, not to make a sound that might rouse Jacobs from his stupor.

Outside, she began to limp home. Whenever a car approached, she crouched in shadows, convinced Jacobs would follow, and this time his hands would find her throat to silence her for good. She couldn't let anyone see her. Pain accompanied every step.

Just as she reached the sidewalk in front of her apartment, she heard a car motor. Her legs felt like rubber. Hurrying, she stumbled.

Jacobs leaned out the car window. "Forgive me. Please forgive me," he pleaded. "I don't know what happened. I passed out. When I came to, I saw...remembered what I'd done. Please don't tell anyone. I'll make it up to you. I promise. I'll make it right."

Cat didn't answer. She turned her back on his begging, and hobbled up the stairs. Inside her apartment, she locked the door, collapsed on the bed.

Who could she tell? Who would believe her? It would be the word of Jacobs the community pillar against her—a woman married to an embezzler and bigamist. Wagging tongues would say she'd asked for it—if they even believed she'd been raped. A married woman. Out cavorting alone at night. Some would figure she'd seduced Jacobs so her husband could blackmail him. Make a little money. Oh, God. Dirk would do exactly that. He wouldn't care a whit what the fallout might be for her and her family. She couldn't let Dirk know.

She ripped off her clothes. Wadded them up. Threw them on the back porch. She'd figure out what to do with them tomorrow. She wouldn't keep them, but neither could she let someone see her put them in her trash. You didn't throw out clothes in the Depression. She set a kettle on the stove to heat water. She couldn't wait. She soaked a washcloth in cold water. She scrubbed her skin raw. Exhausted by fear she slept.

The next morning she took a long, hot soaking bath. Chose a high-necked, long-sleeved dress to hide most of her bruises. She dusted the telltale bluish marks on her chin with sweet-scented face powder.

She rode the bus to the bank, climbed the stairs to the mezzanine, and took her seat at the comptometer. Cat had to keep her job. She needed money to pay off her husband's debts and to help keep her mom, dad and grandmother out of the poorhouse.

Pretend nothing happened. She could will it, she could. Nothing happened.

Beside the comptometer, she found an envelope with her name. An envelope marked "Personal." The first of his letters. The first of Kenneth Jacobs' promises, the odes he penned to assuage his guilt.

"On the head of my dead son, I swear to look after you and your family as long as I live. Forgive me."

* * *

A breeze fluttered the window shade, allowing more strips of sunlight to escape oilcloth trap and flicker across her face. Cat sat up with a start. Though bone tired, she couldn't believe she'd drifted off. She glanced at Jay's crib and smiled. A champion sleeper. Her little boy looked as if he hadn't moved a muscle.

A quiet knock rattled the flimsy door. Was that what woke her? She tiptoed across the room to keep from disturbing Jay and opened the door a crack.

"Pete? I thought Beth said you were helping Bruce harvest tomatoes."

Cat swallowed, afraid her sister-in-law had told her brother everything, that he'd come to forcibly remove her and Jay from Keokuk. Pete looked sad, not agitated.

"We did what we could. Not much left to salvage," he answered. "I'm going to visit Dad at the jail. Wondered if you felt up to coming with me?"

"Of course. Let me make sure Nell can watch Jay."

Cat closed the door. She braced her back against the doorframe as a shiver ran through her. She wanted to see her dad, but the idea of walking into the police station made her stomach cramp. She prayed Chief Dexter wouldn't be there.

THIRTY-EIGHT

Ed's entry to the police station startled David Hooker awake. Telltale creases in the officer's cheek offered clear-cut evidence that he'd been napping on desk duty.

"Hi, David. How's it going?" Ed asked.

David scrubbed at his eyes with his knuckles before he looked around to see if anyone else was about. "Chief's been on the warpath. Don't know whether you heard 'bout that hurricane hitting somewhere up on the East Coast today and killing hundreds, but I'm thinking Dexter's more dangerous than that blow.

"The boss man wanted to know where the hell you went. Said you disappeared soon as you told the fellas you'd found cars belongin' to them Black brothers. Dexter got all squinty-eyed and started yellin'. Said that damned college boy had gotten too big for his britches. I'd play it real cool, if you know what I mean. "

Ed's shoulders slumped. "Is he here?" He felt like he'd been toting moldy bales of hay since daybreak.

His days as a policeman were rapidly dwindling. If Chief Dexter didn't fire—or kill—him, he'd quit. Ed's only acting experience was putting on a top hat to play Abe Lincoln in second grade. Not exactly solid credentials for pulling the wool over Dexter's eyes. How much longer could he stick with this charade, saying "yes sir, no sir" to a bully he longed to beat senseless.

"The Chief hustled outta here half an hour ago," David added. "Said he might not be back today."

Ed smiled. "Okay. I'll write up my report. Maybe that'll buy me a little grace."

"Don't count on it." David's obligatory chuckle sounded forced.

Ed went to his desk and hurriedly wrote up his discovery of Ralph Black's body and his murder scene observations. He described following tire tracks to the abandoned barn and discovering the stashed cars. He pointedly omitted any mention of the strongbox he carted away. He'd since muscled that find into a treehouse on his old family farm.

"Ed?" David rapped lightly on the doorframe to snag his attention. "I need to go out for a bit. Will you hold down the fort?"

"Sure. Take your time. Imagine we've had our excitement for the day."

Ed's heart rate bumped up. Being alone in the station house offered a rare opportunity to search Dexter's office. He'd had that chance only once before. His first foray turned up bits and pieces of evidence that tied the chief to the mob and his brother-in-law's disappearance. But he needed more.

Dexter's arrogance and packrat tendencies worked in Ed's favor. The chief constantly wrote notes to himself and squirreled them away. Based on the scribbles Ed pocketed earlier, he wasn't worried about leaving a paper trail. He seemed convinced his word was gospel. If he said his office was off-limits, no one would dare defy him. If they did, he'd kill them.

The minute Hooker walked outside, Ed slipped into Dexter's office. Just in case Hooker returned earlier than expected, Ed clutched his report. He'd use its delivery as a ruse for entering the forbidden inner sanctum.

On his last sortie into Dexter's office, he'd found the combination to the safe scratched inside a desk pullout. At last, he could use it. His hands shook as the tumblers clicked. He kept one ear tuned to the front office, alert to any sound that might signal company.

The safe opened. His gaze fastened on a leather-bound ledger. He opened it. His fingers trailed down the columns on the first few sheets. *Yes.* A record of payments for a la carte services. The ledger revealed grease-the-palm rates for everything from closing down a competing gambling den to dropping charges against a wife beater.

Ed flipped to the date his brother-in-law disappeared. He froze as he studied a short-hand notation beside a hundred-dollar entry. Clearly Dexter's handwriting. The scribbled text read: *J. Cloyd for Disposal of AU.*

No swami needed to interpret. Jimmy Cloyd, the mob's bagman, paid Dexter one hundred bucks to dispose of Ed's brother-in-law, Al Underwood.

Finally, some proof. A string of curses blossomed in Ed's mind. He clamped his jaw shut to dam up the tidal wave of obscenities. No telling when Hooker would return. Either the chief murdered Al or sent him to his death. He was guilty as sin. Of course, the chief would claim AU had some innocent meaning.

Seething at the flippant entry, Ed tightened his grip on the incriminating journal. He itched to tear the page loose, wad it up, and shove it down Dexter's throat until he quit breathing.

No. Think. He had to take the entire ledger. His friend with the State Police stressed the necessity of documenting the total pattern of Dexter's corruption. If enough mud stuck to him, the slimy bastard couldn't slither away.

Ed closed the safe and unbuttoned his shirt. The ledger's smooth leather felt cool against his skin. His fingers were re-fastening the last button on his shirt when the front door squeaked. He heard Hooker say something and relaxed for a second before he heard Chief Dexter answer.

His heart pounded.

"Who's in my office?" Chief Dexter bellowed. He rounded the corner faster than Ed thought the beefy cop could move.

"Just putting a report on your desk, sir." Ed's heart imitated a jackhammer. Sweat popped on his forehead like corn kernels in a hot fire. He tried to smile, look innocent.

"No one goes in my office when I'm not here. No one." Dexter dialed down his volume. Menace edged his softer tone. "I've had it with you. You're fired. Leave your badge and get out of my sight. Now."

Ed didn't protest, didn't trust himself to utter a word. He had a single goal—to exit the police station alive before Dexter discovered his ledger was missing. Even someone with the chief's IQ could figure who took it.

He tried not to think about what would happen then. Both Dexter and the mobsters he protected would be gunning for him. Time to get his sister and nieces out of town. His new enemies would have no qualms about threatening his loved ones.

THIRTY-NINE

As her brother parked the car, Cat spotted Ed leaving the police station. His long strides suggested fury. He'd barely reached the curb when Chief Dexter burst from the building like a bull escaping a paddock.

"I'd better not see your face 'round here or hear you're interferin' with police business," Dexter yelled at Ed's back. "If'n I do, you'll see what the scenery looks like behind bars."

Cat's temples throbbed. Had Dexter found out about the strongbox, about Ed helping her? Dammit. She wished she could see Ed's face. Dexter's mug was too easy to read. Red blotches mottled his skin.

"Still want to go in, Sis?"

She clamped her brother's arm in a death grip. She wanted to say, "No, hell no." Yet the bad timing might be a godsend. The enraged chief might not mind his tongue. Maybe he'd blurt out something useful.

"Let's go. Dexter might slip up. Maybe Ed uncovered information that points to the real killer. Maybe that's why he's so mad. Besides we need to check on Dad."

Dexter stomped back to the building without a glance in their direction.

Cat tugged on Pete's arm. "Slow down. Let Dexter get to his office. Don't give him any ideas about blocking the door."

A vein in her throat pulsed in wild, chaotic rhythm as she entered the lion's den. She bit the inside of her cheek. The instant pain forced her to focus.

"Officer." Pete kept his voice just above a whisper as he addressed the officer standing at the front desk. "May we see John Reedy?"

Cat considered piping up, speaking loud enough to roust Dexter. No. Plenty of time for confrontations after they saw her dad.

The officer grunted, "Yeah." He nodded toward the stairs leading to the cells below. "Five minutes."

An eye-watering mix of urine and sweat sucker-punched Cat. *Dad's in this hellhole because of me.*

She clutched Pete's arm, gaining comfort from his steadiness. Her father lay on his back, bony elbows locking a blanket over him in the cold, damp cellar. His waxy flesh seemed only loosely attached. His cheek bones jutted up like tent poles against moldy canvas. *I'm going to be sick.*

"Dad?" Pete spoke. "Can you hear me?"

In the eerie silence, she searched for some sign her father heard. That he was alive.

"Dad, are you sick?" Her panicked voice ricocheted off the stone walls.

She choked back angry tears at the hell Dexter was putting her father through. "Dad, please open your eyes."

"Go." The hoarse voice almost knocked Cat to her knees. "I don't want you to see me like this, to remember me this way. Go. Please."

Behind her, she heard Pete's heavy breathing. Her brother's hands settled on her shoulders. "We'll leave, Dad. But this isn't over. We're going to bring you home. I promise."

Cat's constricted throat wouldn't let her say goodbye. She could barely squeak out her last words. "I love you, Dad."

She bolted for the stairs. Furious. She'd climbed almost to the top before Pete grabbed her arm. "Sis, stop. I know you. Don't you jump on Dexter. Hunting more trouble's not the answer. He's itching for a reason to put you in that cell with Dad. Don't give it to him."

She took a shuddering breath. *Dammit.* Pete had it spot on. She wanted to march into Dexter's office and pack her entire one hundred and ten pounds into a punch aimed directly at his nose.

"Okay. I promise I won't fly off the handle. But I need to see Dexter, hear what he has to say for himself."

They approached the officer who'd directed them downstairs. "May we bring Dad some food and clean clothes?" She spoke loud enough for her voice to carry to Dexter's office.

A crash—something being thrown?—suggested Dexter'd heard her request. The chief emerged a moment later, lips stretched in a familiar sneer.

"Well, looky who's come visiting? Daddy's little girl. You're quite the dutiful daughter, aren't you? Letting your father hang for your husband's murder."

Dexter planted himself directly in front of her. His black pupils dilated in anger. "Don't think John Reedy will stop me from seeing you hanged. Maybe I can't prove you murdered your husband, but I'm this close—" his thumb almost caressed the index finger he held an inch from her nose—"to arresting you for Ralph Black's murder."

Pete tried to pull her away. She shook off her brother's arm. "What motive will you manufacture? Why would I kill my brother-in-law, a man I haven't seen in two years?"

Dexter laughed. "Aren't you the game little chippy? The more I see of you the more I can't wait to watch you swing. Your phone is on a party line, Mrs. Black. Your landlord heard you threaten your brother-in-law. Says you promised he'd meet the same fate as your blackmailing husband."

What? The air whooshed out of her lungs. Oh, God. She'd tried to warn Ralph off, not threaten him.

This time Pete gripped Cat's arm in a vice she couldn't break and yanked her back from the brink. "We're leaving."

She stumbled as Pete propelled her toward the door.

FORTY

Ed hustled in the hospital's side door and marched to the nurses' station. He prayed Beth Reedy was on duty. A woman in a white nurse's uniform stood with her back to him. Auburn hair curled beneath the starched white cap. Cat's sister-in-law?

"Mrs. Reedy?" He held his breath.

The smile on Beth's lips faded when she turned and recognized him. He felt like a typhoid carrier. Everyone seemed to know he was tainted with the smell of death. He glanced around. No one loitered within earshot.

"I didn't know how else to send Cat a message," he whispered. "No one's watching your house. Invite her over tonight. I'll drive into the alley about eight. I have to speak with her."

Before Beth could refuse, he cut her off. "Please. I wouldn't ask if it wasn't urgent."

Ed bolted, almost running down the hall and out the door. As he drove toward Garfield Elementary School, his next stop, he tried to conjure up a believable tale for Mrs. Heironymous, his nieces' teacher. He didn't want his request to take his nieces out of school seem desperate. He parked.

On the playground, dozens of chubby legs pumped in a furious game of tag. Recess. The twins were easy to spot. Their coppery curls flashed in the sun like panned gold. High-pitched laughs interspersed shrieks of pleasure.

A hand shaded Mrs. Heironymous' eyes as she watched her young charges. She jumped when Ed touched her arm.

"Didn't mean to frighten you."

The teacher smiled. "Recess is almost over. You wouldn't want to take over for me next period, would you? It's hard to settle them down."

"No, but I will take Susie and Sarah off your hands. One of our cousins up river has been in a bad accident, and Myrtle needs to help out. She asked me to collect the girls. I'm sure she'll make them study while they're gone."

The teacher frowned. "How long will they be away?"

"Sorry, I don't rightly know. My guess is a week."

The girls spotted their uncle and came running. He scooped them up in his arms. "Susie, Sarah, your mom sent me to pick you up. We're going for a car trip."

Though out of breath from their tag game, the little girls found enough oxygen to whoop with joy. They loved car trips, a rare novelty given the cost and scarcity of petrol.

He set the girls back on the ground. "Your mama's expecting us. Say goodbye to Mrs. Heironymous."

The girls giggled a goodbye. Their teacher frowned as she watched him shepherd the twins to his car.

As he opened the car door, Susie jumped up and down, and Sarah clapped her hands. "Oh, goody." Sarah giggled. "Are we going for an extra-long ride?"

"Yes." *Extra, extra long.* "Hop in the car. Time to collect your mom."

As he drove up, Ed caught a glimpse of movement behind the backyard's sagging fence. "You girls stay in the car. I'll gather your mother and be right back," he told the twins.

As he opened a side gate, Myrtle dropped a damp sheet back into her wicker laundry basket and extracted the clothespin from her mouth. Her frown deepened as her gaze traveled to the car where her twins bounced up and down in excitement.

"Why did you collect the girls? What's happened?" Her voice vibrated with panic. "What's wrong?"

Ed stepped directly in front of his sister to block his nieces' view of their mother. If they saw her fright, they might panic, too. The whole damn country had proven how contagious terror could be. He needed Myrtle to stay calm—and move quickly.

He clamped his hands on his sister's shoulders. "Please, listen and keep your voice down. No need to scare Susie and Sarah. Everything will be fine, but I need to get you and the girls out of town. Now. Right this minute. Dexter will come for me—soon. I need to be certain he can't hurt you. We haven't a minute to waste."

Myrt's hand flew to her mouth. "Oh, Lord Jesus. Why? What does the chief know? Oh, God, Ed, I told you to leave Cat's mess alone. I can't lose anyone else. I just can't."

He tightened his grip on his sister's shoulders. "Stop. I can't undo what's done. I have proof Dexter killed Al, and I'm not about to give it back. The chief doesn't know it's missing yet, but he'll find out soon enough. He caught me alone in his office. He'd been put out with me. That was the last straw."

Myrt's eyes widened. Fearing she might go into shock, he gave her a gentle shake. "Stay with me. Do you understand? Leave that laundry basket right where it is. I told Mrs. Hieronymous a cousin had been in an accident, and we had to leave town immediately. I was careful not to say who or where. I'm taking you to Aunt Celia's farm outside Fort Madison. I just told the girls we were going for a drive."

She shook her head. "I need to pack if we won't be back tonight. I can't just leave without clothes for the girls."

"Yes, you can. I'll pack clothes later and get them to you. Meanwhile Celia can scare up something for you and the girls to wear."

He draped his arms around Myrt's shoulders and guided her toward the car. "Smile," he reminded. "Let the girls think this trip is one big lark."

He chucked Myrt under the chin. "I seem to remember that Mom made you a dress out of a seed sack when you were the girls' age? Maybe Aunt Celia still has the pattern."

FORTY-ONE

Jimmy Cloyd swatted Emily on her rump. "Always say I like my women corn-fed and Iowa-bred. I want titties I can grab hold of. You have great knockers, Emily."

"Thanks Jimmy." She cupped her bare breasts and pointed them at him like tommy guns. "I aim to please."

He laughed. He actually liked this broad. Her snaggle-toothed smile could scare the paint off a barn, but she was built like a brick shithouse. And she didn't sass him about nothing. Always done everything he asked. He reached down to button his fly. When he glanced back at Emily, her smile had vanished.

"Jimmy, any way you can get the chief to ease up on the girls when he calls? He whomped on Pauline till she looked like one of them black-and-red barber polls. Can't hardly breathe without holdin' her ribs. Don't know if'n she can work the rest of the week the pain's so bad."

He shook his head. "Sorry, hon. He's the one keepin' the 19 ½ Club open. Don't nobody tell him to mind his Ps and Qs on visits."

As he slipped his shirt on, Jimmy heard a bellow downstairs. "Speak of the devil. I'd say Dexter's here, and he ain't happy."

He buttoned his last button and slapped a sawbuck on the table. "See you next week."

Jimmy slid his hand along the banister as he loped down the stairs. Hearing Chief Dexter raging 'bout one thing or t'other wasn't exactly rare. Too bad his mob bosses needed the jackass. Otherwise he'd be glad to give Dexter the same treatment he showed the ladies. Though Jimmy had no problems killin' folks who needed killin', he had no stomach for torture—'specially women. Wasn't right.

"Jimmy!" Dexter growled. "They told me you was here. Didn't you hear me yellin' for you?"

"Just had some business needed finishing." Jimmy winked, hoping to soften him up.

Dexter grabbed his shirt and shoved him against the wall. "Listen, you halfwit. This is serious."

The chief's mouth hovered an inch from his ear. "You gotta help me find Ed Nelson and kill the son-of-a-bitch."

Jimmy cringed as he tried to dodge the chief's hot fetid breath.

He shoved Dexter away. "Hey, man, keep it down. You don't shout that kinda business, even in a whorehouse."

The chief glared at him, but lowered his voice. He huffed like a runaway locomotive. "He stole my ledger. The shithead opened my safe—don't know how—took my damn book. It's got notes on every payment. If he hands that over to some do-gooder who'll listen, I won't be the only one with his Johnson hanging out."

Jimmy stared back. "You wrote stuff down? With names?"

Dexter backed up a step. "Not exactly, but won't take no genius to figure out who's who. Who'd guess that prissy college boy'd pull a stunt like this. Stealing from *me*."

Jimmy recognized an opportunity to make a buck when one slapped him upside the head. "Settle down, we'll find Ed. But time's come for money to start flowing upriver. If you want me to solve your problem—and forget to tell my bosses what you done—I'm gonna need a little incentive. No. Make that a big incentive."

Dexter clenched and unclenched his fists. Jimmy almost laughed at his struggle for control. The asswipe wanted to beat the tar out of him. But he knew his bare ass was stickin' out over a mighty big barrel.

Jimmy patted the chief's arm. "I'm handling a little job for another party. With a wee bit a plannin', we can take care of my client's problem and yours together. Bury both Ed Nelson and Catherine Reedy for good in one helluva deep dark hole."

FORTY-TWO

"Pete, go on home." Cat touched her brother's arm as he opened the Model T's passenger door for her to climb in. "I want to walk home. I need a few minutes alone. Time to think."

"What's to think about?" He turned to face her, his stare unrelenting. "We can't help Dad. He won't let us. Way things are headed, he'll be dead long before there's a trial. It's past time you and Jay left town."

Cat nodded. "Maybe. Maybe it is."

"Maybe?" Pete's voice shook. "Are you deaf? Dexter just promised to hang you for Ralph's murder."

Her hand settled on her brother's forearm. He shook it off.

"Please understand," she said. "I heard. I'm not stupid. But I just...have to take care of a few things first."

Pete's eyes widened. "What are you up to, Cat? Taking care of a few things could get you killed. You need to leave now."

Her chin jutted out. "I know what I'm doing." Her younger brother could push her buttons. She sighed. *Give him something.* "Tomorrow. I promise. I'll take Jay away tomorrow."

Pete slammed the car door shut. "Fine. I know that look. You've planted your feet like a damn Missouri mule. But I heard your promise, Sis. Tomorrow. You leave at first light or I swear I'll truss you up and carry you off."

She chuckled. "I'd like to see that." Time to let Pete win a round.

"Don't think I won't." His tone sounded no less firm, but his look softened.

God, she didn't deserve this family. Her bullheadedness had brought them to this precipice, and yet they were all willing to leap off the cliff holding her hand.

She dared to reach up and pat Pete's cheek. Her fingers felt the bristles re-emerging from his morning shave. *My not so little brother.*

Cat swallowed. "See you tonight. Don't know if Beth told you but we're having dinner at your house. It'll give Nell a little change of scenery."

Pete nodded. "All right. I know you're smart, Sis. But you can't outsmart evil. You be careful."

***

Cat hesitated at the employee entrance to the bank. Since she'd been fired, she knew it was off-limits. Who cared? She was accused of murder. Why not flaunt custom, too?

She cracked the door wide enough to slip inside. She glanced around. Good. That prissy scarecrow who thought it was his job to keep worker peons away from Jacobs' inner sanctum was nowhere in sight. But the door to the bank president's office was closed. Was he even inside?

She turned the doorknob. Not locked. As the door clicked shut behind her, Jacobs raised his eyes and his mouth dropped open. His face blanched, but he didn't utter a word.

"Surprised to see me?" Cat tried for a conversational tone though she wanted to scream at the man. "Alive and not in jail?"

He stood, and she walked rapidly toward his desk. "Sit down." An order, not a request. "We're going to have us a nice conversation. I'll have my say first. Then you can have a turn."

Jacobs' eyes cut to the door as he reclaimed his chair. "Did anyone see you come in?"

"No. Don't worry. I doubt anyone's going to interrupt us."

Standing directly across from him, she braced her hands on his mahogany desk and leaned in. "I know Ralph Black came to see you yesterday, and you killed him."

"Wha…what? He's dead?" Jacobs' mouth quivered. He looked like a catfish yanked from the river after stupidly swallowing a hook. Could he fake such shock?

"Yes. He's dead. And it's plain as day whoever killed Ralph, murdered Dirk. The police found the brothers' cars stashed side by side in an abandoned barn on property owned by your bank.

Seems only logical to conclude the same murdering son-of-a-bitch who killed the blackmailers tried to kill me. That murdering son-of-a-bitch is you."

"No. No." Jacobs stood. He shook his head, his eyes wild.

"Stop and listen," Cat barked. "I'll tell you when you can talk. I've taken out some life insurance. I wrote down everything that happened the night you raped me. I detailed how Dirk found one of your letters begging forgiveness, promising to take care of Jay, your son. I made eight copies of my new life insurance policy. If I suddenly stop breathing—for any reason—your hoity-toity friends on Grand Avenue and at the Keokuk Country Club get copies. More importantly, a friend will place one copy directly in Martha Jacobs' hands. I'm guessing your wife won't be amused."

Jacobs teetered and grabbed the desk for balance. Shock? Genuine? Was he surprised a mere woman had enough gumption to confront a murderer?

She took a steadying breath. "Will your wife and friends believe me? I think so. Your son inherited your nose, your chin, your ears. Actually, I'm surprised no one's commented on the resemblance. Will you be arrested for murder? Maybe not, but you'll be a pariah in Keokuk. Your life as you know it will be over."

"Cat, please, please. I don't know what you're talking about. Yes, Ralph came to see me. But I swear I didn't know he was dead. I went to the Grand Annex Tavern at noon to meet him—to bring his hush money. He didn't show."

Jacobs fumbled with a desk drawer, pulled out a sack and dumped stacks of twenty-dollar bills on his desk blotter. "See, here's the money I got to pay him off. Think. Would I have put this money together if I planned to kill Ralph?"

"Yes. To use it as bait. You showed it to Ralph then lured him to a spot where you promised to exchange the cash for the letter. Instead you killed him."

The banker slumped in his chair. "Oh, God. No matter what I say you won't believe me. I did not kill those men."

His eyes sought hers. "And I'd never kill you. I … love you."

Love? How could he say the word. He raped me.

"Then answer this. Who else had a motive to kill Ralph Black—a stranger who's been in town less than forty-eight hours?"

His forehead wrinkled. Was he giving the question real thought?

"I don't know. I swear I have no idea."

Cat caught the eye movement. His lips said one thing. A furtive sideways glance told a different story. Cat knew how to recognize a bald-faced lie. If Jacobs wasn't the killer, he had an inkling who might be.

"There's nothing more to say. For Jay's sake, I'll keep quiet so long as you leave me and my family alone." She spun on her heel.

His voice followed her. "Cat, please, how can I help? What can I do?"

She didn't look back. As she fled Jacobs' office, she heard a gasp. *Oh, for cripe's sake.* Maude Burks, the head bank gossip, stood three feet away, juggling rolls of pennies from the cashier stations. The rolled coins dropped on the marble floor. Pennies burst from their wrappers in a gunshot explosion. As the freed coins escaped and rolled across the polished floor, they tinkled in a musical aftershock.

Normal bank sounds hushed. Conversation stopped. All eyes traveled to Maude and then to the cause of the ruckus—Cat, former employee and accused murderer running from the bank president's office.

FORTY-THREE

Jimmy sipped his iced tea, wishing his hostess had left off the damn mint leaf. Got in the way and made him dribble. What was he supposed to do with it anyway—eat it?

Sun sparkled on the Mississippi as a tugboat pushed coal-laden barges toward the locks. Its horn tooted three quick blasts. He recalled standing in the Nauvoo graveyard wishing his employer would give up her cockamamie charade and invite him to her home. Why sweat in the boondocks when they could plot murders comfy-like on a patio?

Now he wished they were back in Nauvoo, wished he'd never blurted out that he knew who she was. Then a veil would hide those glittering, crazy-bitch eyes.

He couldn't shake the feeling her brain was engaged in high gear, feverishly calculating ways to rub him out once he helped solve her "little problems."

She glared at him. "You told Chief Dexter my plan to kidnap the boy and lure Catherine Reedy to the caves?" Her tone was frosty; her stare, pure ice.

Sweat popped out on Jimmy's upper lip. He better be damn careful what he said to this broad. "Well, uh, yes and no. I told the chief my *client* had a plan. Never gave no hint 'bout who t'was. Didn't even let on you was a woman."

The lady's nostrils did that little flare number that made him think of a demented rabbit, but she didn't say boo. Sat there like an empress waiting for her subject to bow and scrape. The silence weighed on him, its own torture.

He put down the iced tea, wiped a wet palm on his trousers. "Bringing Dexter in makes sense. He hates the Reedy dame. Says if'n she and the kid both disappear, he can just claim she run off so she wouldn't have to pay no debt to society for murdering her husband and brother-in-law. It'll wrap things up nice and tidy, and he gets rid of Ed Nelson same time."

"How do you know this young cop will follow that bitch to the cave?" she interrupted. "And why does the chief want this policeman murdered? You're not telling me everything."

Damn. How much should he tell her? He licked his lips.

"I got my sources," Jimmy mumbled. "I got suspicious about Nelson and the Reedy dame after he dropped in for a chat with me. Seemed like he was keen on pinning Dirk Black's murder on someone besides Cat Reedy. So I asked around. A mug I know had too much to drink at the Street Fair and had to piss like a racehorse. Ducked in an alley to relieve hisself and saw the two of 'em, Nelson and the woman, together. Nelson was hidin' her in his car. The drunk ducked behind a trash can. They never saw him. Imagine they still think no one knows about 'em."

She arched an eyebrow. "So that harlot has her hooks in another man. No surprise. Go on, what about the chief? Why does he want Ed Nelson dead? I'm not stupid, Mr. Cloyd. You didn't concoct this joint assault out of the goodness of your heart. What are you getting out of it? Money, I assume."

"Look, lady. Yeah, I'm doin' it for money. Ain't got nothing personal against any of these folks. Matter a fact, I'm a tad queasy 'bout killing some tyke. But I ain't gonna tell you why Dexter wants rid of the cop. Just like I didn't tell him who you were or why you wanted your bodies dead. It ain't my affair."

The woman laughed. "Good answer. Almost. You raised a question. Do you have the stomach to murder that child?"

He sighed. "Won't give me no pleasure, but I can do it."

"Fine. I'll be there to make sure you have no crisis of conscience."

"What d'ya mean—you'll be there?" A shiver ran down his spine. Was she coming along to shoot him?

"You act like a good little sheep dog and herd the Reedy woman and the cop into the cave. But don't you kill them till I get there. You wait for me."

"Uh, lady, pardon me for sayin' so, but that's a rotten idea. For one, it's dangerous. Ed Nelson ain't dumb. He'll be expecting trouble. Could well be some shootin'. For seconds, Chief Dexter's a comin' with me. Figured I might need backup. If you show, Dexter will sure as hell learn who you are."

She smiled. "What'll he do—arrest me for joining his murder spree? No, I'm coming."

She used a polished fingernail to draw a circle on her sweating iced tea glass. "When I visited the bank today, I overheard Maude Burks whispering how the Reedy woman—she called her a brazen hussy—barged out of the bank president's office. Maude said she didn't know what the woman was up to, but figured it was no good."

Jimmy shook his head. "Don't know nothin' bout that."

"You say this Ed person is helping Catherine Reedy. Bet they're planning to run for it. That's what I'd do. Could be she sweet-talked her old employer into lending her some cash. We can't wait. Grab the kid tonight. Then get word to the woman however you choose. Tell her to come to Momiss Cave at sunrise if she wants to see her son alive again."

Jimmy frowned. "Snatchin' the kid at night sounds tricky. Better to wait till the granny's alone with the boy. If Cat's there, she'll fight like a she-demon."

The woman rose. "How you grab the kid's your problem. Remember you're being paid by two clients for one job. Do it."

Jimmy knew an exit line when he heard one. "So when you gonna show? If Cat and Ed follow directions and come at sun up, Dexter and I should have things sorted out by six-thirty. We'll try to keep 'em alive till you get there. No guarantees. Dead is dead."

She smiled. "Aren't you the philosopher? Indeed, dead is dead."

FORTY-FOUR

Cat hid behind a trellis trained with tiny yellow roses. The cascade—her sister-in-law's green thumb at work—provided a fragrant invisibility cloak. No one could see her from the alley, and a plank fence screened her brother's backyard from anyone cruising down the street.

Was anyone watching? No point taking chances.

The image of Ed's green eyes burned in her memory. Her breath hitched at the thought of seeing him, of being alone with him. Her lips trembled recalling the taste of his tender kisses. *Don't.* No point dwelling on might-have-beens. Tonight would be a final meeting. A goodbye.

Beth said Ed sounded frantic to meet her. She'd heard the chief sack him. Was she the reason? Was Ed's life one more she had poisoned?

Cat glanced at her watch. Two minutes until eight. A motor sounded. Ed? Gravel crunched as a Model T rolled in slow motion down the alleyway. She recognized the dented grill. Abandoning her leafy blind, she ran to the car. Ed stretched across the bench seat to open her door.

His face had paled, spotlighting the sprinkling of cinnamon freckles on his skin. Tonight his emerald eyes telegraphed fear.

"Thank God, you got my message," he said. "We need to talk, but you can't be seen with me. Stay down. We'll head to my family farm. I need to show you where I hid the strongbox should anything happen to me."

Anything happen? Had she put Ed in danger? Cat crouched, imitating a human pretzel. Hiding made her feel she'd already been convicted, sentenced to a life of shame. She was guilty, all right. Guilty of keeping secrets from a man who'd tried to help. A decent man.

She abhorred lies and liars. Or so she claimed. But wasn't keeping secrets the same as telling lies?

Ed announced cross streets as the car approached the city limits. "Just passed K Street. The road's deserted. You can sit up."

She craned her head side to side, unkinking the painful knot between her shoulders. For a moment, the night sky scrubbed away all thought. It glowed an eerie green, winking stars knit together in a delicate web of light.

"It's the aurora borealis," Ed said. "Not often we get a display like this."

"It feels like I'm waking inside a fairytale." Transfixed, Cat placed the palm of her hand against the cool glass of the car window. "Makes you realize how small we are, how little our problems matter in the grand scheme." She sighed. "Doesn't make the trouble any easier to bear, does it? Pete and I were at the police station today. We heard Dexter scream at you, fire you. Because of me?"

Ed shook his head. "No." His eyes left the bumpy road to look at her. "He caught me snooping in his office. He was already apoplectic that I'd disappeared for a good part of the day. Catching me in his private bailiwick was the final straw. Don't worry. He hasn't a clue about us. He certainly doesn't know we've been meeting, or that I found Dirk's strongbox."

The breath Cat had been holding escaped in a whoosh. "Thank the Lord. I didn't want to be responsible for one more disaster. I know Myrtle hasn't been able to find work. What will you do for money? Please, take some of the cash from the strongbox. I mean it."

Ed huffed out a sound, part laugh, part grunt. "Haven't thought about money. All I care about is keeping Myrt, my nieces, and you and Jay breathing. Although a bit of cash may come in handy to get all of you to safety."

Her eyebrows knitted in confusion. "Are you saying Chief Dexter would harm your sister and nieces, just because you rifled through a few papers in his holy office?"

He snorted. "I did a bit more than poke around. I stole a ledger. Foolishly, Dexter recorded all the payments he's received from hoodlums for services rendered." He paused. "One of those services was killing my brother-in-law."

"What?" The hairs lifted on the back of Cat's neck. Dexter murdered Al Underwood?

Ed answered her unspoken question. "I'm guessing Jimmy Cloyd did the dirty work and paid the chief to look the other way. Same difference. I signed on with the police force for one reason—to get the goods on Dexter and see him hang."

Ed pulled into the driveway and parked behind a copse of trees. He scurried around to open Cat's door. "Come on." He gripped her hand. "I need to show you something."

He led her to a large oak tree and pointed at the leafy canopy above. "Myrt and I spent more hours in that treehouse than in school. Dad built it. It's rock solid. A great hiding place."

Cat smiled. Any kid would love the hideaway. Even after Ed pointed it out, she had to look hard to separate the treehouse from its feathery skirt of foliage. It would be well hidden until fall winds and winter frosts defrocked the trees.

"I hauled the strongbox up there," he said. "Figured no one would think of looking in a treehouse. How about I show you around?"

Cat took in the sturdy wooden slats nailed to the tree trunk to form a makeshift ladder. Her right foot tested the first rung. After swinging from a three-story Ferris wheel, the climb presented little challenge. "Piece of cake." Climbing ahead of Ed she realized he'd get a good view up her skirt. She almost laughed. As if he hadn't seen all there was to see.

Ed settled her on a blanket spread on the planked floor. He lit a small gas lantern and hung it from a branch poking through the ceiling.

"I figured there might be a time when I needed to hide so I toted up a few comforts. If we hear a car, I'll douse the light."

The treehouse completely circled the giant oak's trunk. A wheel with its own living hub. Ed sat and leaned his back against the tree's tough bark. He pulled her into his arms. Despite the horrors battering her, she found comfort in the strong beat of his heart, steady as the big old grandfather clock in her dad's parlor.

She snuggled into the crook of his arm. "Did you suspect Dexter killed your brother-in-law before you found that ledger?"

He kissed the top of her head. "Yes. Brad, a college friend, is with the State Police. After Al disappeared, Brad told me he had reason to believe Dexter killed Al."

"I still don't understand how Dexter got appointed when family needs forced Chief McPherson to step down," Cat said.

"Yea, McPherson ran a clean operation. Dexter didn't waste any time turning it into a corrupt mess," Ed added. "When the State Police realized what Dexter was up to, they asked Al to be their inside source. I signed on to finish the job he started. The one that cost Al's life. The minute Dexter discovers his ledger's missing, he'll come after me. He can't let me live."

Cat broke free of his sheltering arm to search his face. "What will you do?"

"I took Myrt and the girls to our aunt's farm near Fort Madison. They should be safe there. I'm leaving, too. Tonight. I want you and Jay to come with me."

Cat sucked in a breath. What was he offering—a ride over the county line or a new life?

She twined her fingers in her lap to keep her hands from shaking. She refused to leave herself open to more hurt, new misunderstandings.

She straightened, stared at her hands in the flickering lamplight as if they held some secret. "You needn't worry about me. Pete's convinced me that staying in Keokuk won't help Dad. My brother will whisk Jay and me out of town come morning."

When she snuck a glance at Ed, he averted his eyes. Relief? Of course, he was relieved. What man running for his life would want to be saddled with a woman and a two-year-old?

The silence stretched. His shoulders straightened and he turned back to her. "You don't want to come with me?"

Ed cupped her face, forcing her to meet his gaze. "Cat, I want to keep you safe. But that's not the only reason I'm asking. I want to be with you, with Jay. I want us to be a family."

Tears welled in her eyes. She blinked to ward off the waterworks. God, how she wished for a fairytale ending. Too bad, Ed didn't say he loved her. She'd seen how he looked at her son. Like he was looking at his own boy. Were she and Jay substitutes for his dead wife and baby? Jay deserved a father who loved him, not a ghost.

It has to be real this time. If I can't be with a man who loves me, I'd rather live alone. Settling isn't an option.

She bit her lip. "I can't come with you. I spent the last four years living with a man who didn't love me. I still don't know why Dirk picked me. Maybe he just needed to appear respectable to his marks. Maybe the 'who' he married never mattered."

Ed's face clouded and he started to speak. She put a finger against his lips. "I don't think you have any ulterior motive. But I don't want you to take on Jay and me out of some sense of duty or because you miss the loved ones you've lost. I can take care of myself and my little boy."

He grabbed her shoulders and pulled her tight against him. "My God, Cat. Don't you know I love you?"

He kissed her hard, then pushed back to study her face. "I love you, Cat. I'll ask once more. Please come with me. This nightmare won't last forever. Could you learn to love me? Marry me?"

The tears came. "Learn? How could I not love you? Are you sure?"

"I loved my wife. Loving you doesn't change that. Hannah would want me to be happy. It's possible to love more than one person in this life."

He tilted her chin up. "You're smart, resourceful, beautiful, and perhaps the most honest person I've ever known. I'd trust you with my life."

Cat froze. Honest? How would he feel once he discovered she'd duped Dirk for two years, letting him think Jay was his son? What if she told him about her visit to Jacobs at the bank—how she'd blackmailed her rapist to leave her be? How would he feel about trusting her then?

"What's wrong, Cat? You're trembling. Don't you believe me?"

She nodded. "I only wish I were the woman you imagine me to be. I can lie. I'm damned good at it. Dirk proved an excellent teacher. I've lied to you. Repeatedly. And I'd lie again in a heartbeat. I'd murder, too. I'd do just about anything to keep my son safe."

Ed's eyebrows bunched. "What are you saying?"

"Let me tell you a story. Then we leave. I won't hold you to any promises."

Ed never stopped rubbing her arms and shoulders as she described the rape and its aftermath—the banker's letters begging for forgiveness, the anonymous "gifts" she accepted despite her shame. Cat told him all about Dirk's blackmail scheme and Ralph's determination to cash in.

Finally, she took a long breath and described her afternoon encounter with Jacobs. "He knows he'll be exposed if anyone harms me or my boy," she said. "I made that crystal clear."

She pulled away and looked at Ed. "Don't say a word. You fell in love with a mirage. I understand."

He kissed her so gently it might have been her imagination. "You are exactly who I thought you were, Cat. I love you more than I can say."

She swallowed hard, and the tight lump in her throat slowly dissolved. His eyes didn't lie.

Ed nuzzled her neck, brushed the spot where her pulse advertised her desire with its trip-hammer beat. She ran her hands through his thick mahogany hair. How had she imagined she could say goodbye to this man?

A chill wind rustled the leaves. Cat barely noticed as he unbuttoned her blouse. He trailed kisses along her bared shoulders. The warm kisses felt connected, a delicate web enveloping her, binding her to her lover with invisible threads. Her fingers fumbled with his shirt buttons.

FORTY-FIVE

Jimmy drove slowly down Timea Street. Shades on the Reedy windows were down, no lights. He'd been keeping tabs, knew the routine. Lights flicked on inside the minute dusk settled. The place was empty. Nobody home.

"We goin' in?" Mick asked.

At six-three and a solid two-hundred-thirty pounds, Mick reminded Jimmy of a vicious dog, chained and snarling, eager to bite any ankle in his vicinity. He'd brought the carnie bruiser along for muscle. One woman alone, no problem. But two could be trouble, even if one was an old bat.

"Not just yet," Jimmy answered. "Let's see if they're at the brother's house. They don't go nowhere else."

Jimmy let his car crawl past Pete Reedy's house. Two squirts—a little girl and a chubby toddler—chased fireflies. The little boy tripped over a toy, did a face plant on the scraggly lawn, and wailed. A woman this side of chubby bent over and hoisted the crybaby to her shoulder. "You're okay, Jay. No need for tears."

"You want I should grab him now?" Mick asked.

The man's zeal made Jimmy a tad queasy. "Nah, I don't want to tangle with the brother. Better if we nab the kid at his ma's house. With the old gent in jail, there ain't no men to interfere."

Jimmy cruised back past the vacant Reedy house. He parked on a side street. An alley meandered behind the sad-looking clapboard. Real private. He'd used it before. Snuck into the basement without a hitch to boost the old drunk's gun and bury it in the backyard. He'd never have found the Webley if John Reedy hadn't blabbed to his drinking buddies how he hid his pistol where his grandson couldn't reach it.

The Reedy backyard was a burglar's dream 'cept for the caged varmints. Them minks made more racket than a pack of coyotes at the scent of blood. Good thing the neighbors were used to the furry rats screechin', and paid 'em no never mind.

"What we doin'?" Mick asked.

"Gonna take a little look-see inside. Never been upstairs. Want to get the lay of the land afore we decide the best way to snatch the kid."

The minks limited their protests to a few high-pitched squeals as the men slipped past. The hinged cellar doors jutted a foot above ground. No locks. The Reedys must have figured their moldy cellar wasn't exactly a magnet for thieves. Jimmy grabbed a handle and lifted one planked door, then the other.

Once inside, Mick lowered the warped doors, plunging the men into darkness. Jimmy switched on his Eveready flashlight. He held the long tube like a club. It had come in handy before. They followed its watery beam down a handful of rickety stairs, walked through the basement and climbed a longer flight of stairs to the home's first floor. Mick slid his hunting knife between the door and jamb to unseat the almost-useless latch hook.

Dirty dishes cluttered the kitchen's chipped porcelain sink. Jimmy took a deep whiff. No cooking smells.

"Musta gone to the brother's for feed. Perfect. We can wait, give 'em a surprise homecoming. Got to decide if we jump 'em soon as they walk in or wait for 'em upstairs."

He led the way to the second-floor bedrooms. Mick clomped behind him with the stealth of a newly shod plow horse. "Keep it down, will ya?"

"What's your beef? No one's here."

"Don't give you cause to create a racket. I wanna hear myself think." Jimmy splashed the flashlight around the first bedroom, avoiding the window. "It's the woman's all right. Crib's here." His light dallied on a slip hanging on a hall tree. "That don't belong to some old granny."

Car lights flickered briefly on the shade before they extinguished. A door slammed. Jimmy signaled Mick to stay quiet and switched off the flashlight.

A man's voice floated through the open window. "Do you want me to put Jay to bed for you, Grandmother?"

"No, Pete. Go on home. I'm fine. It's just been a long day. I'll tuck Jay in and pour myself a spot of Wild Irish Rose. Doc Wheeler says wine's good for the digestion, and my stomach feels a little tetchy."

"All right then," the man answered. "I'll bring Cat over in a little bit."

Jimmy smiled in the dark. Couldn't ask for better. The old lady would come upstairs alone with the kid. She'd be easy as pie to handle. He grabbed Mick's shirt collar and yanked his head close enough to whisper in his ear. "Stay behind the door. We'll wait till granny sets the kid in the crib. Then you grab her from behind. Be sure'n clamp a hand over her mouth so she don't scream bloody murder and wake the neighbors."

He couldn't see Mick's expression, but his head bobbed a yes.

The front door closed. A car engine started. The car's lights swept over the shade as it drove away. The stairwell bloomed with light, turning the bedroom from black to gunmetal gray.

Creaking stairs advertised the old lady's dawdling progress. Could she go any slower? Jimmy positioned himself behind the loaded clothes tree. While it didn't hide him entirely, deep shadows offered reasonable camouflage. As an afterthought, he tied a kerchief over half his face just like the bandits in them Roy Rogers' movies.

Chief Dexter promised no one could lay a hand on him for this caper—even if things went squirrelly. Still why take any risks?

"Looks like you're as tired as I am, sweetheart," the woman cooed to the brat in her arms. "You're sound asleep."

Granny didn't bother with the bedroom light. Probably afraid she'd wake the tyke and he'd start squawking afore she could hit her own bottle. She lowered the boy into his crib.

Soon as she straightened, Mick snaked one arm around her middle, picking her up and pinning her arms against her side. He used his free hand to muffle her startled cries.

Jimmy turned on the flashlight and aimed it right in granny's face. Eyes wide with terror, she blinked crazily. A pearl button popped off her dress near where Mick's arm acted as a human vice.

"Quit squirming if you wanna live, old woman," Jimmy warned. "We ain't gonna hurt you or the kid. All you gotta do is deliver a message to your granddaughter."

"Will ya hurry up and tie her?" Mick growled. "She's kickin' like a mule."

Jimmy found what he wanted in the first dresser drawer he slid open. He extracted two pair of stockings. The old lady had no chance to howl before he replaced Mick's meaty paw with a tightly-knotted stocking. He used another to bind her feet.

"Dump her on the bed," Jimmy ordered, "and hold her still so's I can tie her hands to the bed frame." A minute later he'd hogtied her to the iron bedposts. Her frantic eyes cast about the room.

"Give it up, lady. It's over. We got the kid. We won't hurt you or the boy. But if Catherine Reedy Black wants to see her son alive again, she better git to Missouri come dawn. She's to bring her boyfriend—that copper, Ed—and make sure he brings the book he stole. They's to come to the entrance of Momiss Cave seven a.m. sharp. Not a minute sooner or later. And it better be just the two of 'em."

Jimmy studied the old lady. Her chest heaved like one of the ponies he bet on that ran out of wind long before the home stretch. He worried her damn heart would explode before her granddaughter showed. He shrugged. Didn't matter. His client had typed a note, neat as a pin, on her Olivetti. He placed it atop the old woman's ample stomach. The note didn't say boo 'bout no kidnapping, just, "Momiss Cave, 7 a.m.," followed by directions.

They'd get the point, what with the baby missing.

Mick hovered near the bed, playing with his knife. The guy'd begun to creep Jimmy out. He wondered if it might be smarter to dump mountain man before the morning show.

Jimmy walked to the crib. Hard to believe the kid slept straight through the tussle with the old lady. "I'll carry sonny boy," he said. "You drive. Let's get the hell out of here."

FORTY-SIX

Ed parked the car in the alleyway behind Pete Reedy's house, then checked his pocket watch. Almost ten o'clock. He hoped Cat's two-hour absence hadn't caused anyone to pace the floor. Not that he regretted their stolen moments.

Warm light spilled from the back of the house. Good. "Let's go in together. I want to reassure Pete. Your brother needs to believe I'll keep you and Jay safe."

"Pete sometimes forgets he's my little brother." Cat smiled. "Now that he's a head taller, he's somehow cottoned to the notion he can boss me around. Too bad I came of age in the flapper era."

Ed's forehead wrinkled. "Not sure I get your meaning."

She laughed. "Lord knows the Roaring Twenties weren't all fun and games. That's when the mob discovered Keokuk. But, oh what delicious freedom for a young woman. Hard to convince a filly to stay fenced in the paddock when she's roamed the open plain."

Ed grinned. "Exactly where did you roam?"

"Weekends my girlfriends and I took the train to Chicago. We visited all the ballrooms—the Trianon, the Aragon—danced the night away. How I love to dance. Stopped by a few speakeasies, too." She arched an eyebrow. "Any second thoughts, now that you know I'm a flapper?"

He snorted. "Can't say I'm surprised. Based on the stories I heard, you veered off the beaten path in grammar school, by beating up boys. I figured you'd grow up free-spirited." He licked his lips. "And I'd love to see you dance."

They walked arm in arm to the back door. For the first time in years, Ed felt light-hearted, optimistic. He'd pocketed evidence to help end Chief Dexter's reign of terror. He'd found a woman to treasure as long as he drew breath.

The screen door screeched as Cat pushed on it.

Pete jumped up from the kitchen table. "Where have you been?"

His eyes lit on Ed. "Nothing against you. Beth told me you're trying to help. But I don't know what's what these days with Dad in jail, and Dexter making threats left and right."

Ed dipped his chin to show he understood and took no offense. "Sorry if we worried you, but Cat and I had some things to figure out. It's no longer safe for her in Keokuk, and I have to leave, too, if I want to keep breathing."

"That's what I've been telling Sis," Pete interrupted. "I'm—"

"Sorry, let me finish." Ed held up a hand. "I'm driving Cat and Jay out of town tonight. A friend with the State Police arranged a safe place for us to stay in Iowa City. We'll hole up there until Dexter's no longer a threat."

Pete's mouth opened and closed. No sound came out. Beth's Cheshire cat grin indicated she was less surprised.

Cat squeezed Ed's hand. "Let me break the news. We're getting married."

Beth leapt up and hugged her sister-in-law. "Oh, Cat. I'm so happy for you. It's about time for some good news."

Ed snuck a glance at a flummoxed Pete. The man sank into a chair, his expression puzzled.

"Where's Grandmother Nell?" Cat asked. "I want to tell her, and I need to give my baby a big smooch."

"They left an hour ago," Beth answered. "Nell had one of her headaches. She could barely keep her eyes at half-staff. Pete drove them home."

"Imagine they're sound asleep by now," Pete added. "You sure you don't want to wait until morning to leave?"

Ed shook his head. "No, the sooner the better. Cat, you want to explain or should I?"

Beth's smile melted away. "What haven't you told us?"

It took fifteen minutes to bring Pete and Beth up to speed.

When they finished, Pete stood. "You're right. It's best if you leave tonight. I'll drive Cat to the front of Dad's house. If anyone's watching, they'll think she's home for the night. I'll come in for a few minutes and help Cat pack. They'll think I've stayed for a nightcap. When I come out the front door and drive away alone, you can take off out back."

Ed and Cat nodded in unison. "Let's do it," Ed said.

***

Ed moved as stealthily as he could to the back of the Reedy house. The minks' claws—or were they toenails?—made eerie skittering sounds on the packed dirt. Their eyes glowed red like hot pokers. An eerie screech caused him to stumble. His flesh crawled in response to the sense of mindless evil the rodents projected.

He huddled in the shadows by the back porch, waiting for Cat to unlock the door. Heels clicked as someone crossed the linoleum floor.

"Ed?" Cat whispered through the closed door.

"Yes," he whispered back. She opened the door, and he slipped into the darkened kitchen.

She hugged him. "We only turned on lights at the front of the house. Wanted to focus attention there in case anyone's watching."

"Good thinking." He followed her down the hallway where Pete waited at the base of the stairs.

"Cat, you lead the way," Pete suggested. "If Nell wakes, she should see you first and not the hulking shadows of two men."

"Right." Cat kept her voice low.

The trio tiptoed up the stairs. The men paused on the landing while Cat gently knocked on the door to the second bedroom. "Nell? Grandmother? Wake up we need to talk."

No response. Cat opened the door, switched on the light. "Wha..?"

She whirled and called to the men. "She's not in her room." Cat ran toward her own bedroom. "Grandmother?" She flung the door open.

Her scream sent a chill straight to Ed's gut. My God, what now? Was it Jay? He practically mowed Pete down in his rush to reach Cat. Pete, right behind him, hit the light switch.

Ed's gaze raked the room, stuttering for a moment on the empty crib before focusing on Cat. She'd crawled onto the bed. Her fingers frantically pried at the gag stuffed in her grandmother's mouth. The old woman's sagging skin looked waxy. Was she even alive? Her chest moved. Thank God.

As soon as the gag came off, the old lady tried to speak. "They…took…him." The words came out on huffs of breath. "Two men. I'm so sorry, Catherine."

"Why?" Cat sobbed. "Where did they take Jay?"

The old woman swallowed. A shaky hand flew to her forehead. She kneaded the thin skin at her temple. Ed feared she'd pass out. She needed water, but he couldn't move to fetch it. Not until he heard her answer.

Cat saw the typed note and grabbed it. Her eyes scanned the message. "What do they want?"

Mrs. Reedy coughed. "The man said if you want Jay back, you need to come to Momiss Cave at sunrise." The old lady's brow creased. Her skittering gaze confirmed her confusion. "I didn't understand what he said next—you're supposed to 'bring your cop and the book he stole.'" She licked her lips. "What does that mean?"

Ed's heart hammered. *Jesus.* Had Dexter arranged the kidnapping to trap him? He wondered if the chief tried to take his nieces hostage first, then snatched Jay as a substitute. How did they know he and Cat were involved?

"Oh, no." Was he responsible for Cat's latest tragedy? He staggered under the weight of his guilt.

"Cat, I swear to you, we'll get Jay back. I'll return the ledger if that's what it takes. I'll trade my life for Jay's. You are not going to lose your son because of me. I promise."

FORTY-SEVEN

Cat's vision swam. Her grandmother's hoarse voice faded in and out like a St. Louis radio station on the Philco. An ice-cold hand patted her arm.

Jay. My darling Jay. What have they done? What have I done?

Her eyes locked on Ed. His mouth moved. The words ran together in her mind. White noise, no meaning.

Blackness swallowed her.

Strong fingers dug into her shoulder blades shaking her. She wanted the dark. Craved its peace. She batted at the hands, but they wouldn't go away. The jarring rattled her brain, unhinged her jaw. A sharp pain pulsed behind her eyes. She willed her eyelids to open.

Pete? That's right. Pete's here. To help me pack. So Jay and I can go away with Ed.

Her neck muscles felt wilted. She could barely hold her head up. Fingers patted her cheek. Her skin tingled. Her brother's face flitted into view. Then disappeared. Someone propped up her head, held a glass of water to her lips. She blinked. Ed?

She drank. Water dribbled down her chin. She choked. Why was she in bed?

"Sis, stay with us." Pete's tone was sharp. "Jay's been kidnapped. Don't disappear. We need to put our heads together. Help decide the best way to get him back."

The fuzzy blanket wrapping her brain tore free. "Where's Grandmother Nell?"

"I poured her a healthy shot of Wild Irish Rose and put her to bed," Pete answered. "She's no spring chicken, but she has grit. She'll be fine."

Cat stared at the empty crib. *Jay's been kidnapped*. Oh, Lord. He was only a few months older than the Lindbergh baby when they stole him. Murdered him. The soothing black void beckoned. She fought back.

Be strong. For Jay. She'd kill the monsters. Strangle them with her bare hands before they could harm her little one.

"Did Nell know the men?"

Ed cleared his throat. "There were two of them. Only one spoke. Your grandmother said the talker had a squat wrestler's body and stank of cigarettes. Couldn't see his face. Wore a bandana as a mask. My bet's on Jimmy Cloyd."

"Makes sense since he does dirty work for Chief Dexter." Cat struggled to keep her mind focused. "What about the other man?"

"Mrs. Reedy said he was huge. Tattooed forearms, big muscles, horrible scars covering one side of his face. I doubt Keokuk boasts two thugs who look like that. Has to be the Ferris wheel operator—the one who arranged your 'accident'."

Ed took her hand. "This is my doing. Dexter's using your son to force me out in the open, to return the ledger. I—" Cat pulled her hand free and pressed her fingers against his lips.

Her eyes bored into his. "It's not your fault. The Ferris wheel man tried to kill me *before* you stole the ledger. Before Dexter realized you were working against him."

She bit her lip. "Remember? You saw Jimmy huddled with that street fair ogre two days before he tried to kill me. And what about the threat in my mailbox? I agree—Dexter has a hand in the kidnapping, but he had nothing to do with what happened at the Street Fair."

Ed's forehead wrinkled. He stood and began to pace. "I'm not sure I follow. Jimmy must be working for Dexter. Otherwise he wouldn't know about the ledger."

Cat massaged her temples, trying to clear the fog in her brain. "I was wrong about Kenneth Jacobs. This isn't his doing. But we definitely have two enemies, Chief Dexter and Dirk's killer. My bet is on the woman who drove Dirk's car away after his murder. Maybe they've joined forces."

"Mrs. Hamilton?" Skepticism colored Ed's voice. "You think she'd condone kidnapping Jay?"

"It's possible."

She swung her legs off the bed and rotated her head to unkink her neck. She'd made a mistake, fixating on Jacobs. Once she'd convinced herself the banker killed Ralph, she placed him at the eye of her personal hurricane. She'd forgotten the woman. Somehow the villainess claimed a starring role in the murders of Dirk and Ralph Black. This woman—whoever she might be—was a mother. She understood Cat would do anything to save her baby. But what mother could do this to someone else's child?

She raked a hand through her hair. "My guess is Jimmy's working for Dexter and this woman. You say Jimmy's a conniving bastard. It's possible he's keeping his clients in the dark. Maybe they don't even know about one another. That Jimmy's getting paid twice for his work."

She pushed to her feet and walked to the crib. Her fingers trailed along the rail's smooth wood. She'd slept in this same crib—built by her dad—when she was a babe. She picked up the tiny pillow, touched it to her face. She swallowed the racking sob that bubbled to her lips. No. Jay needed her to think logically. She would be as single-minded and ruthless as her enemies.

"If this were only about the ledger, the kidnappers would have insisted you come alone, Ed," she said. "Less messy. Dexter doesn't need me to traipse off to some secret rendezvous. He's confident I'll hang for Ralph's murder. He'd love to see me swing from a rope in public. I think he'd prefer that finale to killing me in private."

Pete broke in. "Sis, suppose you're right. Does it make a difference?"

"I'm not sure. I'm convinced whoever issued the ultimatum doesn't intend for Ed, Jay or me to leave the rendezvous alive. They left us little choice. We can't go to the police. We're boxed in. We have to show. They want Ed and me to disappear. Permanently. And I can't bet on their inherent decency to spare a child."

Her heart sank. "My little boy…he must be terrified."

Ed draped an arm around her shoulders. "He's fine. Jay's their insurance. They need him until we hand over the ledger. Of course, the minute they have it, they'll try to kill us. "

His arm dropped away and he walked to the window. "This afternoon I phoned Brad, my friend in the State Police, when I took Myrt and my nieces to Celia's farm. I wanted a private conversation, and I didn't trust any phone in this town.

"Brad expects to meet us in Iowa City come morning. Even if I chanced phoning him from Keokuk this very minute, he couldn't get men to Missouri by sunrise. There's a risk, too. If the kidnappers have a friend working the switchboard, they might retaliate if we make a call."

Pete interrupted. "The call's no problem. No one will know. I have a key to the telephone office. We can sneak in the back door, bypass the switchboard completely."

"That's good." Ed nodded. "At least I can tell Brad what's happening—even if he can't ride to the rescue."

He lifted the edge of the heavy roll-down shade to peer outside. "The fact Jimmy ordered us to Missouri complicates things. I wonder what kind of clout the Iowa State Police have across state lines."

Cat plucked her son's teddy bear from the crib and idly brushed its fur with her fingers. She took a deep breath, inhaling Jay's baby scent, and steeled herself. She'd get him back.

"Okay, if we meet the kidnappers in the open and give them the ledger, they'll shoot us." She sighed. "Not an option. What can we do? Dexter took Dad's Webley as evidence. Do we even have a weapon?"

"My double-barreled 12-gauge," Pete answered.

"I have a revolver. It's old but it works." Ed's smile slowly grew. "And I know where to find a stash of dynamite. I set plenty of blasts in the CCC."

Ed fell silent. His brows knotted. "I'm trying to remember a talk I had with a fellow in the CCC. A hard chap. Had a bayonet scar down the side of his face. He told stories about hurling petrol bombs to stop Jerry tanks. Burned the tires right off them. We have petrol, and I saw a lot of Mason jars in your basement. If I remember what this bloke said, we can make our own petrol bombs. A lot safer than dynamite under ground."

Pete nodded. "I've heard stories about petrol bombs. They're dangerous. But they might help make it an even fight."

"They ordered us to be there at sunrise," Cat chimed in. "They'll be waiting. I'm sure of it. Can we get there faster? Set our own trap? Pete, you were just down that way helping Bruce harvest tomatoes. Know any shortcuts?"

"I sure do." His brief smile morphed into a frown. "But it's a risk. Don't forget the reason I was down in that bottomland. The Mississippi and the Des Moines rivers are near flood stage and are breaching levees. By now those back roads could be washed out."

Ed chewed his lip "It's a risk we have to take," he said.

"I agree." Cat said. "Where's the chief's ledger?"

"In my car," Ed answered. "Why?"

"What does it look like?"

"Nothing special. Soft cloth cover. Gray, I think. Same kind my nieces use for school work."

"Could we cook up a fake?" she asked.

"Maybe. But the chief would spot a phony soon as he cracked it open. The man has to know his own writing. Looks like hen scratches."

Cat bit her lip. "Maybe we only need to fool him for a minute or two. Just long enough to make an exchange. What does the chief want? Does he want the book destroyed so it can't be used as evidence against him? Or does he want it returned?"

"I'm sure he'd like it back," Ed answered. "It holds plenty of details tailor-made for blackmail. It's insurance should the mob decide he's outlived his usefulness. It gives him leverage to force them to think again."

"Good to know." Cat nodded. "We also know the chief's a certifiable coward. He only hits women and old men who can't fight back. If he's there, he'll order Jimmy to collect the book while he stays hidden."

Pete sighed. "The guns will come out as soon as you turn loose of the ledger—fake or real."

Cat smiled. "True enough. My guess is they plan to ambush us from nice, safe cover after we make the trade. If we get there early enough, maybe we can do them one better."

FORTY-EIGHT

The woman held out her arms for the screaming baby. "Come here, honey," she cooed.

Jimmy shoved the fussy brat at her. One more minute of high-pitched wailing and he'd have strangled the damn kid just to make him shut the hell up.

Since the kid woke, he'd been squealin' louder than a stuck pig. When Mick suggested getting some carnie stripper to look after the boy till morning, Jimmy was all over it. He just hoped no one saw him and Mick sneak the writhing bundle of snot into the back of the tent. The kid let out another shriek.

Glad I never had me one of these.

"Stella, can't you do sumpin' to shut his trap?" Mick growled. "Stick sumpin' in his damn mouth."

The woman cuddled the baby and stared daggers at Mick and Jimmy. "You scared him. That's all. I'll get him settled. Whose kid is he? Why you got him?"

"None of your damn business, woman," Mick answered. "He's a meal ticket—nothin' more."

Stella rocked the boy in her arms, making shushing sounds. The toddler whimpered like a wind-up toy that had done run down. The tyke snuggled his face into the woman's bare tits. Nice and perky with purple pasties on the nipples. Jimmy wouldn't mind a little of that action.

He glanced at Mick, who glared back, and decided he'd better quit admiring the scenery.

"Git, woman," Mick said. "Take the kid to your bed. We'll get him when we need him."

Without another word, the woman opened a tent flap and walked into what Jimmy guessed were sleeping quarters.

"She gonna be a problem?" Jimmy asked.

"Nah, she does what I say. Knows what'll happen if she don't."

Mick flexed his hands, forming transitory fists. Jimmy didn't need a diagram to tell him what the man did to Stella when she pissed him off. While he didn't cotton to using women as punching bags, he didn't stick his nose in other folks' business. He wanted to live a long time.

Mick took a swig from a flask and then offered to share.

Jimmy pushed the rot gut away. "Need to keep me wits about me. Don't you go getting snockered neither. That Ed Nelson ain't no idiot. Has to figure we don't plan to wave goodbye once he hands over the chief's tell-all book. He'll pull something to try'n save the Reedy woman and her kid—not to mention his own skin. We need to be ready."

"What's he gonna do?" Mick snorted. "No chance to run for it after we get our hands on the book. Ain't like there'll be people 'round to help. This place is real private, right?"

Jimmy nodded. "Yeah, it's private. I'd feel better if'n the folks paying us weren't hankerin' to get in on the fun. More bodies mean more ways to mess up. Our lady client's all het up to kill the tyke. Can't figure why. It ain't like he can blab."

Mick chuckled. "Maybe she's heard the kid bawl. An hour listenin' to that racket, and I'm ready to jerk his lungs out of his throat and stuff him in the ground."

Jimmy shrugged. He pulled out his gun to clean it. "Let's go over the plan one more time. We meet Dexter at five-thirty. He'll hide in the bushes, while we stand at the cave opening with the kid. You keep a knife tight to the brat's throat so's Ed and the mother can see. I'll cover 'em with my gun."

He paused to dab oil on his cleaning rag. "Ed'll demand we put down our guns. We agree if'n they ditch theirs first. Then we swap the kid for the ledger like we're on the up and up. That's when Dexter pops outta the bushes pointing both barrels at them. 'Surprise!'"

"So Dexter gets to shoot 'em?" Mick sounded disappointed.

"Nah. We pick up our guns and herd 'em underground. No point having to hump dead bodies inside. That cave's perfect. No diggin' or nothing. Just walk 'em in a little ways and find a cozy hidey-hole for their skeletons."

"What about the lady paying to see 'em die? We waitin' on her?"

"That blood-thirsty bitch ain't gonna keep us twiddling our thumbs. She's too eager for the bloodletting. You keep a close eye on her. Make sure she don't try to add our bodies to the pile."

FORTY-NINE

Thursday, September 22, 1938

Ed killed the car engine and turned to face Cat. "I'm pretty sure no one followed us. If someone was keeping tabs, they'd have stopped us when we picked up the dynamite. But, just to be on the safe side, scoot over and take the wheel. Get ready to drive off if anything happens."

Ed tuned out Cat's protest as he hurried to play lookout for Pete, who'd already reached the telephone company's back door.

"It should only take a minute," Pete whispered to Ed. "Just need to grab tools to tap into one of these lines." He gestured to the wires strung on a pole in the alley. "Doubt if I'll see anyone, but, if I do, I'll say I'm checking a problem. Just watch for police."

Ed strained to hear any sound. The Street Fair sideshows and rides had long since shuttered. But Ed knew from his night patrols that it wasn't too late for drunken gamblers to stumble out the alley entrance of the mob-run club three doors down.

A door creaked, and Ed jumped.

"Told you I'd be fast," Pete said. "Let me make the first call. Tell Beth to take Amy and go sit with Grandmother Nell. The old woman is tough but her health isn't great. I want Beth to invite one of her uncles to join the party with a shotgun."

After Pete called Beth, it was Ed's turn. The phone rang repeatedly.

"Hello, who's calling?" Brad's syrupy voice said he'd been sound asleep. Ed quickly brought him up to date.

"Dammit," Brad swore. "There's no way I can round up the Iowa cavalry and have them in Missouri by sunrise."

Ed sighed. Though he'd expected Brad's answer, hearing the verdict spoken aloud increased his dread.

"Could you get any help from Missouri troopers?" Ed asked.

"Maybe. It would be a lot easier if I weren't asking favors in the middle of the night. I'll do what I can, soon as I can. Figure out some way to hold out till we can get there. I promise you I'm coming."

***

Clouds scudded over the moon, throwing a smoky blanket over the rural landscape. The eerie glow of the aurora borealis had vanished. The gloomy night mirrored Cat's thoughts. She recalled how a Street Fair huckster had bamboozled her niece, claiming to bend a spoon with his mind. Did the mind have unique powers? Was there such a thing as telepathy? She closed her eyes, pictured her baby. *I love you. More than life. Where are you?*

No image. No answer.

"How many toughs do you think Jimmy Cloyd will bring?" Ed wondered aloud. "I'm betting Chief Dexter will be there."

"Yes, Dexter'll come," she answered. "And this time his badge won't protect him. He'll be off his rotten turf."

Though she couldn't read her watch in the dim light, she figured it was nigh on two a.m. Headlights picked up a rabbit's beady eyes as it dashed across the road. Bouncing yellow beams in the rearview mirror said her brother wasn't far off their bumper.

Dipping into a valley, she scanned the road ahead. The headlight beams skimmed over a pool of water. "Ed, there's water ahead. Pete was right. The flooding is worse."

Inky waters lapped at the road's edges. At the bottom of the hill, the gravel road vanished. God Almighty, was it even passable? Could the current sweep the car away?

Ed braked. "I'll check and see how deep it is. Hope to heaven it isn't a washout. I'll be right back."

"Careful." Cat opened her own car door and stood. Mud sucked at her shoes as she watched Pete join Ed.

Her brother had left his car's headlights on. The beams spotlighted the men as they huddled, talking.

"I grabbed the rope we brought," Pete said. "I'll tie you off before you wade in. If it's deep or the current's strong, I can pull you back."

"No argument from me," Ed replied. "Good idea."

Cat ran her hands up and down her arms to ward off the night's damp chill. "Looks like the water's still rising," she said. "What if we can't cross here?"

"We backtrack," Pete answered. "A detour to higher ground will eat up a couple of hours. They'll likely beat us to the site."

Cat swallowed hard. Would Jimmy take these backroads, too? The question raised terrifying possibilities. She tried to shake the image of Jay being swept down river with Jimmy and that carnie thug.

Oh, lord. What if the kidnappers decided to turn tail? After the Lindbergh tragedy, folks wasted zero sympathy on baby stealers. Would they kill her baby and dump him somewhere to avoid getting caught with a tiny hostage?

Don't go there.

"Jesus, will they even show up with the roads flooded?" Cat's voice quavered. "Jimmy's not stupid. If he thinks we'll have time to get help, he won't set up another meet."

She walked down to join the men, and Ed gripped her shoulders. "Let's not borrow trouble before we need to. Let me check the road."

Pete cinched a rope around Ed's waist. "I'll loop my end around that oak to get a little more leverage in case I need to haul you back."

Ed walked to the spot where the road vanished and stepped into the black liquid. Cold water swirled around his ankles. Another step and muddy water soaked his trousers to the knees. His teeth began to chatter like a Tommy gun.

Cat shivered in sympathy. The rippling ooze must feel like an ice bath. She grabbed a broken tree branch from the side of the road and leaned out to hand it to him. "Here, use this stick to test how deep it gets."

He probed ahead. Half of the stick disappeared. "About three feet," Ed called. He probed again with the makeshift depth finder. It didn't sink quite as far. The water was lower, beneath his kneecaps. Cat's heartbeat slowed.

"The cars should make it. I'll drive over first. Cat, ride with Pete. Wait till I get to the other side, then you two follow."

Ed slogged back to dry land, climbed in his car, and cranked the engine. As the car waddled into the muck, water seeped over the floorboards. He gave it more gas, and the Model T plowed through the muddy channel like an eager cocker spaniel. He climbed out on the other side and motioned for them to follow. Though she wasn't Catholic, Cat felt like crossing herself.

Safely on the other side, Cat swapped rides to sit beside Ed. She ran her fingers along the spines of the two ledgers they'd brought—one real, one decoy. "How much longer?"

"Half an hour—unless we get lost."

"Have you been to Momiss Cave before?" she asked.

"No. Myrt and I brought the twins to visit the Mark Twain Caves last summer. They'd read *Huckleberry Finn*, and their teacher told them all about Samuel Clemmons, how he once lived in Keokuk and worked on the newspaper. When I promised we'd visit the cave, the girls were almost as happy as when our dog Brownie had puppies."

He glanced toward Cat and smiled. "Susie and Sarah are tomboys. Wanted to know when I'd build them a raft."

Her head slumped against the side window. She didn't want him to see her face, see her fear. "Someday I'll bring Jay to Tom Sawyer's old stomping grounds for fun. But I doubt I'll be eager to come near Missouri any time soon."

He reached over and stroked her arm. "Could be a blessing they ordered us here. In an odd way, it puts us on equal footing. We'll all be in the dark."

Cat shivered. "I remember when Dad took Pete and me inside a cave up by Iowa City. Bats swooped down. Seemed like a million beating wings. Scared me silly. I pretended to be brave for my little brother. Guess I'd better make believe again. I've heard this cave is enormous. And it's been left just like it was when they discovered it. No torches mounted on walls, no gussying it up to make it easier for tourists to sightsee. We could get lost."

"We'll find out what waits for us in that cave soon enough," Ed said. "Here's Olivet Cemetery. We take the next turnoff." A minute later he swung the car onto the dirt road leading to the caverns.

Neither spoke for a time. Cat shifted in her seat to check her brother's progress.

"I wish Pete hadn't come," she whispered. "What if something happens to him? Who's going to take care of Beth, Amy and the little one on the way—not to mention Grandmother Nell and Dad?"

"No way you could've stopped Pete. You'd do exactly the same if someone kidnapped your niece."

"You're right." She sighed. "I'm just scared. Terrified. People willing to steal a two-year-old seem capable of anything."

A stout, unpretentious wood sign announced their arrival at Momiss Cave. After the trio unpacked their supplies, Pete drove away to stash his car out of sight, while Ed and Cat poured gasoline into six Mason jars and soaked quilt pieces from Nell's sewing basket to make wicks for their petrol bombs.

A twig snapped. Startled, Cat jumped.

"Sorry to scare you," Pete said as he emerged from the woods. "I found a great hiding place. They'll never see my car."

With loops of rope draped over his shoulder, her brother looked like a cowboy ready to wrangle calves.

"You should be sorry for scaring me, Little Brother. But I'm glad to see you. Still plenty of work to do." She waved a four-foot long branch. "I found a nice sturdy stick, reasonably straight. How about sharpening the end so we can skewer our note on it."

Pete pulled out a pocketknife and whittled, while Ed thumbed through the chief's ledger. "Guess Brad can live without this page. Only penny-ante crimes."

He tore out the page, took a pen from his pocket, and printed instructions in bold letters over the chief's hen scratches.

FOLLOW THE RED YARN. BRING JAY, AND WE'LL TRADE. ONLY WAY YOU'LL GET THE BOOK.

A crimson skein was the best eye-catcher Cat could find when she rummaged through Nell's sewing basket. Cat tied the yarn in a red bow, while Ed wedged the sharpened stick between boulders at the mouth of the cave, and speared their note on the end.

Pete picked up the heavy-duty rope he'd contributed and handed one end to Cat. "Ugh." Her nose wrinkled as her fingers fought for purchase. Immersion in the muddy flood waters had added a coating of slime. "It's as slippery as a night crawler, and it stinks."

"It'll do," Pete said. "None of us has been inside this cave before. The rope'll help us stay together and make sure no one falls down a sinkhole."

Ed tied one end around his middle and measured off a few feet before knotting the rope around Cat's waist. Pete tied on last. *Like mules in a pack line.*

The men tested their flashlights. Cat carefully picked up the two petrol bombs she'd volunteered to carry. Sweat soaked the back of her blouse despite a biting wind off the nearby Mississippi. A constant ache of worry about her baby added a layer of clammy perspiration

"Okay. Everyone has two Mason jars, right?" Ed asked. "Pete, you sure you hid your 12-gauge and the dynamite sticks good enough they can't be spotted."

"Yeah," Pete answered. "Hid 'em near that big tree overlooking the entrance. I'll shinny up that oak soon as we get you two settled inside."

Cat watched Ed tuck a revolver into his belt.

"Ready?" he asked.

Cat nodded. "Let's do it while I'm feeling brave."

Ed led. Dank air whispered over Cat's skin as she followed him into the gloom. Her dread deepened. The cavern seemed to breathe, exhaling putrid air from a cold, dark grave. If it frightened her, it would be hell for her little boy.

Ed plunged ahead, his flashlight beam scampering over the uneven limestone floor. Random cobblestone-like bulges and rubble made walking a hazardous game of hopscotch as they lunged one way, then another to keep their balance.

She tugged on the rope linking them. "Not so fast. If I go down, we'll topple like dominoes. We can't afford to break any of these Mason jars. Even if they won't ignite, a spill will stink to high heaven and give Dexter a heads-up."

"Sorry, I'll slow down."

A bat screeched and a whir of wings beat the air near the cave's ceiling.

"Oh, wonderful." She whimpered. "Wish I could forget Mom's tales about bats trying to build nests in human hair."

Ed's flashlight spotlighted a "Y" intersection of passageways. He chose left. "Cat, tie an extra piece of yarn shoulder high on that outcrop. This is our first left. Now we count steps."

She set down her petrol bombs to tie a loose bow. Afraid they'd run out of yarn before they reached their ambush site, they'd decided to tie ribbons periodically on prominent rocks that were at least shoulder high. Pete used his jackknife to cut a generous length for the bow. She fumbled. Her fingers felt like icicles.

Bending to pick the Mason jars back up, she stumbled. Her foot hit a jar. The pungent odor of spilled gasoline assaulted her. "Oh, no. They'll smell it."

Ed turned and hurried to her side. He set down his own jar bombs to clasp her shaking shoulders. "Look at me. It's okay. We have plenty. The good news is the glass didn't break. Don't worry."

He kissed her cheek, then stooped to retrieve his own homemade incendiaries. "We need to keep going."

The passageway steadily widened. Cool moist air oozed around her like a soupy spring fog. At fifty steps what looked to be another corridor snaked left. Ed's flashlight revealed a dead end. They veered right. Just ahead, the tunnel opened on a grand salon.

"See that ledge?" she asked as they approached. "I might be able to flatten myself on that rock shelf. They'd walk right by without seeing me."

Ed nodded. "A possibility."

Twenty-nine more steps brought them inside a room as big as the stage at Keokuk's Grand Theater. Ed's Eveready splashed light around the space, spotlighting a breathtaking collection of water-worn stalactites and smoothed stalagmites. Bold colors leached from the soil stippled the walls, whitewashed in places by concentrated runoff. The ceiling soared. Twenty feet, maybe higher. A boulder adjacent to the entrance could easily hide a plow horse. Dead center, a pale stalagmite erupted from the floor like a giant mushroom.

"My God, I've never seen anything like this," Ed said. "What do you think? Prop Dexter's fake ledger in the center by that stalagmite and put one of our lamps beside it? Will it fool them?"

"I wish I knew." Worry softened her voice. "Dexter may smell a trap, literally."

She took a deep breath. "Do you two smell the gas, or is it just me? I know I got some on my hands when I stumbled and kicked over the jar."

"Dexter won't notice, Sis. He'll be too focused on getting his hands on that book."

She hoped her brother was right and not simply trying to calm her nerves.

She watched Ed subject a boulder to a thorough flashlight exam.

"What are you thinking?" Pete asked.

"I'll hide behind this boulder until they go for the book. Cat, are you sure you want to hole up in that side passage? If so, we could corner them in this main room. Of course, that assumes they'll take our bait. Once they figure out we're between them and the exit, they might be more inclined to play nice."

Cat carefully lowered her Mason jars to the ground and fiddled with the skein of yarn. "Last bow here?" she asked. "Wish I could believe they're gullible enough to follow our red breadcrumbs. Dexter won't come alone, and he won't risk his own neck walking down a path laid out by his enemies. He'll probably send a scouting party. Might even decide to have one of his men hold Jay at the entrance to force us back outside."

"That wouldn't be a bad thing," Pete said. "Remember, I'm out there. If Dexter leaves Jay outside with a single guard, I'll have surprise working for me—as well as my trusty 12-gauge. Don't worry. I won't take a shot if there's any chance of harming a hair on Jay's head."

Ed shone the flashlight on his watch. "Four a.m. You need to leave, Pete. Make sure you're in your hiding place before our company arrives. Stay alert. We may be running like crazy fools when we leave the cave. As soon as we're clear, you throw a stick of dynamite to block the exit. That should give all of us time to get away before Dexter and his thugs dig free."

FIFTY

Sleep eluded her. Too keyed up. She couldn't be late to the party. Could she trust Jimmy Cloyd to carry out his assignment? His squeamishness about killing a toddler troubled her. She had to make certain both mother and child died.

She switched on a bedside lamp and hurried to dress in the dim light. The cold floorboards made her toes curl. Icy tendrils shot up her calves. Her fingers fumbled with the buttons on her long-sleeved dress.

It was nippy for September, and the caves triggered goose bumps in any season. She laced up her sturdy gardening shoes and draped a wool shawl around her shoulders.

Her early departure wouldn't wake a soul. Five years had passed since she'd shared a bedroom—or her bed. She tiptoed down the hall and nudged open the door to her daughter's room. Capitulating to her little girl's fear of the dark, she allowed a miniature lamp to remain lit all night. Light seeped through the flowered shade, tingeing the child's cheeks a soft rose. What a sweet, peaceful face. An innocent's dreamless slumber. She pictured her little girl wakening—the gap-toothed smile, merry blue eyes.

I'm doing this for you, Sweetie. I'm going to protect your future, your inheritance.

Yet the rage boiling in her gut wasn't born only of a mother's love.

If her father were alive, she'd arrange to kill him, too, then spit on the sanctimonious misogynist's corpse. He'd left the family fortune, controlling bank shares, even her ancestors' Grand Avenue mansion, to her husband.

Memories of her father's patronizing lectures still made her grind her teeth. "Daughter, I understand you graduated college. But women have no head for business or money matters. It's your husband's duty to care for you, for your children, to watch over your inheritance. In time, you'll recognize the wisdom of entrusting everything to him."

Wisdom? Her cowardly husband had watched all right—watched their only son die. She wouldn't let him touch her after that betrayal. Why should she? After her daughter's birth, the doctor had told her she wouldn't be able to have another child. Was that why he'd impregnated the strumpet? Was he that keen for a male heir?

She'd kill the little Reedy bastard. He would not be named an heir, not be allowed to steal the money that belonged to her blood. She'd make certain her daughter became the sole recipient of the family fortune—or what was left of it. God knew her spineless spouse had squandered plenty of *her* money. At least she'd reclaimed the five-hundred dollars he'd paid Dirk Black. Money she'd put to better use.

Kenneth had lied when she asked why Ralph Black had called on him at their home. Her miscreant husband had become quite adept at deceit.

Well, she was better.

She entered the library, walked to the gun cabinet, and took out her daddy's pistol. She ran her fingers along its cold metal barrel. She had more sand than Jimmy Cloyd. If he wouldn't shoot the bastard child, she would oblige.

* * *

"Time to go," Jimmy said. "Can't let the chief or Miz High'n Mighty get to the cave afore us. Either one o' them would lay into me faster than a German blitzkrieg if we weren't there waiting for them. Think I'd rather face down ol' Adolf Hitler than the witch who's a payin' us. Go get the kid from Stella, and try not to wake him. My nerves are frayed 'nuff without him howlin' for his mama."

Mick raised the flap that served as a door between sections of the canvas tent and disappeared. Jimmy had to hand it to Stella. Not a peep out of the brat for hours. Maybe she'd let the tyke suck on one of her perky titties.

Jimmy checked his rucksack. A knife, two pistols, a flashlight. "Hey, Mick, hurry it up."

The bruiser stormed in. His face fire-engine red, his fists clenched.

"What's wrong?"

"Stella ain't here. Kid's gone, too. I'll kill her, if'n I find her."

"What? Maybe she stepped out for some air. Never pays to panic." Even as he mouthed the words, Jimmy knew he was screwed. "Where could she go?"

"Damn woman didn't go for no walk," Mick growled. "Took her clothes. She done flew the coop."

Jimmy felt his bowels loosen. Sweat popped above his upper lip. *Shit.* They needed to leave *now.* No time to hunt down some runaway bitch. Musta heard 'em talk 'bout killing the tyke. Decided she'd play Saint Whore. Damnation.

Should he take off, too, forget about the cave? Without the kid, there'd be nuttin' to trade. What would that rich biddy do once she heard tell they'd lost the brat? He shuddered. *Think.*

"Mick, can we grab us another kid 'bout the same size? Maybe if'n we bunched enough blankets around him we could pass him off for a time."

"Ain't no carnie kids that size to snatch, 'cept the lion tamer's, and I ain't tangling with him. His whip's got a longer reach than my knife."

Jimmy paced. "What about that midget? The one who plays barker for the girlie shows?"

Mick hee-hawed. Jimmy'd never heard him laugh before. Not a pleasant sound.

"Joe's a runt, sure 'nough," Mick said. "But he's a head taller than the brat. And he's got a moustache."

"Maybe if he scrunched up. You're big. You could carry him, right? It'll be dark. We could hide his face. I'd pay him."

Mick shrugged. "Druther have Joe's cigar smoke than that kid bleatin' like a sheep on the drive to Missouri."

Jimmy wavered. Maybe he'd go on the lam. Visit his big sis in Des Moines. He could disappear for a month, maybe two. No, the chief t'weren't the forgivin' kind. He'd grip a grudge tighter than his nightstick. So would Miz Moneybags. He couldn't ever come back. And he had it good in Keokuk. He had to show. How could he make this cock-up work?

FIFTY-ONE

Cat slumped against clammy rocks in the cave's grand salon. Pushed beyond exhaustion, she fought to stay awake in the flickering shadows of the underground world. They'd doused their flashlights to conserve batteries. A sputtering oil-lamp, the only light, played peek-a-boo with Ed's face, randomly lighting and concealing his features.

She sucked in a breath as he lined up the five Mason jar petrol bombs. They made her nervous, damn nervous. Before Jay's birth, she'd played "Y" basketball—the half-court style deemed suitable for ladies. She could throw a ball from near center court and hit the hoop. Yet she wondered how far she could toss one of the incendiaries after she lit its quilt wick. Far enough to keep the flames from licking her? Did Ed have the same worries? If so, he kept them to himself.

Ed handed her brother the chief's real tell-all ledger. "If we don't make it out, give this to my friend Brad."

Pete unbuttoned his shirt and slipped the ledger inside. "Count on it. But you'll hand it to Brad yourself in a few hours."

He nodded. "Better hustle. If you run into our visitors on the way out, you won't keep your own skin safe."

Pete kissed Cat's forehead. "Don't fret, Sis. I spotted a perfect perch in that big old oak. Leaves thicker than bees on a hive. Frost hasn't thinned the canopy. They'll never see me. And don't forget I have my 12-gauge and several sticks of dynamite."

Cat touched her hand to his cheek. "Hurry and be extra careful. I love you. If something should happen—"

He pressed two fingers against her lips. "Don't say it. We'll all come through."

Her gaze followed Pete's flashlight until it dimmed and disappeared. The cave swallowed him whole. In her mind, the inky interior had become a sinister being, one that ate light and oozed evil.

Ed walked her to the ledge hideaway they'd agreed on. A rear opening to the rock shelf wasn't visible from the main corridor. He helped her crawl into position.

"You're almost invisible." His head tilted sideways as he assessed the rock ledge she now occupied. "If anyone shines a light along the wall, keep your head down. They won't see you."

He reached into the stone crevice to hold her hand—the only contact possible in the cramped space. "I can't stay long. I need to be in place well before we hear them."

"I understand," she whispered.

* * *

Jimmy waved away Joe's cigar smoke. It felt all wrong, a huge mistake. The midget was dressed in pajamas with little footies. He punctuated his sentences with grand cigar gestures, sprinkling ashes across his baby getup. No wonder crispy brown burns pocked the pink fleece. Every night, Joe got dolled up in this same costume for a racy vaudeville act. He played a tot who enthusiastically fondled the girlie strippers. When he occasionally paused to wink and stroke his moustache, the men packing the tent hooted their approval.

The costume gave Jimmy the willies. But the little man didn't make him as jumpy as Mick. That silent mound of brainless, dripping muscle took up three-quarters of the car's back seat.

Preoccupied, Jimmy hadn't noticed the flooded roadbed until the car plunged in. When the motor coughed like a TB patient and fell silent, Mick never uttered a peep. Just climbed out and pushed them free of the muck. Once the car started, he plopped back in his seat, bouncing the car on its back springs, and adding the stench of rotting decay to Joe's cigar stink.

With any luck, they'd beat their employers to the cave. He'd finally come up with a tale to keep his hide in one piece. Truth be told, he feared Miz Moneybags and the police chief a helluva lot more than the folks he'd been hired to put in the ground.

"Mick, Joe, listen up. Us losin' that brat ain't gonna set well with Chief Dexter or the hoity-toity broad. So here's our story. The kid died. Just quit breathin'—happens all the time. Went to pluck him out of his crib and his face was all blue. Allowin' as how we needed some live squirmin' bait to lure Cat Reedy and her cop out in the open, we drafted little Joe here to play like a kid. Miz High'n Mighty'll be happier than a pig in slop that the brat's already turned toes up, and the chief won't give a shit so long as we get the ledger. That's our story. Got it?"

Both men grunted.

Maybe he'd live through the coming dawn after all.

* * *

"Dammit!" She swore under her breath. She'd taken the main road, certain it wouldn't be flooded. Not yet. She'd never seen the water rise so quickly. Was God testing her? He'd taken her son. Flaunted the evidence that her husband had fornicated with a Jezebel. Now nature conspired to deprive her of seeing justice served. Well, God be damned. She had no plans to play Job. She'd sell her soul if need be. A fair trade to protect her daughter. Surely, her god—the vengeful God of Jacob—wouldn't let her come so close and deny her satisfaction.

She braced her hands on the wheel, envisioning her car as one of those German tanks she'd watched in newsreels—behemoths that rolled through marshes and crossed rocky fields. She jammed her foot on the gas pedal. The car rocketed forward. Muddy water drenched her windshield, blinding her.

She strained to make out the road. Was she even on it? Her mud-caked headlamps were about as useful as guttering candles. As her windshield shed the bulk of the grimy water, it left behind a film of muck that tinted the scene in sepia tones. Yes, she was on the road. She'd escaped the flood waters. She laughed and slogged ahead through the churned mud.

Morning couldn't come soon enough. She'd watch the bitch die. See her husband's bastard spawn take his last breath.

FIFTY-TWO

Jimmy'd barely had time to get his keister out of the car before Dexter advanced on him like a red-faced grizzly.

"It's about time," the chief growled. "I wondered if you was gonna show."

"We got lotsa time," Jimmy interrupted. "Miz Moneybags ain't even here yet. But I need to tell ya about a little change in plan. The kid's dead."

"What?" the chief roared.

Damn. Jimmy shuffled backward as Dexter's meaty hands balled into fists.

"Hold on, okay? It ain't so bad. I got a plan. It'll work. We recruited Joe, here"—he nodded toward the midget exiting the car—"to pretend he's the kid. He'll scrunch into a ball, and Mick'll carry him wrapped in a blanket. We won't let Cat near 'nough to see his face."

Jimmy stole another glance at Dexter's fists and rushed ahead. "Mick'll hold a knife to Joe's head. I'll cover him with a gun and tell Cat to hand over the ledger or else. Joe can squirm a little under the blanket so she can see the bundle's breathin'. Once she hands over the ledger, it don't matter none that we ain't got the brat. We hustle them in the cave and bury 'em all."

"What happened to the kid? Where's his body?"

The chief's tone vibrated with suspicion. Jimmy licked his lips. Having lived through his first batch of lies, he felt a tad more confident about dishing up the next course.

"Don't know what happened to the brat." He shrugged for effect. "Went to pick him up and his lips was all blue. Musta choked or sumpin'. We dumped him in the river. Wasn't about to get caught with no dead baby. We'd be hung for sure."

The chief's chin dipped slightly. A grudging nod. "This better work or you'll wish you could die at the end of a rope. I'll see you suffer a long time. How d'you think your other employer will take the news? I don't care none 'bout the baby 'cept as leverage. But you said the lady was hot to watch all of 'em die. Make sure the deed's done."

Dexter turned at the rattle of an approaching car. "Speak of the devil. You give her the news."

***

She studied the little weasel. Earlier, he'd seemed reluctant to kill the kid. Did he speak the truth? Or was he lying so he didn't have to see it through?

"Lady, I swear on my mother's grave. It's the honest-to-God truth. That kid's dead. I just didn't want to get caught with no dead baby. Bet he's never found."

"He'd better not be found alive. If he is, you'll be the one floating in the river."

She turned her scrutiny to the midget. "Put out that cigar. Even if the mother can't see your face, she'll smell the stink on you. You reek worse than an outhouse."

She strode toward the path that cut across the property she leased to sharecroppers, land that bordered Momiss Cave. "No time to dally. We need to find a place where we can hide our *baby* from sight until we're forced to produce him."

She didn't look back. No need. The men would follow. Her hand caressed the gun hidden beneath her jacket. She'd decide later how many men would be alive to follow her out of the cave.

***

Pete heard the whispering. Disembodied voices accompanied by flickering light. Though it was still dark, the sky had lightened from ebony to a murky gray. The oak leaves that hid him complicated his surveillance. One, two, three distinct light sources. The amber pinpoints didn't exactly offer a head count. The newcomers huddled at the edge of the woods, just shy of the clearing. How did they get here? He hadn't heard a car.

Someone raised a lantern and swiveled. Pete spied a beefy figure through the thick canopy.

"Dammit," the man growled.

Chief Dexter's voice.

"That's Ed's car," Dexter said. "They're here."

"Shhh." A stern warning. A woman's voice. "Dexter, you get out there. They're expecting you. We'll stay back till it's time for the trade."

Pete edged forward in his catbird seat. Who was the lady? Why was she calling the shots?

Dexter shuffled into the clearing, hoisting his lantern shoulder high. Then, as if the possibility of an ambush finally dawned on him, he crouched and scooted to the side of Ed's car. His lantern swayed as he surveyed the Model T's interior. Satisfied, he circled the clearing perimeter, stopping every few feet to peer into the woods. At the mouth of the cave, he spotted the page torn from his missing book. He pulled it free from the stick.

"Dammit." His oath echoed, scaring a nearby owl into noisy flight. "Get over here. They're already holed up inside. Probably lookin' for a good spot to pick us off soon as we follow. Lots of places to hide."

"Don't be such a coward," the woman chastised as she strode into the clearing. "They still think we have the kid. They won't shoot and chance hitting the little brat."

What? Pete's heart raced. Had they left Jay somewhere? He leaned in for a better look at the odd assortment of characters gathered in the flickering lantern light. His foot slipped on wet bark. Catching the nearest branch, he sucked in a ragged breath as a handful of leaves floated to the ground.

No one noticed. He quit holding his breath and returned to his survey.

The woman looked quite tall. At first, he figured it was Deloris Hamilton, the irate widow who'd confronted Cat. Then, he got a better look. It clearly wasn't Mrs. Hamilton. So who was it?

He had no problem identifying Jimmy Cloyd, the bastard. The human hulk next to him had to be the Ferris wheel operator who'd tried to murder his sister. But who was the squirt in PJs, and where the hell was Jay?

"You *will* make this work." The woman's voice could cut glass. "The cave's plenty dark. Harder for our frantic mother to figure out we don't have her son. Once the chief has his book, I'll tell Catherine Reedy Black the good news, that her brat's dead. Let her picture his bloated body floating down river with all the other garbage. Her last vision before I send her to hell."

Pete bit the inside of his cheek to keep from yelling profanities.

God, they'd murdered Jay. Who were these bastards? How could that woman rejoice in a baby's death? Cat would die of grief.

He shook his head. Not the time for sorrow. There'd be years, decades for that. He needed to stop them before they killed anyone else. With Jay gone, there wasn't a single reason not to drop them all.

Pete reached for his 12-gauge then stopped. Maybe, just maybe, he could pick Dexter or the woman off before they found cover. Even if it were broad daylight, he wouldn't have a prayer of taking out all five.

Any shots would allow some of the vermin to scurry into the cave. They'd rush inside, intent on killing Ed. They'd keep Cat alive as a hostage. Of course, they'd kill her soon as they walked her beyond the range of his shooting gallery.

He pulled a dynamite stick from his pack. His index finger stroked the TNT's rough paper exterior as he tried to envision a way to thread it through the intervening tree branches. He shook his head. Disappointed. Best he could do was shake them up, make them run.

The dynamite still seemed a better option than firing his shotgun. Cat and Ed were bound to hear the blast inside the cave.

They'd be warned the enemy had arrived—and they'd know something was very wrong. *Would Sis figure it out?*

He could barely wrap his legs around the big limb he straddled. He locked his ankles together to anchor himself. His fingers searched his pocket for a match. He didn't want to look away and miss something. He struck the match on his belt buckle. Nothing. He struck again. The match flared and blew out. His fingers scrambled for another. It lit on the first strike. He touched the flame to the dynamite fuse.

"My God, Martha, what have you done?" The man's agonized cry rose up directly below Pete.

Startled at the instant his match touched the fuse, Pete watched in horror as the hissing dynamite slipped from his grasp and tumbled toward earth. Lord help me.

* * *

Martha smiled at her husband's horrified expression. Her flashlight played across his face, the tricky shadows made his head resemble a poorly carved Jack-o-lantern.

While his unintended appearance complicated things, it filled her with savage joy. He knew the bastard he'd fathered was dead.

Possibilities cart-wheeled through her brain. Should she shoot him? Or have Dexter take the uninvited guest prisoner? Maybe she'd make him watch his whore die.

What the…?

The ground bucked, and she pitched face first. Her chin crashed into rock-hard soil. Her ears rang, and blood pooled in her mouth. She gagged. The taste metallic, bitter. Damn, she'd bitten her own tongue.

Clumps of earth and rocks rained down, savaging her shoulders and back. She curled her body, raised her arms to shelter her head.

Gradually, the tremors petered out. The dust cloud enveloping her began to settle. She lifted her head to scan the scene. Her eyes narrowed to slits. This wasn't God's wrath. The bastards had beaten them here.

She spotted the chief, on his butt, legs splayed. "Get up!" she bellowed. "Get in the cave before they set off another explosion."

She staggered a couple steps before finding her stride. She wriggled her fingers as she ran. Bent her arms at the elbows. Swiveled her neck to and fro. No serious injuries, just banged up. She didn't stop running until she was sure the cave's gloom hid her from whatever foes lurked outside.

Had her husband brought help? Or was the bitch's note a ruse? Maybe the Reedy woman and her lover weren't even in the cave. Maybe the whore and her new man had set up an ambush to kill them outside the entrance. Why hadn't she thought of that? How had they arrived at the cave so quickly? No way they could have made it so early taking the normal route she'd put in the directions.

Chief Dexter's rank body knocked into her, almost bowling her over as he stumbled inside. Jimmy and his sidekicks—the mountain man and midget—were fast on his heels.

Everyone in her party survived the blast. She scanned the ground outside for her dear husband. Was he dead? She squinted, directing the dim beam of her flashlight to where she'd last seen her fornicating spouse. Through the manmade mud bowl, she spotted two spread-eagled bodies.

Two?

The bodies lay still. Dead or unconscious? Who was the second man?

She squared her shoulders. Time to take charge. No way would she trust what happened next to some male.

She swallowed more blood as she opened her mouth to speak. Her swelling tongue made speech a struggle.

"Chief, is that man on the ground your renegade policeman?"

He shook his head. "No. Can't see his face, but that's not Ed's hair. Wrong color. Could be Cat's brother. Don't matter none. He's down for the count."

"All right." She rose to her full height, stiffened her spine. "Let's find out if the Reedy woman and your cop are inside. You have my permission to kill Nelson, but keep the bitch alive. We'll use her as a—."

Dexter snorted. "Your permission? Damned if'n I'm gonna dance a jig on your say-so, lady. Who d'you think you're talking to? Ain't gonna be no killin' of anyone until I see my book."

"You idiot." She spat out the words like rancid meat. "Do you want to live? If the cop has your ledger, you can pry it from his dead fingers. If he didn't bring it, keeping him alive won't make your stupid book magically reappear. Dead people don't shoot back, and they don't talk. Try to be intelligent for once."

Dexter's nostrils flared.

He wants to hit me. Let him try.

FIFTY-THREE

Cat's eyes snapped open as a stalactite crashed and splintered three feet away. Knifelike shards stabbed her calves. She jerked up, banging the crown of her head on the overhang. She'd dozed and forgotten her bed was a narrow rock shelf, sandwiched between tons of limestone.

The ground shuddered. More rocks tumbled. She levered her prone body into push-up posture and used the palms of her hands and her knees to inch backward. Where was the drop-off?

"Cat, are you all right?" Ed caught her in his flashlight beam. His labored breath told her he'd run to reach her. His fingers found her left hand and covered it. "Keep your head down."

"Help me get free." She hated the panic shading her voice. "I can't risk being trapped, not when Jay needs me."

His light flashed over the length of her body. "You're fine. The rock above you is solid. The explosion came from outside. The aftershock will stop any second."

The corridor walls spat loose stones like a sheller stripping kernels rapid fire from an ear of corn. Then it was over. The rumble petered to a whisper. The trembling ground settled into its ordinary role—bedrock.

Ed extinguished his flashlight, plunging them back into darkness.

"What happened?" Her throat constricted. Impossible to swallow. An explosion outside? Was Pete hurt?

Ed snaked his arm inside the human rookery to give her shoulder a gentle squeeze. "Talk to me. Your eyes look glassy. Did a rock hit you?"

"I'm fine. That was dynamite, right? Pete wasn't supposed to set it off until we were out of the cave. Sweet Jesus, what's happened to him?"

She dug her nails into her palms, trying to gain control. That's when the realization hit. Pete would never, ever set off a charge—even to save his own life—if Jay might be injured.

Bile crawled up her throat. She fought the heaving urge in her spasming diaphragm.

"They didn't bring Jay." She whispered the horrible verdict. "Pete wouldn't risk harming him."

"Cat, you can't know that. Maybe Pete set off the TNT by accident. Maybe he took out some thugs after Dexter carried Jay inside. Or the chief may be playing with his own dynamite. Don't panic."

Rage, not panic, gripped her. A white-hot fury reanimated her limp body. She could almost feel the electricity surge through her brain, relaying steely resolve to every molecule of her body. She would kill Dexter for stealing her son. She wouldn't—couldn't—think where Jay might be if he wasn't here. Couldn't think about Pete being injured. Their fates rested beyond her immediate control, Dexter's didn't. She would stop him, kill him—unless he killed her first.

She sucked in a breath. Ed stooped to bring his face level with hers. She stared into his eyes. "I won't go meekly. I'll fight to my last breath."

She wished she could gauge his reaction. Impossible in the gloom. Did he think she'd fallen over the edge, into insanity? Maybe she had. She felt empowered. She wouldn't play the meek victim. She'd rather die fighting.

Ed's thumb brushed her hand. "I don't know how many are coming, but they'll be here soon. I need to get back. We can't count on Pete to help box them in. We have to play it smart."

His hand lingered a second more, seemingly reluctant to break their tenuous contact. Then he was gone. Ed's revolver lay inches away. Her fingers crept over the cold metal. Her father'd taught her to shoot. When she and Pete were kids, the family camped on islands in the Mississippi. Each morning, she joined her dad on perimeter snake patrol. Though she mostly fired at tin cans for practice, she'd once killed a water moccasin. Human snakes were bigger targets. Easier to hit. Even in the cave's permanent night.

Cat spotted a weaving light, then a second, and a third. The glowing pinpricks moved quickly. Following the red-bow path she'd set out.

"Ed, where you at?" Dexter's tobacco-roughened voice. The police chief had come within hailing distance.

"That little surprise outside t'weren't nice," Dexter chided. "You coulda kilt the kid. Or maybe you don't care 'bout him no more than Cat did 'bout her dead husband. Too bad your buddy screwed up. I'm guessin' t'was Pete who done blew hisself up."

She shook with fury, and clamped her mouth shut to keep a scream from escaping. They'd agreed. Ed would do all the talking. If only one of them spoke, the kidnappers might not realize she and Ed weren't holed up together. They needed surprise for their two-pronged strategy to work. They had to bottle up Dexter and his posse in the cave's grand room long enough to escape with Jay.

Four heads materialized in a hazy cocoon of yellow light. The bobbing flashlights marked their progress. She held her breath as Dexter passed. Jimmy followed less than an arm's length behind the chief. Then a giant lumbered into view. The Ferris wheel operator? The hulking brute carried something wrapped in a blanket. Had she guessed wrong? Was it Jay? The bundle wriggled. In a second the man and his squirming cargo were gone.

A hunched-over female brought up the rear. The woman's flashlight bathed the rocky floor in amber light as she minced forward, tiptoeing around rocks. Scant light danced upward to selectively spotlight her features. It glanced off a Roman nose, tarried on a high cheekbone. The resulting ghoul-like mask hid her eyes in purple shadows.

Martha Jacobs.

In an instant, Jay's kidnapping made insane yet horrible sense. The banker's wife must know Jay was her husband's son. Dirk's blackmail had loosed a hurricane of hate. How had the Jacobs woman come to partner with Dexter?

She despises me—and my boy. Enough to kill us both?

Cat struggled to still her body. Cold sweat meandered down her back. The individual beats of her racing heart melded into a single, chest-crushing tsunami.

Her gaze followed the woman until only her bent back remained visible. She'd joined the rest of the kidnap party inside the cave's grand room. They'd walked by Ed without spotting him. Their lanterns and flashlights cast elongated, dagger-like shadows.

Good. The kidnappers had no way to exit the cave without becoming targets for her pistol or Ed's petrol bombs.

Maybe just maybe we can snatch Jay and escape this damn cave alive.

* * *

"Where's the boy?" Ed demanded.

The group's startled reaction pleased him. Four heads swiveled toward his voice—a voice that came at their backs. For a moment, no one replied.

"Mick's got him," Dexter said. "Got a knife at his throat so you won't try nothin' funny. Where's my book?"

"Propped on that rock in the center," Ed replied. "Put the boy down and let him come to me. Then you can walk over and pick up your damn ledger. Try to retrieve it before Jay's by my side and I'll kill you."

Ed heard muffled whispers. Dexter asking for advice? Not his style.

"Ain't gonna happen, college boy," Dexter growled. "How dumb you think I am? Once you get the boy, you'll shoot us like fish in a barrel. No, I'm gonna send Mick to git my book. He'll carry the kid. If'n you shoot at Mick, you'll plug the brat. If'n you turn a gun on us, Mick'll slit the kid's throat. So sit tight, hotshot."

The jumbo-sized hooligan shuffled toward the book bait, stumbling backward to keep his wriggling bundle between him and the gun he assumed Ed held. Why hadn't the boy uttered a sound? Silence not even a whimper?

"Stop," Ed yelled. "How do I know it's Jay? Uncover his face. Now. Books burn, Dexter. I can torch your tell-all from here if I want to. And I'm betting you need to keep it in tact to protect your hide should your popularity with the mob take a nosedive."

"You're bluffing." The chief laughed. "You'd have to leave your rat hole to set my book on fire. Go ahead. You know what'll happen then."

"Wrong as usual." Ed lobbed a petrol bomb several feet left of the book lure.

An orange fireball exploded. Flames danced. Whirling dervishes of light licked the black cave ceiling.

"I ain't doin' this. Done been burnt up afore." The giant who'd been crawfishing toward Dexter's book heaved his blanketed bundle a good five feet before gunfire ended the panicked goon's dash toward the cave exit.

Ed's throat constricted. What had he done? Had his taunts and the carnie's mutiny pushed Dexter into a blind rage? The chief had gunned down his own man.

I have to get Jay before he's shot, too.

Ed abandoned the boulder's cover and sprinted toward the boy. Was he alive?

"Cat, they're lying!" A man's yell ricocheted off the stone walls. His last word—"lying"—echoed. It punched through Ed's panic.

Who yelled? Why? One of Dexter's flunkies.

"They...killed...Jay." Labored breaths spaced his words. "They murdered our son. They mean to kill you, Cat."

My God, Jacobs. The bastard who'd raped Cat. Another trick?

"No!" Cat's scream froze Ed.

A bullet whizzed past. Instinctively he flopped to the ground. Sprawled in the open, his survival odds seemed worse than a dumb cow in a Chicago slaughterhouse. He had to reach Jay. He struggled to his knees and searched the shadows where the thug had flung his human cargo like a lifeless sack of potatoes.

He stared, blinked, and swore. *Mother of God!* It wasn't Jay. It was that Street Fair midget. His stomach dropped. Had they really murdered Cat's son?

"Die you bastard!" A woman's vengeful cry prodded Ed's brain and feet to engage. Was the specter screaming at him?

A bullet twanged off a rock, peppering his cheek with rock shards. He made a dash for the boulder he'd forsaken. A hard tug on his pants stopped one leg. His arms flailed for balance. The damn midget. Ed bunched a fist, bent, and swung at the charlatan. He felt the jolt all the way to his shoulder. The pretender collapsed in a heap.

Cat screamed again. Now Dexter would know where she hid. Praying she'd use his pistol, he sent a mental message: Do it, Cat! Pull the damn trigger.

Diving behind the boulder, he skidded. Pain knifed through his shoulder as he slammed into one of his petrol bombs. Goosebumps staked claim to all the territory between his shoulder blades. Bloody hell! He gagged on the pungent gasoline fumes soaking his shirt. He needed to lob another bomb to distract the rabble before they closed in on Cat.

Did he dare light a match?

* * *

Tears streamed down Cat's cheeks.

Jay.

Her baby.

Dead.

Her brain behaved like a scratched phonograph record, struggling to move forward but always skipping back. Jacobs' anguished accusation repeated over and over.

Gunfire jolted her out of her emotional coma.

She focused on a shadowy figure hobbling down the rock corridor. His hitched gait suggested serious injury. His voice radiated pain. The banker. Her rapist.

"Die you bastard!" The woman's enraged scream curdled Cat's blood and wrenched her attention to Jacobs' wife.

Pistol in hand, Martha Jacobs aimed at her husband. A single gunshot. It seemed anticlimactic after her scream. Jacobs clutched his chest and staggered two steps, hands outstretched. He fell face forward without uttering a sound, as if he'd decided his wife deserved the last word.

The bloodthirsty woman turned toward Cat. "You're next, whore!"

Cat blinked away tears. *Does she see me?*

No, but the yell told her where to look. A flashlight beam scoured the wall, swept past Cat's rock bed, then swiveled back. Blinded, her eyes squeezed shut as a bullet ricocheted off the ledge below.

Her eyes flew open again. The woman's gun hand was a mere shadow in the glare as the enraged killer tried to correct her aim. The frenzied murderer seemed unable to hold a flashlight and steady her gun at the same time. Yet Cat had no doubt she'd eventually zero in on her trapped target.

Move! Protruding rocks ripped at her stomach and breasts as she frantically scooted backward. Where was Ed's damned gun? She'd dropped it when Jacobs shouted his crushing news. Her fingers scrabbled over the clammy surface. It had to be here. She touched the butt of the pistol, frantically pulled it toward her.

Another bullet slammed into the ledge overhang, stinging her with shrapnel. She gripped the gun, cocked it. She took a deep breath and mentally repeated her dad's lessons. *Don't rush. Brace your hands. Aim.*

The woman stalked toward her, stopped less than ten feet away, and jettisoned her flashlight in favor of a two-handed grip on her gun. *Oh, no.*

Lying on the cave floor, the discarded flashlight silhouetted the woman. Cat recognized her shooter's stance.

Brace. Aim. Fire. Cat's finger pulled the trigger. The woman stood firm. Her snarl worthy of a hyena. Oh my God, had she missed?

Martha Jacobs collapsed forward. Her body draped over an outcrop. All Cat could see was the top of the woman's head.

* * *

Ed's breath escaped in a relieved huff when Jacobs' crazy wife fell. Powerless to protect Cat from the raging woman, he'd felt impotent. His future snatched away without him lifting a finger. He'd raised the gas-filled Mason jar, but couldn't bring himself to throw it. Couldn't risk injuring Cat. Setting her on fire.

Thank God, she'd shot the woman.

He silently thanked the chief, too, for killing Mick and improving what had been lopsided odds. Two down. Three, if he counted the out-cold midget. That left only Dexter and Jimmy. "Only" wasn't the right word. Not to describe two ruthless killers. Assassins didn't panic. Both were better shots than Cat, and he had no gun. Only the petrol bombs that might be the death of him.

Good Lord. Dexter and Jimmy had vanished. Where'd they go? They couldn't have passed him. They had to be cowering behind a rock outcropping. His position's clear view of the only exit gave him the advantage. To leave they had to pass him. The lantern he'd placed in the center of the cavern would help him spot them before they reached the corridor.

Murmured conversation. Ed couldn't decipher the words, but now he knew where Dexter and Jimmy holed up. They couldn't fire at Cat without abandoning their cover. The chief and Jimmy were too savvy to risk that. The killers didn't know he had no gun.

Choking on fumes, Ed ripped off his shirt and heaved it as far as he could. The acrid scent of gas made his eyes water. A cold prickle on his skin told him lighting a match remained risky.

"Cat," he yelled. "Go. If they show themselves, they know I'll shoot them dead. Go, now, check on Pete. Then wait for Brad and the state troopers."

"You traitorous bastard!" Dexter's bellow communicated rage not panic.

"I ain't gonna sit with my thumb up my ass while Cat-the-Bitch-Reedy waltzes out of here and sets up an ambush by some coppers. No way. Try your best to stop me, college boy. Bet you can't."

Dexter's bulky silhouette popped from behind the boulder. My God, what was he doing? He had to believe running was suicide. Damn, damn, damn.

Bullets zinged off the boulder, whizzing by Ed's head. Jimmy providing cover for Dexter's mad dash. The chief's gun blazed, too. Firing in Cat's direction.

Hell, no, he couldn't lose her. *I won't let Cat die.*

His fingers shook as he grabbed a match. He clenched his teeth. Do it!

The match flared. The deadly liquid in the Mason jar sloshed as Ed held it at arm's length from his body. He touched the flame to the gas-soaked quilting. The make-shift wick flared. He drew his arm back, pretended he was hurling a baseball at the running police chief. He heaved the bomb.

A fireball bloomed in the semi-darkness. Brilliant as an exploding star. Blinding.

FIFTY-FOUR

Cat crawled backward, wriggled free of her rock bed. She switched on her flashlight. Though loath to leave Ed alone to face the chief and that scumbag Jimmy, she knew he was right. Pete might be bleeding to death. When—if—the state troopers arrived, she could tell them Ed was inside. She couldn't bear it if Ed died in crossfire.

My baby.

Dead.

The crushing thought wracked her body. She gulped air, forced herself to think about Ed and his family. His twin sister. His nieces. They needed him. She didn't have time to fall to pieces. Not now.

Dexter screamed his defiance. A second later gunfire erupted. She plastered herself against the slimy stone wall. Jagged rocks poked at her ribs. She doused her flashlight and crept along the rock corridor. The slick floor had become sticky. Blood? Her toes stumped into something soft. Oh, God. She'd bungled into Martha Jacobs' body.

Whoosh.

Flames lit the cave behind her.

Her heart jumped as Dexter burst through a ring of fire like some circus lion. Unearthly, high-pitched screams drowned all other sound. Except the gunfire. Dexter kept shooting. At her.

She dropped to the cave floor. Her arm grazed the lifeless woman's thigh. She grappled with the woman's clammy flesh, trying to get a grip on the corpse. She rolled Martha Jacobs' body over her like a heavy quilt. A thick shield, but also dead weight. Cat struggled to move her trapped gun arm.

Dexter. Still coming. Flames leaping from his shirt. The smell of roasted flesh flooded her nostrils. How could he still be alive?

"You stole my daughter, bitch. Now your bastard's dead. Your turn to die."

He fired. The bullet tore into Martha Jacobs' corpse.

Cat's arm slithered free. She aimed at Dexter's chest. Die you son-of-a-bitch. Die now. She pulled the trigger.

Click.

Dammit. Dammit.

She tried again. Click. Her hands shook with frustration. Tears streamed down her face. Why wouldn't the damn gun work? Out of bullets? How many shots had she fired?

Dexter was almost close enough to touch. A fiery devil belched up from hell. His wild eyes fixed on her. His mouth gaped in a soundless scream.

Cat watched, almost detached, waiting to die. To join Jay.

"Drop your weapon!" The command cracked the air like a bullwhip.

"Screw you," Dexter screamed.

A rifle cracked. Dexter went down. His hand brushed her leg.

Cat screamed.

"Who's there? Identify yourself."

"Catherine Black," she wheezed.

"Speak louder. Who are you?"

"Catherine Reedy Black," she repeated.

"Ed Nelson's inside. He's been helping the police. Don't shoot him." Her pleas poured out in a torrent. "There are two other men inside. A midget from the Street Fair, and Jimmy Cloyd. Cloyd has a gun."

She blinked as a flashlight shone in her eyes. She couldn't see the man's features, barely made out his uniform.

"Sweet Jesus," the man swore. "What the bloody hell happened here?"

He pulled her free of both corpses. "We got a call from the Iowa State Police asking for help. Something about a kidnapping and the mob."

She choked back tears. Fought the urge to cough. "They kidnapped my son. They killed him." Her voice wavered. "Please help Ed. Don't let Cloyd kill him, too."

"Jerry, carry this woman outside," the trooper ordered. "Don't worry. We'll get your man out."

Cat wanted to argue. Wanted to stay and make sure Ed was okay. But her limp body seemed powerless to resist the young officer hustling her through the cave. She caught a last glimpse of the man who led the rescue party as he marched ahead flanked by three officers. All carried flashlights and shotguns.

The trooper shouted. "It's over. Come out with your hands up. My orders are to shoot first, ask questions later."

* * *

Ed thanked heaven Cat was safe. Help had arrived, almost too late.

"I'm here," Ed called, raising his empty hands above his sheltering boulder. "I'm not armed, but Jimmy Cloyd has a gun. He's at about ten o'clock from where you're standing."

"Goddammit," Jimmy swore and threw out his pistol. "Don't shoot. I'm coming out. None of it t'was my idea anyway. The Jacobs witch and Chief Dexter forced me to snatch the kid. And the tyke ain't dead. I just told them he was to save my own hide."

Jimmy rose slowly. The trooper's flashlight washed over his face. Ed watched the hoodlum lick his lips. The lying scum. What was he trying to pull? Jimmy had been up to his neck in this mess. No way the chief had forced him to do a damn thing.

"Don't you dare lie, Jimmy," Ed shouted as he walked from behind the boulder. "I'll rip your heart out if you're lying about Jay. If the boy's alive, where is he?"

"I gave him to Mick's girlfriend, Stella, told her to keep him safe. He's alive. I swear it, and I'm the reason he's still breathin'. I'm the hero here, not the villain."

The lead trooper jerked Jimmy's hands behind him to cuff him.

"Outside both of you," the trooper ordered. "Where's this midget the woman mentioned? You, wherever you are, show yourself. Hands up."

"Think he's still out cold," Ed answered. "I decked him. See that heap over there?"

"Pick him up, Stan," the leader ordered. "Let's get out of this moldy dungeon."

* * *

Cat leaned heavily on the young man helping her from the cave. Her muscles no longer responded to her commands. They twitched in aftershocks from her near-death ordeal. Once help arrived for Ed, she allowed herself to wallow in despair. Jay. Dead.

How can I live without my baby?

Outside the cave, the morning sun dazzled. So bright she couldn't see. Her eyes, like her body, had mutinied.

"Cat! You're okay. Thank heaven."

She recognized Pete's voice, blinked rapidly, and tried to focus on the silhouette propped against the base of a big tree. She shook free of her helper and hobbled toward her brother. She collapsed at his side.

"Pete, what happened? The dynamite. Dexter told us you were dead."

"I was up in the tree, watching, just like we'd planned. Dexter, Jimmy, the carnies, and a woman were gathered below, trying to formulate a plan. The woman said Jay was dead. I'm so sorry, Sis. Then the banker showed up. That woman claimed Jay was Jacobs' bastard."

Pete coughed and lowered his eyes. "What the hell was she talking about, Cat?"

"I'll explain later. Please. What happened?"

"I wanted to warn you and Ed, and I figured I'd take out a few bad guys at the same time if I lobbed a stick of dynamite. Lost my grip before I could toss it. Last thing I remember."

"Thanks be, you're alive." Cat kissed her brother's cheek and squeezed his hand. Her eyes returned to the cave entrance. Where was Ed? What was happening?

A minute later, Ed limped from the gloom. Shirtless and bloodied, he looked like a refugee. Fatigue etched his dirty face. Then he saw her and smiled.

She rose. Unable to manage a run, she hobbled in his direction. They met midway and he crushed her in his arms.

"Jay's alive. Jimmy says they didn't kill him."

She pushed back from him so she could search his face. Her heart hammered. "What? Are you sure?"

He nodded. "I'm convinced he's telling the truth."

She broke away to face Jimmy. "What happened to Jay?"

"Your boy's fine," Jimmy mumbled as a trooper shoved him ahead. Hands cuffed behind his back, he teetered as the guard prodded him with a gun.

Cat rushed him. "You stinking monster."

Jimmy never saw the kick coming, her sturdy shoe made a perfect landing between his legs. An unearthly squeal accompanied his collapse. The trooper behind him cringed then grinned.

Cat grabbed the downed prisoner by his hair.

"Hey, Lady," he moaned. "I'm the good guy. Your brat would be dead if'n I hadn't helped. That crazy Jacobs' bitch was keen on killin' him from the get-go. I left the kid with Stella, Mick's whore."

Cat kept a firm grasp on his greasy hair. She'd snatch him bald unless he told her the truth. "Where's Stella? What has she done with my baby?"

Ed fastened his hand around her wrist.

"Let him go, Cat. He's a lying sack of shit. But that midget backs him up. This Stella took off with the boy."

"Hey, you're the kid's mother?" The revived carnie midget's raucous laugh seemed more than obscene. "You're that lady I wanted to hire to twirl her titties."

Ed wound up to cold-cock the little bastard again, but the man ducked behind another trooper's legs.

"Keep talking," Cat ordered, steel in her voice. "Or I swear I'll ask this nice trooper to leave you in my care. You don't want to know what I'll do with parts of your anatomy. Ask Jimmy if I'm serious. Where's my son?"

The midget chuckled. "You're a real ball buster, lady. They shoulda picked on someone else. Your brat was cryin' so they gave him to Stella to keep quiet. She musta heard 'em say they was gonna kill the kid cause she flew the coop with 'im. Took her clothes, too. Don't know where she might a gone. Could be half way to Timbuktu."

Cat turned toward Ed and the lead trooper. "Can we go? We have to hunt for my son. We have to find Jay before he's hurt—or disappears."

Had Stella, attempting to do the right thing, vanished? If she heard Jimmy talk about killing Jay, she also must have heard the plan to murder his mother. Would she assume the baby was an orphan? Decide to run and claim him as her son?

"Can we leave? I'll report in later." Ed's urgent plea gave the trooper another nudge.

"Yeah, your friend Brad vouches for you. He'll be here soon. Pete already gave us the ledger for safekeeping. No reason for you to stay. I'm sure our Iowa brothers know how to find you."

The trooper nodded at Cat. "Good luck, ma'am. Hope you find your son real soon."

Then Ed's bare torso registered on the man, and he shrugged off his jacket. "Here, take this. You need it more than me now that I'm out of that godforsaken hole in the ground."

A field of gooseflesh had sprouted across Ed's bared shoulders. "Thanks."

He slipped on the jacket while Cat helped her brother struggle to an upright position. "Pete, can you walk? Or do we need to carry you?"

"I can make it, if I can lean on Ed. Just can't put weight on my left leg."

"Okay, let's go," Ed said. "I'd say your next stop should be the hospital, but I'm betting you want to go home instead. Good thing you have your very own nurse to patch you up."

Supporting Pete, Ed didn't have a spare arm to wrap around Cat but he reached over and squeezed her hand. "We'll find Jay. Don't worry."

She bit her lip, and tears welled in her eyes. Jay was alive. Thank the Lord. But would she ever see him again? Where would this Stella woman go? Where had she taken her son?

FIFTY-FIVE

Cat finally broke down. Sobs shook her body as the Model T wallowed its way along roads the flood waters had turned into fetid pig pens. When her shoulders finally quit shaking, she glanced at Pete sprawled across the back seat. Asleep or passed out? The jouncing ride couldn't be helping his cracked or broken ribs. But he was alive. So were all the people she loved—Jay, Ed, Grandmother Nell, her dad. And Ed promised her father would be out of jail as soon as Brad arrived on the scene.

Be grateful. Just a few hours ago you'd have sold your soul just to know Jay was alive.

Still the fear of losing him, of never seeing his mischievous grin again, smothered all competing emotions.

Ed seemed to sense her need for solitude. She didn't want to talk. Didn't want to share her fears. She just wanted to reach Keokuk as soon as possible. She tried to organize where to hunt for the woman, who she might ask for help.

It was almost noon when the car pulled to a stop in front of her dad's house. She reached over the seat to give her brother's hand a gentle tap. "Wake up, we're home."

When she looked out the window, she smiled to see her niece, Amy, playing with dolls on the front porch. The little girl looked over at the car just as Pete levered himself upright.

"Daddy, Daddy," she squealed and ran toward the car.

The front door opened and Beth stood in the doorway. She tore off an apron and raced toward Pete.

"Thank the Lord," Beth cried. "You're all here, you're all alive."

Pete hugged Beth and his little girl, one arm around each. The happy scene tore at Cat's heart. Would she ever have such a joyful reunion?

Beth broke free. "Oh, lordy, forgive me, Sis. There's someone here you want to see."

She nodded toward the house. Grandmother Nell had walked out on the porch. She held Jay's hand.

"Jay!"

Cat leapt from the car and sprinted up the stairs. She lifted her son, hugged him, and dotted his plump cheeks with kisses. He squirmed. "Mommy, you're squishing me."

She laughed as she choked back tears of joy and set her son down. She refused to let go of his tiny hand though. Couldn't bring herself to sever the touch, the connection.

Cat looked up and saw Sister Pearl standing next to her grandmother. The nun beamed.

"Sister Pearl found this little troublemaker inside St. Andrews church, asleep on the altar," Nell said. "Must have been too much for the nuns to handle."

The nun chuckled. "Soon as I laid eyes on him, I knew where he belonged. God does work his wonders, though I'd have been a mite happier if this bundle of joy had arrived with a clean nappy and without the sticky cotton candy."

A hand squeezed her shoulder. Cat turned.

"I'm hoping we all have a chance to visit church soon." Ed grinned. "For a wedding. Sorry Sister Pearl, but I think Cat and I plan to walk down the aisle over at the Methodist Church."

Sister Pearl smiled. "I can't argue with God's will. You're all home. That's miracle enough."

Before she was reunited with her son, Cat couldn't think about the future. Didn't dare believe she'd have reason to smile again. Now she wondered if she'd ever stop grinning.

She kissed Ed. The kiss tender at first, then fierce.

She'd truly come home.

EPILOGUE

The ceremony was simple. Since they'd turned Dirk's ill-gotten treasure over to the authorities, there was no money to waste on frills. Cat wore a three-year-old gabardine suit, plain navy. A cheap cat-shaped brooch served as her only jewelry. The pin had been her dad's gift on her fifteenth birthday. At Grandma Nell's insistence, her wedding ensemble included hat and gloves. They were in church, after all, and it wasn't as if she'd need to doff gloves for Ed to slip a ring on her finger. Like other luxuries, a ring would wait.

Ed smiled at her as the Methodist minister led them through their vows. Cat grinned like a schoolgirl. Had she ever been this happy?

It took less than five minutes to say the I do's. They kissed chastely and turned to greet their family. Except for the first pew the church was empty. The nuptials private.

"I'm happy for you Kitty-Kat," her dad whispered in her ear. "Hope you love Ed as much as I did your mom."

Cat kissed his gaunt cheek, relieved her dad seemed a tad stronger, the DTs long passed. His warm breath gave no hint of whisky. But she didn't kid herself. While she'd defeated her own devils, John Reedy wrestled with ones she couldn't see.

Her dad was released from jail the same day Chief Dexter died. The State Police wasted no time appointing Ed as interim police chief until Elmer McPherson, the former chief, could return. Ed wasn't certain he'd stay on. Farming still called to him. In time, maybe he'd be able to buy the family farm back. Meanwhile, it was a job, and Ed would be good at it. Good for Keokuk, too.

Nell stood to the side. Was she crying? A rarity for the lady of the stiff upper lip. Cat leaned forward and bussed her cheek. "Hope Jay isn't too big a bother this weekend. Thanks for watching him until Monday."

Cat and Ed were giving themselves a weekend alone. Not precisely honeymoon. They'd be settling into their new home, the house Ed's brother-in-law, Al Underwood, built for his family. Ed had already helped his twin, Myrt, and his nieces move to the farm where they'd sought refuge with cousins. Susie and Sarah loved the old farmhouse, rolling acreage, and animal menagerie. The cousins welcomed help with chores. Food wasn't a problem. Ed would send money to Myrt every month until he paid for her Keokuk house.

Cat glanced at Ed's nieces as they teased Jay, who was completely enthralled with his new "older" playmates.

Her throat tightened. How could she be so lucky, surrounded by people she loved—Jay, her dad, Nell, Pete, Beth, Amy, and now Ed and his tightknit family.

Would Jacobs' daughter, Dorothy, ever find such happiness?

She hoped so. God help her, she understood Martha's blinding rage. And she forgave Jacobs' sins. Would she even be alive if the banker hadn't followed and confronted his wife?

Jacobs' younger brother, a decent sort, had moved his family to Keokuk, taken over the bank, and adopted his orphaned niece Dorothy. After he found his brother's journal, he wrote Cat. He'd offered Cat money as a salve for the pain his brother and sister-in-law had caused.

Cat told Ed about the offer. No more secrets. No more lies. Ed understood. She didn't want retribution or reparations. Cat wrote back to the younger Jacobs. "Keep that money for Dorothy. It's what Martha would want."

Cat had everything she wanted. Love and a fresh start.

BOOKS BY LINDA LOVELY

Smart Women, Dumb Luck Series
Dead Line (Previously titled Final Accounting, 2012)
Dead Hunt (2014)
Dead Cure (Coming 2016)

Marley Clark Mystery Series
Dear Killer (2011)
No Wake Zone (2012)
With Neighbors Like These (Coming 2016)

Stand Alone Titles
Lies: Secrets Can Kill (2015)

Audiobooks
Dead Line, Dead Hunt, Dear Killer & No Wake Zone are available in audiobook formats.

ABOUT THE AUTHOR

Linda Lovely majored in journalism and has made her living as a writer, primarily in PR. She now focuses on her first love—fiction. In addition to ***Lies***, her published fiction includes novels in two series—MARLEY CLARK MYSTERIES and SMART WOMEN, DUMB LUCK romantic thrillers.

Her manuscripts have earned final spots in 15 contests, including RWA Golden Heart and Daphne du Maurier contests. ***Dear Killer***, the first Marley novel, was a finalist in the RWA Golden Quill published novel competition. ***Dead Line*** made the finals of the National Readers' Choice Awards for Romantic Suspense.

Linda actively supports the Upstate SC Chapter of Sisters in Crime, which she served as president for five years, and she works as volunteer staff for the renowned Writers' Police Academy. She also belongs to Romance Writers of America and International Thriller Writers. A popular speaker, Linda teaches genre fiction classes and often visits with book clubs.

An Iowa native, Linda now lives with her husband beside a South Carolina lake. Her hobbies include reading, swimming, kayaking, tennis, and gardening.

To learn more, visit: www.lindalovely.com.

ABOUT WINDTREE PRESS

Windtree Press sees writers in all their artistic complexity, individuals who may wish to pursue more than one genre, more than one publisher, and more than one distribution mechanism.

Founded in 2011, Windtree Press is an author publishing cooperative that fills the gap between traditional and independent publishing with promotion, distribution, shared expertise and a supportive environment for publication among proven published authors.

Come see what Windtree Press has to offer. You'll be glad you gave us a try. Direct sales of ebooks are available on the Windtree Press website. Windtree digital and print books are also available from a variety of major distributors. Windtree Press books are currently available in more than 200 countries and our print books can be ordered through most bookstores.

For more information, visit our website:
http://windtreepress.com

CPSIA information can be obtained
at www.ICGtesting.com
Printed in the USA
LVHW011719100520
655304LV00001BA/220

9 781943 601271